THE BROKEN WHEEL

DAVID WINGROVE is the Hugo Award-winning co-author (with Brian Aldiss) of *Trillion Year Spree: The History of Science Fiction*. He is also the co-author of the first three MYST books – novelizations of one of the world's bestselling computer games. He lives in north London with his wife and four daughters.

CHUNG KUO

THE BROKEN WHEEL

CHUNG KUO

DAVID WINGROVE

CORVUS

The Broken Wheel was first published as part of *The White Mountain* in Great Britain in 1991 by New English Library.

This revised and updated edition published in special edition hardback, trade paperback, and e-book in Great Britain in 2013 by Corvus, an imprint of Atlantic Books Ltd.

10 9 8 7 6 5 4 3 2 1

A CIP catalogue record for this book is available from the British Library.

Hardback ISBN: 978 0 85789 820 3
Trade paperback ISBN: 978 0 85789 821 0
E-book ISBN: 978 0 85789 822 7

Printed in Great Britain by TJ International Ltd, Padstow, Cornwall.

Corvus
An imprint of Atlantic Books Ltd
Ormond House
26–27 Boswell Street
London
WC1N 3JZ

www.corvus-books.co.uk

CONTENTS

To Lily Jackson
from your grandson David on the occasion of
your ninety-fifth birthday
with a lifetime's love

CHUNG KUO

THE BROKEN WHEEL

Book Seven

The way never acts yet nothing is left undone.
Should lords and princes be able to hold fast to it,
The myriad creatures will be transformed of their own
    accord.
After they are transformed, should desire raise its head,
I shall press it down with the weight of the nameless
    uncarved block.
The nameless uncarved block
Is but freedom from desire,
And if I cease to desire and remain still,
The empire will be at peace of its own accord.
—Lao Tzu, *Tao Te Ching*, Book One, XXXVII (sixth century BC)

INTRODUCTION

Chung Kuo. The words mean 'Middle Kingdom' and since 221BC, when the First Emperor, Ch'in Shih Huang-ti, unified the seven Warring States, it is what the 'black-haired people', the Han, or Chinese, have called their great country. The Middle Kingdom – for them it was the whole world; a world bounded by great mountain chains to the north and west, by the sea to east and south. Beyond was only desert and barbarism. So it was for two thousand years.

By the turn of the twenty-second century, however, Chung Kuo had come to mean much more. For more than a century, the Empire of the Han had encompassed the world, the Earth's bloated population of forty billion contained in vast, hive-like cities that spanned whole continents. The Council of Seven – Han lords, T'ang, each more powerful than the greatest of the ancient emperors – ruled Chung Kuo with an iron authority, their boast that they had ended Change and stopped the Great Wheel turning. But Change was coming.

It had begun twelve years before, when a new generation of powerful young merchants – Dispersionists, formed mainly of *Hung Mao*, or Westerners – had challenged the authority of the Seven, demanding an end to the Edict of Technological Control, the cornerstone of Han stability, and a return to the Western ideal of unfettered progress. In the spate of assassination and counter-assassination that followed, something had to give, and the destruction of the Dispersionist starship, *The New Hope*, signalled the beginning of the 'War-that-wasn't-a-War', an incestuous power struggle fought within the City's levels. The Seven won that War, but at a price they could ill afford. Suddenly they were weak – weaker than they had been in their entire history. The new T'ang were young and inexperienced. Worse than that, they were divided against themselves.

But the War was only the first small sign of greater disturbances to come, for down in the lowest levels of the City, in the lawless regions 'below the Net' and in the overcrowded decks just above, new currents of unrest have awoken. In the years since the War, *Ko Ming* – revolutionary – groups have proliferated, and none more powerful or deadly than the *Ping Tiao*, or Levellers. The War was no longer a struggle for power, but for survival...

PROLOGUE FALLEN PETALS

Summer 2207

The guests are gone from the pavilion high,
In the small garden flowers are whirling around.
Along the winding path the petals lie;
To greet the setting sun, they drift up from the
    ground.

Heartbroken, I cannot bear to sweep them away;
From my eager eyes, spring soon disappears.
I pine with passing, heart's desire lost for aye;
Nothing is left but a robe stained with tears.
—Li Shangyin, *Falling Flowers* (ninth century AD)

Li Yuan reined in his horse and looked up. On the far side of the valley, beyond the tall, narrow spire of Three Swallows Mount, a transporter was banking, heading for the palace, two li distant. As it turned he saw the crest of the *Ywe Lung* emblazoned on its fuselage and frowned, wondering who it was. As far as he knew, his father was expecting no one.

He turned in his saddle, looking about him. The grassy slope led down to a dirt track that followed the stream for a short way then crossed a narrow wooden bridge and snaked south towards Tongjiang. He could follow that path back to the palace or he could finish the ride he had planned, up to the old monastery then south to the beacon. For a moment longer he hesitated, caught in two minds. It was a beautiful morning, the sky a perfect, cloudless blue; the kind of morning when one felt like riding on and on for ever, but he had been out three hours already, so maybe it was best if he got back. Besides, maybe his father needed him. Things had been quiet recently. Too quiet. Maybe something had come up.

He tugged at the reins gently, turning the Arab's head, then spurred her on with his heels, leading her carefully down the slope and along the path, breaking into a canter as he crossed the bridge. He was crossing the long meadow, the palace just ahead of him, when a second transporter passed overhead, the insignia of the Marshal clearly displayed on the undersides of its stubby wings. Yuan slowed, watching as it turned and landed on the far side of the palace, a cold certainty forming in his guts.

It had begun again.

At the stables he all but jumped from the saddle, leaving the groom to skitter about the horse, trying to catch hold of the reins, while he ran on, along the red-tiled path and into the eastern palace.

He stopped, breathless, at the door to his father's suite of rooms, taking the time to calm himself, to run his fingers quickly through his unruly hair, but even as he made to knock, Chung Hu-yan, his father's Chancellor, drew the door of the ante-room open and stepped out, as if expecting him.

'Forgive me, Prince Yuan,' he began, without preamble, 'but your father has asked me if you would excuse him for an hour or so. A small matter has arisen, inconsequential in itself yet urgent.' Yuan hesitated, wondering how far he could push Hu-yan on this, but again Hu-yan pre-empted him.

'It is nothing you can help him with, Prince Yuan. I assure you of that. It is a... *personal* matter, let us say. No one has died, neither is the peace of Chung Kuo threatened, yet the matter is of some delicacy. In view of special circumstances your father thought it best that he consult his cousin, Tsu Ma, and the Marshal. You understand, I hope?'

Yuan stood there a moment longer, trying to read something in Chung Hu-yan's deeply creased face, but the old man's expression was like a wall, shutting him out. He laughed, then nodded.

'I am relieved, Hu-yan. I had thought...'

But he had no need to say. It had been on all their minds these past few months. Where would their enemies strike next? Who would they kill? In many respects this peace was worse than the War that had preceded it; a tenuous, uncertain peace that stretched the nerves almost to breaking point.

He smiled tightly then turned away, hearing the door pulled closed behind him. But even as he walked back he was beginning to wonder what it was that might have brought Tsu Ma so urgently to his father's summons. A *personal matter*... He turned, looking back thoughtfully, then shrugged and turned round, making his way past bowing servants and kneeling maids, hurrying now.

Maybe Fei Yen knew something. She was always hearing snippets of rumour that his own ears hadn't caught, so maybe she knew what this was. And even if she didn't, she had ways of finding such things out. Women's ways.

He laughed and broke into a run. And then maybe he would take her out in the palanquin. One last time before she was too far advanced in her pregnancy. Up to the monastery, perhaps. Or to the beacon.

Yes, they could make a picnic of it. And maybe, afterwards, he would make love to her, gently, carefully, there on the grassy hillside, beneath the big open sky of northern China. One last, memorable time before the child came.

He stopped before her door, hammering at it and calling her name, laughing, all of his earlier fears forgotten, his head filled with the thought of the afternoon ahead.

'What is it, Yuan?' she asked, opening the door to him almost timidly, her smile uncertain. 'Are you drunk?'

In answer he drew her to him, more roughly than he had meant, and lifted her up, crushing her lips with his own. 'Not drunk, my love. But happy...'

Li Shai Tung had taken his guests through to the Summer House. Servants had brought *ch'a* and sweetmeats and then departed, leaving the three men alone. Tolonen stood by the window, looking down the steep slope towards the ornamental lake, while Tsu Ma and Li Shai Tung sat, facing each other, on the far side of the room. So far they had said nothing of importance, but now Li Shai Tung looked up at Tsu Ma and cleared his throat.

'Do you remember the first time you came here? That day you went riding with Yuan and the Lady Fei?'

Tsu Ma met his gaze unflinchingly. 'That was a good day. And the evening that followed, out on the lake.'

Li Shai Tung looked down. 'Ah, yes, Yuan told me of that...'

He smiled – sourly, Tsu Ma thought, fearing the worst.

The old T'ang raised his head again, the smile fading altogether. 'And you recall what we spoke of that day?'

Tsu Ma nodded, his mouth dry, wishing the old man would be more direct. If he knew, why didn't he say something? Why this torment of indirectness? 'We spoke of Yuan's Project, if I remember accurately,' he said, looking across at Tolonen momentarily, recalling that they had appointed the old man to oversee the whole business. But what had this to do with him and Fei Yen? For surely that was why he had been summoned here this morning at such short notice. He looked down, filled with shame for what he had done. 'I am sorry, Shai Tung, I–'

But Li Shai Tung seemed not to have heard. He carried on, as if Tsu Ma had said nothing.

'We spoke afterwards, too, didn't we? A week or so later, if I recall. At which time I made you a party to my thoughts.'

Tsu Ma looked up, frowning. He had heard of indirection, but this... Then he understood. This had nothing to do with Fei Yen and him. Nothing at all. He laughed, relief washing through him.

Li Shai Tung stared at him, astonished. 'I am afraid I find it no laughing matter, cousin.' He half turned, looking at the Marshal. 'Show him the file, Knut.'

Tsu Ma felt himself go cold again. He took the file and opened it, the faintest tremor in his hands. A moment later he looked up, his face a picture of incomprehension.

'What in Hell's name is all this?'

The old T'ang held his head stiffly, his anger barely controlled. 'Inventions. Machines. Devices that would be the ruin of Chung Kuo. Every last one of them breaking the Edict in a dozen, maybe twenty different ways.'

Tsu Ma glanced through the file, amazed by what he saw, then shook his head. 'But where did they come from? Who invented them? And why?'

Tolonen spoke up for the first time. 'They're SimFic mainly. From the traitor Berdichev's papers. We saw them long ago – three, maybe even four years ago – but in a different form from this. Li Shai Tung ordered them destroyed. But here they are again, the same things but better than before.'

'Better?'

Li Shai Tung nodded. 'You recall that we talked of a young boy. A clever one, by the name of Kim Ward. Well, this is his work. Somehow he got hold of these papers and worked on them. The improvements are his. In one sense it's quite amazing, in another horrifying. But the fault does not lie with the boy.'

Tsu Ma shook his head, still not understanding how all of this connected, or why Li Shai Tung should consult him on the matter. 'But if not the boy, then who?'

'That's exactly what I asked the Marshal to find out. He came upon these files by accident, you understand. Six months had passed and I wanted to know what was happening with Yuan's Project. So, secretly, without the Project Director's knowledge, the Marshal trawled the Project's files.'

Tsu Ma leaned back in his chair. 'I see. And you didn't want Yuan to know that you were checking up on him?'

Li Shai Tung nodded. 'It seemed best. It was not that I felt he would lie to me, just that he might act as... a filter, let's say. But this shocked me.'

'Then Li Yuan is responsible for this file? It was he who gave the originals to the boy to work on?'

'Yes...' Bitterness and anger were etched starkly in the old man's face.

'I see...'

He understood. Li Shai Tung had asked for him because he alone could be trusted, for he alone among the Seven knew of the existence of the Project. Even Wu Shih was under the impression that Li Shai Tung was only considering matters. Yes, and he understood the necessity for that, for were it to become common knowledge it could only do them harm. Wang Sau-leyan, certainly, could be counted on to use it to foment trouble in Council and try to break the power of the Li family.

But that was not really the issue. No. The real problem was that Li Shai Tung felt himself affronted. His son had not acted as a son should act. He had lied and cheated, no matter the good intent that lay behind the act. Indeed, to the old man that was probably the worst of it. Not that these things existed, for they could be destroyed as easily as if they had never been, but that Li Yuan had sought to conceal them from him. It was this part of it on which he sought Tsu Ma's advice. For who was closer to his son than Tsu Ma? As close, almost, as a brother...

Li Shai Tung leaned closer. 'What should I do, Tsu Ma? Should I confront him with these... *things*?'

'No...' Tsu Ma took a breath. 'I would say nothing.'

'*Nothing*?'

He nodded, holding the old man's eyes. 'What good would it do? Yuan acted in your best interests. Or so he believes. So I'm sure he believes. There was no desire to harm you, only... an eagerness, let us call it, an impatience in him, that can be set down to his youthfulness. Look upon these as folly. Arrange an accident and have all record of these things destroyed. The Marshal could arrange something for you, I'm certain. But say nothing. Do not damage what is between you and your son, Shai Tung.'

The old man shook his head, momentarily in pain. 'But he has lied to me. Deceived me.'

'No... Forgive me, Shai Tung, but your words are too strong.'

'It is unfilial...'

Tsu Ma swallowed, thinking of his own far greater deceit, then shook his head again. 'He loves you, Shai Tung. He works hard for you. Unstintingly hard. There is nothing he would not do for you. In that he is anything but unfilial. So let things be. After all, no real harm is done.'

His words came strong and heartfelt, as if it were himself he was plead-ing for, and when Li Shai Tung looked up at him again there were tears in the old man's eyes.

'Maybe you are right, Tsu Ma. Maybe I am being too harsh.' He sighed. 'You are a good friend to him. I hope, for his sake, you are ever so.' He turned, looking at the Marshal. 'And you, Knut? What do you say?'

Tolonen hesitated, then lowered his head. 'Tsu Ma is right. I had come here ready to argue otherwise, but having heard him I am inclined to agree. Say nothing. The rest I will arrange.'

'And the boy?'

Tolonen looked briefly at Tsu Ma, then met his master's eyes again. 'I would leave the boy for now, *Chieh Hsia*. Li Yuan will discover for him-self how dangerous the boy is. And who knows, that may prove the most important thing to come from all of this, neh? To learn that knowledge is a two-edged sword?'

Li Shai Tung laughed; but it was an unhealthy, humourless sound. 'Then it will be as you say, good friends. It will be as you say.'

Fei Yen had been quiet for some while, staring out across the circular pool towards the distant mountains. Now she turned, looking back at him.

'Why did you bring me here?'

Li Yuan met her eyes, smiling vaguely, unconscious, it seemed, of the slight edge to her voice.

'Because it's beautiful. And...' He hesitated, a strange, fleeting expres-sion crossing his features, then he looked down. 'I haven't said before, but Han and I used to come here as boys. We would spend whole afternoons here, playing among the ruins. Long ago, it seems now. Long, long ago.' He looked up at her again, searching her eyes, as if for understanding. 'When I rode out this morning, I knew I had to come here. It was as if something called me.'

She turned, shivering, wondering still if he was playing with her. If, despite everything, he *knew*. Behind him the ancient Buddhist stupa stood out against the blue of the sky, its squat base and ungainly spire something alien in that rugged landscape. To its left rested the green silk palanquin he had insisted she be carried in, its long poles hidden in the waist-length grass, the six runners squatting nearby, talking quietly among themselves, their eyes averted. Further up the hillside she could see the entrance to the ruined monastery where she had come so often with Tsu Ma.

It had all come flooding back to her, all the old feelings reawakened, as sharp as ever. *Why now?* she had asked herself, horrified. *Why, when I have finally found peace, does it return to torment me?* She had listened to Yuan abstractedly, knowing Tsu Ma was once more in the palace, and had found herself wanting to run to him and throw herself upon his mercy. But it could not be. She was this man's wife. This *boy's* wife. So she had chosen. And now it could not be undone. Unless that was why the old man had summoned Tsu Ma.

For one brief, dreadful moment she imagined it undone. Imagined herself cast off, free to marry Tsu Ma, and saw the tiny movement of denial he would make. As he had done that time, here, beside the pool. She caught her breath, the pain of that moment returned to her.

I should have been your wife, Tsu Ma. Your strength. Your second self.

Aiya, but it was not to be. It was not her fault that she had fallen for Tsu Ma. No. That had been her fate. But this too was her fate. To be denied him. To be kept from him for ever. To be married to this child. She looked down, swallowing back the bitterness.

'What is it, my love?'

She looked at him, for the moment seeing nothing but his youth, his naivety – those and that awful old-man certainty of his. Then she relented. It was not his fault. He had not chosen to fall in love with her. He had shown nothing but kindness to her. Even so, her heart bled that it was he and not Tsu Ma who had brought her here today.

'It's nothing,' she answered. 'Only the sickness.'

He stared at her, concerned, real sympathy in his expression as he struggled to understand her. But he would never understand her.

'Should we go back?' he asked softly, but she shook her head.

'No. It's all right. It'll pass in a while.'

She looked away again, staring out towards the south and the distant beacon, imagining him there, waiting for her, even now. But there were only ghosts. Distant memories. Those and the pain.

She sighed. Was it always so? Did fate never grant a full measure? Was it the lot of everyone to have this lesser satisfaction – this pale shadow of passion?

And was she to cast that to the winds? To choose nothing rather than this sometimes-bitter compromise? She shook her head, anguished. Oh, she had often thought of telling him; had had the urge to let the words float free from her, like acids, eating into the soft dream of love he had built about him. And what had kept her from that? Was it pity for him? A desire not to be cruel? Or was it simple self-interest?

She turned, looking at him again. Did she love him? Did she?

No. But neither did she hate him. It was as she'd said so often to herself. He was a good man. A good husband. But beyond that...

She closed her eyes, imagining herself in Tsu Ma's arms again, the sheer physical strength of him thrilling beyond words, the strange, mysterious power of him enfolding her until her mind went dark and her nerve ends sang with the sweetness of his touch.

And could Li Yuan do that for her? She shuddered. No. Not in ten thousand years.

'If you would wait here a brief moment, *Shih* Nan, I will let my master know you are here.'

Nan Ho, Li Yuan's Master of the Inner Chambers, returned the First Steward's bow, then, when the man had left, turned, looking about him. It was not often that he found himself in one of the mansions of the Minor Families and he was not going to miss this opportunity of seeing how they lived. He had seen the balcony on his way in; now he crossed the room quickly and stood there just inside the window, looking out across the grounds. Down below the *chao tai hui* – the entertainment – was in full swing, more than a thousand guests filling the space between the old stone walls.

He took a step further, out on to the balcony itself, fascinated by the range of outlandish fashions on display, amused by the exaggerated gestures of some of the more garishly dressed males, then froze, hearing voices in the gallery behind him. He drew in closer to the upright, drawing the long silk curtain across a fraction to conceal himself. It would not do to be seen to be so curious, even if he was here on the Prince's business.

At first he was unaware of the import of what was being said, then a single phrase made him jerk his head about, suddenly attending.

He listened, horrified, the laughter that followed the words chilling him. And as their footsteps went away down the stairs, he came out and, tiptoeing quietly across the tiled floor, leaned over the stairway to catch a sight of the men who had been talking, drawing his head back sharply as they turned on the landing below.

Gods! he thought, all consideration of the business he had come for gone from his mind. He must do something, and immediately, for this matter would not wait. He must nip it in the bud at once.

He was still standing there, his hands gripping the marble of the balustrade, when Pei Ro-han entered the gallery from the far end.

'Master Nan? Is that you?'

He turned, flustered, bowing twice, then hurried forward, kissing Pei's offered ring hand. He straightened up and, after the briefest pause to collect his thoughts, came directly to the point.

'Forgive me, my lord, but something has just happened that I must attend to at once. I was waiting here, just by the window there, when four men entered the gallery, talking among themselves. Not wishing to disturb them, I took a step outside, on to the balcony, yet what I overheard is of the gravest importance. Indeed, I would go so far as to say that it threatens the security of our masters.'

Pei Ro-han had gone very still. There was a small movement in his normally placid face, then he nodded. 'I see. And what do you wish to do, Master Nan?'

In answer Nan Ho went to the balcony again, his head bowed, waiting for Pei to come across. When the old man stood beside him, he pointed out across the heads of the crowd to four men who were making their way to one of the refreshment tents on the far side of the walled garden.

'Those are the men. The two in red silks and the others in lilac and green. If you could detain them on some pretext for an hour or two, I will see if I can bring the Marshal here. He will know best how to deal with this matter.'

'Are you sure that is wise, Master Nan? Should we not, perhaps, simply keep an eye on them and prevent them from leaving?'

Nan Ho shook his head vigorously. 'Forgive me, but, no, my lord. They must be isolated at the earliest opportunity, for what they know is danger-ous. I cannot say more, but the safety of my masters is at stake here and I would be failing in my duty if I did not act.'

Pei smiled, immensely pleased by this show of loyalty. 'I understand, Nan Ho. Then go at once and bring Marshal Tolonen. I, meanwhile, will act my part in this.'

Kim sat there in the semi-darkness, the room lights doused, the soft, pearled glow of the screen casting a faint, silvered radiance over his face and upper arms. He had worked through the night then slept, waking only an hour past, entranced, fearful, filled with the dream he'd had.

Her eyes. He had dreamed of Jelka Tolonen's eyes. Of eyes so blue that he could see the blackness beyond them; could see the stars winking through, each fastened on its silver, silken thread to where he stood, looking through her at the universe. He had woken, shivering, the intensity of the vision scaring him. What did it mean? Why was she there, suddenly, between him and the stars? Why could he not see them clearly, but through the startling blueness of her eyes?

He had lain there a while, open-mouthed with astonishment, then had come and sat here, toying with the comset's graphics, trying to re-create the vision he had had.

A spider. As so often he had been a spider in his dream; a tiny, silvered, dark-eyed creature, throwing out his web, letting the threads fly outward to the stars on tiny spinners that caught the distant sunlight and converted it to silk, flying onward, faster and ever faster to their various destinations. But this time it had been as if a great wind was blowing, gathering all of the threads into a single twisted trunk, drawing them up into the blueness of those eyes that floated like twin planets above where he crouched. Only on the far side of those eyes, where the blue shaded into black, did the trunk seem to blossom, like the branches of a tree, a million tiny threads spread-ing out like the fine capillaries of a root system, thrust deep into the earth of the universe.

Kim shivered, staring down at the thing he had made, first in his dreams and then here in the flatness of the screen. So it had always been for him:

first he would see something and then he would act on what he'd seen. But this? How could he act on this? How could he pass his web through the young girl's eyes?

Or was that what it meant? Was he being too literal? Did this vision have a meaning other than all those that had preceded it?

He shook his head then cleared the screen, only now realizing how fast his heart was beating, how hard it seemed suddenly to breathe. Why was that? What did it mean?

He stood, angry with himself. It was only a dream after all. It didn't *have* to mean anything, surely? He was better off concentrating on finishing off the work for Prince Yuan. Another two, maybe three days should see that done. Then he could send it through. He would ask Barycz for the favour.

He leaned forward, about to bring up the lights, when the screen came alive again. A message was coming through. He leaned back, waiting, one hand touching the keyboard lightly, killing the hardprint facility.

The words appeared in the official Project typescript, headed by the symbol of a skull surrounded by a tiny nimbus of broken lines. It was an instruction for him to go to the medical centre at once for his three-monthly check-up.

Kim sat back thoughtfully. It was too early. He wasn't due his next medical for another ten days. Still, that wasn't so unusual. Not everyone was as punctilious as he. Even so, he would make sure it wasn't one of Spatz's tricks.

He tapped out the locking combination, then put in the code, touching Cap A to scramble it. Cap L would unscramble it when the time came to unlock, but until then Prince Yuan's files would be safe from prying eyes. Yes, they could take the comset apart, component by component, and never find it.

He looked up at the watching camera and smiled, then, going across to the corner, poured water from the jug into the bowl and began to wash.

Tolonen stood and came round his desk, greeting Prince Yuan's Master of the Inner Chambers.

'Master Nan, how pleasant to see you here. What can I do for you?'

Nan Ho bowed low. 'Forgive me, Marshal. I realize how busy you are, but this is a matter of the most extreme urgency.'

'So my equerry leads me to believe. But tell me, what has happened, Master Nan? Is the T'ang's life in danger?'

Nan Ho shook his head. 'It is young Prince Yuan who is threatened by this matter. Neither is it a matter of life but of reputation.'

The old man frowned. 'I don't understand. You mean Prince Yuan's reputation is threatened?'

'I do. I was at Pei Ro-han's mansion on my master's business, when I overheard something. A rumour. A most vile rumour, which, if it were to become common knowledge, might do irreparable damage not only to my master but to the Seven. Such damage might well have political consequences.'

Tolonen was watching him, his lips slightly parted. 'Could you be more specific, Master Nan? I mean, what kind of rumour is this we're talking of?'

Nan Ho lowered his eyes. 'Forgive me, Marshal, but I would rather not say. All I know is that there are no grounds whatsoever for such a rumour and that the perpetrators have but one purpose, to create a most vile nuisance for the Family that you and I deem it an honour to serve.'

He glanced up, seeing that his words had done the trick. At the thought of the Li Clan being harmed in any way, Tolonen had bristled. There was a distinct colour at his neck, and his grey eyes bulged with anger.

'Then what are we to do, Master Nan? What steps might we take to eradicate this vileness?'

Nan Ho smiled inwardly, knowing he had been right to come direct to Tolonen. 'Pei Ro-han has detained the men concerned before they could spread their wicked rumour. He is holding them until our return. If, through them, we can trace the source of these rumours, then we might yet stand a chance of crushing this abomination before it takes root.'

Tolonen gave a terse nod, then went back to his desk, giving brief instructions into his desk-top comset before he turned back.

'The way is cleared for us. We can be at Lord Pei's mansion in half an hour. One of my crack teams will meet us there. Let us hope we are not too late, neh, Master Nan?'

Yes, thought Nan Ho, the tightness at the pit of his stomach returning. *For all our sakes, let us hope we can stop this thing before it spreads.*

*

The two men stood at the barrier, waiting while the Marshal's party passed through on the down transit. When it had gone they turned, their eyes meeting briefly, a strange look passing between them.

'Passes…' the guard seated beyond the barrier said, waving them on with one hand.

Mach flipped open the tiny warrant card he was carrying in his left hand and offered it to the guard. The guard took it without looking at him. 'Face up to the camera,' he said tonelessly.

Mach did as he was told, staring up into the artificial eye. Somewhere in central records it would be matching his retinal prints to his service record. A moment later a green light flashed on the board in front of the guard. He handed the card back, again without looking at Mach, then held out his hand again.

Lehmann came forward a pace and placed his card into the guard's hand. This time the guard's eyes came up lazily, then took a second look as he noted the pallor of the man.

'You sick or something?'

Mach laughed. 'So would you be if you'd been posted to the Net for four years.'

The guard eyed Lehmann with new respect. 'That so, friend?'

Lehmann nodded, tilting his face up to stare at the camera.

'Four years?'

'Three years eight months,' Lehmann corrected him, knowing what was in the false record DeVore had prepared for him.

The guard nodded, reading from the screen in front of him. 'Says here you were decorated, too. What was that for?'

'Some bastard Triad runner got too nosy,' Lehmann said, staring back at him menacingly. 'I broke his jaw.'

The guard laughed uncomfortably and handed back the card. 'Okay. You can go through. And thanks …'

Out of earshot Mach leaned close. 'Not so heavy, friend.'

Lehmann simply looked at him.

Mach shrugged. 'Okay. Let's get on with this. We'll start with the boxes at the top of the deck.'

They took the deck-lift up, passing through a second checkpoint, then sought out the maintenance shaft that led to the first of the eighteen communications boxes that serviced this deck.

Crouched in the narrow tunnel above the floor-mounted box, Lehmann took a small cloth bag from the pocket of his tunic. Tilting his head forward, he tapped first one and then the other of the false lenses out into his hand, placing them into the bag.

Mach was already unscrewing the first of the four restraining bolts. He looked up at Lehmann, noting what he was doing. 'Are you sure you ought to do that? There are cameras in these tunnels, too.'

Lehmann tucked the bag away. 'It'll be okay. Besides, I can't focus properly with those false retinas in place.'

Mach laughed. 'So DeVore doesn't think of everything.'

Lehmann shook his head 'Not at all. He's very thorough. Whose man do you think is in charge of the tunnel cameras?'

Mach slowed, then nodded thoughtfully. 'Uhuh? And how do you think he does that? I mean, he's got a lot of friends, your man DeVore. It seems odd, don't you think? How long is it since he quit Security? Eight years now? Ten?'

'It's called loyalty,' Lehmann said coldly. 'I thought you understood that. Besides, there are many who feel as you and I. Many who'd like to see things change.'

Mach shook his head slowly, as if he still didn't understand, then got to work on the second of the bolts.

'You think that's strange, don't you?' Lehmann said after a moment. 'You think that only you low-level types should want to change how things are, but you're wrong. You don't have to be on the bottom of this shit-heap to see how fuck-awful things are. Take me. From birth I was set to inherit. Riches beyond your imagination. But it was never enough. I never wanted to be rich. I wanted to be free. Free of all the restraints this world of ours sets upon us. Chains they are. It's a prison, this world of ours, boxing us in, and I hate that. I've always hated it.'

Mach stared up at him, surprised and, to a small degree, amused. He had never suspected that the albino had so much feeling in him. He had always thought him cold, like a dead thing. This hatred was unexpected. It hinted at a side to him that even DeVore knew nothing of.

The second bolt came free. He set to work on the third.

'I bet you hated your parents, too, didn't you?'

Lehmann knelt, watching Mach's hands as they turned the bolt. 'I never knew them. My father never came to see me. My mother… well, I killed my mother.'

'You…' Mach looked back at him, roaring with laughter, then fell silent. 'You mean, you really did? You *killed* her?'

Lehmann nodded. 'She was a rich Han's concubine. An arfidis addict too. She disgusted me. She was like the rest of them, soft, corrupt. Like this world. I set fire to her, in her rooms. I'd like to do the same to all of them. To burn the whole thing to a shell and pull it down.'

Mach took a deep breath through his nose, then set to work again. 'I see. And DeVore knows this, does he?'

'No. He thinks I'm someone else, *something* else.'

'I see. But why tell me?'

'Because you're not what he thinks you are either.' Lehmann reached across him, beginning to unscrew the final bolt. 'DeVore sees only enemies or pale shadows of himself. That's how he thinks. Black and white. As if this were all one great big game of *wei chi*.'

Mach laughed. 'You surprise me. I'd have thought…' Then he laughed again. 'I'm sorry. I'm doing what you said he does, aren't I? Assuming you're something that you're not.'

The last screw came loose. Between them they gently lifted the plate from the connecting pins and set it to one side. Beneath the plate was a panel, inset with tiny slip-in instruction cards. At the base of the panel was a keyboard. Lehmann tapped in the cut-out code he'd memorized then leaned close, studying the panel. His pale, thin fingers searched the board, then plucked five of the translucent cards from different locations. He slipped them into the pouch at his waist, then reached into his jacket and took out the first of the eighteen tiny sealed packets. When a certain signal was routed through this board, these five would be triggered, forming a circuit that overrode the standard instruction codes. To the back-up system it would seem as if the panel was functioning normally, but to all intents and purposes it would be dead. And with all eighteen boxes triggered in this way, communications to the deck would be effectively cut off.

He slotted the five wafer-thin cards into place, reset the cut-out code, then, with Mach's help, lowered the plate back on to the connecting pins.

'There,' Mach said. 'One down, seventeen to go. Pretty easy, huh?'

'Easy enough,' Lehmann said, taking one of the restraining bolts and beginning to screw it down. 'But only if you've the nerve, the vision and the intelligence to plan it properly.'

Mach laughed. 'And a few old friends, turning a blind eye.'

Lehmann turned his head slightly, meeting Mach's eyes. 'Maybe. And a reason for doing it, neh?'

Kim had heard the alarm from three decks down but made nothing of it, yet coming out of the transit he remembered it again. Pulse quickening, he began to run towards his room.

Even before he turned the corner into his corridor he saw signs of what had happened. A long snake of hose ran from the corner hydrant, flaccid now. On the far side of it, water had pooled. But that was not what had alerted him. It was the scent of burning plastics.

He leapt the hose, took three small, splashing steps, then stopped. The door to his room was open, the fire-hose curving inside. Even from where he stood he could see how charred the lintel was, could see the ashy residue of sludge littering the floor outside.

'What in the gods' names...?'

T'ai Cho jerked his head round the door. 'Kim!' he cried, coming out into the corridor, and his face lit up. 'Oh, thank the gods you're safe. I thought...'

He let himself be embraced, then went inside, facing the worst. It was gone. All of it. His comset was unrecognizable, fused into the worktop as if the whole were some strange, smooth sculpture of twisted black marble. The walls were black, as was the ceiling. The floor was awash with the same dark sludge that had oozed into the corridor.

'What happened?' he asked, looking about him, the extent of his loss – his books, his clothes, the tiny things he'd called his own – slowly sinking in. 'I thought this kind of thing couldn't happen? There are sprinklers, aren't there? And air-seals.'

T'ai Cho glanced at one of the maintenance men who were standing around, then looked back at Kim. 'They failed, it seems. Faulty wiring.'

Kim laughed sourly, the irony not lost on him. 'Faulty wiring? But I thought the boxes used instruction cards.'

One of the men spoke up. 'That's right. But two of the cards were wrongly encoded. It happens sometimes. It's something we can't check up on. A mistake at the factory... You know how it is.'

Only too well, Kim thought. *But who did this? Who ordered it done? Spatz? Or someone higher than him? Not Prince Yuan, anyway, because he wanted what was destroyed here today.*

He sighed, then shook his head. It would take weeks, months perhaps, to put it all together again. And if he did? Well, maybe it would be for nothing after all. Maybe they would strike again, just as he came to the end of his task, making sure nothing ever got to Li Yuan.

He turned, looking at his old friend. 'You shouldn't have worried, T'ai Cho. But I'm glad you did. I was having my three-monthly medical. They say I'm fine. A slight vitamin C deficiency, but otherwise...' He laughed. 'It was fortunate, neh? I could have been sleeping.'

'Yes,' T'ai Cho said, holding the boy to him again. 'We should thank the gods, neh?'

Yes, thought Kim. *Or whoever it was decided I was not as disposable as my work.*

Nan Ho stood in the cool of the passageway outside the room, mopping his brow, the feeling of nausea passing slowly from him. Though ten minutes had passed, his hands still trembled and his clothes were soaked with his own sweat. In all his forty years he had seen nothing like it. The man's screams had been bad enough, but the look in his eyes, that expression of sheer terror and hopelessness, had been too much to bear.

If he closed his eyes he could still see it. Could see the echoing kitchen all about him, the prisoner tied naked to the table, his hands and feet bound tight with cords that bruised and cut the flesh. He bared his teeth, remembering the way the masked man had turned, the oiled muscles of his upper arms flexing effortlessly as he lifted the tongs from the red-hot brazier and turned them in the half-light. He could see the faint wisp of smoke that rose towards the ceiling, could hear the faint crackle as the coal was lifted into the cooler air, even before he saw the glowing coal itself. But most of all he could see the panic in the young man's eyes and recalled what he had thought.

Forgive me, Fan Ming-yu, but I had to do this. For my master.

The man had begun to babble, to refute all he had been saying only a moment before, but the torturer's movements seemed inexorable. The coal came down, slowly, ever so slowly it seemed, and the man's words melted into shrieks of fearful protest. His body lifted, squirming, desperate, but all of its attempts to escape only brought it closer to the implement of its suffering.

The torturer held back a moment. One leather-gloved hand pushed the man's hip down, gently, almost tenderly it seemed. Then, with the kind of care one might see from a craftsman, tracing fine patterns on to silver, he brought the coal down delicately, pressing it tightly against the man's left testicle.

Nan Ho had shuddered and stepped back, swallowing bile. He had glanced, horrified, at Tolonen, seeing how the old man looked on impassively, then had looked back at the man, unable to believe what he had seen, appalled and yet fascinated by the damage the coal had done. Then, turning away, he had staggered out, his legs almost giving way under him, the screams of the man filling his head, the smell of charred flesh making him want to retch.

He stood there a moment longer, calming himself, trying to fit what he had just witnessed into the tightly ordered pattern of the world he knew, then shook his head. It was not his fault. He had had no choice in the matter. If his master had been any other man, or if the Lady Fei had chosen any other man but Tsu Ma to be her lover. But... as it was, this had to be. To let the truth be known, that was unthinkable.

Tolonen came outside. He stood there, staring at Nan Ho a moment, then reached out and held his shoulder. 'I am sorry, Master Nan. I didn't mean it to upset you. It's just that I felt you ought to be there, to hear the man's confession for yourself.' He let his hand fall, then shrugged. 'There are more efficient ways of inflicting pain, of course, but none as effective in loosening a tongue. The more barbaric the means of torture, we find, the quicker the man will talk.'

Nan Ho swallowed, then found his voice again. 'And what did you discover?'

'I have a list of all those he spoke to. Few, fortunately. And his source.'

'His source?'

'It seems you acted not a moment too soon, Master Nan. Fan Ming-yu had just come from his lover. A young man named Yen Shih-fa.'

Nan Ho's eyes widened. 'I know the man. He is a groom at the stables.'

'Yes,' Tolonen smiled grimly. 'I have contacted Tongjiang already and had the man arrested. With the very minimum of fuss, you understand. They are bringing him here even now.'

Nan Ho nodded abstractedly. 'And what will you do?'

The Marshal swallowed, a momentary bitterness clouding his features. 'What can I do? It is as you said, Master Nan. This rumour cannot be allowed to spread. But how to prevent that? Normally I would trust to the word of such *ch'un tzu*, but in a matter of this seriousness it would not be enough to trust to their silence. A man's word is one thing, but the security of the State is another. No, neither would it serve to demote them below the Net. These four are men of influence. Small influence, admittedly, but their absence would be noticed and commented upon. No, in the circumstances we must act boldly, I'm afraid.'

Nan Ho shuddered. 'You mean they must die.'

Tolonen smiled. 'Nothing quite so drastic, Master Nan. It is a matter of a small operation.' He traced a tiny line across the side of his skull. 'An incision here, another there...'

'And their families?'

'Their families will be told that they took an overdose of something illicit. Pei Ro-han's surgeons had to operate to save them, but unfortunately there was damage – serious damage – to those parts of the brain that control speech and memory. Most unfortunate, neh? But the T'ang, in his generosity, will offer compensation.'

Nan Ho stared at the Marshal, surprised. 'You know this?'

'I have already written the memorandum. It will be on Li Shai Tung's desk this evening.'

'Ah, then the matter is concluded?'

'Yes. I think we can safely say that.'

'And the groom? Yen Shih-fa?'

Tolonen looked down, clearly angry. 'Yen Shih-fa will die. After we have made sure he has done no further mischief.'

Nan Ho bowed his head. 'I understand...' Yet he felt no satisfaction, only a sense of dread necessity; that, and a slowly mounting anger at his young master's wife. This was *her* fault, the worthless bitch. This was the price of *her* selfishness, *her* wantonness.

Tolonen was watching him sympathetically. 'You have served your master well, Nan Ho. You were right. If this rumour *had* taken root...'

Nan Ho gave the slightest nod. He had hoped to keep the details from Tolonen, but it had not proved possible. Even so, no harm had been done. Fang Ming-yu's insistence on the truth of what he had said – that Tsu Ma *had* slept with the Lady Fei – had shocked and outraged the old man. Nan Ho had seen for himself the fury in Tolonen's face as he leaned over the man, spittle flecking his lips as he called him a liar and a filthy scandal-monger. And thank the gods for that. No. Not for one moment had the Marshal believed it could be true. Tsu Ma and the Lady Fei. No. It was unthinkable!

And so it must remain. For a lifetime, if necessary. But how long would it be before another whispered the secret to one they trusted? How long before the rumour trickled out again, flowing from ear to ear like the tributaries of a great river?

And then?

'I am pleased that it has all worked out so well, Marshal,' he said, meeting the old man's eyes briefly. 'But now, if you need me no longer, I must see Pei Ro-han. I have yet to complete the business I came here for.'

'Of course. You have done all that needs to be done here, Master Nan. For which I thank you. I can deal with the rest.'

'Good. Then you'll excuse me.'

He bowed and was beginning to turn away when Tolonen called him back.

'Forgive me, Master Nan, but one small thing. This morning, as I understand it, was the first time Tsu Ma had visited Tongjiang for three, almost four months. Now, without saying for a moment that I believe it to be true, such rumours have no credibility – even among such carrion as these – unless there are some few small circumstances to back them up. What crossed my mind, therefore, was that this was possibly some old tale, renewed, perhaps, by Tsu Ma's visit this morning. I wondered...' He hesitated, clearly embarrassed by what he was about to say. 'Well, to be frank, I wondered if you had heard any whisper of this rumour before today, Master Nan. Whether...'

But Nan Ho was shaking his head. 'Personally I think it more likely that the T'ang's visit put the idea into the young groom's head. Dig a little and I'm sure you'll find a reason for his malice. It would not be the first time that such mischief has come from personal disappointment.'

Tolonen considered that, then nodded, satisfied. 'Well, it was just a passing thought. Go now, Master Nan. And may the gods reward you for what
you have done here today.'

It had taken the best part of six hours to work their way down through the
deck, but now they had only this last box to deal with and they were done.
Both men had been quiet for some time, but now Mach looked across at his
pale companion and laughed.

'What is it?' Lehmann asked tonelessly, concentrating on unscrewing
the last of the restraining bolts.

'I was just thinking...'

Again he laughed. This time Lehmann raised his eyes, searching his
face. 'Thinking what?'

'Just about what you might have become. With your father's money, I
mean. You could have been a right bastard, neh? Beating them at their own
game. Making deals. Controlling the markets. Undercutting your competitors or stealing their patents. Did that never appeal to you?'

Lehmann looked down again. 'I considered it. But, then, I considered
a lot of things. But to answer you, Shih Mach. No, it never appealed to me.
But this...' He eased the bolt out and set it down. 'This is what I've always
wanted to do.'

'Always?' Mach helped him remove the plate, then sat back on his
haunches, watching.

'Since I can remember,' Lehmann went on, tapping the cut-out code into
the keyboard, 'I've always fought against the system. Ever since I knew I
could. In small ways at first. And later...'

Mach waited, but Lehmann seemed to have finished.

'Are you really as nihilistic as you seem, Stefan Lehmann? Is there nothing you believe in?'

Lehmann's pale, thin fingers hovered over the panel a moment, then
quickly plucked the five tiny cards from their slots. Mach had watched
Lehmann do this eighteen times now, noting how he took his time, double-
checking, making absolutely sure he took the right ones. It was impressive
in a way, this kind of obsessive care. And necessary in this case, because the
configuration of each panel was different. But there was also something

machine-like about the way Lehmann went about it.

He waited, knowing the albino would answer him when he was good and ready; watching him take out the tiny sealed packet and break it open then slip the replacement cards into their respective slots.

'There,' Lehmann said. 'That's all of them. Do you want to test the circuit out?'

Mach was about to answer when there was a banging on the tunnel wall beneath them.

'Shit!' Mach hissed between his teeth. 'What the fuck is that?'

Lehmann had turned at the noise, now he waited, perfectly still, like a lizard about to take its prey. 'Wait,' he mouthed. 'It may be nothing.'

There was silence. Mach counted. He had got to eight when the banging came again, louder than before and closer, almost beneath their feet. Moments later a head appeared at the hatchway further along.

'Hey!' the guard said, turning to face them. 'Are you authorized to be in there?'

Mach laughed. 'Well, if we're not we're in trouble, aren't we?'

The guard was pulling himself up into the tunnel, hissing with the effort. Mach looked at Lehmann quickly, indicating that he should do nothing. With the barest nod Lehmann leaned back, resting his head against the tunnel wall, his eyes closed.

The guard scrambled up, then came closer, his body hunched up in the narrow space. He was a young, dark-haired officer with the kind of bearing that suggested he had come out of cadet-training only months before. 'What are you doing here?' he asked officiously, one hand resting lightly on his sidearm.

Mach smiled, shaking his head. 'Don't you read your sheets?'

The young guard bristled, offended by Mach's offhand manner. 'That's precisely why I'm here. I've already checked. There's no mention of any maintenance work on the sheets.'

Mach shrugged. 'And that's our fault? You should get on to Admin and find out what arsehole fucked things up, but don't get on our backs. Here.' He reached inside his tunic and pulled out the papers DeVore had had forged for them.

He watched the guard's face; saw how the sight of something official-looking mollified him.

'Well? Are you satisfied?' Mach asked, putting out his hand to take the papers back.

The guard drew back a step, his eyes taking in the open box, the exposed panel. 'I still don't understand. What exactly are you doing there? It says here that you're supposed to be testing the ComNet, but you can do that without looking at the boxes, surely?'

Mach stared back at him, his lips parted, momentarily at a loss, but Lehmann came to the rescue. He leaned forward casually and plucked one of the tiny cards from the panel in front of him, handing it to the guard.

'Have you ever seen one of these?'

The guard studied the clear plastic of the card then looked back at Lehmann. 'Yes, I—'

'And you know how they function?'

'Vaguely, yes, I—'

Lehmann laughed. Cold, scathing laughter. 'You don't know a fucking thing, do you, soldier boy? For instance, did you know that if even a single one of these instruction cards gets put in the wrong slot then the whole net can be fucked up. Urgent information can be misrouted, emergency calls never get to their destinations. That's why we take such pains. That's why we look at every box. Carefully. Meticulously. To make sure it doesn't happen. Understand me?' He looked up at the guard savagely. 'Okay, you've been a good boy and done all your checking, now just piss off and let us get on with the job, neh? Before we register a complaint to your superior officer for harassment.'

Mach saw the anger in the young guard's face, the swallowed retort. Then the papers were thrust back into his hand and the guard was backing away down the tunnel.

'That was good,' Mach said quietly when he was gone. 'He'll be no more trouble, that's for sure.'

Lehmann looked at him, then shook his head. 'Here,' he said, handing him the plate. 'You finish this. I'm going after our friend.'

Mach narrowed his eyes. 'Are you sure that's wise? I mean, he seemed satisfied with your explanation. And if you were to kill him...'

Lehmann turned, his face for that brief moment very close to Mach's, his pink eyes searching the *Ping Tiao* leader's.

'You asked if I believed in anything, Mach. Well, there's one thing I do believe in – I believe in making sure.'

Li Yuan rode ahead, finding the path down the hillside. Behind him came the palanquin, swaying gently, the six carriers finding their footholds on the gentle slope with practised certainty, their low grunts carrying on the still evening air.

Li Yuan turned in his saddle, looking back. The sun was setting in the west, beyond the Ta Pa Shan. In its dying light the pale yellow silks of the palanquin seemed dyed a bloody red. He laughed and turned back, spurring his horse on. It had been a wonderful day. A day he would remember for a long time. And Fei Yen? Despite her sickness, Fei had looked more beautiful than ever. And even if they had not made love, simply to be with her had somehow been enough.

He threw his head back, feeling the cool breeze on his neck and face. Yes, motherhood suited Fei Yen. They would have many sons. A dozen, fifteen sons. Enough to fill Tongjiang. And daughters too. Daughters who would look like Fei Yen. And then, when he was old and silver-haired, he would have a hundred grandchildren; would gather his pretties about his throne and tell them of a summer day – this day – when he had gone up to the ruins with their grandmother, the Lady Fei, and wished them into being.

He laughed, enjoying the thought, then slowed, seeing lights floating, dancing in the darkness up ahead. Looking back, he raised a hand, signalling for the carriers to stop, then eased his mount forward a pace or two. No, he was not mistaken, the lights were coming on towards them. Then he understood. They were lanterns. Someone – Nan Ho, most likely – had thought to send out lantern-bearers to light their way home.

He turned, signalling the carriers to come on, then spurred the Arab forward again, going down to meet the party from the palace.

He met them halfway across the long meadow. There were twenty bearers, their ancient oil-filled lanterns mounted on ten ch'i wooden poles. Coming up behind were a dozen guards and two of the young grooms from the stables. Ahead of them all, marching along stiffly, like a young boy playing at soldiers, was Nan Ho.

'Master Nan!' he hailed. 'How good of you to think of coming to greet us.'

Nan Ho bowed low. Behind him the tiny procession had stopped, their heads bowed. 'It was but my duty, my lord.'

Li Yuan drew closer, leaning towards Nan Ho, his voice lowered. 'And the business I sent you on?'

'It is all arranged,' Nan Ho answered quietly. 'The Lord Pei has taken on the matter as his personal responsibility. Your maids will have the very best of husbands.'

'Good.' Li Yuan straightened up in his saddle, then clapped his hands, delighted that Pearl Heart and Sweet Rose would finally have their reward. 'Good. Then let us go and escort the Lady Fei, neh, Master Nan?'

Li Yuan galloped ahead, meeting the palanquin at the edge of the long meadow. 'Stop!' he called. 'Set the palanquin down. We shall wait for the bearers to come.'

As the chair was lowered there was the soft rustle of silk from inside as Fei Yen stirred. 'Yuan?' she called sleepily. 'Yuan, what's happening?'

He signalled to one of the men to lift back the heavy silk at the front of the palanquin, then stepped forward, helping Fei Yen raise herself into a sitting position. Then he stepped back again, pointing out across the meadow.

'See what Master Nan has arranged for us, my love.'

She laughed softly, delighted. The darkness of the great meadow seemed suddenly enchanted, the soft glow of the lanterns like giant fireflies floating at the ends of their tall poles. Beyond them on the far side of the meadow, the walls of the great palace of Tongjiang were a burnished gold in the sun's last rays, the red, steeply tiled roofs like flames.

'It's beautiful,' she said. 'Like something from a fairy-tale.'

He laughed, seeing how the lamplight seemed to float in the liquid darkness of her eyes. 'Yes. And you the fairy princess, my love. But come, let me sit with you. One should share such magic, neh?'

He climbed up next to his wife then turned, easing himself into the great cushioned seat next to her.

'All right, Master Nan. We're ready.'

Nan Ho bowed, then set about arranging things, lining up the lantern-bearers to either side of the palanquin then assigning six of the guards to double up as carriers. He looked about him. Without being told, the two grooms had taken charge of the Arab and were petting her gently.

Good, thought Nan Ho, signalling for the remaining guards to form up behind the palanquin. But his satisfaction was tainted. He looked at his master and at his wife and felt sick at heart. How beautiful it all looked in the light of the lanterns, how perfect, and yet...

He looked down, remembering what he had done, what he had seen that day, and felt bitter anger. *Things should be as they seem*, he thought. *No*, he corrected himself: *things should seem as they truly are*.

He raised his hand. At the signal the carriers lifted the palanquin with low grunts. Then, as he moved out ahead of them, the procession began, making its slow way across the great meadow, the darkness gathering all about them.

'Well, how did it go?'

Lehmann threw the pouch down on the desk in front of DeVore. 'There was a slight hitch, but all the circuits are in place. I had to kill a man. A Security guard. But your man there, Hanssen, is seeing to that.'

DeVore studied Lehmann a moment. 'And nobody else saw you?'

'Only the guards at the barriers.'

'Good.' DeVore looked down, fingering the pouch, knowing that it contained all the communication circuits they had replaced, then pushed it aside. 'Then we're all set, neh? Ten days from now we can strike. There was no problem with Mach, I assume?'

Lehmann shook his head. 'No. He seems as keen as us to get at them.'

DeVore smiled. *As he ought to be*. 'Okay. Get showered and changed. I'll see you at supper for debriefing.'

When Lehmann was gone he got up and went across the room, looking at the detailed diagram of Security Central that he'd pinned on the wall. Bremen was the very heart of City Europe's Security forces, their 'invulnerable' fortress. But it was that very assumption of invulnerability that made them weak. In ten days' time they would find that out. Would taste the bitter fruit of their arrogance.

He laughed and went back to his desk, then reached across, drawing the folder towards him. He had been studying it all afternoon, ever since the messenger had brought it. It was a complete file of all the boy's work; a copy of the file Marshal Tolonen had taken with him to Tongjiang that very morning; a copy made in Tolonen's own office by Tolonen's own equerry, a young man he had recruited to his cause five years earlier, when the boy had still been a cadet.

He smiled, remembering how he had initiated the boy, how he had made him swear the secret oath. It was so easy. They were all so keen; so young and fresh and ripe for some new ideology – for some new thing they could believe in. And he, DeVore, was that new thing. He was the man whose time would come. That was what he told them, and they believed him. He could see it in their eyes; that urgency to serve some new and better cause – something finer and more abstract than this tedious world of levels. He called them his brotherhood and they responded with a fierceness born of hunger. The hunger to be free of this world ruled by the Han. To be free men again, self-governing and self-sustaining. And he fed that hunger in them, giving them a reason for their existence – to see a better world. However long it took.

He opened the file, flicking through the papers, stopping here and there to admire the beauty of a design, the simple elegance of a formula. He had underestimated the boy. Had thought him simply clever. Super-clever, perhaps, but nothing more. This file, however, proved him wrong. The boy was unique. A genius of the first order. What he had accomplished with these simple prototypes was astonishing. Why, there was enough here to keep several Companies busy for years. He smiled. As it was, he would send them off to Mars, to his contacts there, and see what they could make of them.

He leaned back in his chair, stretching out his arms. It would be time, soon, to take the boy and use him. For now, however, other schemes prevailed. Bremen and the Plantations, they were his immediate targets – the first shots in this new stage of the War. And afterwards?

DeVore laughed, then leaned forward, closing the file. The wise man chose his plays carefully. As in *wei chi*, it did not do to play too rigidly. The master player kept a dozen subtle plays in his head at once, prepared to use whichever best suited the circumstances. And he had more than enough schemes to keep the Seven busy.

But first Bremen. First he would hit them where it hurt most. Where they least expected him to strike.

Only then would he consider his next move. Only then would he know where to place the next stone on the board.

PART FOURTEEN   AT THE BRIDGE OF CH'IN

Summer 2207

The white glare recedes to the Western hills,
High in the distance sapphire blossoms rise.
Where shall there be an end of old and new?
A thousand years have whirled away in the wind.
The sands of the ocean change to stone,
Fishes puff bubbles at the bridge of Ch'in.
The empty shine streams on into the distance,
The bronze pillars melt away with the years.
—Li Ho, *On And On For Ever*, ninth century AD

Chapter 57

SCORCHED EARTH

L i Shai Tung stood beside the pool. Across from him, at the entrance to the arboretum, a single lamp had been lit, its light reflecting darkly in the smoked-glass panels of the walls, misting a pallid green through leaves of fern and palm. But where the great T'ang stood it was dark.

These days he courted darkness like a friend. At night, when sleep evaded him, he came here, staring down through layers of blackness at the dark, submerged forms of his carp. Their slow and peaceful movements lulled him, easing the pain in his eyes, the tenseness in his stomach. Often he would stand for hours, unmoving, his black silks pulled close about his thin and ancient body. Then, for a time, the tiredness would leave him, as if it had no place here in the cool, penumbral silence.

Then ghosts would come. Images imprinted on the blackness, filling the dark with the vivid shapes of memory. The face of Han Ch'in, smiling up at him, a half-eaten apple in his hand from the orchard at Tongjiang. Lin Yua, his first wife, bowing demurely before him on their wedding night, her small breasts cupped in her hands, like an offering. Or his father, Li Ch'ing, laughing, a bird perched on the index finger of each hand, two days before the accident that killed him. These and others crowded back, like guests at a death feast. But of this he told no one, not even his physician. These, strangely, were his comfort. Without them the darkness would have been oppressive, would have been blackness, pure and simple.

Sometimes he would call a name, softly, in a whisper, and that one would come to him, eyes alight with laughter. So he remembered them now, in joy and at their best. Shades from a summer land.

He had been standing there more than two hours when a servant came. He knew at once that it was serious – they would not have disturbed him otherwise. He felt the tenseness return like bands of iron about his chest and brow; felt the tiredness seep back into his bones.

'Who calls me?'

The servant bowed low. 'It is the Marshal, *Chieh Hsia*.'

He went out, shedding the darkness like a cloak. In his study the viewing screen was bright, filled by Tolonen's face. Li Shai Tung sat in the big chair, moving Minister Heng's memorandum to one side. For a moment he sat there, composing himself, then stretched forward and touched the contact-pad.

'What is it, Knut? What evil keeps you from your bed?'

'Your servant never sleeps,' Tolonen offered, but his smile was half-hearted and his face was ashen. Seeing that, Li Shai Tung went cold. *Who is it now?* he asked himself. *Wei Feng? Tsu Ma? Who have they killed this time?*

The Marshal turned and the image on the screen turned with him. He was sending from a mobile unit. Behind him a wide corridor stretched away, its walls blackened by smoke. Further down, men were working in emergency lighting.

'Where are you, Knut? What has been happening?'

'I'm at the Bremen fortress, *Chieh Hsia*. In the barracks of Security Central.' Tolonen's face, to the right of the screen, continued to stare back down the corridor for a moment, then turned to face his T'ang again. 'Things are bad here, *Chieh Hsia*. I think you should come and see for yourself. It seems like the work of the *Ping Tiao*, but...' Tolonen hesitated, his old, familiar face etched with deep concern. He gave a small shudder, then began again. 'It's just that this is different, *Chieh Hsia*. Totally different from anything they've ever done before.'

Li Shai Tung considered a moment, then nodded. The skin of his face felt tight, almost painful. He took a shallow breath, then spoke. 'I'll come, Knut. I'll be there as soon as I can.'

★

It was hard to recognize the place. The whole deck was gutted. Over fifteen thousand people were dead. Damage had spread to nearby stacks and to the decks above and below, but that was minimal compared to what had happened here. Li Shai Tung walked beside his Marshal, turning his bloodless face from side to side as he walked, seeing the ugly mounds of congealed tar – all that was left of once-human bodies – that were piled up by the sealed exits, conscious of the all-pervading stench of burned flesh, sickly sweet and horrible. At the end of Main the two men stopped.

'Are you certain?' There were tears in the old T'ang's eyes as he looked at his Marshal. His face was creased with pain, his hands clasped tightly together.

Tolonen took a pouch from his tunic pocket and handed it across. 'They left these. So that we would know.'

The pouch contained five small, stylized fish. Two of the golden pendants had melted, the others shone like new. The fish was the symbol of the *Ping Tiao*.

Li Shai Tung spilled them into his palm. 'Where were these found?'

'On the other side of the seals. There were more, we're certain, but the heat...'

Li Shai Tung shuddered, then let the fish fall from his fingers. They had turned the deck into a giant oven and cooked everyone inside – men, women and their children. Sudden anger twisted like a spear in his guts. '*Why*? What do they want, Knut? What do they want?' One hand jerked out nervously, then withdrew. 'This is the worst of it. The killings. The senseless deaths. For what?'

Tolonen had said it once before, years ago, to his old friend, Klaus Ebert; now he said the words again, this time to his T'ang. 'They want to pull it down. All of it. Whatever it costs.'

Li Shai Tung stared at him, then looked away. 'No...' he began, as if to deny it; but for once denial was impossible. This was what he had feared, his darkest dream made real. A sign of things to come.

He had been ill of late. For the first time in a long, healthy life he had been confined to bed. That too seemed a sign. An indication that things were slipping from him. Control – it began with one's own body and spread outward.

He nodded to himself, seeing it now. This was personal. An attack upon his person. For he *was* the State. *Was* the City.

There was a sickness loose, a virus in the veins of the world. Corruption was rife. Dispersionism, Levelling, even this current obsession in the Above with longevity – all these were symptoms of it. The actions of such groups were subtle, invidious, not immediately evident, yet ultimately they proved fatal. Expectations had changed and that had undermined the stability of everything.

They want to pull it down.

'What did they do here, Knut? How did they do this?'

'We've had to make some assumptions, but some things are known for certain. Bremen Central Maintenance report that all communications to Deck Nine were cut at second bell.'

'All?' Li Shai Tung shook his head, astonished. 'Is that possible, Knut?'

'That was part of the problem. They didn't believe it either, so they wasted an hour checking for faults in the system at their end. They didn't think to send anyone to make a physical check.'

Li Shai Tung grimaced. 'Would it have made a difference?'

'No difference, *Chieh Hsia*. There was no chance of doing anything after the first ten minutes. They set their fires on four different levels. Big, messy, chemical things. Then they rigged the ventilators to pump oxygen-rich air through the system at increased capacity.'

'And the seals?'

Tolonen swallowed. 'There was no chance anyone could have got out. They'd blown the transit and derailed the bolt. All the inter-level lifts were jammed. That was part of the communications blackout. The whole deck must have been in darkness.'

'And that's it?' Li Shai Tung felt sickened by the callousness of it all.

Tolonen hesitated, then spoke again. 'This was done by experts, *Chieh Hsia*. Knowledgeable men, superbly trained, efficiently organized. Our own special services men could have done no better ...'

Li Shai Tung looked back at him. 'Say it, Knut,' he said softly. 'Don't keep it to yourself. Even if it proves wrong, say it.'

Tolonen met his eyes, then nodded. 'All of this speaks of money. Big money. The technology needed to cut off a deck's communications – it's all too much for normal *Ping Tiao* funding. Out of their range. There has to be a backer.'

The T'ang considered a moment. 'Then it's still going on. We didn't win the War after all. Not finally.'

Tolonen looked down. Li Shai Tung's manner disturbed him. Since his illness he had been different. Off balance and indecisive, withdrawn, almost melancholy. The sickness had robbed him of more than his strength; it had taken some of his sharpness, his quickness of mind. It fell upon the Marshal to lead him through this maze.

'Maybe. But more important is finding out who the traitor is in our midst.'

'Ah...' Li Shai Tung's eyes searched his face, then looked away. 'At what level have they infiltrated?'

'Staff.'

He said it without hesitation, knowing that it had to be that high up the chain of command. No one else could have shaped things in this manner. To seal off a deck, that took clout. More than the *Ping Tiao* possessed.

Li Shai Tung turned away again, following his own thoughts. Maybe Yuan was right. Maybe they should act now. Wire them all. Control them like machines. But his instinct was against it. He had held back from acting on the Project's early findings. Even this – this outrage – could not change his mind so far.

'It's bad, Knut. It's as if you could not trust your own hands to shave your throat...'

Tolonen laughed; a short, bitter bark of laughter.

The old T'ang turned. 'You have it in hand. You, at least, I trust.'

The Marshal met his master's eyes, touched by what had been said, knowing that this was what shaped his life and gave it meaning. To have this man's respect, his total trust. Without thinking, he knelt at Li Shai Tung's feet.

'I shall find the man and deal with him, *Chieh Hsia*. Were it my own son.'

At that moment, on the far side of the world, Li Yuan was walking down a path on the estate in Tongjiang. He could smell the blossom in the air, apple and plum, and beneath those the sharper, sweeter scent of cherry. It reminded him of how much time had passed since he had been here; of how little had changed while he had been gone.

At the top of the terrace he stopped, looking out across the valley, down the wide sweep of marble steps towards the lake. He smiled, seeing her, there on the far side of the lake, walking between the trees. For a moment he simply looked, his heart quickening just to see her, then he went down, taking the steps in twos and threes.

He was only a few paces from her when she turned.

'Li Yuan! You didn't say...'

'I'm sorry, I...' But his words faltered as he noted the roundness of her, the fullness of her belly. He glanced up, meeting her eyes briefly, then looked down again. *My son*, he thought. *My son.*

'I'm well.'

'You look wonderful,' he said, taking her in his arms, conscious of the weeks that had passed since he had last held her. But he was careful now and released her quickly, taking her hands, surprised by how small they were, how delicate. He had forgotten.

No, not forgotten. Simply not remembered.

He laughed softly. 'How far along are you?'

'More than halfway now. Twenty-seven weeks.'

He nodded, then reached down to touch the roundness, feeling how firm she was beneath the silks she wore, like the ripened fruit in the branches above their heads.

'I wondered...' she began, looking back at him, then fell silent, dropping her head.

'Wondered?' He stared at her, realizing suddenly what had been bothering him. 'Besides, what's this? Have you no smiles to welcome your husband home?'

He reached out, lifting her chin gently with his fingers, smiling, but his smile brought no response. She turned from him petulantly, looking down at her feet. Leaf shadow fell across the perfection of her face, patches of sunlight catching in the lustrous darkness of her hair, but her lips were pursed.

'I've brought you presents,' he said softly. 'Up in the house. Why don't you come and see?'

She glanced at him, then away. This time he saw the coldness in her eyes. 'How long this time, Li Yuan? A day? Two days before you're gone again?'

He sighed and looked down at her hand. It lay limply in his own, palm upwards, the fingers gently bent.

'I'm not just any man, Fei Yen. My responsibilities are great, especially at this time. My father needs me.' He shook his head, trying to understand what she was feeling, but he could not help but feel angered by her lack of welcome. It was not *his* fault, after all. He had thought she would be pleased to see him.

'If I'm away a lot, it can't be helped. Not just now. I would rather be here, believe me, my love. I really would...'

She seemed to relent a little; momentarily her hand returned the pressure of his own, but her face was still turned away.

'I never see you,' she said quietly. 'You're never here.'

A bird alighted from a branch nearby. He looked up, following its flight. When he looked back it was to find her watching him, her dark eyes chiding him.

'It's odd,' he said, ignoring what she had said. 'This place... it's changed so little over the years. I used to play here as a child, ten, twelve years ago. And even then I imagined how it had been like this for centuries. Unchanged. Unchanging. Only the normal cycle of the seasons. I'd help the servants pick the apple crop, carrying empty baskets over to them. And then, later, I'd have quite insufferable belly-aches from all the fruit I'd gorged.' He laughed, seeing how her eyes had softened as he spoke. 'Like any child,' he added, after a moment, conscious of the lie, yet thinking of a past where it had really been so. Back before the City, when such childish pleasures were commonplace.

For a moment he simply looked at her. Then, smiling, he squeezed her hand gently. 'Come. Let's go back.'

On the bridge he paused and stood there, looking out across the lake, watching the swans moving on the water, conscious of the warmth of her hand in his own.

'How long this time?' she asked, her voice softer, less insistent than before.

'A week,' he said, turning to look at her. 'Maybe longer. It depends on whether things keep quiet.'

She smiled – the first smile she had given him in weeks. 'That's good. I'm tired of being alone. I had too much of it before.'

'I know. But things will change. I promise you, Fei. It will be better from now on.'

'I hope so. It's so hard here on my own.'

Hard? He looked across the placid lake towards the orchard, wondering what she meant. He saw only softness here. Only respite from the harsh realities of life. From deals and duties. Smelled only the healthy scents of growth.

He smiled and looked at her again. 'I decided something, Fei. While I was away.'

She looked back at him. 'What's that?'

'The boy,' he said, placing his hand on her swollen belly once more. 'I've decided we'll call him Han.'

Lehmann woke him, then stood there while he dressed, waiting.

DeVore turned, lacing his tunic. 'When did the news break?'

'Ten minutes back. They've cleared all channels pending the announcement. Wei Feng is to speak.'

DeVore raised an eyebrow. 'Not Li Shai Tung?' He laughed. 'Good. That shows how much we've rattled him.' He turned, glancing across the room at the timer on the wall, then looked back at Lehmann. 'Is that the time?'

Lehmann nodded.

DeVore looked down thoughtfully. It was almost four hours since the attacks. He had expected them to react quicker than this. But that was not what was worrying him.

'Has Wiegand reported back?'

'Not yet.'

DeVore went into the adjoining room and sat in the chair, facing the big screen, his fingers brushing the controls on the chair's arm to activate it. Lehmann came and stood behind him.

The *Ywe Lung* – the wheel of dragons, symbol of the Seven – filled the screen. So it did before every official announcement, but this time the backdrop to the wheel was white, signifying death.

Throughout Chung Kuo, tens of billions would be sitting before their screens, waiting pensively, speculating about the meaning of this break in regular programming. It had been a common feature of the War-that-wasn't-a-War, but the screens had been empty of such announcements for some while. That would give it added flavour.

He looked back at Lehmann. 'When Wiegand calls in, have him switched through. I want to know what's been going on. He should have reported back to me long before this.'

'I've arranged it already.'

'Good.' He turned back, smiling, imagining the effect this was having on the Seven. They would be scurrying about like termites into whose nest a great stick had just been poked; firing off orders here, there and everywhere; readying themselves against further attacks; not knowing where the next blow might fall.

Things had been quiet these last few months. Deliberately so, for he had wanted to lull the Seven into a false sense of security before he struck. It was not the act itself but the context of the act that mattered. In time of war, people's imaginations were dulled by a surfeit of tragedy, but in peacetime such acts took on a dreadful significance. So it was here.

They would expect him to follow up – to strike again while they were in disarray – but this time he wouldn't. Not immediately. He would let things settle before he struck again, choosing his targets carefully, aiming always at maximizing the impact of his actions, allowing the Seven to spend their strength fighting shadows while he gathered his. Until their nerves were raw and their will to fight crippled. Then – and only then – would he throw his full strength against them.

He let his head fall back against the thick leather cushioning, relaxing for the first time in days, a sense of well-being flooding through him. Victory would not come overnight but, then, that was not his aim. His was a patient game and time was on his side. Each year brought greater problems for Chung Kuo – increased the weight of numbers that lay heavy on the back of government. He had only to wait, like a dog harrying a great stag, nipping at the heels of the beast, weakening it, until it fell.

Martial music played from the speakers on either side of the screen. Then, abruptly, the image changed. The face of Wei Feng, T'ang of East Asia, filled the screen, the old man's features lined with sorrow.

'People of Chung Kuo, I have sad news…' he began, the very informality of his words unexpected, the tears welling in the corners of the old man's eyes adding to the immense sense of wounded dignity that emanated from him.

DeVore sat forward, suddenly tense. What had gone wrong?

He listened as Wei Feng spoke of the tragedy that had befallen Bremen, watching the pictures dispassionately, waiting for the old man to add something more – some further piece of news. But there was nothing. Nothing at all. And then Wei Feng was done and the screen cleared, showing the *Ywe Lung* with its pure white backdrop.

DeVore sat there a moment longer, then pulled himself up out of the chair, turning to face Lehmann.

'They didn't do it... The bastards didn't do it!'

He was about to say something more when the panel on his desk began to flash urgently. He switched the call through, then turned, resting on the edge of the desk, facing the screen.

He had expected Wiegand. But it wasn't Wiegand's face that filled the screen. It was that of Hans Ebert.

'What in hell's name has been happening, Howard? I've just had to spend two hours with the Special Investigation boys being grilled! Bremen, for the gods' sakes! The stupid bastards attacked Bremen!'

DeVore looked down momentarily. He had deliberately not told Ebert anything about their designs on Bremen, knowing that Tolonen would screen all his highest-ranking officers – even his future son-in-law – for knowledge of the attack. Caught out once that way, Tolonen's first thought would be that he had once again been infiltrated at staff level. It did not surprise him, therefore, to learn that Tolonen had acted so quickly.

'I know,' he said simply, meeting Ebert's eyes.

'What do you mean, you *know*? Were you involved in that?'

Ignoring Ebert's anger, he nodded, speaking softly, quickly, giving his reasons. But Ebert wasn't to be placated so simply.

'I want a meeting,' Ebert said, his eyes blazing. '*Today!* I want to know what else you've got planned.'

DeVore hesitated, not for the first time finding Ebert's manner deeply offensive, then nodded his agreement. Ebert was too important to his plans just now. He needn't tell him everything, of course. Just enough to give him the illusion of being trusted.

'Okay. This afternoon,' DeVore said, betraying nothing of his thoughts. 'At Mu Chua's. I'll see you there, Hans. After fourth bell.'

He broke contact, then sat back.

'Damn him!' he said, worried that he had still heard nothing. He turned. 'Stefan! Find out where the hell Wiegand is. I want to know what's been happening.'

He watched the albino go, then looked about the room, his sense of well-being replaced by a growing certainty.

Lehmann confirmed it moments later. 'Wiegand's dead,' he said, coming back into the room. 'Along with another fifty of our men and more than a hundred and fifty Ping Tiao.'

DeVore sat down heavily. 'What happened?'

Lehmann shook his head. 'That's all we know. We've intercepted Security reports from the Poznan and Krakov garrisons. It looks like they knew we were coming.'

DeVore looked down. Gods! Then the harvest was untouched, City Europe's vast granaries still intact. He could not have had worse news.

He shuddered. This changed things dramatically. What had been designed to weaken the Seven had served only to make them more determined.

He had known all along what the probable effect of a single strike against Bremen would have. Had known how outraged people would be by the assault on the soldiers' living quarters – the killing of innocent women and children. That was why he had planned the two things to hit them at the same time. With the East European Plantations on fire and the safe haven of Bremen breached, he had expected to sow the seeds of fear in City Europe. But fear had turned to anger, and what ought to have been a devastating psychological blow for the Seven had been transformed into its opposite.

No wonder Wei Feng had spoken as he had. That sense of great moral indignation the old man had conveyed had been deeply felt. And there was no doubting that the watching billions would have shared it. So now the Seven had the support of the masses of Chung Kuo. Sanction, if they wanted it, to take whatever measures they wished against their enemies.

DeVore sighed and looked down at his hands. No. Things could not have turned out worse.

But how? How had they known? Despair turned to sudden anger in him. He stood abruptly. Wiegand! It had to be Wiegand! Which meant that the report of his death was false; a fabrication put out for them to overhear. Which meant...

For a moment he followed the chain of logic that led out from that thought, then sat again, shaking his head. No, not Wiegand. His instinct was against it. In any case, Wiegand didn't have either the balls or the imagination for such a thing. And yet, if not Wiegand, then who?

Again he sighed, deciding to put the base on full alert. In case he was wrong. In case Wiegand had made a deal and was planning to lead Tolonen back here to the Wilds.

Emily Ascher was angry. Very angry. She trembled as she faced her four compatriots on the central committee of the *Ping Tiao*, her arm outstretched, her finger stabbing towards Gesell, the words spat out venomously.

'What you did was *vile*, Bent. You've tainted us all. Betrayed us.'

Gesell glanced at Mach then looked back at his ex-lover, his whole manner defensive. The failure of the attack on the Plantations had shaken him badly and he was only now beginning to understand what effect the Bremen backlash would have on their organization. Even so, he was not prepared to admit he had been wrong.

'I knew you'd react like this. It's exactly why we had to keep it from you. You would have vetoed it –'

She gave a high-pitched laugh, astonished by him. 'Of *course* I would! And rightly so. This could destroy us –'

Gesell lifted his hand, as if to brush aside the accusation. 'You don't understand. If our attack on the Plantations had succeeded –'

She batted his hand away angrily. 'I understand things perfectly. This was a major policy decision and I wasn't consulted.' She turned her head, looking across at the other woman in the room. 'And you, Mao Liang? Were *you* told?'

Mao Liang looked down, shaking her head, saying nothing. But that wasn't so surprising: since she had replaced Emily in Gesell's bed, it was as if she had lost her own identity.

She looked back at Gesell. 'I understand, all right. It's back to old patterns. Old men meeting in closed rooms, deciding things for others.' She made a sound of pure disgust. 'You know, I really believed we were beyond all that. But it was all lip-service, wasn't it, Bent? All the time you were fucking me, you really despised me as a person... After all, I was only a *woman*. An inferior being. Not to be trusted with *serious* matters.'

'You're wrong –' Gesell began, stung by her words.

'I don't know how you've the face to tell me I'm wrong after what you've done. And you, Mach. I know this was all your idea.'

Mach was watching her, his eyes narrowed slightly. 'There was good reason not to involve you. You were doing so well at recruiting new members.'

Again she laughed, not believing what she was hearing. 'And what's that worth now? All that hard work, and now you've pissed it all away. My word. I gave them my word as to what we were, and you've shat on it.'

'We're *Ko Ming*,' Gesell began, a slight edge to his voice now. 'Revolutionaries, not fucking hospital workers. You can't change things and have clean hands. It isn't possible!'

She stared back at him witheringly. '*Murderers*, that's what they're calling us. Heartless butchers. And who can blame them? We destroyed any credibility we had last night.'

'I disagree.'

She turned, looking at him. 'You can disagree as much as you like, Jan Mach, but it's true. As of last night this organization is dead. You killed it. You and this prick here. Didn't you see the trivee pictures of the children who died? Didn't you see the shots of those beautiful, blond-haired children playing with their mothers? Didn't something in you respond to that?'

'Propaganda –' began Quinn, the newest of them, but a look from Gesell silenced him.

Ascher looked from one to the other of them, seeing how they avoided her eyes. 'No? Isn't there one of you with the guts to admit it? *We* did that. The *Ping Tiao*. And this time there's nothing we can do to repair the damage. We're fucked.'

'No,' Mach said. 'There is a way.'

She snorted. 'You're impossible! What way? What could we possibly do that could even begin to balance things in our favour?'

'Wait and see,' Mach said, meeting her eyes coldly. 'Just wait and see.'

DeVore sat back on the sofa, looking about him at the once opulently furnished room, noting how the fabrics had worn, the colours faded since he had last come here. He picked up one of the cushions beside him and studied it a moment, reading the Mandarin pictograms sewn into the velvet. *Here men forget their cares.* He smiled. So it had been, once. But now?

He looked up as Mu Chua entered, one of her girls following with a fully laden tray. She smiled at him, lines tightening about her eyes and at the corners of her mouth.

'I thought you might like some *ch'a* while you were waiting, *Shih* Reynolds.'

He sat forward, giving the slightest bow of his head. 'That's kind of you, Mother.'

As the girl knelt and poured the *ch'a*, DeVore studied Mu Chua. She too was much older, much more worn than he remembered her. In her sixties now, she seemed drawn, the legendary ampleness of her figure a thing of the past. Death showed itself in her: in the sudden angularity of her limbs and the taut wiriness of her muscles; in the slackness of the flesh at neck and arm and breast. He had known her in better days, though it was unlikely she remembered him.

She was watching him, as if aware of how he looked at her. Even so, when she spoke again, her smile returned, as strong as ever. He smiled back at her. Though the body failed, the spirit lived on, in spite of all she'd suffered.

'Shall I let him know you're here?'

He shook his head, then took the offered bowl from the girl. 'No, Mu Chua. I'll wait.'

She hesitated, her eyes flicking to the girl then back to him. 'In that case, is there anything you'd like?'

Again he smiled. 'No. Though I thank you. Just let him know I'm here. When he's done, that is.'

He watched her go, then looked about him, wondering. Mu Chua's old protector, the Triad boss, Feng Chung, had died three years back, leaving a power vacuum down here below the Net. Rival Triads had fought a long and bloody war for the dead man's territory, culminating in the victory of Lu Ming-Shao, or 'Whiskers Lu' as he was better known. No respecter of fine detail, Lu had claimed Mu Chua's House of the Ninth Ecstasy as his own, letting Mu Chua stay on as Madam, nominally in charge of things. But the truth was that Lu ran things his way these days, using Mu Chua's as a clearing house for drugs and other things, as well as for entertaining his Above clients.

Things had changed, and in the process Mu Chua's had lost its shine. The girls here were no longer quite so carefree, and violence, once banned from the house, was now a regular feature of their lives.

So the world changes, thought DeVore, considering whether he should make Whiskers Lu an offer for the place.

'Has something amused you?'

He turned sharply, surprised that he'd not heard Ebert enter, then saw that the Major was bare-footed, a silk *pau* drawn loosely about his otherwise naked body.

DeVore set the *ch'a* bowl down beside him and stood, facing Ebert.

'I thought you were in a hurry to see me?'

Ebert smiled and walked past him, pulling at the bell rope to summon one of the girls. He turned back, the smile still on his lips. 'I was. But I've had time to think things through.' He laughed softly. 'I ought to thank you, Howard. You knew that Tolonen would screen his staff officers, didn't you?'

DeVore nodded.

'I thought so.'

There was a movement to their right, a rustling of the curtains, and then a girl entered, her head lowered. 'You called, Masters?'

'Bring us a bottle of your best wine and two...' He looked at DeVore, then corrected himself, 'No, make that just one glass.'

When she was gone, DeVore looked down, for the first time letting his anger show.

'What the fuck are you up to, Hans?'

Ebert blinked, surprised by DeVore's sudden hostility. Then, bridling, he turned, facing him. 'What do you mean?'

'I ought to kill you.'

'Kill me? Why?'

'For what you did. It didn't take much to piece it together. There was really no other possibility. No one else knew enough about our plans to attack the Plantations. It had to be you who blew the whistle.'

Ebert hesitated. 'Ah... that.' Then, unbelievably, he gave a little laugh. 'I'm afraid I had to, Howard. One of our captains got a whiff of things. If it had been one of my own men I could have done something about it, but the man had already put in his report. I had to act quickly. If they'd taken them alive...'

DeVore was breathing strangely, as if preparing to launch himself at the bigger man.

'I'm sure you see it, Howard,' Ebert continued, looking away from him.

'It's like in *wei chi*. You have to sacrifice a group sometimes, for the sake of the game. Well, it was like that. It was either act or lose the whole game. I did it for the best.'

You did it to save your own arse, thought DeVore, calming himself, trying to keep from killing Ebert there and then. It wouldn't do to be too hasty. And maybe Ebert was right, whatever his real motive. Maybe it had prevented a far worse calamity. At least the fortresses were safe. But it still left him with the problem of dealing with the *Ping Tiao*.

'So Wiegand's dead?'

Ebert nodded. 'I made sure of that myself.'

Yes, he thought. *I bet you did*. He forced himself to unclench his fists, then turned away. It was the closest he had come to losing control. *Don't let it get to you*, he told himself, but it did no good. There was something about Ebert that made him want to let fly, whatever the consequences. But, no – that was Tolonen's way, not his. It was what made the old man so weak. And Ebert, too. But he was not like that. He used his anger; made it work *for* him, not against him.

The girl brought the wine, then left them. As Ebert turned to pour, DeVore studied him, wondering, not for the first time, what Hans Ebert would have been had he not been born heir to GenSyn. A low-level bully, perhaps. A hireling of some bigger, more capable man, but essentially the same callous, selfish type, full of braggadocio, his dick bigger than his brain.

Or was that fair? Wasn't there also something vaguely heroic about Ebert – something that circumstance might have moulded otherwise? Was it his fault that he had been allowed everything, denied nothing?

He watched Ebert turn, smiling, and nodded to himself. Yes, it *was* his fault. Ebert was a weak man beneath it all, and his weakness had cost them dearly. He would pay for it. Not now – he was needed now – but later, when he had served his purpose.

'*Kan pei!*' Ebert said, raising his glass. 'Anyway, Howard. I've better news.'

DeVore narrowed his eyes. What else had Ebert been up to?

Ebert drank heavily from his glass, then sat, facing DeVore. 'You're always complaining about being underfunded. Well...' his smile broadened, as if at his own cleverness '...I've found us some new backers. Acquaint-ances of mine.'

'Acquaintances?'

Ebert laughed. 'Friends... People sympathetic to what we're doing.'

DeVore felt the tension creep back into his limbs. 'What have you said?'

Ebert's face cleared, became suddenly sharper. 'Oh, nothing specific, don't worry. I'm not stupid. I sounded them first. Let them talk. Then, later on, I spoke to them in private. These are people I trust, you understand? People I've known a long time.'

DeVore took a long breath. Maybe, but he would check them out himself. Thoroughly. Because, when it came down to it, he didn't trust Ebert's judgment.

'What sums are you talking about?'

'Enough to let you finish building your fortresses.'

DeVore gave a small laugh. Did Ebert know how much that was, or was he just guessing? One thing was certain: he had never told Hans Ebert how much even one of the great underground fortresses cost.

'That's good, Hans. I'll have to meet these friends of yours.'

Mu Chua closed the door behind her, furious with Ebert. She had seen the bruises on the girl's arms and back. The bastard! There'd been no need. The girl was only fourteen. If he'd wanted that he should have said. She'd have sent in one of the older girls. They, at least, were hardened to it.

She stood still, closing her eyes, calming down. He would be out to see her any moment and it wouldn't do to let him see how angry she was. Word could get back to Lu Ming-Shao, and then there'd be hell to pay.

She shuddered. Life here could still be sweet – some days – but too often it was like today: a brutish struggle simply to survive.

She went to her desk and busied herself, making out his bill, charging him for the two sessions and for the wine and *ch'a*. She paused, frowning, as she thought of his guest. There was something strangely familiar about *Shih* Reynolds – as if they'd met some time in the past – but she couldn't place him. He seemed a nice enough man, but could that really be said of anyone who associated with that young bastard? For once she wished she had overheard what they had been talking about. She could have – after all, Lu Ming-Shao had put in the surveillance equipment only four months back – but a lifetime's habits were hard to break. She had never spied on her clients and she didn't intend to start now, not unless Lu specifically ordered her to.

Mu Chua froze, hearing Ebert's voice outside, then turned in time to greet him as he came through the door into her office.

'Was it everything you wished for, Master?'

He laughed and reached out to touch her breast familiarly. 'It was *good*, Mu Chua. Very good. I'd forgotten how good a house you run.'

Her smile widened, though inside she felt something shrivel up at his touch. Few men touched her these days, preferring younger flesh than hers. Even so, there was something horrible about the thought of being used by him.

'I'm pleased,' she said, bowing her head. 'Here,' she said, presenting her bill, the figures written in Mandarin on the bright red paper.

He smiled and, without looking at the bill, handed her a single credit chip. She looked down, then bowed her head again.

'Why, thank you, Master. You are too generous.'

He laughed, freeing her breasts from her robe and studying them a moment. Then, as if satisfied, he turned to go.

'Forgive me, Major Ebert...' she began, taking a step towards him.

He stopped and turned. 'Yes, Mother Chua?'

'I was wondering... about the girl.'

Ebert frowned. 'The girl?'

Mu Chua averted her eyes. 'Golden Heart. You remember, surely? The thirteen-year-old you bought here. That time you came with the other soldiers.'

He laughed, a strangely cold laugh. 'Ah, yes... I'd forgotten that I got her here.'

'Well?'

He looked at her, then turned away, impatient now. 'Look, I'm busy, Mu Chua. I'm Major now, I have my duties...'

She looked at him desperately, then bowed her head again, her lips formed into a smile. 'Of course. Forgive me, Major.' But inwardly she seethed. Busy! Not too busy, it seemed, to spend more than two hours fucking her girls!

As the door closed behind him she spat at the space where he had been standing, then stood there, tucking her breasts back inside her robe, watching her spittle dribble slowly down the red, lacquered surface of the door.

'You bastard,' she said softly. 'I only wanted a word. Just to know how she is – whether she's still alive.'

She looked down at the credit in her hand. It was for a thousand *yuan* – more than four times what she had billed him for – but he had treated it as nothing.

Perhaps that's why, she thought, closing her hand tightly over it. *You have no values because you don't know what anything is really worth. You think you can buy anything.*

Well, maybe he could. Even so, there was something lost in being as he was. He lacked decency.

She went to the drawer of her desk and pulled out the strong box, opening it with the old-fashioned key that hung about her neck. Rummaging about amongst the credit chips, she found two for two hundred and fifty *yuan* and removed them, replacing them with Ebert's thousand. Then, smiling to herself, she felt amongst her underclothes and, after wetting herself with her finger, placed the two chips firmly up her clout.

She had almost saved enough now. Almost. Another month – two at the most – and she could get out of here. Away from Whiskers Lu and bastards like Ebert. And maybe she would go into business on her own again. For, after all, men were always men. They might talk and dress differently up there, but beneath it all they were the same creatures.

She laughed, wondering suddenly how many *li* of First Level cock she'd had up her in the fifty years she had been in the business. No. In that respect, nothing ever changed. They might talk of purity, but their acts always betrayed them. It was why she had thrived over the years – because of that darkness they all carried about in them. Men. They might all say they were above it, but, try as they would, it was the one thing they could not climb the levels to escape.

Fei Yen stood there before him, her silk robes held open, revealing her nakedness.

'Please, Yuan... It won't hurt me.'

His eyes went to her breasts, traced the swollen curve of her belly, then returned to her face. He wanted her so much that it hurt, but there was the child to think of.

'*Please...*'

The tone in her voice, the *need* expressed in it, made him shiver then reach out to touch her. 'The doctors...' he began, but she was shaking her head, her eyes – those beautiful, liquid-dark eyes of hers – pleading with him.

'What do they know? Can they feel what I feel? No... So come, Yuan. Make love to me. Don't you know how much I've missed you?'

He shuddered, feeling her fingers on his neck, then nodded, letting her undress him, but he still felt wrong about it.

'I could have hurt you...' he said, lying beside her afterwards, his hand caressing her stomach tenderly.

She took his hand and held it still. 'Don't be silly. I'd have told you if it hurt.' She gave a little shudder, then looked down, smiling. 'Besides, I want our child to be lusty, don't you? I want him to know that his mother is loved.'

Her eyes met his provocatively, then looked away.

Tolonen bowed deeply, then stepped forward, handing Li Shai Tung the report Hans Ebert had prepared on the planned attack on the Plantations.

'It's all here?' the T'ang asked, his eyes meeting Tolonen's briefly before they returned to the opening page of the report.

'Everything we discussed, *Chieh Hsia*.'

'And copies have gone to all the generals?'

'And to their T'ang, no doubt.'

Li Shai Tung smiled bleakly. 'Good.' He had been closeted with his Ministers since first light and had had no time to refresh his mind about the details. Now, in the few minutes that remained to him before the Council of the Seven met, he took the time to look through the file.

Halfway through he looked up. 'You know, Knut, sometimes I wish I could direct input all this. It would make things so much easier.'

Tolonen smiled, tracing the tiny slot behind his ear with his right index finger, then shook his head. 'It would not be right to break with tradition, *Chieh Hsia*. Besides, you have servants and Ministers to assist you in such matters.'

Yes, thought the T'ang, *and as you've so often said, it would only be another way in which my enemies could get to me. I've heard they can do it now. Programmes that destroy the mind's ability to reason. Like the food I eat, it would need to be 'tasted'. No, perhaps you're right, Knut Tolonen. It would only build more walls between Chung Kuo and I, and the gods know there are enough already.*

He finished the document quickly, then closed it, looking back at Tolonen. 'Is there anything else?'

Tolonen paused, then lowered his voice slightly. 'One thing, *Chieh Hsia*. In view of how things are developing, shouldn't we inform Prince Yuan?'

Li Shai Tung considered a moment, then shook his head. 'No, Knut. Yuan has worked hard these last few weeks. He needs time with that wife of his.' He smiled, his own tiredness showing at the corners of his mouth. 'You know how Yuan is. If he knew, he would be back here instantly, and there's nothing he can really do to help. So let it be. If I need him, I'll instruct Master Nan to brief him fully. Until then, let him rest.'

'*Chieh Hsia*.'

Li Shai Tung watched his old friend stride away, then turned, pulling at his beard thoughtfully. The session ahead was certain to be difficult and it might have helped to have had Yuan at his side, but he remembered the last time, when Wang Sau-leyan had insisted on the Prince leaving. Well, he would give him no opportunity to pull such strokes this time. It was too important. For what he was about to suggest...

Twenty years too late. He knew that now. Knew how vulnerable they had become in that time. But it had to be said, even if it split the Council. Because unless it was faced – and faced immediately – there could be no future.

He looked about him at the cold grandeur of the marble hallway, his eyes coming to rest on the great wheel of the *Ywe Lung* carved into the huge double doors, then shook his head. This was the turning point. Whatever they decided today, there was no turning back from this, no further chance to right things. The cusp was upon them.

And beyond?

Li Shai Tung felt a small ripple of fear pass down his spine, then turned and went across to the great doorway, the four shaven-headed guards bowing low before they turned and pushed back the heavy doors.

★

Wei Feng, T'ang of East Asia, sat forward in his chair and looked about him at the informal circle of his fellow T'ang, his face stern, his whole manner immensely dignified. It was he who had called this emergency meeting of the Council; he who, as the most senior of the Seven, hosted it now, at his palace of Chung Ning in Ning Hsia province. Seeing him lean forward, the other T'ang fell silent, waiting for him to speak.

'Well, cousins, we have all read the reports, and I think we would all agree that a major disaster was only narrowly averted, thanks to the quick action of Li Shai Tung's Security forces. A disaster which, whilst its immediate consequences would have befallen one of our number alone, would have damaged every one of us, for are not the seven One and the one Seven?'

There was nodding from all quarters, even from Wang Sau-leyan. Wei Feng looked about him, satisfied, then spoke again.

'It is, of course, why we are here today. The attack on Bremen and the planned attacks on the East European Plantations are significant enough in themselves, but they have far wider implications. It is to these wider implications – to the underlying causes and the long-term prospects for Chung Kuo – that we must address ourselves.'

Wei Feng looked briefly at his old friend, Li Shai Tung, then lifted one hand from the arm of his chair, seventy-five years of command forming that tiny, almost effortless gesture. All of his long experience, the whole majesty of his power was gathered momentarily in his raised hand, while his seated form seemed to emanate an aura of solemn purpose and iron-willed determination. His eyes traced the circle of his fellow T'ang.

'These are special circumstances, my cousins. Very special. I can think of no occasion on which the threat to the stability of Chung Kuo has been greater than it is now.'

There was a low murmur of agreement, a nodding of heads. To Li Shai Tung it felt suddenly like old times, with the Council as one not merely in its policy but in its sentiments. He looked across at Wang Sau-leyan and saw how the young T'ang of Africa was watching him, his eyes filled with sympathetic understanding. It was unexpected, but not, when he considered it, surprising, for this – as Wei Feng had said – threatened them all. If some good were to come of all that horror, let it be this – that it had served to unify the Seven.

He looked back at Wei Feng, listening.

'Not even in the darkest days of the War was there a time when we did not believe in the ultimate and inevitable triumph of the order which we represent. But can we say so with such confidence today? Bremen was more than a tragedy for all those who lost friends and family in the attack – it was a show of power. A statement of potentiality. What *we* must discover is this: who wields that power? What is that potentiality? The very fact that we cannot answer these questions immediately concerns me, for it indicates just how much we have lost control of things. For Bremen to have happened... it ought to have been unthinkable. But now we must face facts – must begin to think the unthinkable.'

Wei Feng turned slightly, the fingers of his hand opening out, pointed towards Li Shai Tung.

'Cousins! It is time to say openly what has hitherto remained unexpressed. Li Shai Tung, will you begin?'

Their eyes turned expectantly to the T'ang of Europe.

'Cousins,' Li Shai Tung began softly, 'I wish I had come to you in better days and spoken of these things, rather than have had adversity push me to it. But you must understand that what I say here today is no hasty, ill-considered reaction to Bremen, but has matured in me over many years. Forgive me also if what I say seems at times to border on a lecture. It is not meant so, I assure you. Yet it seemed to me that I must set these things out clearly before you, if only to see whether my eyes and my brain deceived me in this matter, or whether my vision and my reason hold good.'

'We are listening, cousin Li,' Tsu Ma said, his expression willing Li Shai Tung to go on – to say what had to be said.

Li Shai Tung looked about him, seeing that same encouragement mirrored in the faces of the other T'ang, even in the pallid, moon-like face of Wang Sau-leyan. 'Very well,' he said, keeping his eyes on Wang Sau-leyan, 'but you must hear me out.'

'Of course,' Wei Feng said quickly, wanting to smooth over any possibility of friction between the two T'ang. 'There will be ample time afterwards to discuss these matters fully. So speak out, Shai Tung. We are all ears.'

Li Shai Tung looked down, searching inside himself for the right words, knowing there was no easy way to put it. Then, looking up, his face suddenly set, determined, he began.

'You have all read Major Ebert's report, so you understand just how close the *Ping Tiao* came to succeeding in their scheme to destroy large areas of the East European Plantations. What you haven't seen, however, is a second report I commissioned. A report to ascertain the probable economic and social consequences had the *Ping Tiao* succeeded.'

He saw how they looked among themselves and knew that the matter had been in all their minds.

'It was, of necessity, a hastily compiled report, and I have since commissioned another to consider the matter in much greater detail. However, the results of that first report make fascinating and – without exaggerating the matter – frightening reading. Before I come to those results, however, let me undertake a brief résumé of the situation with regard to food production and population increase over the past fifteen-year period.'

He saw how Wang Sau-leyan looked down and felt his stomach tighten, instinct telling him he would have to fight the younger T'ang on this. Well, so be it. It was too important a matter to back down over.

He cleared his throat. 'Back in 2192 the official population figure for the whole of Chung Kuo was just short of thirty-four billion – a figure that excluded, of course, the populations of both Net and Clay. I mention this fact because, whilst the figure for the Clay might, with good reason, be overlooked, that for the Net cannot. The relationship of Net to City is an important one economically, particularly in terms of food production, for whilst we have no jurisdiction over the Net, we nonetheless produce all the food consumed there.

'Unofficial estimates for 2192 placed the population of the Net at just over three billion. However, the growing number of demotions over the period, added to an ever-increasing birth rate down there have given rise to latest estimates of at least twice that number, with the highest estimate indicating a below-Net population of eight billion.

'Over the same period the population of the City has also climbed, though not with anything like the same rate of growth. The census of 2200 revealed a rounded-up figure of 37.8 billion – a growth rate of just under half a billion a year.'

Li Shai Tung paused, recalling the reports his father had once shown him from more than two hundred years ago – World Population Reports compiled by an ancient body called the United Nations. They had contained an underlying assumption that, as Man's material condition improved, so his numbers would stabilize, but the truth was otherwise. One law alone governed the growth of numbers – the capacity of Humankind to feed itself. As health standards had improved, so infant mortality rates had plummeted. At the same time life expectancy had increased dramatically. With vast areas of the City being opened up yearly, the population of Chung Kuo had grown exponentially for the first century of the City's existence. It had doubled, from four to eight billion, from eight to sixteen, then from sixteen to thirty-two, each doubling a matter of only thirty years. Against such vast and unchecked growth the United Nations' estimate of the world's population stabilizing at 10.2 billion was laughable. What had happened was more like the ancient tale of the Emperor and the *wei chi* board.

In the tale the Emperor had granted the peasant his wish – for one grain of rice on the first square of the board, twice as much on the second, twice as much again on the third and so on – not realizing how vast the final total was, how far beyond his means to give. So it was with the Seven. They had guaranteed the masses of Chung Kuo unlimited food, shelter and medical care, with no check upon their numbers. It was madness. A madness that could be tolerated no longer.

He looked about him; saw how they were waiting for him, as if they knew where his words led.

'That rate of growth has not, thankfully, maintained itself over the last seven years. However, births are still outstripping deaths by two to one, and the current figure of thirty-nine and a half billion is still enough to cause us major concern, particularly in view of the growing problems with food production.'

So here he was, at last, speaking about it.

He looked across at Wu Shih, then back to Tsu Ma, seeing how tense his fellow T'ang had grown. Even Wei Feng was looking down, disturbed by the direction Li Shai Tung's words had taken. He pressed on.

'As you know, for the past twenty years I have been trying to anticipate these problems – to find solutions without taking what seems to me now the inevitable step. The number of orbital farms, for instance, has been increased eight hundred per cent in the past fifteen years, resulting in fifty-five per cent of all Chung Kuo's food now being grown off-planet. That success, however, has caused us new problems. There is the danger of cluttering up the skies; the problem of repairing and maintaining such vast and complex machineries; the need to build at least four and possibly as many as twelve new spaceports, capacity at the present ports being strained to the limit. Added to this, the cost of ferrying down the produce, of processing it and distributing it, has grown year by year. And then, as we all know, there have been accidents.'

He saw, once again, how they looked among themselves. This was the Great Unsaid. If the Seven could be said to have a taboo it was this – the relationship of food production to population growth. It was Chung Kuo's oldest problem – as old as the First Emperor, Ch'in Shih Huang Ti himself – yet for a century or more they had refused to discuss it, even to mention it. And why? Because that relationship underpinned the one great freedom they had promised the people of Chung Kuo – the one freedom upon which the whole great edifice of Family and Seven depended, *the right to have an unlimited number of children*. Take that away and the belief in Family was undermined; a belief that was sacrosanct – that was the very foundation stone of their great State, for were they not themselves the *fathers* of their people?

Yes. But now that had to change. A new relationship had to be forged, less satisfactory than the old, yet necessary, because without it there would be nothing. No Seven, no State, nothing but anarchy.

'We know these things,' he said softly, 'yet we say nothing of them. But now it is time to do our sums: to balance the one against the other and see where such figures lead us. All of which brings me back to the report I commissioned and its central question – what would have happened if the *Ping Tiao* had succeeded in their attack on the Plantations?'

'Li Shai Tung... ?' It was Wei Feng.

'Yes, cousin?'

'Will we be given copies of this report?'

'Of course.'

Wei Feng met his eyes briefly, his expression deeply troubled. 'Good. But let me say how... unorthodox I find this – to speak of a document none of us has seen. It is not how we normally transact our business.'

Li Shai Tung lowered his head, respecting his old friend's feelings. 'I understand, cousin, but these are not normal times, neither is this matter... *orthodox*. It was simply that I did not feel I could submit such a document for the record. However, when the detailed report is ready I shall ensure each of you receives a copy.'

Wei Feng nodded, but it was clear he was far from happy with the way things had developed, despite his words about 'thinking the unthinkable'. Li Shai Tung studied him a moment, trying to gauge how strongly he felt on the matter, then looked away, resuming his speech.

'However, from our first and admittedly hurried estimates, we believe that the Ping Tiao attack would have destroyed as much as thirty-five per cent of the East European growing areas. In terms of overall food production this equates with approximately ten per cent of City Europe's total.'

He leaned forward slightly.

'Were this merely a matter of percentage reductions the problem would be a relatively minor one – and, indeed, short term, for the growing areas could be redeveloped within three months – but the fact is that we have developed a distribution network that is immensely fragile. If you will forgive the analogy, we are like an army encamped in enemy territory that has tried to keep its supply lines as short as possible. This has meant that food from the Plantations has traditionally been used to feed the eastern Hsien of City Europe, while the food brought down from the orbitals – landed in the six spaceports on the west and southern coasts – has been used to feed the west and south of the City. If the Plantations failed it would mean shipping vast amounts of grain, meat and other edibles across the continent. It is not impossible, but it would be difficult to organize and immensely costly.'

He paused significantly. 'That, however, would be the least of our problems. Because production has not kept pace with population growth, the physical amount of food consumed by our citizenry has dropped considerably over the past fifteen years. On average, people now eat ten per cent less than they did in 2192. To ask them to cut their consumption by a further ten per cent – as we would undoubtedly have had to in the short term – would, I am told, return us to the situation we faced a year ago, with widespread rioting in the lower levels. The potential damage of that is, as you can imagine, inestimable.

'But let me come to my final point – the point at which my worries become your worries. For what we are really talking of here is not a question of logistics – of finding administrative solutions to large-scale problems

– but an ongoing situation of destabilization. Such an attack, we could be certain, would be but the first, and each subsequent attack would find us more vulnerable, our resources stretched much further, our options fewer. What we are talking of is a downward spiral with the only end in sight our own. My counsellors estimate that it would need only a twenty-five per cent reduction in food supplies to make City Europe effectively ungovernable. And what can happen in Europe can, I am assured, be duplicated elsewhere. So you see, cousins, this matter has brought to our attention just how vulnerable we are in this, the most important and yet most neglected area of government.'

He fell silent, noting the air of unease that had fallen over the meeting. It was Wu Shih, T'ang of North America, who spoke.

'And what is your answer?'

Li Shai Tung took a small, shuddering breath. 'For too long we have been running hard to try to catch up with ourselves. The time has come when we can do that no longer. Our legs cannot hold us. We must have controls. Now, before it is too late.'

'*Controls?*' Wang Sau-leyan asked, a faint puzzlement in his face.

Li Shai Tung looked back at him, nodding. But even now it was hard to say the words themselves. Hard to throw off the shroud of silence that surrounded this matter and speak of it directly. He raised himself slightly in his chair, then forced himself to say it.

'What I mean is this. We must limit the number of children a man might have.'

The silence that greeted his words was worse than anything Li Shai Tung had ever experienced in Council. He looked at Tsu Ma.

'You see the need, don't you, Tsu Ma?'

Tsu Ma met his eyes firmly, only the faintness of his smile suggesting his discomfort. 'I understand your concern, dear friend. And what you said – there is undeniably a deal of truth in it. But is there no other way?'

Li Shai Tung shook his head. 'Do you think I would even raise the matter if I thought there were another way? No. We must take this drastic action and take it soon. The only real question is how we go about it, how we can make this great change while maintaining the status quo.'

Wei Feng pulled at his beard, disturbed by this talk. 'Forgive me, Shai Tung, but I do not agree. You talk of these things as if they *must* come about, but I cannot see that. The attack on the Plantations would, I agree, have had serious repercussions, yet now we are forewarned. Surely we can take measures to prevent further attacks? When you said to me earlier that you wished to take decisive action, I thought you meant something else.'

'What else could I have meant?'

Wei Feng's ancient features were suddenly unyielding. 'It's obvious, surely, cousin? We must take measures to crush these revolutionaries. Enforce a curfew in the lower levels. Undertake level-by-level searches. Offer rewards for information on these bastards.'

Li Shai Tung looked down. *That was not what he meant. The solution was not so simple. The dragon of Change had many heads – cut off one and two more grew in its place. No, they had to be far more radical than that. They had to go to the source of the problem. Right down to the root.*

'Forgive me, cousin Feng, but I have already taken such measures as you suggest. I have already authorized young Ebert to strike back at the *Ping Tiao*. But that will do nothing to assuage the problem I was talking of earlier. We must act, before this trickle of revolutionary activity becomes a flood.'

Wu Shih was nodding. 'I understand what you are saying, Shai Tung, but don't you think that your cure might prove more drastic than the disease? After all, there is nothing more sacred than a man's right to have children. Threaten that and you might alienate not just the revolutionary elements but the whole of Chung Kuo.'

'And yet there are precedents.'

Wei Feng snorted. 'You mean the *Ko Ming* emperors? And where did that end? What did that achieve?'

It was true. Under Mao Tse-tung the *Ko Ming* had tried to solve this problem more than two hundred years before, but their attempt to create the one-child family had only had limited success. It had worked in the towns, but in the countryside the peasants had continued having six, often a dozen children. And though the situations were far from parallel, the basic underlying attitude was unchanged. Chung Kuo was a society embedded in the concept of the Family, and in the right to have sons. Such a change would need to be enforced.

He looked back at Wu Shih. 'There would be trouble, I agree. A great deal of trouble. But nothing like what must ultimately come about if we continue to ignore this problem.' He looked about him, his voice raised momentarily, passionate in its belief. 'Don't you *see* it, any of you? We *must* do this! We have no choice!'

'You wish to put this to a vote, Shai Tung?' Wei Feng asked, watching him through narrowed eyes.

A vote? He had not expected that. All he had wanted was for them to carry the idea forward – to agree to bring the concept into the realm of their discussions. To take the first step. A vote at this stage could prevent all that – could remove the idea from the agenda for good.

He began to shake his head, but Wang Sau-leyan spoke up, taking up Wei Feng's challenge.

'I think a vote would be a good idea, cousins. It would clarify how we feel on this matter. As Shai Tung says, the facts are clear, the problem real. We cannot simply ignore it. I for one support Shai Tung's proposal. Though we must think carefully how and when we introduce such measures, there is no denying the need for their introduction.'

Li Shai Tung looked up, astonished. Wang Sau-leyan... *supporting* him! He looked across at Tsu Ma, then at Wu Shih. Then perhaps...

Wei Feng turned in his chair, facing him. 'I take it you support your own proposal, Shai Tung?'

'I do.'

'Then that is two for the proposal.'

He looked at Wu Shih. The T'ang of North America looked across at Li Shai Tung, then slowly shook his head.

'And one against.'

Tsu Ma was next. He hesitated, then nodded his agreement.

'Three for, one against.'

Next was Chi Hsing, T'ang of the Australias. 'No,' he said, looking at Li Shai Tung apologetically. 'Forgive me, Shai Tung, but I think Wu Shih is right.'

Three for, two against.

On the other side of Wang Sau-leyan sat Hou Tung-po, T'ang of South America, his smooth, unbearded cheeks making him seem even younger than his friend, Wang. Li Shai Tung studied him, wondering if, in this as in most things, he would follow Wang's line.

'Well, Tung-po?' Wei Feng asked. 'You have two children now. Two sons. Would you have one of them not exist?'

Li Shai Tung sat forward angrily. 'That is unfair, Wei Feng!'

Wei Feng lifted his chin. 'Is it? You mean that the Seven would be exceptions to the general rule?'

Li Shai Tung hesitated. He had not considered that. He had thought of it only in general terms.

'Don't you see where all this leads us, Shai Tung?' Wei Feng asked, his voice suddenly much softer, his whole manner conciliatory. 'Can't you see the great depth of bitterness such a policy would bring in its wake? You talk of the end of Chung Kuo, of having no alternative, yet in this we truly have no alternative. The freedom to have children – that *must* be sacrosanct. And we must find other solutions, Shai Tung. As we always have. Isn't that the very reason for our existence? Isn't that the *purpose* of the Seven – to keep the balance?'

'And if the balance is already lost?'

Wei Feng looked back at him, deep sadness in his eyes, then turned, looking back at Hou Tung-po. 'Well, Tung-po?'

The young T'ang glanced at Li Shai Tung, then shook his head.

Three for. Three against. And there was no doubt which way Wei Feng would vote. Li Shai Tung shivered. Then the nightmare must come. As sure as he saw it in his dreams, the City falling beneath a great tidal wave of blood. And afterwards?

He thought of the dream his son, Li Yuan, had had, so long ago. The dream of a great white mountain of bones, filling the plain where the City had once stood. He thought of it and shuddered.

'And you, Wei Feng?' he asked, meeting his old friend's eyes, his own lacking all hope.

'I say no, Li Shai Tung. I say no.'

Outside, in the great entrance hall, Tsu Ma drew Li Shai Tung aside, leaning close to whisper to him.

'I wish a word with you, Shai Tung. In private, where no one can overhear us.'

Li Shai Tung frowned. This was unlike Tsu Ma. 'What is it?'

'In private, please, cousin.'

They went into one of the small adjoining rooms and closed the door behind them.

'Well, Tsu Ma? What is it?'

Tsu Ma came and stood very close, keeping his voice low, the movements of his lips hidden from the view of any overseeing cameras.

'I must warn you, Shai Tung. There is a spy in your household. Someone very close to you.'

'A spy?' He shook his head. 'What do you mean?'

'I mean just that. A spy. How else do you think Wang Sau-leyan has been able to anticipate you? He knew what you were going to say to the Council. Why else do you think he supported you? Because he knew he could afford to. Because he had briefed those two puppets of his to vote with Wei Feng.'

Li Shai Tung stared back at Tsu Ma, astonished not merely at this revelation but by the clear disrespect he was showing to his fellow T'ang, Hou Tung-po and Chi Hsing.

'How do you know?' he asked, his own voice a hoarse whisper now. It was unheard of. Unthinkable.

Tsu Ma laughed softly, and leaned even closer. 'I have my own spies, Shai Tung. That's how I know.'

Li Shai Tung nodded vaguely, but inside he felt numbness, real shock, at the implications of what Tsu Ma was saying. For it meant that the Seven could no longer trust each other. Were no longer, in effect, Seven, but merely seven men, pretending to act as one. This was an ill day. He shook his head. 'And what... ?'

He stopped, turning, as the knocking on the door came again.

'Come in!' said Tsu Ma, stepping back from him.

It was Wei Feng's Chancellor, Ch'in Tao Fan. He bowed low.

'Forgive me, *Chieh Hsia*, but my master asks if you would kindly return. Urgent news has come in. Something he feels you both should see.'

They followed Ch'in through, finding the other five T'ang gathered in Wei Feng's study before a huge wallscreen. The picture was frozen. It showed a shaven-headed Han, kneeling, a knife held before him.

'What is this?' Li Shai Tung asked, looking at Wei Feng.

'Watch,' Wei Feng answered. 'All of you, watch.'

As the camera backed away, a large 'big-character' poster was revealed behind the kneeling man, its crude message painted in bright red ink on the white in Mandarin, an English translation underneath in black.

PING TIAO INNOCENT
OF BREMEN TRAGEDY
WE OFFER OUR BODIES
IN SYMPATHY WITH
THOSE WHO DIED

The camera focused on the man once more. He was breathing slowly now, gathering himself about the point of his knife. Then, with a great contortion of his features, he cut deep into his belly, drawing the knife slowly, agonizingly across, disembowelling himself.

Li Shai Tung shuddered. *Our bodies...* did that mean? He turned to Wei Feng. 'How many of them were there?'

'Two, maybe three hundred, scattered throughout the City. But the poster was the same everywhere. It was all very tightly coordinated. Their deaths were all within a minute of each other, timed to coincide with the very hour of the original attack.'

'And were they all Han?' Tsu Ma asked, his features registering the shock they all felt.

Wei Feng shook his head. 'No. They were evenly distributed, Han and Hung Mao. Whoever arranged this knew what he was doing. It was quite masterful.'

'And a lie,' said Wu Shih angrily.

'Of course. But the masses will see it otherwise. If I had known I would have stopped the pictures going out.'

'And the rumours?' Tsu Ma shook his head. 'No, you could not have hushed this up, Wei Feng. It would have spread like wildfire. But you are right. Whoever organized this understood the power of the gesture. It has changed things totally. Before it we had a mandate to act as we wished against them. But now...'

Li Shai Tung laughed bitterly. 'It changes nothing, cousin. I will crush them anyway.'

'Is that wise?' Wei Feng asked, looking about him to gauge what the others felt.

'Wise or not, it is how I will act. Unless my cousins wish it otherwise?'

Li Shai Tung looked about him, challenging them, a strange defiance in his eyes, then turned and hurried from the room, his every movement expressive of barely controlled anger.

'Follow him, Tsu Ma,' Wei Feng said, reaching out to touch his arm. 'Catch up with him and try to make him see sense. I understand his anger, but you are right – this changes things. You must make him see that.'

Tsu Ma smiled, then looked away, as if following Li Shai Tung's progress through the walls. 'I will try, Wei Feng. But I promise nothing. Bremen has woken something in our cousin. Something hard and fierce. I fear it will not sleep until he has assuaged it.'

'Maybe so. But we must try. For all our sakes.'

Chapter 58

GODS OF THE FLESH

'**K**uan Yin preserve us! What is that?'

DeVore turned, looking at his new lieutenant. 'Haven't you ever seen one of these, Schwarz?' He stroked the blind snout of the nearest head, the primitive nervous system of the beast responding to the gentleness of his touch. 'It's a *jou tung wu*, my friend, a meat-animal.'

The *jou tung wu* filled the whole of the left-hand side of the factory floor, its vast pink bulk contained within a rectangular mesh of ice. It was a huge mountain of flesh, a hundred *ch'i* to a side and almost twenty *ch'i* in height. Along one side of it, like the teats of a giant pig, three dozen heads jutted from the flesh: long, eyeless snouts with shovel jaws that snuffled and gobbled in the conveyor-belt trough that moved constantly before them.

The stench of it was overpowering. It had been present even in the lift coming up, permeating the whole of the stack, marking the men who tended it with its rich, indelible scent.

The factory was dimly lit, the ceiling somewhere in the darkness high overhead. A group of technicians stood off to one side, talking softly, nervously amongst themselves.

Schwarz shuddered. 'Why does it have to be so dark in here?'

DeVore glanced at him. 'It's light-sensitive, that's why,' he said, as if that were all there was to it, but he didn't like it either. Why had Gesell wanted to meet them here? Was the lighting a factor? Was the bastard planning something?

DeVore looked past Schwarz at Lehmann. 'Stefan. Here.'

Lehmann came across and stood there silently, like a machine waiting to be instructed.

'I want no trouble here,' DeVore said, his voice loud enough to carry to the technicians. 'Even if Gesell threatens me, I want you to hold off. Understand me? He'll be angry. Justifiably so. But I don't want to make things any more difficult than they are.'

Lehmann nodded and moved back.

There was the sound of a door sliding back at the far end of the factory. A moment later five figures emerged from the shadows. Gesell, the woman, Ascher, and three others – big men they hadn't seen before. Looking at them, DeVore realized they were bodyguards and wondered why Gesell had suddenly found the need to have them.

The *Ping Tiao* leader wasted no time. He strode across and planted himself before DeVore, his legs set apart, his eyes blazing, the three men formed menacingly into a crescent at his back.

'You've got some talking to do this time, *Shih* Turner. And you'd better make it good!'

It was the second time Gesell had threatened DeVore. Schwarz made to take a step forward, but found Lehmann's hand on his arm, restraining him.

'You're upset,' DeVore said calmly. 'I understand that. It was a fuck-up and it cost us dearly. Both of us.'

Gesell gave a small laugh of astonishment. '*You?* What did it cost you? Nothing! You made sure you kept your hands clean, didn't you?'

'Are you suggesting that what happened was *my* fault? As I understand it, one of your squads moved into place too early. That tipped off a Security captain. He reported in to his senior commander. At that point the plug had to be pulled. The thing wouldn't have worked. If you calmed down a while and thought it through, you'd see that. My man on staff *had* to do what he did. If he hadn't, they'd have been in place, waiting for your assault squads. They'd have taken some of them alive. And then where would you be? They may have been brave men, *Shih* Gesell, but the T'ang's servants have ways of getting information from even the most stubborn of men.

'As for what I lost, I lost a great deal. My fortunes are bound up with yours. Your failure hurt me badly. My backers are very angry.'

DeVore fell silent, letting the truth of what he'd said sink in.

Gesell was very agitated, on the verge of striking DeVore, but he had been listening – thinking through what DeVore had been saying – and some part of him knew that it was true. Even so, his anger remained, unassuaged.

He drew his knife. 'You unctuous bastard –'

DeVore pushed the blade aside. 'That'll solve nothing.'

Gesell turned away, leaning against the edge of the trough, the *jou tung wu* in front of him. For a moment he stood there, his whole body tensed. Then, in a frenzy of rage, he stabbed at the nearest head, sticking it again and again with his knife, the blood spurting with each angry thrust, the eyeless face lifting in torment, the long mouth shrieking with pain, a shriek that was taken up all along the line of heads, a great ripple running through the vast slab of red-pink flesh.

Gesell shuddered and stepped back, looking about him, his eyes blinking, then threw the knife down. He looked at DeVore blankly, then turned away, while, behind him, the blind snouts shrieked and shrieked, filling the foetid darkness with their distress.

The technicians had held back. Now one of them, appalled by what the *Ping Tiao* leader had done, hurried across, skirting Gesell. He jabbed a needle-gun against the wounded head, then began rubbing salve into the cuts, murmuring to the beast all the while as if it were a child. After a moment the head slumped.

Slowly the noise subsided, the heads grew calm again, those nearest falling into a matching stupor.

'Still,' DeVore said after a moment, 'you've contained the damage rather well. I couldn't have done better myself.'

He saw how Gesell glanced uncertainly at Ascher and knew at once that he'd had nothing to do with the ritual suicides. He was about to make comment when a voice came from the darkness to his left.

'You liked that? That was my idea.'

DeVore turned slowly, recognizing Mach's voice. He narrowed his eyes, not understanding. Mach was the last person he would have expected to have tried to save the reputation of the *Ping Tiao*. No. The collapse of the 'Levellers' could only bolster the fortunes of his own secret movement-within-a-movement, the *Yu*.

Unless... He turned back, watching Gesell's face as Mach came towards him.

Of course! Gesell was out! Mach was now the *de facto* leader of the *Ping Tiao*. It was what he had sensed earlier; why Gesell had been so touchy. Why he had begun to surround himself with thugs. Gesell knew. Even if it hadn't been said, he knew. And was afraid.

Mach seemed taller, broader at the shoulder than before. Then DeVore understood. He was wearing uniform – the uniform of the Security Reserve Corps. His long dark hair was coiled tightly in a bun at the back of his head and he had shaved off the beard he usually wore. He strode across casually, smiling tightly at Gesell, then turned his back on his colleagues.

'You've balls, Turner, I'll grant you that. If I'd been in your shoes, this is the last place I'd have come.'

DeVore smiled. 'I gambled. Guessed that the surprise of seeing me here would make you listen to me. Even your friend, the hot-head over there.'

Gesell glared back at him, but said nothing. It was as if Mach's presence neutralized him.

Mach was nodding. 'I'm sorry about that. Bent lets things get on top of him at times. But he's a good man. He wants what I want.'

DeVore looked from one to the other, trying to make out exactly what their new relationship was. But one thing was clear: Mach was number one. He alone spoke for the *Ping Tiao* now. Overnight the illusion of equality – of committee – had dissipated, leaving a naked power struggle. A struggle that Mach had clearly won. But had he won anything of substance? Had he won it only to see the *Ping Tiao* destroyed? If so, he seemed remarkably calm about it.

'And what *do* you want?' he asked. 'Something new, or the same old formula?'

Mach laughed. 'Does it matter? Are you interested any longer?'

'I'm here, aren't I?'

Mach nodded, a slightly more thoughtful expression coming to his face. 'Yes.' Again he laughed. It was strange. He seemed more relaxed than DeVore had ever seen him. A man free of cares, not burdened by them.

'You know, I was genuinely surprised when you contacted us. I wondered what you could possibly want. After Bremen I thought you'd have nothing to do with us. I did what I could to repair the damage, but...' He shrugged. 'Well, we all know how it is. We are small fish in the great sea of the people, and if the sea turns against us...'

DeVore smiled inwardly. So Mach knew his Mao. But had he Mao's dour patience? Had he the steel in him to wait long years to see his vision made real? His creation of the *Yu* suggested that he had. And that was why he had come. To keep in touch with Mach. To cast off the *Ping Tiao* and take up with the *Yu*. But it seemed that Mach had not yet done with the *Ping Tiao*. Why? Were the *Yu* not ready yet? Did he need the *Ping Tiao* a while longer – as a mask, perhaps, to his other activities?

He looked down, deciding how to play it, then smiled, meeting Mach's eyes again.

'Let's just say that I believe in you, *Shih* Mach. What happened was unfortunate. Tragic, let's say. But not irreparable. We have patience, you and I. The patience to rebuild from the ashes, neh?'

Mach narrowed his eyes. 'And you think you can help?'

DeVore reached into his tunic pocket and took out the ten slender chips, handing them across to Mach.

Mach looked at them then laughed. 'Half a million *yuan*. And that'll solve all our problems?'

'That and four of my best propaganda men. They'll run a leaflet campaign in the lower levels. They'll reconstruct what happened at Bremen until even the most cynical unbeliever will have it on trust that the Seven butchered fifteen thousand of their own to justify a campaign against the *Ping Tiao*.'

Mach laughed. 'And you think that will work?'

DeVore shook his head. 'I *know* it'll work. The Big Lie always does.'

'And in return?'

'You attack the Plantations.'

Mach's eyes widened. 'You're mad. They'll be waiting for us now.'

'Like they were at Bremen?'

Mach considered. 'I take your point. But not now. We've lost too many men. It'll take time to heal our wounds, and even more to train others to take the place of those we lost.'

'How long?'

'A year, perhaps. Six months at the very least.'

DeVore shook his head. 'Too long. Call it a month and I can promise twenty times the money I've just given you.'

Mach's mouth opened slightly, surprised. Then he shook his head. 'For once it's not a question of money. Or haven't you heard? The T'ang's men raided more than a dozen of our cells this afternoon. To all intents and purposes the *Ping Tiao* has ceased to exist in large parts of City Europe. Elsewhere we're down to a bare skeleton. That's where I've been, inspecting the damage.'

DeVore looked past Mach at the others. No wonder the woman had been so quiet. They had known. Even so, his reasoning remained sound. Until the fortresses were ready, he needed an organization like the *Ping Tiao* to burrow away at the foundations of the City and keep the Seven under pressure. The *Ping Tiao*, or maybe the *Yu*. When the *Yu* were ready.

He was silent a moment. 'I see. Then you had best use my men to bolster your numbers, *Shih* Mach. Five hundred should be enough, don't you think? I'll arrange for Schwarz here to report to you two days from now. You'll have command, naturally.'

Mach narrowed his eyes. 'I don't understand. Why don't you just attack them yourself? I don't see what you get out of doing it this way.'

'You don't trust me, then?'

'Damn right, I don't!' Mach laughed and half moved away, then turned back, coming right up close to DeVore.

'Okay. Let's have no more games between us, *Major*. I know who you are, and I know what you've done. I've known it some while now. It explains a lot. But this... this just doesn't fit together.'

DeVore stared back at him, undaunted. *Of course he knew. Who did he think let him know?*

'Start thinking clearly, Mach. How could I get that many men into position without Security finding out about it? No. I need you, Mach. I need you to find false identities for these men. To find them places to live. To organize things for me. Beyond that we both need this. In my case to placate my backers; to let them see that something real, something tangible is being done against the Seven. You to bring new blood to your movement; to prove that the *Ping Tiao* isn't moribund.'

Mach looked away thoughtfully, then nodded. 'All right. We'll do as you say. But I want the funds up front, and I want them three days from now. As token of your good faith.'

It would be difficult, but not impossible. In any case, Ebert would pay. He'd fucked things up, so he could foot the bill.

DeVore offered his hand. 'Agreed.'

Mach hesitated, then took his hand. 'Good. Three days, then. I'll let you know where we'll meet and when.'

As he made his way back to the transporter, DeVore considered what had been said and done. Whatever happened now, Gesell was dead. After the raid on the Plantations if necessary, but before if it could be arranged. That was the last time he would put himself at risk with that fool.

He smiled. It had all seemed very bleak yesterday, when the news had first broken, but it was going to be all right. Maybe even better than before, in fact, because this gave him a chance to work much closer with Mach. To make him his tool.

In that Mach and the *jou tung wu* were alike. Neither was conscious of the role they served. Of how they were fattened only to be slaughtered. For that was their ultimate purpose in life. To eat shit and feed others. The *jou tung wu* to feed the *mei yu jen wen*, the 'sub-humans' of the City, and Mach – a finer, tastier meat – to feed himself.

He laughed. *Yes, Mach, I mean to eat you. To make your skull my rice bowl and feast upon your brains. Because that's how it is in this little world of ours. It's man eat man, and always has been.*

He slowed as he came closer to the transporter, checking for signs that anything was wrong, then, satisfied, he ducked inside, leaving his lieutenants to follow in the second craft.

He sat down at once, strapping himself in, the craft rising steeply even before the door was fully closed, the pilot following his earlier instructions to the letter, making sure there was no possibility of pursuit, no chance of ambush.

As the ground fell away he smiled, thinking of the equation he had made in his head. Yes, they were all meat-animals, every last one of them, himself included. But he could dream. Ah, yes, he could dream. And in his dreams he saw them – finer, cleaner beasts, all trace of grossness excised from their natures. Tall, slender creatures, sculpted like glass yet hard as steel. Creatures of ice, designed to survive the very worst the universe could throw at them. Survivors.

No... More than that. *Inheritors.*

He laughed. That was it – the name he had been looking for. *Inheritors.* He keyed the word into his wrist set, then closed his eyes and let his head fall back, relaxing.

Yes. But first he must destroy what stopped them from coming into being. In that, Tsao Ch'un had been right. The new could not come into being while the old remained. His inheritors could not stand tall and straight in that cramped little world of levels. So the old must go. The levels must be levelled, the walls torn down, the universe opened up again. In order that they might exist. In order that things could go forward again – onward to that ultimate of mind's total control of matter. Only then could they stop. Only then could there be surcease.

He shivered. That was the dream. The reason, no, the motivating force behind each action that he took – the dark wind blowing hard and cold at his back. To bring them into being. Creatures of ice. Creatures *better* than himself. What finer aim was there? What *finer* aim?

Hans Ebert stopped in the doorway, lowering his head in a bow of respect, then came on, the fully laden tray held out before him. As he came near, Nocenzi, Tolonen and the T'ang moved back slightly, letting him put it down in the space they had cleared. They had been closeted together three hours now, discussing the matter of reprisals and the new Security measures.

Li Shai Tung smiled, accepting a bowl of *ch'a* from the young Major. 'You shouldn't have, Hans. I would have sent a servant.'

Ebert's head remained lowered a moment longer. 'You were in deep discussion, *Chieh Hsia*. I felt it best to see to things myself.'

The old T'ang laughed softly. 'Well, Hans, I'm glad you did. I did not realize how much time had passed, or how thirsty I had grown.'

The T'ang made to sip from the bowl, but Ebert cleared his throat. 'Forgive me, *Chieh Hsia*. But if you'd permit me?'

Li Shai Tung frowned, then saw what Ebert meant. He handed him the bowl, then watched as the young man sipped, then wiped where his lips had touched with a cloth before handing back the bowl.

The T'ang looked at Tolonen and Nocenzi and saw how his own pleasure was mirrored in their faces. Ebert was a splendid young man, and he had been right to insist on tasting the *ch'a* before he himself had drunk it.

'One cannot be too careful, *Chieh Hsia*.'

Li Shai Tung nodded. 'You are quite right, Hans. What would your father say, neh?'

'To you, nothing, *Chieh Hsia*. But he would most certainly have chastised me for failing in my duties as his son if I had let you sip the *ch'a* untasted.'

Again the answer pleased the three older men greatly. With a last bow to his T'ang, Ebert turned and began to pour for the General and the Marshal.

'Well, Knut,' continued the T'ang , where he had left off, 'do you think we got them all?'

Tolonen straightened slightly, taking the bowl from Ebert before he answered.

'Not all, *Chieh Hsia*, but I'd warrant it'll be a year or more before we have any more trouble from them, if then. Hans did a fine job. And it was good that we acted when we did. If we had left it even an hour later we wouldn't have got anyone to inform on the scum and we would never have got to those cells. As it was...'

As it was they had practically destroyed the *Ping Tiao*. After the awfulness of Bremen there had been smiles again. Grim smiles of satisfaction at a job well done.

'I wish I had known,' the T'ang said, looking away. 'I might have pushed things a little less hard in Council. Might have waited a while and tried to convince my fellow T'ang rather than coerce them.'

'Forgive me, *Chieh Hsia*, but you acted as you had to,' Nocenzi said, his voice free of doubt. 'Whether the threat be from the *Ping Tiao* or from another group, the problem remains. And as long as population outstrips food production, it can only get worse.'

'Yes, Vittorio, but what can I do? The Council will hear nothing of population measures and I have done all that can be done to increase productivity. What remains?'

Nocenzi looked to Tolonen, who gave the slightest nod, then turned to young Ebert. 'Hans, you know the facts and figures. Would you like to spell it out for us?'

Ebert looked to his T'ang, then set his *ch'a* down. '*Chieh Hsia*?'

'Go ahead, Major.'

Ebert hesitated, then bowed his head. 'Forgive me, *Chieh Hsia*, but when I learned what had been planned against the Plantations, I decided, after consultation with Marshal Tolonen, to commission a report. One separate from those you had asked us to compile.'

The T'ang looked briefly at Tolonen, then frowned. 'I see. And what was in this report?'

'It was quite simple, *Chieh Hsia*. Indeed, it asked but one highly specific question. What would it cost in terms of manpower and finances to guard the Plantations adequately?'

'And the results of your report?'

Tolonen interrupted. 'You must understand, *Chieh Hsia*, that Ebert acted only under my strict orders. Neither would I have mentioned this had you been successful in Council. It's just that I felt we should be prepared for the worst eventuality. For the failure of our action against the *Ping Tiao* and the... the hostility, let us say, of the Seven to your scheme.'

The T'ang looked down, then laughed. 'I am not angry, Knut. Gods, no. I'm glad to have such fine men as you three tending to my interests. If I seem angry, it is at the need for us to take such measures. At the wastefulness of it all. Surely there's no need for us to breed and breed until we choke on our own excess of flesh!'

He looked about him angrily, then calmed, nodding to himself. 'Well, Hans? What would the cost be?'

Ebert bowed. 'In men we're talking of a further half-million, *Chieh Hsia*. Six hundred and fifty thousand, to be absolutely safe. In money – for food, billeting, equipment, salaries and so forth – it works out to something like eighty-five thousand *yuan* per man, or a total of somewhere between forty-two and fifty-five billion *yuan* per year.

'However, this scenario presumes that we *have* half a million trained Security guards ready for placement. The truth is, if we took this number of men from their present duties there would be a substantial increase in criminal activity throughout the levels, not to say a dramatic rise in civil disturbance at the very bottom of the City. It would reduce current strength by over twenty-five per cent, and that could well result in a complete breakdown of law and order in the lowest fifty levels.'

'And the alternative?'

'To take a much smaller number, say, fifty thousand, from present strength, then recruit to make up numbers. This, too, creates problems, primarily in training. To accommodate such an influx we would have to expand our training programme considerably. And the cost... forgive me, *Chieh Hsia*, but that alone would account for an estimated twenty billion, even before we equipped and trained the first recruit.'

Li Shai Tung considered a moment, then shook his head. 'I don't like it, ch'un tzu. To finance this would mean making cuts elsewhere, and who knows what troubles that would bring? But what choice do we have? Without enough food...'

He shrugged. It came back to the same thing every time. Population and food. Food and population. How fill the ever-growing rice bowl of Chung Kuo?

Tolonen hesitated, then bowed his head. 'Might I suggest a solution, Chieh Hsia?'

'Of course.'

'Then what of this? What if we were to adopt part of Hans's scheme? Aim for a force of, say, a quarter of a million, to be stationed on the Plantations, concentrated at key points to maximize their effectiveness. This to be phased in by degrees, at a rate of, say, fifty thousand every six months. That would take the strain off the training facilities while at the same time minimizing the social effects.'

'But that would take too long, surely?'

'Forgive me, Chieh Hsia, but the one thing Hans neglects to mention in his report is the effectiveness of his action against the Ping Tiao. If our problems of recruitment and training are great, imagine theirs. They've been routed. They won't easily recover from that. As I said earlier, it'll be a year at the very least before they're in any fit state to cause us problems, and there's no terrorist group of comparable size to take their place.'

The T'ang considered a moment, then nodded. 'All right. We shall do as you say, Knut. Draw up the orders and I'll sign them.' He turned, looking at Ebert. 'You have served me well today, Hans Ebert, and I shall not forget it. Neither shall my son. But come, let's drink this fine ch'a you brought before it cools.'

The three men bowed as one. 'Chieh Hsia...'

Li Yuan looked up from the document he was reading and yawned.

'You should take a break, my lord,' Chang Shih-sen, his personal secretary, said, looking across at him from his desk on the far side of the room. 'I'll finish off. There are only a few things remaining.'

Li Yuan smiled. They had been working since seven and it was almost midday. 'A good idea, Shih-sen. But it's strange that my father hasn't contacted me. Do you think he's all right?'

'I am certain of it, my lord. You would be the first to hear were your father ill.'

'Yes...' He looked down at Minister Heng's memorandum again, then nodded. 'It's interesting, this business with the Shepherd boy, don't you think?'

'My lord...' Chang Shih-sen was watching him, smiling.

Li Yuan laughed. 'All right. I know when I'm being bullied for my own good. I'll go, Shih-sen. But make sure you get an acknowledgment off to Heng Yu this afternoon. I've kept him waiting two days as it is.'

'Of course, my lord. Now go. Enjoy the sunshine while you can.'

Li Yuan went out into the brightness of the Eastern Courtyard, standing there a moment at the top of the broad steps, his hand resting on the cool stone of the balustrade. He looked about him, feeling totally at peace with the world. There was such order here. Such balance. He stretched, easing the tiredness of sitting from his limbs, then went down, taking the steps two at a time before hurrying across the grass, his silk *pau* flapping about him.

There was no sign of Fei Yen and her maids in the gardens, or in the long walk. The ancient, wall-enclosed space was still and silent. At the stone arch he turned, considering whether he should go to her rooms, then decided not to. She needed her rest. Now more than ever. For their son's sake.

As ever, the thought of it made him feel strange. He looked across at the ancient, twisted shapes of the junipers that rested in the shade of the palace walls, then turned his head, tracing the curved shape of the pool with his eyes. He held himself still, listening, and was rewarded with the singing of a bird, the sound distant, from across the valley. He smiled, sniffing the cool, late morning air, finding a faint scent of herbs underlying it.

It was a good day to be alive.

He turned, looking at the great upright of the arch, then let his fingers trace the complex, interwoven patterns in the stone. All this had stood here a thousand years and yet the pattern seemed freshly cut into the stone. As if time had no power here.

He turned, making his way towards the stables. It had been some time since he had seen his horses. Too long. He would spend an hour and make a fuss of them. And later, perhaps, he would exercise Fei's horse, Tai Huo.

The great barn of the stables was warm and musty. The grooms looked up from their work as he entered, then hurried forward to form a line, bowing from the waist.

'Please ...' he said. 'Carry on. I'll not disturb you.'

They backed away respectfully, then turned, continuing with their chores. He watched them a while, some part of him envying the simplicity of their existence, then he looked upwards, drawing in the strong, heady scents of the barn – scents that seemed inseparable from the darkly golden shadows of the stalls.

Slowly he went down the line, greeting each of the horses in its stall. The dark-maned barb, Hei Jian – 'Black Sword' – lifted her broad muzzle in greeting, letting him pat then smooth her flank. Mei Feng – 'Honey Wind' – the elegant Akhal-teke, was more skittish, almost petulant, but after a moment he relented, letting Li Yuan smooth the honey-gold of his flank, his sharp ears pricked up. He was the youngest of the six horses, and the most recently acquired, a descendant of horses that had served the wild herdsmen of West Asia thousands of years earlier.

Next was his brother's horse, the black Arab he had renamed Chi Chu – 'Sunrise'. He spent some time with it, rubbing his cheek against its neck, feeling a kinship with the mare that he felt with none of the others. Beside it was the white Arab, the horse he had bought for Fei Yen, Tai Huo – 'Great Fire'. He smiled, seeing the creature, remembering the night he had brought Fei Yen blindfolded to the stables to see him for the first time. That time they had made love in the stall.

He turned, looking past the horse's rump, then frowned. The fifth stall was empty. The Andalusian – his father's present to him on his twelfth birthday – was not there. He went out and stood there at the head of the stall, looking into the empty space, then turned, summoning the nearest of the grooms.

'Where is the Andalusian?'

The groom bowed low, a distinct colour in his cheeks. 'I... I...' he stammered.

Li Yuan turned, looking back at the stall, his sense of wrongness grow-ing. From outside he heard a clamour of voices. A moment later a tall figure appeared in the great doorway. Hung Feng-chan, the Chief Groom.

'My lord...' he began hesitantly.

Li Yuan turned, facing him. 'What is it, Hung?'

Hung Feng-chan bowed low. 'The Andalusian is being... exercised, my lord.'

Li Yuan frowned, his eyes returning to the empty stall. 'Exercised? I thought they were only exercised first thing. Is something wrong with the animal?'

'My lord, I–'

'The gods help us, Hung! What is it? Are you keeping something from me?'

He looked about him, seeing how the grooms had stopped their work and were looking on, their flat Han faces frightened now.

'Is the horse *dead*, Hung? Is that it?'

Hung bowed his head lower. 'No, my lord–'

'Then, in the gods' names, what *is* it?'

'Nan Hsin is being ridden, my lord.'

Li Yuan straightened up, suddenly angry. 'Ridden? Who gave permission for anyone to ride the beast?'

Hung Feng-chan was silent, his head bowed so low that it almost touched his slightly bent knees.

Li Yuan's bark of anger was unexpected. 'Well, Hung? Who is riding Nan Hsin? Or must I have it beaten from you?'

Hung raised his head, his eyes beseeching his young master. 'My lord, forgive me. I tried to talk her out of it...'

'Tried to...' He stopped, sudden understanding coming to him. Fei Yen. He was talking about Fei Yen. It couldn't be anyone else. No one else would have dared countermand his orders. But Fei was seven months pregnant. She couldn't go riding, not in her condition. The child...

He rushed past the Chief Groom and stood in the great doorway, looking out. The palace was to his left, the hills far off to the right. He looked, scanning the long slope for a sight of her, but there was nothing. Then he turned back, concern for her making him forget himself momentarily, all control gone from his voice, naked fear shaping his words.

'Where is she, Hung? Where in the gods' names is she?'

'I... I don't know, my lord.'

Li Yuan strode across to him and took his arms, shaking him. 'Kuan Yin preserve us, Hung! You mean you let her go out, alone, unsupervised, in *her* condition?'

Hung shook his head miserably. 'She forbade me, my lord. She said...'

'*Forbade* you? What nonsense is this, Hung? Didn't you realize how dangerous, how *stupid* this is?'

'My lord, I–'

Li Yuan pushed him away. 'Get out of my sight!' He looked about him, furious now. 'Go! All of you! Now! I don't want to see any of you here again!'

There was a moment's hesitation, then they began to leave, bowing low as they moved about him. Hung was last.

'My lord... ?' he pleaded.

But Li Yuan had turned his back on the Chief Groom. 'Just go, Hung Feng-chan. Go now, before I make you pay for your foolishness.'

Hung Feng-chan hesitated a moment longer, then, bowing to the back of his prince, he turned and left dejectedly, leaving Li Yuan alone.

Hans Ebert ran up the steps of the Ebert Mansion, grinning, immensely pleased with his day's work. It had been easy to manipulate the old men. They had been off balance, frightened by the sudden escalation of events, only too eager to believe the worst-case scenario he had spelled out for them. But the truth was otherwise. A good general could police the East European Plantations with a mere hundred thousand men, and at a cost only a tenth of what he had mentioned. As for the effect on the levels, that too had been exaggerated, though even he had to admit that it wasn't known precisely what effect such an attack would have at the lowest levels of the City.

He went through to his suite of rooms to shower and change. As he stripped off, he stood over his personal comset, scrolling through until he came upon a cryptic message from his uncle.

Beattie asks if you'll settle his bar bill for him. He says a thousand will cover it.
Love, your Uncle Lutz.

Beattie was DeVore. Now what did DeVore want ten million for? Ebert kicked off his shorts and went across to the shower, the water switching on as soon as he stepped beneath the spray. Whatever DeVore wanted, it was probably best to give him just now. To pacify him. It would be easy enough to reroute that much. He would get on to it later. Just now, however, he felt like making his regular sacrifice to the gods of the flesh. He closed his eyes, letting the lukewarm jets play on him invigoratingly. Yes, it would be good to have an hour with the *mui tsai*. To get rid of all the tensions that had built up over the last few days.

He laughed, feeling his sex stir at the thought of her.

'You were a bargain, my lovely,' he said softly. 'If I'd paid ten times as much, you'd have been a bargain.'

The thought was not an idle one. For some time now he had thought of duplicating her. Of transferring those qualities that made her such a good companion to a vat-made model. After all, what wouldn't the Supernal pay for such delicious talents? GenSyn could charge five times the price of their current models. Fifty times, if they handled the publicity properly.

Yes, he could see the campaign now. All the different, subtle ways of suggesting it without actually saying it: of hiding the true function of their latest model and yet letting it be known...

He laughed then stepped out, into the drying chamber, letting the warm air play across his body. Or maybe he would keep her for himself. After all, why should every jumped-up little merchant be able to buy such pleasures?

He threw on a light silk gown and went through, down a small flight of steps into the central space. The mansion was shaped irregularly, forming a giant G about the gardens. A small wooden bridge led across a narrow stream to a series of arbours. Underfoot was a design of plum blossom, picked out in small pale pink and grey pebbles, while on every side small red-painted wooden buildings, constructed in the Han style, lay half-hidden among the trees, their gently sloping roofs overhanging the narrow ribbon of water that threaded its way backwards and forwards across the gardens.

The gardens were much older than the house. Or at least their design was, for his grandfather had had them modelled on an ancient Han original, naming them the Gardens of Peace and Prosperity. The Han character for longevity was carved everywhere, into stone and wood, and inlaid into mosaic at the bottom of the clear, fast-running stream. Translucent, paper-covered windows surrounded the garden on all sides, while here and there a moon door opened on to new vistas – another tiny garden or a suite of rooms.

Hans stopped in the middle of the gardens, leaning on the carved wooden balustrade, looking down at his reflection in the still, green water of the central pond. Life was good. Life was very good. He laughed, then looked across at the three ancient pomegranate trees on the far side of the pool, noting how their trunks were shaped like flowing water; how they seemed to rest there, doubled in the stillness of the water. Then, as he watched, a fish surfaced, rippling the mirror, making the trees dance violently, their long, dark trunks undulating like snakes.

And then he heard it, unmistakable. The sound of a baby crying.

He turned, puzzled. *A baby? Here? Impossible. There were no children here.* He listened then heard it again, clearer now, from somewhere to his left. In the servants' quarters.

He made his way around the pool and across the high-arched stone bridge, then stood there, concentrating, all thoughts of the *mui tsai* gone.

A baby. It was unmistakably a baby. But who would dare bring a baby here? The servants knew the house rules. His mother's nerves were bad. They knew that, and they knew the rules...

He pulled the robe tighter about him, then climbed the steps, hauling himself up on to the terrace that ran the length of the servants' quarters. The sound came regularly now; a whining, mewling sound, more animal than human. An awful, irritating sound.

He went inside, finding the first room empty. But the noise was louder here, much louder, and he could hear a second sound beneath it – the sound of a woman trying to calm the child.

'Hush now...' the voice said softly. 'Hush, my pretty one.'

He frowned, recognizing the voice. It was Golden Heart, the girl he had bought from Mu Chua's sing-song house ten years back. The girl he had taunted Fest with before he'd killed him.

Yes, Golden Heart. But what was she doing with a baby?

He made his way through, slowly, silently, until he stood there in the doorway of her room, looking in. The girl was crouched over a cot, her back to him, cooing softly to the child. The crying had stopped now and the baby seemed to be sleeping. But whose child was it? And who had given permission for it to be brought into the house? If his mother found out she would have them dismissed on the spot.

'Golden Heart?'

The girl started, then turned to face him, the blood drained from her face.

'Excellency...' she said breathlessly, bowing low, her body placed between him and the cot, as if to hide the child.

He stepped into the room, looking past her. 'What's happening here?'

She half turned her head, clearly frightened, taking one small step backwards so that she bumped against the edge of the cot.

'Whose child is that?'

She looked up at him, her eyes wide with fear. 'Excellency...' she repeated, her voice small, intimidated.

He saw and understood. He would get nothing out of her by frightening her, but it was important that he know whose child it was and why it had been brought here. Whoever it was, they would have to go, because this was too serious a breach of house rules to be overlooked. He moved closer, then crouched down before the girl, taking her hands and looking up into her face.

'I'm not angry with you, Golden Heart,' he said softly, 'but you know the rules. The child shouldn't be here. If you'll tell me who the mother is, I'll arrange for her to take the child away, but you can't keep her here. You know you can't.'

He saw doubt war with a strange, wild hope in her face and looked down, puzzled. What was happening here? He looked up at her again, his smile encouraging her.

'Come, Golden Heart. I'll not be angry. You were only taking care of it, after all. Just tell me who the mother is.'

She looked away, swallowing almost painfully. Again there was that strange struggle in her face, then she looked back at him, her eyes burning wildly.

'The child is yours. Your son.'

'Mine?' He laughed sourly, shaking his head. 'How can it be mine?'

'And mine,' she said softly, uncertainly. '*Our* child...'

He stood, cold anger spreading through him. 'What is this nonsense? How could *you* have a child? You were sterilized years ago.'

She bowed her head, taken aback by the sudden sharpness of his voice. 'I know...' she said. 'But I had it reversed. There's a place...'

'Gods!' he said quietly, understanding what she had done. Of course. He saw it now. She must have stolen some jewellery or something to pay for it. But the child...

He pushed past her, looking down at the sleeping infant. It was a large baby, five or six months in age, with definite Eurasian features. But how had she kept him hidden? How kept her pregnancy from being noticed?

'No... I don't believe you.'

She came and stood beside him, resting her hands against the rail of the cot, her chest rising and falling violently, a strange expectation in her face. Then she bent down and lifted the child from the cot, cradling him.

'It's true,' she said, turning, offering the child to him. 'He's yours, Hans. When I knew I'd fallen I had him removed and tended in a false uterus. After the birth I had him placed in a nursery. I'd visit him there. And sometimes I'd bring him back here. Like today.'

'Secretly,' he said, his voice calm, distant, a thousand li from his thoughts.

'Yes...' she said, lowering her head slightly, willing now to be chastised. But still she held the child out to him, as if he should take it and acknowledge it.

'No,' he said, after a moment. 'No, Golden Heart. You had no child. Don't you understand that? That thing you hold doesn't exist. It can't be allowed to exist. GenSyn is a complex business and you had no right to meddle in it. That thing would be an impediment. A legal nightmare. It would... *inconvenience* things. Can't you see that?'

A muscle twitched beneath her left eye, otherwise she made no sign that she had understood the meaning of his words.

'It's all right,' he said. 'You won't be punished for your foolishness. But this...' he lifted his hand vaguely, indicating the sleeping child '...this can't be allowed. I'll have someone take it now and destroy it.'

Her whimper of fear surprised him. He looked at her, saw the tears that were welling in her eyes, and shook his head. *Didn't she understand? Had she no sense at all?*

'You had no right, Golden Heart. You belong to me. You do what *I* say, not what *you* want. And this... this is ridiculous. Did you really think you could get away with it? Did you really believe for a moment...?'

He laughed, but the laughter masked his anger. No. It was not on. And now his mood was broken. He had been looking forward to the *mui tsai*, but now even the thought of sex was suddenly repugnant to him. Damn her! Damn the stupid girl with her addle-brained broodiness! He should have known something was up. Should have sensed it. Well, she'd not have another chance, that was certain. He'd have the doctors make sure of it this time. Have them make it irreversible.

And the child? It was as he'd said. The child didn't exist. It could not be allowed to exist. Because GenSyn would be threatened by its existence, the very structure of the company undermined by the possibility of a long, protracted inheritance battle in the courts.

He looked at the girl again, at the pathetic bundle she held out before her, and shook his head. Then he turned away, calling out as he did so, summoning his servants to him.

Li Shai Tung's figure filled the tiny overhead screen, his face grave, the white robes of mourning he wore flowing loosely about him as he came slowly down the steps to make his offering before the memorial plaque. Beneath the screen, its polished surface illuminated by the flickering light from the monitor, another, smaller plaque had been set into the foot of the wall, listing all those who had died in this small section of the deck.

Axel Haavikko knelt before the plaque, his head bowed, his shoulders hunched forward. His face was gaunt, his eyes red from weeping. He had not slept since the news had come.

He had thought himself alive again, reborn after years of self-destruction – years spent in idle, worthless dissipation – that moment in Tolonen's office twelve years before, when Hans Ebert had betrayed him, put behind him finally, his life redeemed by his friendship with Karr and Chen, made sense of by their common determination to expose Ebert – to show him for the hollow, lying shit he was. But all that was as nothing now. The light that had burned in him anew had gone out. His sister was dead. Vesa, his beloved Vesa, was dead. And nothing – *nothing* – could redeem the waste of that.

He took a shivering breath then looked up again, seeing the image of the T'ang reflected in the plaque where Vesa's name lay. Vesa Haavikko. It was all that remained of her now. That and the relentless ghosts of memory.

On that morning he had gone walking with her. Had held her arm and shared her laughter. They had got up early and gone down to see the old men and their birds in the treelined Main at the bottom of Bremen stack.

Had sat at a café and talked about their plans for the future. And afterwards he had kissed her cheek and left her to go on duty, never for a moment suspecting that it was the last time he would ever see her.

He moaned softly, pressing his hands against his thighs in anguish. *Why her? She had done nothing. If anyone, it was he who deserved punishment. So why her?*

He swallowed painfully, then shook his head, but the truth would not be denied. She was dead. His beloved Vesa was dead. Soul-mate and conscience, the best part of himself, she was no more.

He frowned then looked down, suddenly bitter, angry with himself. It was his fault. He had brought her here, after all. After long years of neglect he had finally brought her to him. And to what end?

A tear welled and trickled down his cheek.

He shuddered, then put his hand up to his face. His jaw ached from where he had been gritting his teeth, trying to fend off the images that came – those dreadful imaginings of her final moments that tore at him, leaving him broken, wishing only for an end to things.

An end... Yes, there would be an end to everything. But first he had a score to settle. One final duty to perform.

He took a deep breath, summoning the energy to rise, then grew still, hearing a noise behind him: a gentle sobbing. He half turned and saw her there, kneeling just behind him to his right, a young woman, a *Hung Mao*, dressed in mourning clothes. Beside her, his tiny hand clutching hers, stood a child, a Han, bemusement in his three-year-old face.

He looked down, swallowing. The sight of the boy clutching his mother's hand threw him back across the years; brought back the memory of himself, standing there before his mother's plaque; of looking down and seeing Vesa's hand, there in his own, her fingers laced into his, her face looking up at him, not understanding. Two she had been, he five. And yet so old he had felt that day; so brave, they'd said, to keep from crying.

No, he had never cried for his mother. But now he would. For mother and sister and all. For the death of all that was good and decent in the world.

Li Yuan was standing in the stable doorway when she returned, his arms folded across his chest, his face closed to her. He helped her from the saddle, coldly silent, his manner over-careful, exaggeratedly polite.

She stared at him, amused by this rare display of anger, trying to make him acknowledge her presence, but he would not meet her eyes.

'There,' she said, pressing one hand against the small of her back to ease the ache. 'No harm done.'

She smiled and went to kiss him.

He drew back sharply, glaring at her, then took her hand roughly and led her into the dark warmth of the stable. She went reluctantly, annoyed with him now, thinking him childish.

Inside he settled the horse in its stall then came back to her, making her sit, standing over her, his hands on his hips, his eyes wide with anger.

'What in hell's name do you think you were doing?'

She looked away. 'I was riding, that's all.'

'Riding...' he murmured, then raised his voice. 'I said you weren't to ride!'

She looked up, indignation rising in her. 'I'm not a child, Li Yuan. I can decide for myself what's best for me!'

He laughed scornfully then turned, taking three steps away from her. 'You can decide?' He looked directly at her, his expression openly contemptuous. 'You... You're seven months pregnant and you think riding is best for you?'

'No harm was done,' she repeated, tossing her head. She would not be lectured by him! Not in ten thousand years! She turned her face aside, shaking now with anger.

He came across and stood there, over her, for a moment the image of his father, his voice low but menacing. 'You say that you're not a child, Fei Yen, yet you've acted like one. How could you be so stupid?'

Her eyes flared. Who was he to call her stupid? This... this... boy! He had gone too far. She pulled herself up awkwardly from the chair and pushed past him. 'I shall ride when I like! You'll not prevent me!'

'Oh, won't I?' He laughed, but his mouth was shaped cruelly and his eyes were lit with sudden determination. 'Watch! I'll show you how...'

She was suddenly afraid. She watched him stride across the straw-strewn tiles, coldness in her stomach. He wouldn't... But then the certainty of it hit her and she cried out – 'No-o-o!' – knowing what he meant to do. She screamed it at his back, then went after him, nausea mixing with her fear and anger.

At the far end of the stable he turned, abruptly, so that she almost ran into him. He seized her upper arms, his fingers gripping the flesh tightly, making her wince.

'You'll stand here and watch. You'll witness the price of your stupidity!'

There was so much anger, so much real venom in his words that she swayed, feeling faint, paralysed into inaction by this sudden change in him. As she watched, he took the power-gun from the rack and checked its charge, then went down the row of horses.

At the end stall he paused and turned to look at her, then went in, his hand smoothing the flank of the dark horse, caressing its long face, before he placed the stubby gun against its temple.

'Goodbye,' he whispered, then squeezed the trigger, administering the high-voltage shock.

The horse gave a great snort then collapsed on to the floor of the stall, dead. Fei Yen, watching, saw how he shuddered, then stepped back, looking at what he'd done, his face muscles twitching violently.

Appalled, she watched him move down the stalls, her horror mounting as the seconds passed.

Five mounts lay dead on the straw. Only the last of them remained, the horse in the third stall, the black Arab that had once been Han's. She stood there, her hands clenched into tight fists, looking in at it. She mouthed its secret name, cold numbness gripping her, then turned, looking at Li Yuan.

Li Yuan was breathing deeply now. He stood there in the entrance to the stall, for a moment unaware of the woman at his side, looking in at the beautiful beast that stood so proudly before him, its head turned, its dark eyes watching him. His anger had drained from him, leaving only a bitter residue: a sickness gnawing at the marrow of his bones. He shook his head, wanting to cry out for all the pain and anger she had made him feel, then turned and looked at her, seeing now how ill her beauty sat on her.

Like a mask, hiding her selfishness.

He bit his lip, struggling with what he felt, trying to master it. There was the taste of blood in his mouth.

For a moment longer he stood there, trembling, the gun raised, pointed at her. Then he threw it down.

For a time afterwards he stood there, his hands empty, staring down at the red earth floor, at the golden spill of straw that covered it, blankness at the very core of him. When he looked up again she was gone. Beyond the stable doors the sky was a vivid blue. In the distance the mountains showed green and grey and white, swathed in mist.

He went out and stood there, looking out into the beauty of the day, letting his numbness seep down out of him, into the earth. Then he turned back and went inside again, bending down to pick up the gun.

The child – that was all that mattered now, all that was important. To make the Seven strong again.

'I'm sorry, Han,' he whispered gently, laying his face against the horse's neck. 'The gods know I didn't wish for this.' Then, tears blurring his vision, he stepped back and rested the gun against the horse's temple, easing back the trigger.

Chapter 59

THE WAY OF DECEPTION

F ei Yen went back to her father's house. For a week Li Yuan did nothing, hoping she would return of her own free will, then, when there
was no sign of her returning, he went to see her, taking time off from
his duties.

The Yin house defences tracked him from twenty *li* out, checking and
rechecking his codes before granting him permission to set down. He
landed his private craft in the military complex at the back of the estate, in a
shadowy hangar where the sharp, sweet scents of pine and lemon mingled
with the smell of machine oils.

Two of Yin Tsu's three sons, Sung and Chan, were waiting there to greet
him, bowed low, keeping a respectful silence.

The palace was on an island at the centre of a lake; an elegant, two-storey
building in the Ming style, its red, corbelled roof gently sloped, its broad,
panelled windows reminiscent of older times. Seeing it, Li Yuan smiled, his
past memories tinged with present sadness.

The two sons rowed him across the lake, careful not to embarrass him
with their attentions. Fei's father, Yin Tsu, was waiting on the landing stage
before the palace, standing beneath an ancient willow whose shadow dap-
pled the sunlit water.

He bowed low as Li Yuan stepped from the boat.

'You are welcome, Li Yuan. To what do I owe this honour?'

Yin Tsu was a small, neat man. His pure white hair was cut short about his neck in an almost occidental style, slicked back from his high forehead. He held himself stiffly now, yet despite his white hair and seventy-four years he was a sprightly man with a disposition towards smiles and laughter. Just now, however, his small, fine features seemed morose, the tiny webs of lines at the corners of his eyes and mouth drawn much deeper than before.

Li Yuan took his hands. Small hands, like a woman's, the skin smooth, almost silky, the fingernails grown long.

'I need to see my wife, Honoured Father-in-Law. I must talk with her.'

A faint breeze was blowing off the water. Fallen leaves brushed against their feet then slowly drifted on.

Yin Tsu nodded his head. Looking at him, Li Yuan saw the original of his wife's finely featured face. There was something delicate about it; some quality that seemed closer to sculpture than genetic chance.

'Come through. I'll have her join us.'

Li Yuan bowed and followed the old man. Inside, it was cool. Servants brought ch'a and sweetmeats while Yin Tsu went to speak to his daughter. Li Yuan sat there, waiting, rehearsing what he would say.

After a while Yin Tsu returned, taking a seat across from him.

'Fei Yen will not be long. She wants a moment to prepare herself. You understand?'

'Of course. I would have notified you, Yin Tsu, but I did not know when I could come.'

The old man lifted his chin and looked down his tiny nose at his son-in-law. Unspoken words lay in the depth of his eyes. Then he nodded, his features settling into an expression of sadness and resignation.

'Talk to her, Yuan. But, please, you must only talk. This is still my house. Agreed?'

Li Yuan bowed his head. Yin Tsu was one of his father's oldest friends. An affront to him would be as an affront to his father.

'If she will not listen, that will be an end to it, Yin Tsu. But I must try. It is my duty as a husband to try.'

His words, like his manner, were stilted and awkward. They hid how much he was feeling at that moment: how much this meant to him.

Yin Tsu went to the window, staring out across the lake. It was diffi-cult for him too. There was tenseness to each small movement of his that revealed how deeply he felt about all this. But, then, that was hardly surprising. He had seen his hopes dashed once before, when Yuan's brother Han had been killed.

Li Yuan sipped at his ch'a then set it down. He tried to smile, but the muscles in his cheeks pulled the smile too tight. From time to time a nerve would jump beneath his eye, causing a faint twitch. He had not been sleeping well since she had left.

'How is she?' he asked, turning to face Yin Tsu.

'In good health. The child grows daily.' The old man glanced across then looked back at the lake. His tiny hands were folded together across his stomach.

'That's good.'

On the far side of the room, beside a lacquered screen, stood a cage on a long, slender pole. In the cage was a nightingale. For now it rested silently on its perch, but once it had sung for him – on that day he had come here with his father to see Yin Tsu and ask him for his daughter's hand in marriage.

He sat there, feeling leaden. She had left him on the evening of the argument. Had gone without a word, taking nothing, leaving him to think on what he had done.

'And how is Li Shai Tung?'

Li Yuan looked up blankly. 'I beg your pardon, Honoured Father?'

'Your father. How is he?'

'Ah,' he breathed in deeply, returning to himself. 'He is fine now, thank you. A little weak, but...'

'None of us are growing any younger.' The old man shook his head then came across and sat again, a faint smile on his lips. 'Not that we would even if we could, neh, Yuan?'

Yin Tsu's remark was far from innocuous. He was referring to the new longevity process. Already, it was said, more than a thousand of the Above had had the operation and were taking the drugs regularly. And that without concrete evidence of the efficacy of the treatment – without knowing whether there were any traceable side-effects. Such men were desperate, it seemed. They would grasp at any promise of extended life.

'Only ill can come of it, Yuan. I guarantee.' He leaned forward, lifting the lid to look into the ch'a kettle, then summoned the servant across. While the servant hurried to replenish it, Li Yuan considered what lay behind his father-in-law's words. This was more than small talk, he realized. Yin Tsu was talking to him not as a son but as a future colleague. It was his way of saying that, whatever transpired, they would remain friends and associates. The interests of the Families – both Major and Minor – superseded all else. As they had to.

When the servant had gone again, Yin Tsu leaned forward, his voice a whisper, as if he were afraid of being overheard.

'If it helps at all, Li Yuan, my sympathy's with you. She acted rashly. But she's a headstrong young woman, I warn you. You'll not alter that with bit and bridle.'

Li Yuan sighed then sipped at his ch'a. It was true. But he had wanted her both as she was and as he wanted her; like caging fire. He glanced up at Yin Tsu and saw the concern there, the deep-rooted sympathy. And yet in this the old man would support his daughter. He had sheltered her; given her refuge against her husband. He could sympathize but he would not help.

There was a sound, then movement, from the far end of the room. Li Yuan looked up and saw her in the doorway. He stood up as Yin Tsu looked round.

'Fei Yen... Come through. Li Yuan is here to see you.'

Li Yuan stepped forward, moving to greet her, but she walked past him, as though he were not there. He turned, pained by her action, watching her embrace her father gently.

She seemed paler than he remembered her, but her tiny form was well rounded now, seven and a half months into its term. He wanted to touch the roundness of the belly, feel the movements of the growing child within. For all her coldness to him, he felt as he had always felt towards her. All of it flooded back, stronger than ever: all the tenderness and pain; all of his unfathomable love for her.

'Fei Yen...' he began, but found he could say no more than that. What could he say? How might he persuade her to return? He looked pleadingly at Yin Tsu. The old man saw and, giving the slightest of nods, moved back, away from his daughter.

'Forgive me, Fei, but I must leave now. I have urgent business to attend to.'

'Father...' she began, her hand going out to touch him, but he shook his head.

'This is between you two alone, Fei. You must settle it here and now. This indecision is unhealthy.'

She bowed her head, then sat.

'Come...' Yin Tsu beckoned to him. He hesitated, seeing how she was sitting, her head down, her face closed to him, then went across and sat, facing her. Yin Tsu stood there a moment longer, looking from one to the other. Then, without another word, he left.

For a time neither spoke or looked at the other. It was as if an impenetrable screen lay between them. Then, unexpectedly, she spoke.

'My father talks as if there were something to decide. But I made my decision when I left you.' She looked up at him, her bottom lip strangely curled, almost pinched. It gave her mouth a look of bitterness. Her eyes were cold, defiant. And yet beautiful. 'I'm not coming back, Li Yuan. Not ever.'

He looked at her, meeting her scorn and defiance, her anger and bitterness, and finding only his own love for her. She was all he had ever wanted in a woman. All he would ever want.

He looked down, staring at his perfectly manicured nails as if they held some clue to things.

'I came to say that I'm sorry, Fei. That I was wrong.'

When he looked up again he saw that she had turned her face aside. But her body was hunched and tensed, her neck braced, the muscles stretched and taut. She seemed to draw each breath with care, her hands pressed to her breasts as if to hold in all she was feeling.

'I was wrong, Fei. I... *overreacted.*'

'You *killed* them!' She spat the words out between her teeth.

You almost killed my child... But he bit back the retort that had come to mind, closing his eyes, calming himself. 'I know...'

There was a second silence, longer, more awkward than the first. Fei Yen broke this one too. She stood, making to leave.

He went across and held her arm, keeping her there. She looked down at his hand where it gripped her arm, then up at his face. It was a harsh, unsparing look, a look of unfeigned dislike. There was defiance in her eyes, but she made no move to take his hand away.

'We have not resolved this.'

'*Resolved...*' She poured all the scorn she could muster into the word. 'I'll tell you how you could *resolve* this, Li Yuan.' She turned to face him, glaring at him, the roundness of her stomach pressed up hard against him. 'You could take this from my belly and keep it safe until its term was up! That's what you could do!' The words were hard, unfeeling. She laughed bitterly, sneering at him. 'Then you could take your gun and –'

He put his hand over her mouth.

She stepped back, freeing herself from his grip. Then she looked at him, rubbing her arm where he had held it, her eyes watching him all the while, no trace of warmth in them.

'You never loved me,' she said. 'Never. I know that now. It was envy. Envy of your brother. You wanted everything he had. Yes, that was it, wasn't it?' She nodded, a look of triumph, a hideous smile of understanding on her lips.

It was cruel. Cruel and untrue. He had loved his brother dearly. Had loved her too. Still loved her, even now, for all she was saying. More than the world itself.

But he could not say it. His face had frozen to a mask. His mouth was dry, his tongue stilled by her anger and bitterness and scorn.

For a moment longer he watched her, knowing that it ended here; that all he had wanted was in ruins. He had killed it in the stables that day. He turned and went to the door, determined to go, not to look back, but she called out to him.

'One thing you should know before you leave.'

He turned, facing her across the room. 'What is it?'

'The child.' She smiled, an ugly movement of the mouth that was the imperfect copy of a smile. 'It isn't yours.' She shook her head, still smiling. 'Do you hear me, Li Yuan? The child isn't yours.'

In the cage at the far end of the room the bird was singing. Its sweet notes filled the silence.

He turned away, moving one leg at a time until he was gone from there, keeping his face a blank, his thoughts in check. But as he walked he could hear her voice, almost kind for once.

One thing, it said, then laughed. *One thing.*

'Is this it?' DeVore asked, studying the statue of the horse minutely, trying to discern any difference in its appearance.

The man looked across at him and smiled. 'Of course. What were you expecting? Something in an old lead bottle, marked with a skull and cross-bones? No, that's it, all right. It'd make arsenic seem like honeydew, yet it's as untraceable as melted snow.'

DeVore stood back, looking at the man again. He was nothing like the archetypal scientist. Not in his dress, which was eccentrically Han, or in his manner, which was that of a low-level drug dealer. Even his speech – scattered, as it was, with tiny bits of arcane knowledge – seemed to smack of things illicit or alchemical. Yet he was good. Very good indeed, if Ebert could be trusted on the matter.

'Well? Are you happy with it, or would you like me to explain it once more?'

DeVore laughed. 'There's no need. I have it by heart.'

The toxicologist laughed. 'That's good. And so will your friend, neh? Whoever he is.'

DeVore smiled. *And if you knew exactly who that was, you would as soon sell me this as cut your own throat.*

He nodded. 'Shall we settle, then? My friend told me you liked cash. Bearer credits. Shall we call it fifty thousand?'

He saw the light of greed in the man's eyes and smiled inwardly.

'I thought a hundred. After all, it was a difficult job. That genetic pattern... I've not seen its like before. I'd say that was someone special. Someone well bred. It was hard finding the chemical key to break those chains down. I... well, let's say I had to improvise. To work at the very limit of my talents. I'd say that deserved rewarding, wouldn't you?'

DeVore hesitated, going through the motions of considering the matter, then bowed his head. 'As you say. But if it doesn't work...'

'Oh, it *will* work, my friend. I'd stake my life on it. The man's as good as dead, whoever he is. As I said, it's perfectly harmless to anyone else, but as soon as *he* handles it the bacteria will be activated. The rest...' he laughed '... is history.'

'Good.' DeVore felt in his jacket pocket and took out the ten bearer credits – the slender chips identical in almost every respect to those he had given Mach a week earlier. Only in one crucial respect were they different: these had been smeared with a special bacterium – one designed to match the toxicologist's DNA. A bacterium prepared only days earlier by the man's greatest rival from skin traces DeVore had taken on his first visit here.

DeVore watched the man handle then pocket the chips. *Dead,* he thought, smiling, reaching out to pick up the statue the man had treated for him. *Or as good as, give a week or two.*

And himself? Well, he was the last person to take such chances. He had made sure he wore a false skin over both hands before handling the things. Just in case.

Because one never knew, did one? And a poisoner *was* a poisoner after all.

He smiled, holding the ancient statue to his chest, then laughed, seeing how the man joined his laughter, as if sharing the cruel joke he was about to play.

'And there's no antidote? No possible way of stopping this thing once it's begun?'

The man shook his head then gave another bark of laughter. 'Not a chance in hell.'

It was dark where Chen sat. Across from him a ceiling panel flickered intermittently, as if threatening to come brightly, vividly alive again, but never managing more than a brief, fitful glow. Chen had been nursing the same drink for more than an hour, waiting for Haavikko to come, his ill ease growing with every passing minute. More than ten years had passed since he had last sat in the Stone Dragon – years in which he had changed profoundly – yet the place remained unchanged.

Still the same shit-hole, he thought. A place you did well to escape from as quickly as you could. As he had.

But now he was back, if only briefly. Still, Haavikko could hardly have known, could he?

No. Even so, the coincidence made Chen's flesh crawl. He looked about him uncomfortably, as if the ghost of Kao Jyan or the more substantial figure of Whiskers Lu should manifest themselves from the darkness and the all-pervading fug to haunt him.

'You want wings?'

He glanced at the thin young girl who had approached him and shook his head, letting disgust and genuine hostility shape his expression.

'You prefer I suck you? Here, at table?'

He leaned towards her slightly. 'Vanish, scab, or I'll slit you throat to tail.'

She made a vulgar hand sign and slipped back into the darkness, but she wasn't the first to have approached him. They were all out to sell something. Drugs or sex or worse. For a price you could do anything you liked down here. It hadn't been so in his day, but now it was. Now the Net was little different from the Clay.

He sat back. Even the smell of the place nauseated him. But that was hardly surprising: the air filters couldn't have been changed in thirty years. The air was recycled, yes, but that meant little here. He swallowed, keeping the bile from rising. How many times had each breath he took been breathed before? How many foul and cankered mouths had sighed their last, drug-soured breath into this putrid mix?

Too many, he thought. *Far, far too many.*

He looked across. There was someone in the doorway. Someone tall and straight and wholly out of place in this setting. Haavikko. He'd come at last.

He got up and went across, embracing his friend then holding him off at arm's length, staring up into his face.

'Axel... how are you? It's been a long time since you came to us. Wang Ti and the boys... they've missed you. And I... well, I was worried. I'd heard...' He paused then shook his head, unable to say.

Haavikko looked aside momentarily then met his friend's eyes. 'I'm sorry, Chen, but it's been hard. Some days I've felt...' He shrugged then formed his face into a sad little smile. 'Well... I've got what you asked for. I had to cheat a little, and lie rather a lot, not to mention a little bit of burglary, but then it's hard being an honest man when all about you are thieves and liars. One must pretend to take on their colouring a little simply to survive, neh?'

Chen stared at him a moment, surprised by the hardness in his voice. His sister's death had changed him. Chen squeezed his shoulder gently, turning him towards his table.

'Come. Let's sit down. You can tell me what you've been up to while I go through the file.'

Axel sat. 'You remember Mu Chua's?'

Chen took the seat across from him. 'No. I don't think I do.'

'The House of the Ninth Ecstasy?'

Chen laughed. 'Ah... Is that still going?'

Haavikko stared down at his hands. 'Yes, it's still going. And guess what? Our friend Ebert is still frequenting it. It seems he visited there no more than a week back.'

Chen looked up, frowning. 'Ebert? Here? Why would he bother?'

Haavikko looked back at him, bitter resentment in his eyes. 'He had a meeting, it seems. With a *Shih* Reynolds.'

'How do you know this?'

'The Madame, Mu Chua, told me. It's funny... I didn't even raise the matter of Ebert, she just seemed to want to talk about him. She was telling me about this girl she'd sold to Ebert – a fourteen-year-old named Golden Heart. I remember it, strangely enough. It was more than ten years back, so the girl could well be dead now, but Mu Chua was anxious to find out about her, as if the girl were her daughter or something. Anyway, she told me about a dream this girl had had – about a tiger coming from the west and mating with her and about a pale grey snake that died. It seems this was a powerful dream – something she couldn't get out of her mind – and she wanted me to find out what became of the girl. I said I would and in return she promised to let me know if Ebert or his friend returned. It could be useful, don't you think?'

'This Reynolds – do we know who he is or what he was meeting Ebert about?'

'Nothing, I'm afraid. But Mu Chua thinks he's been there before. She said there was something familiar about him.'

'*Ping Tiao*, perhaps?'

'Perhaps...'

Chen looked down at the file, touching his wrist band to make it glow, illuminating the page beneath his fingers. For a while he was silent, reading, then he looked up, frowning.

'Is this all?'

Haavikko looked back at him blankly a moment, his mind clearly elsewhere, then nodded. 'That's it. Not much, is it?'

Chen considered a moment then grunted. Hans Ebert had supposedly instigated an investigation into the disappearance of his friend, Fest, but the investigation had never actually happened. No witnesses had been called, no leads followed up. All that existed was this slender file.

'And Fest? Is there any sign of him?'

Haavikko shook his head. 'He's dead. That's what the file means. They did it. Ebert and Auden. Because we'd got to Fest, perhaps, or maybe for some other reason – I've heard since that Fest was getting a bit too talkative for Ebert's liking even before we approached him. But whatever, they did it. That file makes me certain of it.'

Chen nodded. 'So what now?'

Haavikko smiled tightly. 'The girl, Golden Heart. I'm going to find out what happened to her.'

'And then?'

Haavikko shrugged. 'I'm not sure. Let's see where this leads.'

'And Ebert?'

Haavikko looked away, the tightness in his face revealing the depth of what he felt.

'At first I thought of killing him. Of walking up to him in the Officers' Club and putting a bullet through his brain. But it wouldn't have brought her back. Besides, I want everyone to know what he is. To see him as I see him.'

Chen was quiet a moment then reached out and touched Haavikko's arm, as if consoling a child. 'Don't worry,' he said softly. 'We'll get him, Axel. I swear we will.'

Klaus Ebert stood on the steps of his mansion, his hands extended to the Marshal. Jelka watched as he embraced her father then stood back, one hand resting on Tolonen's shoulder. She could see how deep their friendship ran, how close they were. More like brothers than friends.

Ebert turned, offering his hands to her, his eyes lighting at the sight of her.

He held her close, whispering at her ear. 'You really are quite beautiful, Jelka. Hans is very lucky.' But his smile only made her feel guilty. Was it really so hard to do this for them?

'Come. We've prepared a feast,' Ebert said, turning, putting his arm about her shoulders. He led her through, into the vast, high-ceilinged hallway.

She turned her head, looking back at her father, and saw how he was smiling at her. A fierce, uncompromising smile of pride.

It all went well until she saw him. Until she looked across the room and met his eyes. Then it came back to her: her deep-rooted fear of him – something much greater than dislike. Dread, perhaps. Or the feeling she had in her dreams sometimes. That fear of drowning in darkness. Of cold, sightless suffocation.

She looked down, afraid that her eyes would reveal what she was thinking. It was a gesture that, to a watching eye, seemed the very archetype of feminine modesty: the bride obedient, her husband's thing, to be done with as he willed. But it wasn't so.

Her thoughts disturbed her. They hung like a veil at the back of her eyes, darkening all she saw. Head bowed, she sat beside her future mother-in-law, a sense of horror growing in her by the moment.

'Jelka?'

The voice was soft, almost tender, but it was Hans Ebert who stood before her, straight-backed and cruelly handsome. She looked up, past the silvered buttons of his dark blue dress uniform to his face. And met his eyes. Cold, selfish eyes, little different from how she had remembered them but now alert to her. Alert and open to her womanhood. Surprised by what he saw.

She looked away, frightened by what she saw – by the sudden interest where before there had only been indifference. *Like a curse,* she thought. *My mother's curse, handed down to me. Her dying gift.* But her mouth said simply, 'Hans,' acknowledging his greeting.

'You're looking very nice,' he said, his voice clear, resonant.

She looked up, the strength of his voice, its utter conviction, surprising her. Her beauty had somehow pierced the shell of his self-regard. He was looking down at her with something close to awe. He had expected a child, not a woman. And not a beautiful woman, at that. Yes, he was surprised by her, but there was also something else – something more predatory in that look.

She had changed in his eyes. Had become something he wanted.

His sisters stood behind him, no longer taller than her. They watched her enviously. She had eclipsed them overnight and now they hated her. Hated her beauty.

'Come! Drinks, everyone!' Klaus Ebert called, smiling at her as he passed, oblivious of the dark, unseen currents of feeling that swirled all about him in the room. And all the while his son watched her. Her future husband, his eyes dark with the knowledge of possession.

She looked away, studying the palatial vastness of the room. It was a hundred *ch'i* across, high-ceilinged and six-sided, each wall divided into five by tall, red-painted pillars. The walls were a dark, almost primal green, double doors set into the centre of each wall. Those doors filled the space between floor and ceiling, pillar and pillar. Vast doors that made her feel as though she had shrunk in size. GenSyn giants stood before the pillars to either side of each door, the dark green uniforms of the half-men blending in with the studded leather of the door covering.

A border of tiles, glassy black and bright with darkness, surrounded the central hexagonal space. Huge, claw-footed plinths rested on this polished darkness, each bearing a man-sized vase: brutal-lipped and heavy vases, decorated in violent swirls of red and green and black. Elongated animals coiled about the thick trunk of each vase, facing each other with bared fangs and flaring eyes. On the walls beyond hung huge, wall-sized canvases in thick gilt frames, so dark as to seem in permanent shadow; visions of some ancient forest hell, where huntsmen ran on foot, axe or bow in hand, after a wounded stag. Again there was the green of primal forest, the black of shadows, the red of blood; these three repeated in each frame, melting into one another as in a mist.

A dark red carpet lay lush, luxuriant beneath her feet, while the ceiling above was the black of a starless night.

A voice spoke to her, close by. She smelled a sickly sweetness, masking some deeper, stronger scent. Turning, she met a pink-eyed stare. A three-toed hand held out a glass. The voice was burred, deep, sounding in the creature's throat. She looked at it aghast, then took the offered glass.

The creature smiled and poured the blood-red liquid into the slender crystal. Again she saw the lace at its cuffs, the neat whiteness of its collar. But now she saw the bright, red roughness of the sprouting hairs on its neck, the meat-pink colour of its flesh, and felt her skin crawl in aversion.

She stood and brushed past it, spilling her wine over the creature's jacket, the stain a vivid slash of colour on the ice-white velvet of its sleeve.

The creature's eyes flared briefly, following her figure as she crossed the room towards her father. Then it looked down at its sleeve, its brutal lips curled back with distaste at the spoiled perfection there.

Li Shai Tung sat at his desk, his hands resting lightly to either side of the tiny porcelain figure, his face a mask of pain and bitter disappointment. He had tried to deny it, but there was no doubting it now. Tsu Ma's last message made it clear. It was Wang Ta Chuan. Wang, his trusted Master of the Inner Palace, who was the traitor.

The old T'ang shuddered. First the boy, Chung Hsin, and now Wang Ta Chuan. Was there no end to this foulness? Was there *no one* he could trust?

He had done as Tsu Ma had suggested after the last meeting of the Council; had looked for the spy within his household and concluded that only four people had been privy to the information Wang Sau-leyan had used against him; four of his most senior and trusted men: Chung Hu-yan, his Chancellor; Nan Ho, Master of Yuan's chambers; Li Feng Chuang, his brother and advisor; and Wang Ta Chuan.

At first it had seemed unthinkable that any one of them could have betrayed him. But he had done as Tsu Ma said; had brought each to him separately and sown in them – casually, in confidence – a single tiny seed of information, different in each instance.

And then he had waited to hear what Tsu Ma's spies reported back, hoping beyond hope that there would be nothing. But this morning it had come. Word that the false seed had sprouted in Wang Sau-leyan's ear.

He groaned then leaned forward, pressing the summons pad. At once Chung Hu-yan appeared at the door, his head bowed.

'*Chieh Hsia?*'

Li Shai Tung smiled, comforted by the sight of his Chancellor.

'Bring Wang Ta Chuan to me, Hu-yan. Bring him, then close the doors and leave me with him.'

Li Shai Tung saw the slight query in his Chancellor's eyes. Chung Hu-yan had been with him too long for him not to sense his moods. Even so, he said nothing, merely bowed and turned away, doing his master's bidding without question.

'A good man...' he said softly, then sat back, closing his eyes, trying to compose himself.

Wang Ta Chuan was a traitor. There was no doubt about it. But he would have it from the man's lips. Would have him bow before him and admit it.

And then?

He banged the table angrily, making the tiny porcelain statue shudder.

The man would have to die. Yet his family might live. *If* he confessed. *If* he admitted of his own free will what he had done. Otherwise they too would have to die. His wives, his sons, and all his pretty grandchildren – all to the third generation, as the law demanded. And all because of his foolishness, his foulness.

Why? he asked himself for the hundredth time since he had known. Why had Wang Ta Chuan betrayed him? Was it envy? Was it repayment for some slight he felt had been made to him? Or was it something darker, nastier than that? Did Wang Sau-leyan have some kind of hold on him? Or was it simply greed?

He shook his head, not understanding. Surely Wang had all he wanted? Status, riches, a fine, healthy family. What more did a man need?

Li Shai Tung reached out and drew the statue to him, studying it while he mulled over these thoughts, turning it in his hands, some part of him admiring the ancient craftsman's skill – the beauty of the soft blue glaze, the perfect, lifelike shape of the horse.

It was strange how this had returned to him. Young Ebert had brought it to him only that morning, having recovered it in a raid on one of the *Ping Tiao* cells. It was one of the three that had been taken from the safe in Helmstadt Armoury and its discovery in the hands of the *Ping Tiao* had confirmed what he had always believed.

But now the *Ping Tiao* were broken, the horse returned. There would be no more trouble from that source.

There was a knocking on the outer doors. He looked up then set the statue to one side. 'Come!' he said imperiously, straightening in his chair.

Chung Hu-yan escorted the Master of the Inner Palace into the room then backed away, closing the doors behind him.

'*Chieh Hsia?*' Wang Ta Chuan said, bowing low, his manner no less respectful, no less solicitous than it had always been.

'Come closer,' Li Shai Tung ordered. 'Come kneel before the desk.'

Wang Ta Chuan lifted his head briefly, surprised by his T'ang's request, then did as he was told.

'Have I displeased you, *Chieh Hsia?*'

Li Shai Tung hesitated, then decided to broach the matter directly, but before he could open his mouth, the doors to his study burst open and Li Yuan stormed in.

'Yuan! What is the meaning of this?' he said, starting up from his chair.

'I am sorry, Father, but I *had* to see you. It's Fei... Sh ...' Li Yuan hesitated, taking in the sight of the kneeling man, then went across and touched his shoulder. 'Wang Ta Chuan, would you leave us? I must talk with my father.'

'*Yuan!*' The violence of the word surprised both the Prince and the kneeling servant. 'Be quiet, boy! Have you forgotten where you are?'

Li Yuan swallowed, then bowed low.

'Good!' Li Shai Tung said angrily. 'Now, hold your tongue and take a seat. I have urgent business with Master Wang. Business that cannot be put off.'

He came from behind the desk and stood there over Wang Ta Chuan. 'Have you something to tell me, Wang Ta Chuan?'

'*Chieh Hsia?*' The tone – of surprise and mild indignation – was perfect, but Li Shai Tung was not fooled. To be a traitor – to be the perfect copy of a loyal man – one needed such tricks. Tricks of voice and gesture. Those and a stock of ready smiles.

'You would rather have it otherwise, then, Master Wang? You would rather I told you?'

He saw the mask slip. Saw the sudden calculation in the face and felt himself go cold. So it was true.

Li Yuan had stood. He took a step towards the T'ang. 'What is this, Father?'

'Be quiet, Yuan!' he said again, taking a step towards him, the hem of his robes brushing against the kneeling man's hands.

'*Father!*'

He turned at Yuan's warning, but he was too slow. Wang Ta Chuan had grabbed the hem of the T'ang's ceremonial *pau*, twisting the silk about his wrist, while his other hand searched amongst his robes, emerging with a knife.

Li Shai Tung tried to draw back, but Wang Ta Chuan tugged at the cloth viciously, pulling him off balance. Yet even as the T'ang began to fall, Li Yuan was moving past him, high-kicking the knife from Wang's hands then spinning on his hips to follow through with a second kick that broke the servant's nose.

Li Shai Tung edged back, watching as his son crouched over the fallen man.

'No, Yuan... No!'

But it was no use. Li Yuan was as if possessed. His breath hissed from him as he kicked and punched the fallen man. Then, as if coming to, he stepped back, swaying, his eyes glazed.

'Gods...' Li Shai Tung said, pulling himself up against the edge of the desk, getting his breath.

Li Yuan turned, looking at him, his eyes wide. 'He tried to kill you, Father! Why? What had he done?'

The old T'ang swallowed drily then looked away, shaking his head, trying to control himself; trying not to give voice to the pain he felt. For a moment he could say nothing, then he looked back at his son.

'He was a spy, Yuan. For Wang Sau-leyan. He passed on information to our cousin.'

The last word was said with a venom, a bitterness that surprised them both.

Li Yuan stared at his father, astonished. 'A traitor?' He turned, looking down at the dead man. 'For a moment I thought it was one of those things. Those copies that came in from Mars. I thought...'

He stopped, swallowing, realizing what he had done.

Li Shai Tung watched his son a moment longer, then went back round his desk and took his seat again. For a time he was silent, staring at his hands, then he looked up. 'I must thank you, Yuan. You saved my life just then. Even so, you should not have killed him. Now we will never know the reason for his treachery. Neither can I confront our cousin without the man's confession.'

'Forgive me, Father. I was not myself.'

'No... I could see that.' He hesitated, then looked at his son more thoughtfully. 'Tell me. When you came in just now – what did you want? What was so important that it made you forget yourself like that?'

For a moment it seemed that Yuan would answer. Then he shook his head.

'Forgive me, Father, it was nothing.'

Li Shai Tung studied his son a moment longer then nodded and reached out, holding the tiny statue to him as if to draw comfort from it.

Klaus Ebert and the Marshal stood there, face to face, their glasses raised to each other.

'To our grandchildren!'

Ebert nodded his satisfaction then leaned closer. 'I must say, Jelka is lovelier than ever, Knut. A real beauty she's become. She must remind you of Jenny.'

'Very much...'

Tolonen turned, looking across. Jelka was sitting beside Klaus's wife, Berta, her hands folded in her lap, her blonde hair set off perfectly by the flowing sky-blue dress she was wearing. As he watched, Hans went across and stood there over her, handsome, dashingly elegant. It was the perfect match. Tolonen turned back, almost content, only the vaguest unease troubling him. She was still young, after all. It was only natural for her to have doubts.

'Hans will be good for her,' he said, meeting his old friend's eyes. 'She needs a steadying influence.'

Klaus nodded then moved closer. 'Talking of which, Knut, I've been hearing things. Unsettling things.' He lowered his voice, his words for the Marshal only. 'I hear that some of the young bucks are up to old tricks. That some of them are in rather deep. And more than youthful pranks.'

Tolonen stared at him a moment then nodded curtly. He had heard something similar. 'So it is, I'm sad to say. The times breed restlessness in our young men. They are good apples gone bad.'

Ebert's face showed a momentary distaste. 'Is it our fault, Knut? Were we too strict as fathers?'

'You and I?' Tolonen laughed softly. 'Not we, Klaus. But others?' He considered. 'No, there's a rottenness at the very core of things. Li Shai Tung has said as much himself. It is as if Mankind cannot live without being at its own throat. Peace, that's at the root of it. We have been at peace too long, it seems.'

It was almost dissent. Klaus Ebert stiffened, hearing this bitterness from his friend's lips. Things were bad indeed if the Marshal had such thoughts in his head.

'Ach, I have lived too long!' Tolonen added, and the sudden ironic tone in his voice brought back memories of their youth, so that both men smiled and touched each other's arms.

'All will be well, Klaus, I promise you. We'll come to the root of things soon enough. And then...' He made a movement of pulling up and then discarding a plant. 'Then we shall be done with it.'

They looked at each other grimly, a look of understanding passing between them. They knew the world and its ways. Few illusions remained to them these days.

Tolonen turned to get a fresh drink, and caught sight of Jelka, getting up hastily, the contents of her glass splashing over the serving creature who stood beside her. He frowned as she came across.

'What is it, my love? You look like you've seen a ghost!'

She shook her head, but for the moment could not speak. There was distinct colour in her cheeks.

Klaus Ebert looked at her, concerned. 'Did my creature offend you, Jelka?' He looked at her tenderly then glared at the creature across the room.

'No...' She held on to her father's arm, surprised by her reaction to the creature. 'It's just...'

'Did it frighten you?' her father asked gently.

She laughed. 'Yes. It did. It... surprised me, that's all. I'm not used to them.'

Ebert relaxed. 'It's my fault, Jelka. I forget. They're such gentle, sophisticated creatures, you see. Bred to be so.'

She looked at him, curious now. 'But why?' She was confused by this. 'I mean, why are they like that? Like goats?'

Ebert shrugged. 'I suppose it's what we're used to. My great-grandfather first had them as servants and they've been in the household ever since. But they really are the most gentle of creatures. Their manners are impeccable. And their dress sense is immaculate.'

She thought of the fine silk of the creature's sleeves then shuddered, recalling childhood tales of animals that talked.

That and the musk beneath the scent, the darkness at the back of those blood-pink eyes. Impeccable, immaculate, and yet still an animal at the back of all. A beast for all its breeding.

She turned to look but the serving creature had gone, as if it sensed it was no longer welcome. Good manners, she thought, but there was little amusement to be had from it. The thing had scared her.

'They breed true,' Ebert added. 'In fact, they're the first of our vat-bred creatures to attain that evolutionary step. We're justly proud of them.'

Jelka looked back at her future father-in-law, wondering at his pride in the goat-thing he had made. But there was only human kindness in his face.

She looked away, confused. So maybe it was her. Maybe she was out of step.

But it was ugly, she thought. The thing was ugly. Then, relenting, she smiled and took the glass of wine Klaus Ebert was holding out to her.

An hour later the ritual began.

Overhead the lighting dimmed. At the far end of the room the huge doors slowly opened.

It was dark in the hallway beyond, yet the machine glowed from within. Like a pearled and bloated egg, its outer skin as dark as smoked glass, it floated soundlessly above the tiled floor, a tightly focused circle of light directly beneath it. Two GenSyn giants guided it, easing it gently between the pillars of the door and out across the jet-black marble of the tiles.

Jelka watched it come, her stomach tight with fear. This was her fate. Unavoidable, implacable, it came, gliding towards her as in a dream, its outer case shielding its inner brilliance; masking the stark simplicity of its purpose.

She held her father's arm tightly, conscious of him at her side, of how proudly he stood there. For him this moment held no threat. Today his family was joined to Klaus Ebert's by contract – something he had wished for since his youth. And how could that be wrong?

The machine stopped. The GenSyn servants backed away, closing the doors behind them. Slowly the machine sank into the lush carpeting: dark yet pregnant with its inner light.

Beyond it, in the shadows, a stranger stood at Klaus Ebert's side. The two were talking, their hushed tones drifting across to where she stood. The man was much smaller than Ebert; a tiny creature dressed entirely in red. The Consensor. He looked at her with a brief, almost dismissive glance then turned back.

Dry-mouthed, she watched him turn to the machine and begin to ready it for the ceremony.

'Nu shi Tolonen?' He stood before her, one hand extended.

It was time.

She took his hand. A small, cool hand, dry to the touch. Looking down, she saw that he wore gloves: fine sheaths of black, through which the intense pallor of his skin showed. Holding her hand, he led her to the machine.

The casing irised before her, spilling light. She hesitated then stepped up, into the brilliance.

He placed her hands on the touch-sensitive pads and clamped them there, then pushed her face gently but firmly against the moulded screen of transparent ice, reaching round her to attach the cap to her skull, the girdle about her waist. The movements of his hands were gentle, and for a time her fear receded, lost in the soothing comfort of his touch, but then, abruptly, he moved back and the door irised closed behind her, leaving her alone, facing the empty space beyond the partition.

There was a moment of doubt so great her stomach seemed to fall away. Then the wall facing her irised open and Hans Ebert stepped up into the machine.

Her heart began to hammer in her breast. She waited, exposed to him, her body held fast against the ice-clear partition.

He smiled at her, letting the Consensor do his work. In a moment he was secured, his face pressed close against her own, his hands to hers, only the thinnest sheet of ice between them.

She stared into his eyes, unable to look away, wanting to close her eyes and tear herself away, she felt so vulnerable, so hideously exposed to him. The feeling grew in her, until she stood there, cowed before his relentless stare, reduced to a frightened child. And then he spoke.

'Don't be afraid. I'd never hurt you.'

The words seemed to come from a thousand lí away, distant, disembodied; from the vast emptiness beyond the surface of his pale blue eyes. And yet, at the same time, it was as if the words had formed in her head, unmediated by tongue or lip.

And still he looked at her. Looked through her. Seeing all she was thinking. Understanding everything she was feeling. Emptying her. Until there was nothing there but her fear of him.

Then, in her mind, something happened. A wall blew in and three men in black stepped through. There was the smell of burning and something lay on the floor beside her, hideously disfigured, bright slivers of metal jutting from its bloodied flesh.

She saw this vividly. And in the eyes that faced hers something happened: the pupils widened, responding to something in her own. For a moment she looked outwards, recognizing Hans Ebert, then the memory grabbed at her again and she looked back inwards, seeing the three men come towards her, their guns raised.

Strangely, the memory calmed her. *I survived*, she thought. *I danced my way to life.*

The partition between them darkened momentarily, leaving them isolated. Then it cleared, a circular pattern of pictograms forming in the ice; a tiny circle of coded information displayed before each of their pupils, duplicated so that each half of their brains could read and comprehend. Genotypings. Blood samplings. Brain scans. Fertility ratings. Jelka felt the girdle tighten, then a momentary pain as it probed her.

Figures changed. The ice glowed green. They were a perfect genetic match. The machine stored the figures dispassionately, noting them down on the contract.

The green tinge faded with the pictograms. Again she found herself staring into his eyes.

He was smiling. The skin surrounding his eyes was pulled tight in little creases, his eyes much brighter than before.

'You're beautiful,' said the voice in her head. 'We'll be good together. Strong, healthy sons, you'll give me. Sons we'll both be proud of.'

She pictured the words forming in the darkness behind his eyes: saw them lift and float across, piercing the ice between them; entering her through her eyes.

Her fear had subsided. She was herself again. Now, when she looked at him, she saw only how cruel he was, how selfish. It was there, at the front of his eyes, like a coded pictogram.

As the machine began its litany she calmed herself, steeling herself to outface him: *You'll not defeat me, Hans Ebert. I'm stronger than you think. I'll survive you.*

She smiled, and her lips moved, saying, 'Yes,' sealing the contract, putting her verbal mark to the retinal prints and ECG traces the machine had already registered as her identifying signature. But in her head the 'Yes' remained conditional.

I'll dance my way to life, she thought. *See if I don't.*

★

DeVore looked down at the indicator at his wrist then peeled off the gas mask. Outside, his men were mopping up, stripping the corpses before they set fire to the level.

Gesell was unconscious on the bed, the Han girl beside him.

He pulled back the sheet, looking down at them. The woman had small, firm breasts with large, dark nipples and a scar that ran from her left hip almost to her knee. DeVore smiled and leaned forward, running a finger slowly down the clean-shaven slit of her sex. *Too bad*, he thought. *Too bad.*

He looked across. Gesell lay on his side, one arm cradling his head. A thick dark growth of hair covered his arms and legs, sprouted luxuriantly at his groin and beneath his arms. His penis lay there, like a newborn chick in a nest, folded softly into itself.

Looking at the man, DeVore felt a tight knot of anger constrict his throat. It would be easy to kill them now. Never let them wake. But it wasn't enough. He wanted Gesell to know. Wanted to spit in his face before he died.

Yes. For all the threats he'd made. All the shit he'd made him eat.

He drew the needle-gun from his pocket and fitted a cartridge, then pushed it against Gesell's chest, just above the heart. Discarding the empty cartridge, he fitted another and did the same to the girl. Then he stepped back, waiting for the antidote to take effect.

The woman was the first to wake. She turned slightly, moving towards Gesell, then froze, sniffing the air.

'I'd keep very still if I were you, Mao Liang.'

She turned her head, her eyes taking in his dark form, then gave a tiny nod.

'Good... Your boyfriend will be back with us in a moment. It's him I want. So behave yourself and you won't get hurt. Understand?'

Again she nodded then shifted back slightly as Gesell stirred.

DeVore smiled, drawing the gun from inside his tunic. 'Good morning, friend. I'm sorry to have to disturb your sleep like this, but we've business.'

Gesell sat up slowly, knuckling his eyes, then went very still, seeing the gun in DeVore's hand.

'How the fuck did you get in here?' he said softly, his eyes narrowed.

'I *bought* my way in. Your guards were only too happy to sell you to me.'

'Sell...' Understanding came to his face. He glanced at the girl then looked back at DeVore, some eternal element of defiance in his nature making him stubborn to the last.

'Mach will get you for this, you fucker.'

DeVore shrugged. 'Maybe. But it won't help you, eh, Bent? Because you're dead. And all those things you believed in – they're dead too. I've wiped them out. There's only you left. You and the girl here.'

He saw the movement almost peripherally; saw how her hand searched beneath the pillow and then drew back; heard the tiny click as she took off the safety.

He fired twice as she lifted the gun, the weighted bullets punching two neat holes in her chest, just below her heart. She fell back, dead.

Gesell moved forward sharply then stopped, seeing how DeVore's gun was trained on him, pointed directly at his head.

'You were always a loudmouth, Gesell.'

Gesell glared at him. 'We should never have worked with you. Emily was right. You never cared for anyone but yourself.'

'Did I ever say otherwise?'

Gesell sat back, his face tense. 'So why don't you do it? Get it over with?'

'I will... don't worry, but not with this.'

He threw the gun down. Gesell stared back at him a moment then made his move, scrambling for the gun. DeVore stepped back, drawing the spray can from his pocket, watching as Gesell turned and pointed the gun at him.

'It's empty.'

Gesell pulled the trigger. It clicked then clicked again.

DeVore smiled then stepped closer, lifting the spray, his finger holding down the button as the fine particles hissed from the nozzle.

He watched Gesell tear at the thin film of opaque, almost translucent ice that had formed about his head and shoulders; saw how his fingers fought to free an air-hole in the soft, elastic stuff, but already it was growing hard. Desperation made Gesell throw himself about, bellowing; but the sound was distant, muted. It came from behind a screen that cut him off from the air itself.

DeVore emptied the can then cast it aside, stepping back from the struggling figure. Gesell's arms and hands were stuck now – welded firmly to his face. For a moment longer he staggered about then fell down, his legs kicking weakly. Then he lay still.

DeVore stood over Gesell a moment, studying his face, satisfied by the look of panic, of utter torment he could see through the hard, glass-like mask, then looked up. Mach was watching him from the door.

'He's dead?'

DeVore nodded. 'And the woman, too, I'm afraid. She drew a gun on me.'

Mach shrugged. 'It's all right. It would have been difficult. She was in love with him.'

'And Ascher?'

Mach shook his head. 'There's no trace of her.'

DeVore considered that a moment then nodded. 'I'll find her for you.'

'Thanks.' Mach hesitated then came in, looking down at Gesell. 'I liked him, you know. I really did. But sooner or later he would have killed me. He was like that.'

DeVore stood then reached out, touching Mach's arm. 'Okay. We've finished here. Let's be gone. Before the T'ang's men get here.'

Chapter 60

CARP POOL AND TORTOISE SHELL

K im turned in his seat, looking at Hammond. 'What do you think he wants?'

Hammond glanced at him then looked away nervously, conscious of the overhead camera.

Kim looked down. So it was like that. Director Spatz was putting pressure on him. Well, it made sense. After all, it wasn't every day that Prince Yuan came to visit the Project.

He looked about him, noting how Spatz had had his suite of offices decorated especially for the occasion, the furnishings replaced. It was a common joke on the Project that Spatz's offices were larger – and cost more in upkeep – than the rest of the Project put together. But that was only to be expected. It was how arseholes like Spatz behaved.

Kim had been on the Wiring Project for almost a year now, though for most of that time he had been kept out of things by Spatz. Even so, he had learned a lot, keeping what he knew from Spatz and his cronies. From the outset he had been dismayed to learn how little they'd progressed. It was not that they didn't know about the brain. The basic information they needed had been discovered more than two centuries before. It was simply that they couldn't apply it. They had tried out various 'templates' – all of them embellishments on what already existed – but none of them had shown the kind of delicacy required. In terms of what they were doing, they were crude, heavy-handed models, more likely to destroy the brain than control it; systems of blocks and stimulae that set off whole chains of unwanted chemical and electrical responses. As it was, the wiring system they had was worthless. A frontal lobotomy was of more use. Unless one wanted a population of twitching, jerking puppets.

And now, in less than five hours, Prince Yuan would arrive for his first annual inspection. But Spatz was taking no chances. He remembered the last visit he had had – from Marshal Tolonen – and was determined to keep Kim away from things.

Well, let him try, Kim thought. *Let him try.*

As if on cue, Spatz arrived, Ellis, his assistant, trailing behind him, a thick stack of paper files under his arm. He had seen this aspect of official-dom before. Most of the time they shunned real paperwork, preferring to keep as much as possible on computer, yet whenever the big guns arrived out would come thick stacks of paper.

And maybe it worked. Maybe it *did* impress their superiors.

'Ward,' Spatz said coldly, matter-of-factly, not even glancing at Kim as he sat behind his desk.

'Yes, *Shih* Spatz?'

He saw the tightening of the man's face at his refusal to use his full title. Spatz was a fool when it came to science, but he knew disrespect when he saw it. Spatz looked up at Ellis and took the files from him, sorting through them with a great show of self-importance, before finally setting them aside and looking across at Kim.

'I understand you've requested an interview with Prince Yuan.'

Kim stared back at him, making no response, wanting to see how Spatz would deal with his intransigence; how he would cope with this direct assault on his authority.

'Well...' Spatz masked his anger with a smile. His face set, he raised a hand and clicked his fingers. At once Ellis went across and opened the door.

Kim heard footsteps behind him. It was the Communications Officer, Barycz. He marched up to the desk and handed over two slender files to add to the pile at Spatz's elbow.

Are you trying to build a wall against me, Spatz? Kim thought, smiling inwardly. *Because it won't work. Not today, anyway. Because today Prince Yuan will be here. And I'll let him know exactly what you've been doing. You know that, and it scares you. Which is why I'm here. So that you can offer me some kind of deal.*

But it won't work. Because there's nothing you can offer me. Nothing at all.

Spatz studied the first of the files for a while then held it out to Hammond.

Kim saw the movement in Hammond's face and knew, at once, that the file was to do with himself.

Hammond read through the file, the colour draining from his face, then looked up at Spatz again. 'But this...'

Spatz looked away. 'What's the matter, *Shih* Hammond?'

Hammond glanced at Kim fearfully.

'Is it a problem, *Shih* Hammond?' Spatz said, turning to look at his Senior Technician. 'You only have to countersign. Or is there something you wish to query?'

Kim smiled sourly. He understood. They had constructed a new personnel file. A false one, smearing him.

'Sign it, Joel,' he said. 'It doesn't matter.'

Spatz looked at him and smiled. The kind of smile a snake makes before it unhinges its jaws and swallows an egg.

Hammond hesitated then signed.

'Good,' Spatz said, taking the document back. Then, his smile broadening, he passed the second file to Ellis. 'Give this to the boy.'

Kim looked up as Ellis approached, conscious of the look of apology in the Assistant Director's eyes.

'What is this?'

Spatz laughed humourlessly. 'Why don't you open it and see?'

Kim looked across. Hammond was looking down, his shoulders hunched forward, as if he knew already what was in the second file.

Kim opened the folder and caught his breath. Inside was a sheaf of paper. Hammond's poems and his own replies. A full record of the secret messages they had passed between them.

He looked at Spatz. 'So you knew?' But he knew at once that neither Spatz nor Barycz was behind this. They were too dull-witted. There was no way either of them could have worked out what was going on. No, this was someone else. Someone much sharper than either of them. But who?

Spatz leaned forward, his sense of dignity struggling with his need to gloat.

'You thought you were being clever, didn't you, Ward? A regular little smart-arse. I bet you thought you were *so* superior, neh?' He laughed then sat back, all humour draining from his face. 'For your part in this, you're under report, Hammond, from this moment. But you, Ward – you're *out*.'

'Out?' Kim laughed. 'Forgive me, *Shih* Spatz, but you can't do that. I'm Prince Yuan's appointment. Surely only he can say whether I'm out or not.'

Spatz glanced at him disdainfully. 'A formality. He'll have my recommendation, backed by the personnel file and the complaints of disruption filed against you by several staff members.'

Out of the corner of his eye he saw Hammond start forward. 'But you promised –'

Spatz interrupted, his face hard. 'I promised nothing. Now for the gods' sakes, hold your tongue! Even better, leave the room. You've served your purpose.'

Hammond rose slowly. 'I've served my purpose, eh? Too fucking right I have.' He leaned forward, setting his hands firmly on the edge of the desk, facing the Director. As if sensing what he intended, Spatz drew the file towards him then handed it to Ellis at his side.

'If you say another word...'

Hammond laughed, but his face was filled with loathing for the man in front of him. 'Oh, I've nothing more to say, Director Spatz. Just this...'

He drew his head back and spat; powerfully, cleanly, catching Spatz in the centre of his face.

Spatz cried out, rubbing at his face with the sleeve of his gown, then, realizing what he had done, he swore.

'You bastard, Hammond! My silks...' Spatz stood, his face livid with anger, his hands trembling. 'Get out! Get your things and be gone! As from this moment you're off the Project.'

For a moment longer Hammond stood there, glaring at him, then he moved back, a tiny shudder passing through him.

'Joel, I...' Kim began, reaching out to him, but Hammond stepped back, looking about him as if coming to from a bad dream.

'No. It's fine, Kim. Really it is. I'll survive. The Net can't be worse than this. At least I won't have to pawn myself every day to *hsiao jen* like this pig-brained cretin here!'

Spatz trembled with rage. 'Guards!' he yelled. 'Get the guards here, now!'

Hammond laughed. 'Don't bother. I'm going. But fuck you, Spatz. Fuck you to hell. I hope Prince Yuan has your arse for what you're trying to do here today.' He turned then bent down, embracing Kim. 'Good luck, Kim,' he whispered. 'I'm sorry. Truly I am.'

Kim held him out at arm's length. 'It's all right. I understand. You're a good man, Joel Hammond.'

He stood, watching him go, then turned back, facing Spatz.

'So what now?'

Spatz ignored him, leaning forward to talk into the intercom. 'Send in the nurse. We're ready now.'

Kim looked at Ellis; saw how the man refused to meet his eyes. Then at Barycz. Barycz was pretending to study the chart on the wall behind Spatz.

'Prince Yuan will ask about me,' Kim said. 'He's certain to.'

Spatz smiled coldly. 'Of course he will. But you won't be there, will you?'

He heard the door open, the nurse come in.

'And then he'll ask why I'm not there–' he began, but the words were choked off. He felt the hypodermic gun pressed against his neck and tried to squirm away, struggling against the strong hand that held his shoulder, but it was too late.

The hand released him. Slumping down into the chair, he felt a fiery cold spreading through his veins, leaving him numb, his nerve-ends frozen.

'I-wb...' he said, his eyes glazing. 'I-jibw...'

Then he fell forward, scattering the sheaf of poems across the floor beside him.

Li Yuan stepped down from his craft and sighed, looking about him. The roof of the City stretched away from him like a vast field of snow, empty but for the small group of officials who were gathered, heads bowed, beside the open hatchway.

He looked north to where the City ended abruptly on the shores of the icy Baltic, then turned to smile at his personal secretary, Chang Shih-sen.

'Have you ever seen it when the cloud is low, Chang? The cloud seems to spill from the City's edge like water over a fall. But slowly, very slowly, as in a dream.'

'I have never seen that, my lord, but I should imagine it was beautiful.'

Li Yuan nodded. 'Very beautiful. I saw it once at sunset. All the colours of the sky seemed captured in those endless folds of whiteness.'

Chang Shih-sen nodded, then, softly, mindful of his place, added. 'They are waiting, my lord.'

Li Yuan looked back at him and smiled. 'Let them wait. The day is beautiful. Besides, I wish a moment to myself before I join them.'

'My lord...' Chang backed away, bowing.

Li Yuan turned, moving out from the shadow of the craft into the mid-afternoon sunlight. Chang was a good man. Kind, hard-working, thoughtful. But so had been his father's Master of the Inner Palace, Wang Ta Chuan. It made one think. When the fate of so many were in one's hands, who *could* one trust?

He took a deep breath, enjoying the freshness, the warmth of the sunlight on his arms and back. Last night, for the first time since he had married Fei Yen, he had summoned a woman to his bed – one of the serving girls from the kitchens – purging himself of the need that had raged in his blood like a poison. Now he was himself again.

Or almost himself. For he would never again be wholly as he had been. Fei Yen had changed that.

Who was it? he wondered for the thousandth time. *Who slept with you while I was gone? Was it one of my servants? Or was it someone you knew before our time together?*

He huffed out his sudden irritation. It was no good dwelling on it. Madness lay that way. No, best set such thoughts aside, lest he find himself thinking of nothing else.

And what use would I then be to my father?

He shivered, then, calming himself, turned back and summoned Chang.

'Is this all?'

Spatz, standing before the seated Prince, bowed his head. 'I am afraid so, my lord. But you must understand – I have been working under the most severe restraints.'

Li Yuan looked up, his disappointment clear. 'Just what do you mean, Director?'

Spatz kept his head lowered, not meeting the Prince's eyes. 'To begin with, I have been effectively two short on my team throughout my time here.'

Li Yuan leaned forward. 'I do not understand you, Director. There is no mention in your report of such a thing.'

'Forgive me, my lord, but the matter I am referring to is in the second file. I felt it best to keep the main report to matters of... science.'

The Prince sat back, irritated by the man's manner. If he'd had his way, Spatz would have been replaced as Director, but Spatz had been his father's appointment, like Tolonen.

He set the top file aside and opened the second one. It was a personnel report on the boy, Ward.

Li Yuan looked up, surprised. Could Spatz have known? No. He couldn't possibly have known about Kim and the special projects. But that too had been a disappointment. After the first report he had heard nothing from the boy. Nothing for ten months. At first he had assumed that it was taking much longer than the boy had estimated or that his work on the Project was taking up his time, but this explained it all.

He read it through then looked up again, shaking his head. The boy had been at best lethargic, uncooperative, at worst disruptive to the point of actual physical violence.

'Why was I not told of this before now?'

Spatz hesitated. 'I... I wished to be charitable to the boy, my lord. To give him every chance to change his ways and prove himself. I was conscious of his importance to you. Of your special interest. So...'

Li Yuan raised his hand. 'I understand. Can I see the boy?'

'Of course, my lord. But you must understand his condition. I am told it is a result of his "re-structuring" at the clinic. Occasionally he falls into a kind of torpor where he won't speak or even acknowledge that anyone is there.'

'I see.' Li Yuan kept the depth of his disappointment from his face. 'And is he like that now?'

'I am afraid so, my lord.'

'And his tutor, T'ai Cho?'

Spatz gave a small shrug of resignation. 'A good man, but his loyalty to the boy is... shall we say, misguided. He is too involved, my lord. His only thought is to keep the boy from harm. I'm afraid you'll get little sense from him either.'

Li Yuan studied Spatz a moment longer then closed the file.

'You wish to see the boy, my lord?'

Li Yuan sighed then shook his head. 'No. I think I've seen enough.' He stood. 'I'm disappointed, Spatz. Hugely disappointed. I expected far greater progress than this. Still, things are on the right lines. I note that you've made some headway towards solving things on the technical front. That's good, but I want more. I want a working model twelve months from now.'

'My lord...' The note of pure panic in the Director's voice was almost comical, yet Li Yuan had never felt less like laughing.

'Twelve months. Understand me? For my part, I'll make sure you have another dozen men – the best scientists I can recruit from the Companies. As for funding, you're quite correct, Director. It *is* inadequate. Which is why I'm tripling it from this moment.'

For the first time Spatz's head came up and his eyes searched him out. 'My lord, you are too generous.'

Li Yuan laughed sourly. 'Generosity has nothing to do with it, Director Spatz. I want a job done and I want it done properly. We under-funded. We didn't see the scale of the thing. Well, now we'll put that right. But I want results this time.'

'And the boy?'

Li Yuan stood, handing the main copies of the files to Chang Shih-sen, then looked back at Spatz.

'The matter of the boy will be dealt with. You need worry yourself no further in that regard, Director.'

Barycz locked the door of the communications room then went to his desk and activated the screen. He tapped in the code and waited, knowing the signal was being scrambled through as many as a dozen sub-routes before it got to its destination. The screen flickered wildly then cleared, and DeVore's face stared out at him.

'Is it done?'

Barycz swallowed nervously then nodded. 'I've despatched copies of the files to your man. He should have them within the hour.'

'Good. And the boy? He's out of it, I hope?'

Barycz bowed his head. 'I've done everything as you ordered it, *Shih* Loehr. However, there is one small complication. The Director has ordered Hammond off the Project. With immediate effect.'

DeVore looked away a moment then nodded. 'Fine. I'll see to that.' He looked back at Barycz, smiling. 'You've done well, Barycz. There'll be a bonus for you.'

Barycz bowed his head again. 'You are too kind...' When he looked up again the screen was dark.

He smiled, pleased with himself, then sat back, wondering how generous Loehr planned to be. Maybe he'd have enough to move up a deck – to buy a place in the Hundreds.

Barycz sniffed thoughtfully then laughed, recalling how Hammond had spat in the Director's face.

'Served the bastard right...' he said quietly. Yes. He was not a spiteful man, but he had enjoyed the sight of Spatz getting his deserts.

Lehmann stood in the doorway, looking in. 'Ebert's here.'

DeVore looked up from the *wei chi* board and smiled. 'Okay. I'll be up in a while. Take him through into the private suite and get one of the stewards to look after him. Tell him I won't be long.'

DeVore watched his lieutenant go then stood. He had been practising new openings. Experimenting. Seeing if he could break down old habits. That was the only trouble with *wei chi* – it was not a game to be played against oneself. One needed a steady supply of opponents, men as good as oneself – better if one really wished to improve one's game. But he had no one.

He stretched and looked about him, feeling good, noticing his furs where he had left them in the corner of the room. He had been out early, before sunrise; had gone out alone, hunting snow foxes. The pelts of five were hanging in the kitchens, drying out, the scant meat of the foxes gone into a stew – a special meal to celebrate.

Yes, things were going well. Only a few weeks ago things had seemed bleak, but now the board was filling nicely with his plays. In the north, the *Ping Tiao* were effectively destroyed and Mach's *Yu* were primed to step into the resultant power vacuum. In the east his men were in position, awaiting only his order to attack the Plantations, while to the west he was building up a new shape – seeking new allies among the elite of City North America. Added to these were two much subtler plays – the poisoned statue and his plans for the Wiring Project. All were coming to fruition. Soon the shapes on the board would change and a new phase of the game would begin – the middle game – in which his pieces would be in the ascendant.

And what was Ebert's role in all this? He had ambitions, that was clear now. Ambitions above being a puppet ruler. Well, let Ebert have them. When the time came, he would cut him down to size. Until then he would seem to trust him more.

DeVore laughed. In the meantime, maybe he would offer him the girl, the lookalike. She had been meant for Tolonen – as a 'gift' to replace his murdered daughter – but Jelka's survival had meant a change of plans. He studied the board thoughtfully then nodded. Yes, he would give Ebert the lookalike as an early wedding gift. To do with as he wished.

He smiled then leaned across and placed a white stone on the board, breaching the space between two of the black masses, threatening to cut.

Hans Ebert stood by the open hatchway of the transporter, his left hand gripping the overhead strap tightly as the craft rose steeply from the mountainside.

DeVore's 'gift' was crouched behind him against the far wall of the craft, as far from the open hatchway as she could. He could sense her there behind him and felt the hairs rise along his spine and at the back of his neck.

The bastard. The devious fucking bastard.

He smiled tightly and waved a hand at the slowly diminishing figure on the hillside far below. Then, as the craft began to bank away, he turned, looking at the girl, smiling at her reassuringly, keeping his true feelings from showing.

Games. It was all one big game to DeVore. He understood that now. And this – this 'gift' of the girl – that was part of the play, too. To unsettle him, perhaps. Or mock him. Well... he'd not let him.

He moved past her brusquely and went through into the cockpit. Auden turned, looking at him.

'What is it, Hans?'

He took a breath then shook his head. 'Nothing. But you'd best have this.' He took the sealed letter DeVore had given him and handed it across. 'It's to Lever. DeVore wants you to hand it to him when you meet the Americans at the spaceport. It's an invitation.'

Auden tucked it away. 'What else?'

Ebert smiled. Auden was a good man. He understood things without having to be told. 'It's just that I don't trust him. Especially when he "puts all his stones on the table". He's up to something.'

Auden laughed. 'Like what?'

Ebert stared out through the frosted glass, noting the bleakness of their surroundings. 'I don't know. It's just a feeling. And then there's his gift...'

Auden narrowed his eyes. 'So what are you going to do with her?'

Ebert turned back, meeting his eyes briefly, then jerked away, pulling the cockpit door closed behind him.

The girl looked up as Ebert came back into the hold, her eyes wide, filled with fear. He stopped, staring at her, appalled by the likeness, then went across and stood by the open hatchway, looking outwards, his neat-cut hair barely moving in the icy wind.

'I'm sorry,' he said, against the roar of the wind. 'I didn't mean to frighten you.' He glanced round, smiling. 'Here... come across. I want to show you something.'

She didn't move, only pressed tighter against the far wall of the cabin.

'Come...' he said, as softly as he could against the noise. 'You've nothing to be afraid of. I just want to show you, that's all.'

He watched her, saw how fear battled in her with a need to obey. *Yes, he* thought, *DeVore would have instilled that in you, wouldn't he?* She kept looking down, biting her lip then glancing up at him again, in two minds.

Yes, and you're like her, he thought. *Physically, anyway. But you aren't her. You're just a common peasant girl he's had changed in his labs. And the gods alone know what he's done to you. But the real Jelka wouldn't be cowering there. She would have come across of her own free will. To defy me. Just to prove to me that I didn't frighten her.*

He smiled and looked down, remembering that moment in the machine when she had glared back at him. It had been then, perhaps, that he had first realized his true feelings for her. Then that he had first articulated it inside his head.

I'm in love with you, Jelka Tolonen, he had thought, surprised. *In love.*

So unexpected. So totally unexpected.

And afterwards, when she had gone, he had found himself thinking of her. Finding the image of her, there, entangled in his thoughts of other things. How strange that had been. So strange to find himself so vulnerable.

And now this...

He went to her and took her arm, coaxing her gently, almost tenderly across, then stood there, one arm holding tightly about her slender waist, the other reaching up to hold the strap. The wind whipped her long, golden hair back and chilled her face, but he made her look.

'There,' he said. 'Isn't that magnificent?'

He looked sideways at her; saw how she opened her eyes, fighting against the fear she felt, battling with it, trying to see the beauty there in that desolate place.

DeVore's thing. His 'gift'.

For a moment there was nothing. Then the tiniest of smiles came to her lips, the muscles about her eyes relaxing slightly as she saw.

He shivered then drew his arm back and up, forcing her head down.

He watched the tiny figure fall away from the craft, twisting silently in the air, a tiny star of darkness against the white, growing smaller by the second, then shuddered again, a strange mixture of pain and incomprehension making him shake his head and moan.

No. There would be no impediments. Not this time. No possessive old women or mad whores with their love children. And certainly no copies.

No. Because he wanted the real Jelka, not some copy. Even if she hated him. Or maybe *because* she hated him. Yes, that was it perhaps. Because underneath it all she was as strong as him and that strength appealed to him, making her a challenge. A challenge he could not turn his back on.

For you will love me, Jelka Tolonen. You will.

He watched the body hit in a spray of snow then turned away, the roar of the wind abating as he drew the hatch closed behind him.

Emily Ascher turned from the door then caught her breath, the pay-lock key falling from her hand, clattering across the bare ice floor.

'You...'

DeVore looked back at her from where he sat on the edge of her bed and smiled. 'Yes, me.'

He saw her look from him to the key, judging the distance, assessing the possibility of getting out of the room alive, and smiled inwardly.

She looked back at him, her eyes narrowed. 'How did you find me?'

He tilted his head, looking her up and down, his keen eyes searching for the tell-tale bulge of a concealed weapon.

'It wasn't so hard. I've had someone trailing you since that meeting at the meat warehouse. I knew then that you were planning to get out.'

'You did?' She laughed, but her face was hard. 'That's strange. Because I had no plans to. Not until last night.'

He smiled. 'Then you got out in good time. They're all dead. Or had you heard?'

He saw the way her breathing changed, how the colour drained from her face.

'And Gesell?'

He nodded, watching her. 'I made sure of him myself.'

Her lips parted slightly then she looked down. 'I guess it was... inevitable.' But when she looked back at him he saw the hatred in her eyes and knew he had been right. She was still in love with Gesell.

Such a waste, he thought. *Had the worm understood how lucky he had been to share his bed with two such strong women?*

No. Probably not. Like all his kind, he took things without thinking of their worth.

'Mach helped me,' he said, watching her closely now, his hand resting loosely on the gun in his pocket. 'He arranged it all.'

'Why?' she asked. 'I don't understand. He wanted it to work more than any of us.'

'He still does. But he wants to start again, without the taint of Bremen. New blood, with new ideals, fresh ideas.'

She stared back at him a moment then shook her head. 'But still with you, neh?'

'Is that why you got out? Because of my involvement?'

She hesitated then nodded, meeting the challenge of his eyes. 'It changed, after you came. It was different before, sharper, but then... well, you saw what happened. It wasn't like that before.'

'No...' He seemed almost to agree. 'Well, that's past, neh?'

'Is it?'

He nodded, sitting back slightly, the gun in his pocket covering her now.

'So what now? What do you want of me?'

His smile broadened. 'It's not what I want. It's what Mach wants. And he wants you dead.'

Again that slight tremor of the breasts, that slight change in breathing, quickly controlled. She had guts, that was certain. More, perhaps, than any of them. But he had seen that much at once. Had singled her out because of it.

'I'm unarmed,' she said, raising her hands slowly.

'So I see,' he said. 'So?'

She laughed, almost relaxed. 'No... It wouldn't worry you at all, would it? To kill an unarmed woman.'

'No, it wouldn't. But who said I was going to kill you?'

Her eyes narrowed. 'Aren't you, then?'

He shook his head then reached into his left pocket and pulled out a wallet. It held a pass, a new set of identity documents, two five-hundred *yuan* credit chips and a ticket for the intercontinental jet.

'Here,' he said, throwing it to her.

She caught it deftly, opened it, then looked up sharply at him. 'I don't understand...'

'There's a price,' he said. 'I promised Mach I'd bring something back. To prove I'd dealt with you. A finger.'

He saw the small shiver pass through her. 'I see.'

'It shouldn't hurt. I'll freeze the hand and cauterize the wound. There'll be no pain. Discomfort, yes, but nothing more.'

She looked down, a strangely pained expression on her face, then looked up again. 'Why? I mean, why are you doing this? What's your motive?'

'Do I have to have one?'

She nodded. 'It's how you are.'

He shrugged. 'So you've told me before. But you're wrong.'

'No strings, then?'

'No strings. You give me a finger and I give you your freedom and a new life in North America.'

She laughed, still not trusting him. 'It's too easy. Too...' She shook her head.

He stood. 'You're wondering why. Why should that cold, calculating bastard DeVore do this for me? What does he want? Well, I'll tell you. It's very simple. I wanted to prove that you were wrong about me.'

She studied him a moment then went across and bent down, recovering the pay-key.

'Well?' he asked. 'Have we a deal?'

She looked up at him. 'Have I a choice?'

'Yes. You can walk out of here, right now. I'll not stop you. But if you do, Mach will come after you with everything he's got. Because he'll not feel safe until you're dead.'

'And you?'

DeVore smiled. 'Oh, I'm safe. I'm always safe.'

Slowly the great globe of Chung Kuo turned in space, moving through sunlight and darkness, the blank faces of its continents glistening like ice caps beneath huge swirls of cloud. Three hours had passed by the measure of men and in Sichuan Province, in the great palace at Tongjiang, Li Shai Tung sat with his son in the dim-lit silence of his study, reading through the report General Nocenzi had brought. Li Yuan stood at his father's side, scanning each sheet as his father finished with it.

The report concerned a number of items taken in a raid the previous evening on a gaming club frequented by the sons of several important Company heads. More than a dozen of the young men had been taken, together with a quantity of seditious material: posters and pamphlets, secret diaries and detailed accounts of illicit meetings. Much of the material confirmed what Tolonen had said only the day before. There was a new wave of unrest; a new tide, running for change.

They were good men – exemplary young men, it might be said – from families whose ties to the Seven went back to the foundation of the City. Men who, in other circumstances, might have served his father well. But a disease was rife among them, a foulness that, once infected, could not be shaken from the blood.

And the disease? Li Yuan looked across at the pile of folders balanced on the far side of his father's desk. There were three of them, each bulging with handwritten ice-vellum sheets. He had not had time to compare more than a few paragraphs scattered throughout each text, but he had seen enough to know that their contents were practically identical. He reached across and picked one up, flicking through the first few pages. He had seen the original in Berdichev's papers more than a year ago, amongst the material Karr had brought back with him from Mars, but had never thought to see another.

He read the title page. *The Aristotle File. Being the True History of Western Science. By Soren Berdichev.*

The document had become the classic of dissent for these young men, each copy painstakingly written out in longhand.

His father turned in his seat, looking up at him. 'Well, Yuan? What do you think?'

He set the file down. 'It is as you said, Father. The thing is a cancer. We must cut it out, before it spreads.'

The old T'ang smiled, pleased with his son. 'If we can.'

'You think it might already be too late?'

Li Shai Tung shrugged. 'A document like this is a powerful thing, Yuan.' He smiled then stood, touching his son's arm. 'But come... let us feed the fish. It is a while since we had the chance to talk.'

Li Yuan followed his father into the semi-darkness of the arboretum, his mind filled with misgivings.

Inside, Li Shai Tung turned, facing his son, the carp pool behind him. 'I come here whenever I need to think.'

Li Yuan looked about him and nodded. He understood. When his father was absent, he would come here himself and stand beside the pool, staring down into the water as if emptying himself into its depths, letting his thoughts become the fish, drifting, gliding slowly, almost listlessly in the water, then rising swiftly to breach the surface, imbued with sudden purpose.

The old T'ang smiled, seeing how his son stared down into the water; so like himself in some respects.

'Sometimes I think it needs a pike...'

Li Yuan looked up surprised. 'A pike in a carp pool, Father? But it would eat the other fish!'

Li Shai Tung nodded earnestly. 'And maybe that is what was wrong with Chung Kuo. Maybe our great carp pool needed a pike. To keep the numbers down and add that missing element of sharpness. Maybe that is what we are seeing now. Maybe our present troubles are merely the consequence of all those years of peace.'

'Things decay...' Yuan said, conscious of how far their talk had come; of how far his father's words were from what he normally professed to believe.

'Yes...' Li Shai Tung nodded and eased himself back on to the great saddle of a turtle shell that was placed beside the pool. 'And perhaps a pike is loose in the depths.'

Li Yuan moved to the side of the pool, the toes of his boots overlapping the tiled edge.

'Have you made up your mind yet, Yuan?'

The question was unconnected to anything they had been discussing, but once again he understood. In this sense they had never been closer. His father meant the boy, Kim.

'Yes, Father. I have decided.'

'And?'

Yuan turned his head, looking across at his father. Li Shai Tung sat there, his feet spread, the cane resting against one knee. Yuan could see his dead brother, Han Ch'in, in that posture of his father's. Could see how his father would have resembled Han when he was younger, as if age had been given to him and youth to Han. But Han was long dead and youth with it. Only old age remained. Only the crumbling patterns of their forefathers.

'I was wrong,' he said after a moment. 'The reports are unequivocal. It hasn't worked out. And now this... this matter of the sons and their "New European" movement. I can't help but think the two are connected – that the boy is responsible for this.'

Li Shai Tung's regretful smile mirrored his son's. 'It *is* connected, Yuan. Without the boy there would be no file.' He looked clearly at his son. 'Then you will act upon my warrant and have the boy terminated?'

Li Yuan met his father's eyes, part of him still hesitant, even now. Then he nodded.

'Good. And do not trouble yourself, Yuan. You did all you could. It seems to me that the boy's end was fated.'

Li Yuan had looked down; now he looked up again, surprised by his father's words. Li Shai Tung saw this and laughed. 'You find it odd for me to talk of fate, neh?'

'You have always spoken of it with scorn.'

'Maybe so, yet any man must at some point question whether it is chance or fate that brings things to pass; whether he is the author or merely the agent of his actions.'

'And you, Father? What do you think?'

Li Shai Tung stood, leaning heavily upon the silver-headed cane he had come to use so often these days; the cane with the dragon's head that Han Ch'in had bought him on his fiftieth birthday.

'It is said that in the time of Shang they would take a tortoise shell and cover it with ink then throw it into a fire. When it dried, a diviner would read the cracks and lines in the scorched shell. They believed, you see, that the tortoise was an animal of great purity – in its hard-soft form they saw the meeting of Yin and Yang, of Heaven and Earth. Later they would inscribe the shells with questions put to their ancestors. As if the dead could answer.'

Li Yuan smiled, reassured by the ironic tone of his father's words. For a moment he had thought...

'And maybe they were right, Yuan. Maybe it is all written. But then one must ask what it is the gods want of us. They seem to give and take without design. To build things up, only to cast them down. To give a man great joy, only to snatch it away, leaving him in great despair. And to what end, Yuan? To what end?'

Yuan answered softly, touched to the core by his father's words. 'I don't know, Father. Truly I don't.'

Li Shai Tung shook his head bitterly. 'Bones and tortoise shells...' He laughed and touched the great turtle shell behind him with his cane. 'They say this is a copy of the great Luoshu shell, Yuan. It was a present to your mother from my father, on the day of our wedding. The pattern on its back is meant to be a charm, you see, for easing childbirth.'

Yuan looked away. It was as if his father felt a need to torture himself; to surround himself with the symbols of lost joy.

'You know the story, Yuan? It was in the reign of Yu, oh... more than four thousand years ago now, when the turtle crawled up out of the Luo River, bearing the markings on its back.'

Yuan knew the story well. Every child did. But he let his father talk, finding it strange that only now should they reach this point of intimacy between them; now, when things were darkest, his own life blighted by the failure of his dreams, his father's by ill health.

'Three lines of three figures were marked out there on the shell, as plain as could be seen, the Yin numbers in the corners, the Yang numbers in the centre, and each line – horizontal, vertical and diagonal – adding up to fifteen. Of course, it was hailed at once as a magic square – as a sign that supernatural powers were at work in the world. But we know better, neh, Yuan? We know there are no magic charms to aid us in our troubles – only our reason and our will. And if *they* fail...'

Li Shai Tung heaved a sigh, then sat heavily on the great saddle of the shell. He looked up at his son wearily.

'But what is the answer, Yuan? What might we do that we have not already done?'

Li Yuan looked across at his father, his eyes narrowed. 'Cast oracles?'

The T'ang laughed softly. 'Like our forefathers, neh?'

The old man looked away; stared down into the depths of the pool. Beyond him the moon was framed within the darkness of the window. The night was perfect, like the velvet worn about the neck of a young girl.

'I hoped for peace, Yuan. Longed for it. But...' He shook his head.

'What, then, Father? What should we do?'

'Do?' Li Shai Tung laughed, a soft, unfamiliar sound. 'Prepare ourselves, Yuan. That's all. Take care our friends are true. Sleep only when we're safe.'

It was an uncharacteristically vague answer.

Yuan looked down, then broached the subject he had been avoiding all evening. 'Are you well, Father? I had heard...'

'Heard what?' Li Shai Tung turned, his tone suddenly sharp, commanding.

Li Yuan almost smiled, but checked himself, knowing his father's eagle eye was on him. 'Only that you were not at your best, Father. No more than that. Headaches. Mild stomach upsets. But do not be angry with me. A son should be concerned for his father's health.'

Li Shai Tung grunted. 'Not at my best, eh? Well, that's true of us all after thirty. We're never again at our best.' He was silent a moment then turned, tapping his cane against the tiled floor. 'Maybe that's true of all things – that they're never at their best after a while. Men and the things men build.'

'Particulars, Father. Particulars.'

The old man stared at him a moment then nodded. 'So I've always lectured you, Yuan. You learn well. You always did. You were always suited for this.'

There was a long silence between them. Han Ch'in's death lay there in that silence, cold, heavy, unmentionable: a dark stone of grief in the guts of each that neither had managed to pass.

'And Fei Yen?'

It was the first time his father had mentioned the separation. The matter was not yet public knowledge.

Li Yuan sighed. 'It's still the same.'

There was real pain in Li Shai Tung's face. 'You should command her, Yuan. Order her to come home.'

Li Yuan shook his head, controlling what he felt. 'With great respect, Father, I know what's best in this. She hates me. I know that now. To have her in my home would weaken me.'

Li Shai Tung was watching his son closely, his shoulders slightly hunched. 'Ah...' He lifted his chin. 'I did not know that, Yuan. I...' Again he sighed. 'I'm sorry, Yuan, but the child. What of the child?'

Li Yuan swallowed then raised his head again, facing the matter squarely. 'The child is not mine. Fei Yen was unfaithful. The child belongs to another man.'

The old man came closer; came round the pool and stood there, facing his son.

'You know this for certain?'

'No, but I know it. Fei Yen herself—'

'No. I don't mean "know it" in some vague sense, I mean *know* it, for good and certain.' His voice had grown fierce, commanding once more. 'This is important, Yuan. I'm surprised at you. You should have seen to this.'

Li Yuan nodded. It was so, but he had not wanted to face it. Had not wanted to know for good and certain. He had been quite happy to accept her word.

'You must go to her and offer her divorce terms, Yuan. At once. But you will make the offer conditional. You understand?'

Again he nodded, understanding. There would need to be tests. Tests to ascertain the father of the child. Genotyping. Then he would know. Know for good and certain. He gritted his teeth, feeling the pain like a needle in his guts.

'Good,' said the T'ang, seeing that what he had wanted was accomplished. 'There must be no room for doubt in the future. If your son is to rule, he must be uncontested. Your son, not some cuckoo in the nest.'

The words stung Li Yuan, but that was their aim. His father knew when to spare and when to goad.

'And then?' Li Yuan felt drained suddenly; empty of thought.

'And then you marry again. Not one wife, but two. Six if need be, Yuan. Have sons. Make the family strong again. *Provide*.'

He nodded, unable to conceive of life with any other woman but Fei Yen, but for now obedient to his father's wishes.

'*Love!*' There was a strange bitterness to his father's voice. An edge. 'It's never enough, Yuan. Remember that. It always fails you in the end. Always.'

Li Yuan looked up, meeting his father's eyes, seeing the love and hurt and pain there where for others there was nothing.

'All love?'

The T'ang nodded and reached out to hold his son's shoulder. 'All love, Yuan. Even this.'

There was a pounding at the outer doors. Li Shai Tung woke, drenched in sweat, the dream of his first wife, Lin Yua, and that dreadful night so clear that, for a moment, he thought the banging on the doors a part of it. He sat up, feeling weak, disoriented. The banging came again.

'Gods help us... what is it now?' he muttered, getting up slowly and pulling on his gown.

He went across and stood there, facing the doors. 'Who is it?'

'It is I, *Chieh Hsia*. Your Chancellor, Chung Hu-yan.'

He shivered. Chung Hu-yan. As in the dream. As on the night Lin Yua had died, giving birth to his son, Yuan. For a moment he could not answer him.

'*Chieh Hsia*,' came the voice again. 'Are you all right?'

He turned, looking about him, then turned back. No. He was here. He wasn't dreaming. Seventeen, almost eighteen years had passed and he was here, in his palace, and the knocking on the door, the voice – both were real.

'Hold on, Chung. I'm coming...'

He heard how weak his voice sounded, how indecisive, and shivered. Sweat trickled down his inner arms, formed on his forehead. Why was everything suddenly so difficult?

He fumbled with the lock then drew back the catch. Stepping back, he watched the doors open. Chung Hu-yan stood there, flanked by two guards.

'What is it, Chung?' he said, his voice quavering, seeing the fear in his Chancellor's face.

Chung Hu-yan bowed low. 'News has come, *Chieh Hsia*. Bad news.'

Bad news... He felt his stomach tighten. Li Yuan was dead. Or Tsu Ma. Or...

'What is it, Chung?' he said again, unconscious of the repetition.

In answer Chung moved aside. Tolonen was standing there, his face ashen.

'*Chieh Hsia*...' the Marshal began, then went down on one knee, bowing his head low. 'I have failed you, my lord... failed you.'

Li Shai Tung half turned, looking to see who was standing behind him, but there was no one. He frowned then turned back. 'Failed, Knut? How failed?'

'The Plantations...' Tolonen said, then looked up at him again, tears in his eyes. 'The Plantations are on fire.'

CHUNG KUO

Chapter 61

THE BROKEN WHEEL

A huge window filled the end of the corridor where the tunnel turned to the right, intersecting with the boarding hatch. She stood there a moment, looking out across the pre-dawn darkness of the space-port, barely conscious of the passengers pushing by, knowing that this was probably the last view she would ever have of City Europe – the City in which she had spent her whole life. But that life was over now and a new one lay ahead. Emily Ascher was dead, killed in a fictitious accident three days back. She was Mary Jennings now, a blonde from Atlanta Canton, returning to the eastern seaboard after a two-year secondment to the European arm of her Company.

She had sat up until late, learning the brief she had been sent, then had snatched three hours before the call had come. That had been an hour back. Now she stood, quite literally, on the threshold of a new life, hesitating, wondering even now if she had done the right thing.

Was it really too late to go back – to make her peace with Mach? She sighed and let her fingers move slowly down the dark, smooth surface of the glass. Yes. DeVore might have been lying when he had said he had no motive in helping her, but he was right about Mach wanting her dead. She had given Mach no option. No one left the *Ping Tiao*. Not voluntarily, anyway. And certainly not alive.

Even so, wasn't there some other choice? Some other option than putting herself in debt to DeVore?

She looked down at her bandaged left hand then smiled cynically at her reflection in the darkened glass. If there had been she would not be here. Besides, there were things she had to do. Important things. And maybe she could do them just as well in America. If DeVore let her.

It was a big if, but she was prepared to take the chance. The only other choice was death, and while she didn't fear death, it was hardly worth pre-empting things. No. She would reserve that option. Would keep it as her final bargaining counter. Just in case DeVore proved difficult. And maybe she'd even take him with her. If she could.

Her smile broadened, lost its hard edge. She turned, joining the line of boarding passengers, holding out her pass to the tiny Han stewardess, then moved down the aisle towards her seat.

She was about to sit when the steward touched her arm.

'Forgive me, *Fu Jen*, but have you a reserved ticket for that seat?'

She turned, straightening up, then held out her ticket for inspection, looking the man up and down as she did so. He was a squat, broad-shouldered Han with one of those hard, anonymous faces some of them had. She knew what he was at once. One of those minor officials who gloried in their pettiness.

He made a great pretence of studying her ticket, turning it over then turning it back. His eyes flicked up to her face, took in her clothes, her lack of jewellery, before returning to her face again – the disdain in them barely masked. He shook his head.

'If you would follow me, *Fu Jen*...'

He turned, making his way back down the aisle towards the cramped third- and fourth-class seats at the tail of the rocket, but she stood where she was, her stomach tightening, anticipating the tussle to come.

Realizing that she wasn't following him, he came back, his whole manner suddenly, quite brutally, antagonistic.

'You must come, *Fu Jen*. These seats are reserved for others.'

She shook her head. 'I have a ticket.'

He tucked the ticket down into the top pocket of his official tunic. 'Forgive me, *Fu Jen*, but there has been a mistake. As I said, these seats are reserved. Paid for in advance.'

The emphasis on the last few words gave his game away. For a moment she had thought that this might be DeVore's final little game with her, but now she knew. The steward was out to extract some squeeze from her. To get her to pay for what was already rightfully hers. She glared at him, despising him, then turned and sat. If he just so much as tried to make her budge...

He leaned over her, angry now. 'Fu Jen! You must move! Now! At once! Or I will call the captain!'

She was about to answer him when a hand appeared on the steward's shoulder and drew him back sharply.

It was a big man. A *Hung Mao*. He pushed the Han steward back unceremoniously, a scathing look of contempt on his face. 'Have you left your senses, man? The lady has paid for her seat. Now return her ticket and leave her alone, or I'll report you to the port authorities – understand me, *hsiao jen?*'

The steward opened his mouth then closed it again, seeing the Security warrant card the man was holding out. Lowering his eyes, he took the ticket from his pocket and handed it across.

'Good!' The man handed it to her with a smile then turned back. 'Now get lost, you little fucker. If I so much as see you in this section during the flight...'

The Han swallowed and backed away hurriedly.

The man turned back, looking at her. 'I'm sorry about that. They always try it on. A single woman, travelling alone. Your kind is usually good for fifty *yuan* at least.'

She looked at her ticket, a small shudder of indignation passing through her, then looked back at him, smiling. 'Thank you. I appreciate your help, but I would have been all right.'

He nodded. 'Maybe. But a mutual friend asked me to look after you.'

'Ah...' She narrowed her eyes then tilted her head slightly, indicating the warrant card he still held in one hand. 'And that's real?'

He laughed. 'Of course. Look, can I sit for a moment? There are one or two things we need to sort out.'

She hesitated then gave a small nod. No strings, eh? But it was just as she'd expected. She had known all along that DeVore would have some reason for helping her out.

'What is it?' she asked, turning in her seat to study him as he sat down beside her.

'These...' He handed her a wallet and a set of cards. The cards were in the name of Rachel DeValerian; the wallet contained a set of references for Mary Jennings, including the documentation for a degree in economics, and a letter of introduction to Michael Lever, the director of a company called MemSys. A letter dated two days from then.

She looked up at him. 'I don't understand.'

He smiled. 'You'll need a job over there. Well, the Levers will have a vacancy for an economist on their personal staff. As of tomorrow.'

How do you know? she was going to ask, but his smile was answer enough. If DeVore said there was going to be a vacancy, there would be a vacancy. But why the Levers? And what about the other identity?

'What's this?' she asked, holding out the DeValerian cards.

He shrugged. 'I'm only the messenger. Our friend said you would know what to do with them.'

'I see.' She studied them a moment then put them away. Then DeVore meant her to set up her own movement. To recruit. She smiled and looked up again. 'What else?'

He returned her smile, briefly covering her left hand with his right. 'Nothing. But I'll be back in a second if you need me. Enjoy the flight.' He stood. 'Okay. See you in Boston.'

'Boston? I thought we were going to New York?'

He shook his head then leaned forward. 'Hadn't you heard? New York is closed. Wu Shih is holding an emergency meeting of the Seven and there's a two-hundred-li exclusion zone about Manhattan.'

She frowned. 'I didn't know. What's up?'

He laughed then leaned forward and touched his finger to the panel on the seatback in front of her. At once the screen lit up, showing a scene of devastation.

'There!' he said. 'That's what's up.'

The two men sat on the high wall of the dyke as the dawn came, looking out across the flat expanse of blackened fields, watching the figures move almost somnolently in the darkness below. The tart smell of burned crops seemed to taint every breath they took, despite the filters both wore. They were dressed in the uniform of reserve corps volunteers, and though only one of the two wore it legitimately, it would have been hard to tell which.

Great palls of smoke lifted above the distant horizon, turning the dawn light ochre, while, two li out, a convoy of transporters sped westwards, heading back towards the safety of the City.

DeVore smiled and sat back. He took a pack of mint drops from his top pocket and offered one to his companion. Mach looked at the packet a moment then took one. For a while both men were quiet, contemplating the scene, then Mach spoke.

'What now?'

DeVore met Mach's eyes. 'Now we melt away. Like ghosts.'

Mach smiled. 'And then?'

'Then nothing. Not for a long time. You go underground. Recruit. Build your movement up again. I'll provide whatever finance you need. But you must do nothing. Not until we're ready.'

'And the Seven?'

DeVore looked down. 'The Seven will look to strengthen their defences. But they will have to spread themselves thin. Too thin, perhaps. Besides, they've their own problems. There's a split in Council.'

Mach stared at the other man a moment, wide-eyed, wondering, as he had so often lately, how DeVore came to know so much. And why it was that such a man should want to fight *against* the Seven.

'Why do you hate them so much?'

DeVore looked back at him. 'Why do you?'

'Because the world they've made is a prison. For everyone. But especially for those lower down.'

'And you care about that?'

Mach nodded. 'Out here... this is real, don't you think? But that inside...' He shuddered and looked away, his eyes going off to the horizon. 'Well, it's never made sense to me, why human beings should have to live like that. Penned in like meat-animals. Hemmed in by rules. Sorted by money into their levels. I always hated it. Even when I was a child of five or six. And I used to feel so impotent about it.'

'But not now?'

'No. Not now. Now I've a direction for my anger.'

They were silent again then Mach turned his head, looking at DeVore. 'What of Ascher?'

DeVore shook his head. 'She's vanished. I thought we had her, but she slipped through our fingers. She's good, you know.'

Mach smiled. 'Yes. She was always the best of us. Even Gesell realized that. But she was inflexible. She was always letting her idealism get in the way of practicalities. It was inevitable that she'd break with us.'

'So what will you do?'

'Do? Nothing. Oh, I'll cover my back, don't worry. But if I know our Emily, she'll have found some way of getting out of City Europe. She was always talking of setting up somewhere else – of spreading our influence. She's a good organizer. I'd wager good money we'll hear from her again.'

DeVore smiled, thinking of her – at that very moment – on the jet to America, and of her left index finger, frozen in its medical case, heading out for Mars. 'Yes,' he said. 'We shall. I'm sure we shall.'

They stood there on the high stone balcony, the seven great lords of Chung Kuo, the sky a perfect blue overhead, the early morning sunlight glistening from the imperial yellow of their silks. Below them the great garden stretched away, flanked by the two great rivers, the whole enclosed within a single, unbroken wall, its lakes and pagodas, its tiny woods and flower beds, its bridges and shaded walkways a pleasure to behold. A curl of red stone steps, shaped like a dragon's tail, led down. Slowly, their talk a low murmur barely discernible above the call of the caged birds in the trees, they made their way down, Wu Shih, their host, leading the way.

At the foot of the steps he turned, looking back. Beyond the gathered T'ang his palace sat atop its artificial mound, firmly embedded, as if it had always been there, its pure white walls topped with steep roofs of red tile, the whole great structure capped by a slender six-storey pagoda that stood out, silhouetted against the sky. He nodded, satisfied, then put out his arm, inviting his cousins into his garden.

There was the soft tinkling of pagoda bells in the wind, the scent of jasmine and forsythia, of gardenia and chrysanthemum wafting to them through the great moon door in the wall. They stepped through, into another world – a world of ancient delights, of strict order made to seem like casual occurrence, of a thousand shades of green contrasted against the grey of stone, the white of walls, the red of tile. It was, though Wu

Shih himself made no such claim, the greatest garden in Chung Kuo – the Garden of Supreme Excellence – formed of a dozen separate gardens, each modelled on a famous original.

Their business was done, agreement reached as to the way ahead. Now it was time to relax, to unburden themselves, and where better than here where symmetry and disorder, artistry and chance, met in such perfect balance?

Wu Shih looked about him, immensely pleased. The garden had been built by his great-great-grandfather, but, like his father and his father's father, he had made his own small changes to the original scheme, extending the garden to the north, so that it now filled the whole of the ancient island of Manhattan.

'It is a beautiful garden, cousin,' Wang Sau-leyan said, turning to him and smiling pleasantly. 'There are few pleasures as sweet in life as that derived from a harmoniously created garden.'

Wu Shih smiled, surprised for the second time that morning at Wang Sau-leyan. It was as if he were a changed man, all rudeness, all abrasiveness gone from his manner. Earlier, in Council, he had gone out of his way to assure Li Shai Tung of his support, even pre-empting Wei Feng's offer of help by giving Li Shai Tung a substantial amount of grain from his own reserves. The generosity of the offer had surprised them all and had prompted a whole spate of spontaneous offers. The session had ended with the seven of them grinning broadly, their earlier mood of despondency cast aside, their sense of unity rebuilt. They were Seven again. Seven.

Wu Shih reached out and touched the young T'ang's arm. 'If there is heaven on earth it is here, in the garden.'

Wang Sau-leyan gave the slightest bow of his head, as if in deference to Wu Shih's greater age and experience. Again Wu Shih found himself pleased by the gesture. Perhaps they had been mistaken about Wang Sau-leyan. Perhaps it was only youth and the shock of his father's murder, his brother's suicide, that had made him so. That and the uncertainty of things.

Wang Sau-leyan turned, indicating the ancient, rusted sign bolted high up on the trunk of a nearby juniper.

'Tell me, Wu Shih. What is the meaning of that sign? All else here is Han. But that...'

'That?' Wu Shih laughed softly, drawing the attention of the other T'ang. 'That is a joke of my great-great-grandfather's, cousin Wang. You see, before he built this garden, part of the greatest city of the Americans sat upon this site. It was from here that they effectively ran their great republic of sixty-nine states. And here, where we are walking right now, was the very heart of their financial empire. The story goes that my great-great-grandfather came to see with his own eyes the destruction of their great city and that, seeing the sign, he smiled, appreciating the play on words. After all, what is more Han than a wall? Hence he ordered the sign kept. And so this path is known, even now, by its original name. Wall Street.'

The watching T'ang smiled, appreciating the story.

'We would do well to learn from them,' Wei Feng said, reaching up to pick a leaf from the branch. He put it to his mouth and tasted it, then looked back at Wang Sau-leyan, his ancient face creased into a smile. 'They tried too hard. Their ambition always exceeded their grasp. Like their ridiculous scheme to colonize the stars.'

Again Wang Sau-leyan gave the slightest bow. 'I agree, cousin. And yet we still use the craft they designed and built. Like much else they made.'

'True,' Wei Feng answered. 'I did not say that all they did was bad. Yet they had no sense of rightness. Of *balance*. What they did, they did carelessly, without thought. In that respect we would do well not to be like them. It was thoughtlessness that brought their empire low.'

'And arrogance,' added Wu Shih, looking about him. 'But come. Let us move on. I have arranged for *ch'a* to be served in the pavilion beside the lake. There will be entertainments, too.'

There were smiles at that. It had been some time since they had had the chance for such indulgences. Wu Shih turned, leading them along the *lang*, the covered walkway, then up a twist of wooden steps and out on to a broad gallery above a concealed lake.

A low wooden balustrade was raised on pillars above a tangle of sculpted rock, forming a square about the circle of the lake, the wood painted bright red, the pictogram for immortality cut into it in a repeated pattern. The broad, richly green leaves of lotus choked the water, while, in a thatched *ting* on the far side of the lake, a group of musicians began to play, the ancient sound drifting across to where the Seven sat.

Li Shai Tung sat back in his chair, looking about him at his fellow T'ang. For the first time in months the cloud had lifted from his spirits, the tightness in his stomach vanished. And he was not alone, he could see that now.

They all seemed brighter; refreshed and strengthened by the morning's events. So it was. So it had to be. He had not realized how important it was before now; had not understood how much their strength depended on them being of a single mind. And now that Wang Sau-leyan had come to his senses they would be strong again. It was only a matter of will.

He looked across at the young T'ang of Africa, and smiled. 'I am grateful for your support, cousin Wang. If there is something I might do for you in return?'

Wang Sau-leyan smiled and looked about him, his broad face momentarily the image of his father's when he had been younger, then he looked down. It was a gesture of considerable modesty. 'In the present circumstances it is enough that we help each other, neh?' He looked up, meeting Li Shai Tung's eyes. 'I am a proud man, Li Shai Tung, but not too proud to admit it when I have been wrong – and I was wrong about the threat from the *Ping Tiao*. If my offer helps make amends, I am satisfied.'

Li Shai Tung looked about him, a smile of intense satisfaction lighting his face. He turned back to the young T'ang, nodding. 'Your kind words refresh me, cousin Wang. There is great wisdom in knowing when one is wrong. Indeed, I have heard it called the first step on the path to true benevolence.'

Wang Sau-leyan lowered his head but said nothing. For a while they were quiet, listening to the ancient music. Servants moved among them, serving *ch'a* and sweetmeats, their pale green silks blending with the colours of the garden.

'Beautiful,' said Tsu Ma, when it had finished. There was a strange wistfulness to his expression. 'It is some time since I heard that last piece played so well.'

'Indeed...' began Wu Shih, then stopped, turning as his Chancellor appeared at the far end of the gallery. 'Come, Fen...' he said, signalling him to come closer. 'What is it?'

Fen Cho-hsien stopped some paces from his T'ang, bowing to each of the other T'ang in turn before facing his master again and bowing low. 'I would not have bothered you, *Chieh Hsia*, but an urgent message has just arrived. It seems that Lord Li's general has been taken ill.'

Li Shai Tung leaned forward anxiously. 'Nocenzi, ill? What in the gods' names is wrong with him?'

Fen turned, facing Li Shai Tung, lowering his eyes. 'Forgive me, *Chieh*

Hsia, but no one seems to know. It seems, however, that he is extremely ill. And not just him, but his wife and children, too. Indeed, if the report is accurate, his wife is already dead, and two of his children.'

Li Shai Tung looked down, groaning softly. Gods, was there no end to this? He looked up again, tears in his eyes, the tightness returned to his stomach.

'You will forgive me, cousins, if I return at once?'

There was a murmur of sympathy. All eyes were on the old T'ang, noting his sudden frailty, the way his shoulders hunched forward at this latest calamity. But it was Wang Sau-leyan who rose and helped him from his chair; who walked with him, his arm about his shoulder, to the steps.

Li Shai Tung turned, looking up into the young T'ang's face, holding his arm briefly, gratefully. 'Thank you, Sau-leyan. You are your father's son.' Then he turned back, going down the twist of steps, letting Wu Shih's Chancellor lead him, head bowed, back down Wall Street to the dragon steps and his waiting craft.

Kim woke and lay there in the darkness, strangely alert, listening. For a moment he didn't understand. There was nothing. Nothing at all. Then he shivered. Of course... That was it. The silence was too perfect. There was always some noise or other from the corridors outside, but just now there was nothing.

He sat up then threw back the sheet. For a moment he paused, stretching, working the last traces of the drug from his limbs, then crouched, listening again.

Nothing.

He crossed the room and stood there by the door, his mind running through possibilities. Maybe they had moved him. Or maybe they had closed down the Project and abandoned him. Left him to his fate. But he was not satisfied with either explanation. He reached out, trying the lock.

The door hissed back. Outside, the corridor was dark, empty. Only at the far end was there a light. On the wall outside the guard-room.

He shivered, the hairs on his neck and back rising. The overhead cameras were dead, the red wink of their operational lights switched off. And at the far end of the corridor, beyond the wall-mounted lamp, the door to the Project was open, the barrier up.

Something was wrong.

He stood there a moment, not certain what to do, then let instinct take over. Turning to his left, he ran, making for T'ai Cho's room and the labs beyond, hoping it wasn't too late.

T'ai Cho's room was empty. Kim turned, tensing, hearing the soft murmur of voices further along the corridor, then relaxed. They were voices he knew. He hurried towards them then slowed. The door to the labs was wide open, as if it had been jammed. That too was wrong. It was supposed to be closed when not in use, on a time-lock.

He twirled about, looking back down the dimly lit corridor. The few wall lights that were working were back-ups. Emergency lighting only. The main power system must have gone down. But was that an accident? Or had it been done deliberately?

He stepped inside, cautious now, glancing across to his right where Spatz's office was. He could see the Director through the open doorway, cursing, pounding the keyboard on his desk computer, trying to get some response from it. As he watched, Spatz tried the emergency phone then threw the handset down angrily.

Then maybe it had just happened. Maybe the shut-down had been what had woken him.

He ducked low and scuttled across the open space between the door and the first row of desks, hoping Spatz wouldn't glimpse him, then ran along the corridor between the desks until he came to the end. The main labs were to the left, the voices louder. T'ai Cho's was among them.

He hesitated, looking back the way he'd come, but the corridor was empty. He went on, coming out into the labs.

They were seated on the far side, some in chairs, some leaning on the desk. All of them were there except Hammond. They looked round as he entered, their talk faltering.

'Kim!' T'ai Cho said, getting up.

Kim put up his hand, as if to fend off his friend. 'You've got to get out! Now!'

Ellis, the Director's Assistant, smiled and shook his head. 'It's all right. It's only a power failure. Spatz has gone to sort things out.'

Kim looked about him. A few of them were vaguely uneasy, but nothing more. It was clear they agreed with Ellis.

'No!' he said, trying to keep the panic from his voice. 'The guards have gone and all the doors are jammed open. Can't you see what that means? We've got to get out! Something's going to happen!'

Ellis stood up. 'Are you sure? The guards really aren't there?'

Kim nodded urgently. He could feel the tension like a coil in him; could feel responses waking in him that he hadn't felt since... well, since they'd tried to reconstruct him. He could feel his heart hammering in his chest, his blood coursing like a dark, hot tide. Above all he could feel his senses heightened by the danger they were in.

He grabbed T'ai Cho's arm, dragging him back. T'ai Cho began resisting, but Kim held on tenaciously. 'Come on!' he begged. 'Before they come!'

'What in the gods' names are you talking about?'

'*Come on!*' he pleaded. 'You've got to come! All of you!'

He could see how his words had changed them. They were looking at each other anxiously now.

'Come on!' Ellis said. 'Kim could be right!'

They made for the outer offices, but it was too late. As Kim tugged T'ai Cho round the corner he could see them coming down the corridor, not forty *ch'i* away. There were four of them, dressed in black, suited up and masked, huge lantern guns cradled against their chests. Seeing the tall figure of T'ai Cho, the first of them raised his gun and fired.

Kim pulled T'ai Cho down then scrambled back, feeling the converted warmth of the gun's discharge in the air, accompanied by a sharp, sweet scent that might almost have been pleasant had it not signalled something so deadly.

'Get back!' he yelled to the others behind him, but even as he said it he understood. They were trapped here. Like the GenSyn apes they had been experimenting on. Unarmed, with no means of escape.

'Dead...' he said softly to himself.

Dead. As if they'd never been.

The assassin backed away, shuddering, glad that his mask filtered out the stench of burned flesh that filled the room. He felt a small shiver ripple down his back. He hadn't expected them to act as they had. Hadn't believed that they would just get down on their knees and die, heads bowed.

But maybe that was what made them different from him. Made them watchers, not doers; passive, not active. Even so, the way they had just accepted their deaths made him feel odd. It wasn't that he felt pity for them, far from it – their passivity revolted him. Himself, he would have died fighting for his life, scratching and clawing his way out of existence. But it was the way they made him feel. As if they'd robbed him of something.

He turned away. The others had gone already – had gone to fetch the boy and plant the explosives. Time, then, to get out. He took a couple of paces then stopped, twisting round.

Nerves, he thought. *It's only nerves. It's only one of the apes, scuttling about in its cage.* Even so, he went back, making sure, remembering what DeVore had said about taking pains.

He stopped, his right boot almost touching the leg of one of the dead men, and looked about him, frowning. The four apes lay on the floor of their cages, drugged. 'Funny...' he began. Then, without warning, his legs were grabbed from behind, throwing him forward on to the pile of bodies.

He turned, gasping, his gun gone from him, but the creature was on him in an instant, something hard smashing down into his face, breaking his nose. He groaned, the hot pain of the blow flooding his senses, stunning him.

He put his hands up to his face, astonished. 'What the hell?'

This time the blow came to the side of his head, just beside his left eye.

'Kuan Yin!' he screeched, pulling his head back sharply, coughing as blood began to fill his mouth. He reached out wildly, trying to grasp the creature, but it had moved away. He sat forward, squinting through a blood haze at what looked no more than a child. But not just a child. This was like something out of a nightmare.

It stood there, hunched and spindly, the weight held threateningly in one tiny hand, its big, dark, staring eyes fixed murderously on him, its mouth set in a snarl of deadly intent.

'Gods...' he whispered, feeling himself go cold. Was this what they were making here? These... *things*?

But even as the thought came to him, the creature gave an unearthly yell and leapt on him – leapt high, like something demented – and brought the weight down hard, robbing him of breath.

★

Li Shai Tung turned, angered by what he had seen, and confronted the Chief Surgeon.

'What in the gods' names did this to him, Chang Li?'

Chang Li fell to his knees, his head bent low. 'Forgive me, *Chieh Hsia*, but the cause of the General's affliction is not yet known. We are carrying out an autopsy on his wife and children, but as yet...'

'The children?' Li Shai Tung took a long breath, calming himself. His eyes were red, his cheeks wet with tears. His right hand gripped at his left shoulder almost convulsively, then let it go, flinging itself outward in a gesture of despair.

'Will he live?'

Again the Chief Surgeon lowered his head. 'It is too early to say, *Chieh Hsia*. Whatever it was, it was strong enough to kill his wife and two of his children within the hour. Nocenzi and his other daughter... well... they're both very ill.'

'And you've definitely ruled out some kind of poison in the food?'

Chang Li nodded. 'That is so, *Chieh Hsia*. It seems the Nocenzis were eating with friends when they were stricken – sharing from the same serving bowls, the same ricepot. And yet the three who ate with them are totally unharmed.'

Li Shai Tung shuddered then beckoned the man to get up. 'Thank you, Chang Li. But tell me what you can, neh? As soon as anything is known. And do not tell the General yet of the loss of his wife or children. Let him grow stronger before you break the news. I would not have him survive this only to die of a broken heart.'

Chang Li bowed his head. 'It shall be as you say, *Chieh Hsia*.'

'Good.' He turned, making his way across to the great hallway of the hospital, his guards and retainers at a respectful distance. Nocenzi had been conscious when he'd seen him. Even so, he had looked like a ghost of his former self, all his *ch'i*, his vital energy, drained from him. His voice had been as faint as the whisper of a breeze against silk.

'Forgive me, *Chieh Hsia*,' he had said, 'but you will need a new general now.'

He had taken Nocenzi's hand, denying him, but Nocenzi had insisted, squeezing his hand weakly, not releasing it until the T'ang accepted his resignation.

He stopped, remembering the moment, then leaned forward slightly, a mild wash of pain in his arms and lower abdomen making him feel giddy. It passed and he straightened up, but a moment later it returned, stronger, burning like a coal in his guts. He groaned and stumbled forward, almost falling against the tiled floor, but one of his courtiers caught him just in time.

'*Chieh Hsia!*'

There was a strong babble of concerned voices, a thicket of hands reaching out to steady him, but Li Shai Tung was conscious only of the way his skin stung as if it were stretched too tightly over his bones – how his eyes smarted as if hot water had been thrown into them. He took a shuddering breath then felt the pain spear through him again.

Gods! What was this?

Doctors were hurrying to him now, lifting him with careful, expert hands, speaking soothingly as they helped support him and half carry him back towards the wards.

The pain was ebbing now, the strength returning to his limbs.

'Wait...' he said softly. Then, when they seemed not to hear him, he repeated it, stronger this time, commanding them. 'Hold there!'

At once they moved back, releasing him, but stayed closed enough to catch him if he fell. Chang Li was there now. He had hurried back when he had heard.

'*Chieh Hsia*... what is it?'

Li Shai Tung straightened, taking a breath. The pain had left him feeling a little light-headed, but otherwise he seemed all right.

'I'm fine now,' he said. 'It was but a momentary cramp, that's all. My stomach. Hasty eating and my anxiety for the General's welfare, I'm sure.'

He saw how Chang Li looked at him, uncertain how to act, and almost laughed.

'If it worries you so much, Surgeon Chang, you might send two of your best men to accompany me on the journey home. But I must get back. There is much to be done. I must see my son and speak to him. And I have a new general to appoint.'

He smiled, looking about him, seeing his smile mirrored uncertainly in thirty faces. 'I, above all others, cannot afford to be ill. Where would Chung Kuo be if we who ruled were always being sick?'

There was laughter, but it lacked the heartiness, the sincerity of the laughter he was accustomed to from those surrounding him. He could hear the fear in their voices and understood its origin. And, in some small way, was reassured by it. It was when the laughter ceased altogether that one had to worry. When fear gave way to relief and a different kind of laughter.

He looked about him, his head lifted, his heart suddenly warmed by their concern for him, then turned and began making his way back to the imperial craft.

Yin Tsu welcomed the Prince and brought him *ch'a*.

'You know why I've come?' Li Yuan asked, trying to conceal the pain he felt.

Yin Tsu bowed his head, his ancient face deeply lined. 'I know, Li Yuan. And I am sorry that this day has come. My house is greatly saddened.'

Li Yuan nodded uncomfortably. The last thing he had wished for was to hurt the old man, but it could not be helped. Even so, this was a bitter business. Twice Yin Tsu had thought to link his line with kings, and twice he had been denied that honour.

'You will not lose by this, Yin Tsu,' he said softly, his heart going out to the old man. 'Your sons...'

But it was only half-true. After all, what could he give Yin's sons to balance the scale? Nothing. Or as good as.

Yin Tsu bowed lower.

'Can I see her, Father?'

It was the last time he would call him that and he could see the pain it brought to the old man's face. *This was not my doing*, he thought, watching Yin Tsu straighten up then go to bring her.

He was back almost at once, leading his daughter.

Fei Yen sat across from him, her head bowed, waiting. She was more than eight months now, so this had to be dealt with at once. The child might come any day. Even so, he was determined to be gentle with her.

'How are you?' he asked tenderly, concerned for her in spite of all that had happened between them.

'I am well, my lord,' she answered, subdued, unable to look at him. She knew how things stood. Knew why he had come.

'Fei Yen, this is... painful for me. But you knew when we wed that I was not as other men – that my life, my choices were not those of normal men.'

He sighed deeply, finding it hard to say what he must. He raised his chin, looking at Yin Tsu, who nodded, his face held rigid in a grimace of pain. 'My Family... I must ensure my line. Make certain.'

These were evasions. He had yet to say it direct. He took another breath and spoke.

'You say it is not my child. But I must be sure of that. There must be tests. And then, if it is so, we must be divorced. For no claim can be permitted if the child is not mine. You must be clear on that, Fei Yen.'

Again Yin Tsu nodded. Beside him his daughter was still, silent.

He looked away, momentarily overcome by the strength of what he still felt for her, then forced himself to be insistent.

'Will you do as I say, Fei Yen?'

She looked up at him. Her eyes were wet with tears. Dark, almond eyes that pierced him with their beauty. 'I will do whatever you wish, my lord.'

He stared at her, wanting to cross the space between them and kiss away her tears; to forgive her everything and start again. Even now. Even after all she had done to him. But she had left him no alternative. This thing could not be changed. In this he could not trust to what he felt, for feeling had failed him. His father was right. What good was feeling when the world was dark and hostile? Besides, his son must be *his* son.

'Then it shall be done,' he said bluntly, almost angrily. 'Tomorrow.'

He stood then walked across the room, touching the old man's arm briefly, sympathetically. 'And we shall speak again tomorrow, Yin Tsu. When things are better known.'

The old Han squatted at the entrance to the corridor, waiting there patiently, knowing that the dream had been a true dream, one of those he could not afford to ignore. Beside him, against the wall, he had placed those things he had seen himself use in the dream – a blanket and his old porcelain water-bottle.

This level was almost deserted. The great clothing factory that took up most of it had shut down its operations more than four hours back and only a handful of Security guards and maintenance engineers were to be found down here now. The old man smiled, recalling how he had slipped past the guards like a shadow.

His name was Tuan Ti Fo and, though he squatted like a young man, his muscles uncomplaining under him, he was as old as the great City itself. Older still. This knowledge he kept to himself, for to others he was simply Old Tuan, his age, like his origins, undefined. He lived simply, some would say frugally, in his rooms eight levels up from where he now waited. And though many knew him, few could claim to be close to the peaceful, white-haired old man. He kept himself very much to himself, studying the ancient books he kept in the box beside his bed, doing his exercises, or playing himself at *wei chi* – long games that could take a day, sometimes even a week to complete.

The corridor he was facing was less than twenty *ch'i* long; a narrow, dimly lit affair that was little more than a feeder tunnel to the mainten-ance hatch in the ceiling at its far end. Tuan Ti Fo watched, knowing what would happen, his ancient eyes half-lidded, his breathing unaltered as the hatch juddered once, twice, then dropped, swinging violently on the hinge. A moment later a foot appeared – a child's foot – followed by a leg, a stead-ying hand. He watched the boy emerge, legs first, then drop.

Tuan Ti Fo lifted himself slightly, staring into the dimness. For a time the boy lay where he had fallen, then he rolled over on to his side, a small whim-per – of pain, perhaps, or fear – carrying to where the old Han crouched.

In the dream this was the moment when he had acted. And so now. Nodding gently to himself, he reached beside him for the blanket.

Tuan Ti Fo moved silently, effortlessly through the darkness. For a moment he knelt beside the boy, looking down at him; again, as in the dream – the reality of it no clearer than the vision he had had. He smiled, then, unfolding the blanket, began to wrap the sleeping boy in it.

The boy murmured softly as he lifted him then began to struggle. Tuan Ti Fo waited, his arms cradling the boy firmly yet reassuringly against his chest until he calmed. Only then did he carry him back to the entrance.

Tuan Ti Fo crouched down, the boy balanced in his lap, the small, dark, tousled head resting against his chest, and reached out for the water-bottle. He drew the hinged stopper back and put the mouth of the bottle to the child's lips, wetting them. Waiting a moment, he placed it to the boy's mouth again. This time the lips parted, taking in a little of the water.

It was enough. The mild drug in the liquid would help calm him – would make him sleep until the shock of his ordeal had passed.

Tuan Ti Fo stoppered the bottle and fixed it to the small hook on his belt, then straightened up. He had not really noticed before but the boy weighed almost nothing in his arms. He looked down at the child, surprised, as if the boy would vanish at any moment, leaving him holding nothing.

'You're a strange one,' he said softly, moving outside the dream a moment. 'It's many years since the gods sent me one to tend.'

So it was. Many, many years. And why this one? Maybe it had something to do with the other dreams – the dreams of dead, dark lands and of huge, brilliant webs, stretched out like stringed beads, burning in the darkness of the sky. Dreams of wells and spires and falling Cities. Dreams filled with suffering and strangeness.

And what was the boy's role in all of that? Why had the gods chosen *him* to do their work?

Tuan Ti Fo smiled, knowing it was not for him to ask, or for them to answer. Then, letting his actions be shaped once more by the dream, he set off, carrying the boy back down the broad main corridor towards the guard post and the lift beyond.

The doctors were gone, his ministers and advisors dismissed. Now, at last, the great T'ang was alone.

Li Shai Tung stood there a moment, his arm outstretched, one hand resting against the doorframe as he got his breath. The upright against which he rested stretched up like a great squared pillar into the ceiling high overhead, white-painted, the simplicity of its design emphasized by the seven pictograms carved into the wood and picked out in gold leaf – the characters forming couplets with those on the matching upright. Servants had opened the two huge, white-lacquered doors earlier; now he stood there, looking into the Hall of Eternal Peace and Tranquillity. To one side, just in view, stood a magnificent funerary couch, the grey stone of its side engraved with images of gardens and pavilions in which ancient scholars sat enthroned while the women of the household wove and prepared food, sang or played the ancient *pi-p'a*. Facing it was a broad, red-lacquered screen, the *Ywe Lung* – the circle of dragons, symbolizing the power and authority of the Seven – set like a huge, golden mandala in its centre.

He sighed heavily then went inside, leaving the great doors ajar, too tired to turn and pull them closed behind him. It was true what they had said: he *ought* to get to bed and rest; *ought* to take a break from his duties for a day or so and let Li Yuan take up his burden as Regent. But it was not easy to break the habits of a lifetime. Besides, there was something he had to do before he rested. Something he had put off far too long.

He crossed the room then slowly lowered himself to his knees before the great tablet, conscious of how the gold leaf of the *Ywe Lung* seemed to flow in the wavering light of the candles; how the red lacquer of the background seemed to burn. He had never noticed that before. Neither had he noticed how the smoke from the perfumed candles seemed to form words – Han pictograms – in the still, dry air. Chance, meaningless words, like the throw of yarrow stalks or the pattern on a fire-charred tortoise shell.

He shivered. It was cold, silent in the room, the scent of the candles reminding him of the tomb beneath the earth at Tongjiang. Or was it just the silence, the wavering light?

He swallowed drily. The ache in his bones was worse than before. He felt drawn, close to exhaustion, his skin stretched tight like parchment over his brittle bones. It would be good to rest. Good to lie there, thoughtless, in the darkness. Yes... but he would do this one last thing before he slept.

Reaching out, he took two of the scented sticks from the porcelain jar in front of him and held them in the thread of laser light until they lit. Then, bowing respectfully, he set them in the jar before the tiny image of his great-great-grandfather. At once the image seemed to swell, losing a degree of substance as it gained in size.

The life-size image of the old man seemed to look down at Li Shai Tung, its dark eyes magnificent, its whole form filled with power.

His great-great-grandfather, Li Hang Ch'i, had been a tall, immensely dignified man. For posterity he had dressed himself in the imperial style of one hundred and ten years earlier, a simpler, more brutal style, without embellishment. One heavily bejewelled hand stroked his long, white, unbraided beard, while the other held a silver riding crop – an affectation that was meant to symbolize his love of horses.

'What is it, Shai Tung? Why do you summon me from the dead lands?'

Li Shai Tung felt a faint ripple of unease pass through him.

'I wished to ask you something, Honourable Grandfather.'

Li Hang Ch'i made a small motion of his chin, lifting it slightly as if considering his grandson's words; a gesture that Li Shai Tung recognized immediately as his own.

Even in that we are not free, he thought. We but ape the actions of our ancestors, unconsciously, slavishly, those things we consider most distinctly ours – that strange interplay of mind and nerve and sinew that we term gesture – formed a hundred generations before their use in us.

Again he shivered, lowering his head, conscious of his own weariness; of how far below his great-great-grandfather's exacting standards he had fallen. At that moment he felt but a poor copy of Li Hang Ch'i.

'Ask,' the figure answered. 'Whatever you wish.'

Li Shai Tung hesitated then looked up. 'Forgive me, most respected Grandfather, but the question I would ask you is a difficult one. One that has plagued me for some while. It is this. Are we good or evil men?'

The hologram's face flickered momentarily, the programme uncertain what facial expression was called for by the question. Then it formed itself into the semblance of a frown, the whole countenance becoming stern, implacable.

'What a question, Shai Tung! You ask whether we are good or evil men. But is that something one can ask? After all, how can one judge? By our acts? So some might argue. Yet are our acts good or evil in themselves? Surely only the gods can say that much.' He shook his head, staring down at his descendant as if disappointed in him. 'I cannot speak for the gods, but for myself I say this. We did as we had to. How else *could* we have acted?'

Li Shai Tung took a long, shuddering breath. It was as if, for that brief moment, his great-great-grandfather had been there, really there, before him in the room. He had sensed his powerful presence behind the smokescreen of the hologrammic image. Had felt the overpowering certainty of the man behind the words and, again, recognized the echo in himself. So he had once argued. So he had answered his own son, that time when Yuan had come to him with his dream – that awful nightmare he had had of the great mountain of bones filling the plain where the City had been.

Back then he had sounded so certain – so sure of things – but even then he had questioned it, at some deeper level. Had gone to his room afterwards and lain there until the dawn, unable to sleep, Yuan's words burning brightly in his skull. *Are we good or evil men?*

But it had begun before then, earlier that year, when he had visited Hal Shepherd in the Domain. It had been then that the seed of doubt had entered him; then – in that long conversation with Hal's son, Ben – that he had begun to question it all.

He sat back, studying the hologram a moment, conscious of how it waited for him, displaying that unquestioning patience that distinguished the mechanical from the human. It was almost solid. Almost. For through the seemingly substantial chest of his great-great-grandfather he could glimpse the hazed, refracted image of the *Ywe Lung*, the great wheel of dragons broken by the planes of his ancestor's body.

He groaned softly and stretched, trying to ease the various pains he felt. His knees ached and there was a growing warmth in his back. *I ought to be in bed*, he thought, *not worrying myself about such things*. But he could not help himself. Something urged him on. He stared up into that ancient, implacable face and spoke again.

'Was there no other choice, then, Grandfather? No other path we might have taken? Were things as inevitable as they seem? Was it all written?'

Li Hang Ch'i shook his head, his face like the ancient, burnished ivory of a statue, and raised the silver riding crop threateningly.

'There *was* no other choice.'

Li Shai Tung shivered, his voice suddenly small. 'Then we were right to deny the *Hung Mao* their heritage?'

'It was that or see the world destroyed.'

Li Shai Tung bowed his head. 'Then...' He paused, seeing how the eyes of the hologram were on him. Again it was as if something stared through them from the other side. Something powerful and menacing. Something that, by all reason, should not be there. 'Then what we did was right?'

The figure shifted slightly, relaxing, lowering the riding crop.

'Make no mistake, Shai Tung. We did as we had to. We cannot allow ourselves the empty luxury of doubt.'

'Ah...' Li Shai Tung stared back at the hologram a moment longer then, sighing, he plucked the scented sticks from the offering bowl, and threw them aside.

At once the image shrank, diminishing to its former size.

He leaned back, a sharp sense of anger overwhelming him. At himself for the doubts that ate at him, and at his ancestor for giving him nothing more than a string of empty platitudes. *We did as we had to...* He shook his head, bitterly disappointed. Was there to be no certainty for him, then? No clear answer to what he had asked?

No. And maybe that was what had kept him from visiting this place these last five years: the knowledge that he could no longer share their unquestioning certainty. That, and the awful, erosive consciousness of his own inner emptiness. He shuddered. Sometimes it felt as if he had less substance than the images in this room. As if, in the blink of an eye, his being would turn to breath as the gods drew the scent sticks from the offering bowl.

He rubbed at his eyes then yawned, his tiredness returned to him like ashes in the blood. It was late. Much too late. Not only that, but it was suddenly quite hot in here. He felt flushed and there was a prickling sensation in his legs and hands. He hauled his tired bones upright then stood there, swaying slightly, feeling breathless, a sudden cold washing through his limbs, making him tremble.

It's nothing, he thought. *Only my age.* Yet for a moment he found his mind clouding. Had he imagined it, or had Chung Hu-yan come to him only an hour back with news of another attack?

He put his hand up to his face, as if to clear the cobwebs from his thoughts, then shrugged. No. An hour past he had been with his Ministers. Even so, the image of Chung Hu-yan waking him with awful news persisted, until he realized what it was.

'Lin Yua...' he said softly, his voice broken by the sudden pain he felt. 'Lin Yua, my little peach... Why did you have to die? Why did you have to leave me all alone down here?'

He shivered, suddenly cold again, his teeth chattering. Yes, he would send for Surgeon Hua. But later – in the morning, when he could put up with the old boy's fussing.

Sleep, he heard a voice say, close by his ear. *Sleep now, Li Shai Tung. The day is done.*

He turned, his eyes resting momentarily upon the dim, grey shape of the funerary couch. Then, turning back, he made a final bow to the row of tiny images. *Like breath,* he thought. *Or flames, dancing in a glass.*

★

It was dark in the room. Li Yuan lay on his back in the huge bed, staring up into the shadows. The woman beside him was sleeping, her leg against his own, warm, strangely comforting.

It was a moment of thoughtlessness, of utter repose. He lay there, aware of the weight of his body pressing down into the softness of the bed, of the rise and fall of his chest with each breath, the flow of his blood. He felt at rest, the dark weight of tension lifted by the woman.

In the darkness he reached out to touch her flank then lay back, closing his eyes.

For a time he slept. Then, in the depths of sleep he heard the summons and pulled himself up, hand over hand, back to the surface of consciousness.

Nan Ho stood in the doorway, his eyes averted. Li Yuan rose, knowing it was important, letting Master Nan wrap the cloak about his nakedness.

He took the call in his study, beneath the portrait of his grandfather, Li Ch'ing, knowing at once what it was. The face of his father's surgeon, Hua, filled the screen, the old man's features more expressive than a thousand words.

'He's dead,' Li Yuan said simply.

'Yes, *Chieh Hsia*,' the old man answered, bowing his head.

Chieh Hsia... He shivered.

'How did it happen?'

'In his sleep. There was no pain.'

Li Yuan nodded, but something nagged at him. 'Touch nothing, Surgeon Hua. I want the room sealed until I get there. And, Hua, tell no one else. I must make calls first. Arrange things.'

'*Chieh Hsia*.'

Li Yuan sat there, looking up at the image of his father's father, wondering why he felt so little. He closed his eyes, thinking of his father as he'd last seen him. Of his strength, masked by the surface frailness.

For a moment longer he sat there, trying to feel the sorrow he knew he owed his father, but it was kept from him. It was not yet real. Touch – touch alone – would make it real. Momentarily his mind strayed and he thought of Fei Yen and the child in her belly. Of Tsu Ma and of his dead brother, Han Ch'in. All of it confused, sleep-muddled in his brain. Then it cleared and the old man's face came into focus.

'And so it comes to me,' he said quietly, as if to the painting. But the burden of it, the reality of what he had become while he had slept, had not yet touched him.

He thought of the calls he must make to tell the other T'ang, but for the moment he felt no impulse towards action. Time seemed suspended. He looked down at his hands, at the prince's ring of power, and frowned. Then, as a concession, he made the call to summon the transporter.

He went back to his room, then out on to the veranda beyond. The woman woke and came to him, naked, her soft warmth pressed against his back in the cool, pre-dawn air.

He turned to her, smiling sadly. 'No. Go back inside.'

Alone again, he turned and stared out across the shadowed lands of his estate towards the distant mountains. The moon was a low, pale crescent above one of the smaller peaks, far to his right. He stared at it a while, hollow, emptied of all feeling, then looked away sharply, bitter with himself.

Somehow the moment had no meaning. It should have meant so much, but it was empty. The moon, the mountains, the man – *himself* – standing there in the darkness: none of it made sense to him. They were fragments, broken pieces of some nonsense puzzle, adding to nothing. He turned away, his feeling of anguish at the nothingness of it all overwhelming him. It wasn't death, it was life that frightened him. The senselessness of life.

He stood there a long time, letting the feeling ebb. Then, when it was gone, he returned to his study, preparing himself to make his calls.

Tolonen stood in the centre of the chaos, looking about him. The floor was cluttered underfoot, the walls black with soot. Dark plastic sacks were piled up against the wall to one side. They were all that remained of the men who had worked here on the Project.

'There were no survivors, Captain?'

The young officer stepped forward and bowed. 'Only the tutor, sir. We found him thirty levels down, bound and drugged.'

Tolonen frowned. 'And the others?'

'Apart from T'ai Cho there were eighteen men on the Project, excluding guards. We've identified seventeen separate corpses. Add to that the other one – Hammond – and it accounts for everyone.'

'I see. And the records?'

'All gone, sir. The main files were destroyed in the explosion, but they also managed to get to the back-ups and destroy them.'

Tolonen stared at him, astonished. 'All of them? Even those held by Prince Yuan?'

'It appears so. Of course, the Prince himself has not yet been spoken to, but his secretary, Chang Shih-sen, advises me that the copies he was given on his last visit are gone.'

'Gone?' Tolonen swallowed drily. He was still too shocked to take it in. How could it have happened? They had taken the strictest measures to ensure that the Project remained not merely 'invisible' in terms of its security profile but that, in the unlikely event of sabotage, there would be copies of everything. But somehow all their endeavours had come to nothing. The assassins had walked in here as if they owned the place and had destroyed everything. Erasing every last trace of the Project.

DeVore. It had to be DeVore. But why? How in the gods' names could he possibly benefit from this?

'Let me see the reports.'

The officer turned away, returning a moment later with a clipboard to which were attached the preliminary, handwritten reports. Tolonen took them from him and flicked through quickly.

'Very good,' he said finally, looking up. 'You've been very thorough, Captain. I...'

He paused, looking past the Captain. His daughter Jelka was standing in the doorway at the end of the corridor.

'What is it?'

Jelka smiled uncertainly at him then came closer. 'I wanted to see. I...'

Tolonen looked back at her a moment then shrugged. 'All right. But it's not very pleasant.'

He watched her come into the room and look about her. Saw how she approached the sacks and lifted one of the labels then let it fall from her hand with a slight shudder. Even so, he could see something of himself in her; that same hardness in the face of adversity. But there was more than that – it was almost as if she was looking for something.

'What is it?' he said after a moment.

She turned, looking at him, focusing on the clipboard he still held. 'Can I see that?'

'It's nothing,' he said. 'Technical stuff mainly. Assessments of explosive materials used. Post-mortem examinations of remains. That kind of thing.'

'I know,' she said, coming closer. 'Can I see it? Please, Daddy.'

Out of the corner of an eye he saw the Captain smile faintly. He had been about to say no to her, but that decided him. After all, she was the Marshal's daughter. He had taught her much over the years. Perhaps she, in turn, could teach the young officer something.

He handed her the file, watching her flick through it quickly, again as if she was looking for something specific. Then, astonishingly, she looked up at him, a great beam of a smile on her face.

'I knew it!' she said. 'I sensed it as soon as I came in. He's alive! This proves it!'

Tolonen gave a short laugh then glanced briefly at the Captain, before taking the clipboard back from his daughter and holding it open at the place she indicated. 'What in the gods' names are you talking about? Who's alive?'

'The boy. Ward. He isn't there! Don't you see? Look at the Chief Pathologist's report. All the corpses he examined were those of adults – of fully grown men. But Kim wasn't more than a child. Not physically. Which means that whoever the seventeenth victim was, he wasn't on the Project.'

'And Kim's alive.'

'Yes...'

He stared back at her, realizing what it might mean. The boy had a perfect memory. So good that it was almost impossible for him to forget anything. Which meant...

He laughed then grew still. Unless they'd taken him captive. Unless whoever had done this had meant to destroy everything but him. But, then, why had they taken the tutor, T'ai Cho, and afterwards released him? Or had that been a mistake?

'Gods...' he said softly. If DeVore had the boy, he also had the only complete record of the Project's work – the basis of a system that could directly control vast numbers of people. It was a frightening thought. His worst nightmare come true. If DeVore had him.

He turned, watching his daughter. She was looking about her, her eyes taking in everything, just as he'd taught her. He followed her through, the young Captain trailing them.

'What is it?' he said quietly, afraid to disturb her concentration. 'What are you looking for?'

She turned, looking back at him, the smile still there. 'He got out. I know he did.'

He shivered, not wanting to know. But she had been right about the other thing, so maybe she was right about this. They went through the ruins of the outer office and into the dark, fire-blackened space beyond where they had found most of the bodies.

'There!' she said, triumphantly, pointing halfway up the back wall. 'There! That's where he went.'

Tolonen looked. Halfway up the wall there was a slightly darker square set into the blackness. He moved closer, then realized what it was. A ventilation shaft.

'I don't see how...' he began, but even as he said it he changed his mind and nodded. Of course. The boy had been small enough, wiry enough. And after all, he had come from the Clay. There was his past record of violence to consider. If anyone could have survived this, it was Kim. So maybe Jelka was right. Maybe he *had* got out this way.

Tolonen turned, looking at the young officer. 'Get one of your experts in here now, Captain. I want him to investigate that vent for any sign that someone might have used it to escape.'

'Sir!'

He stood there, Jelka cradled against him, his arm about her shoulders, while they tested the narrow tunnel for clues. It was difficult, because the vent was too small for a grown man to get into, but with the use of extension arms and mechanicals they worked their way slowly down the shaft.

After twenty minutes the squad leader turned and came across to Tolonen. He bowed then gave a small, apologetic shrug.

'Forgive me, Marshal, but it seems unlikely he got out this way. The vent is badly charred. It sustained a lot of fire damage when the labs went up. Besides that, it leads down through the main generator rooms below. He would have been sliced to pieces by the fans down there.'

Tolonen was inclined to agree. It was unlikely that the boy had got out, even if DeVore hadn't taken him. But when he looked down and met his daughter's eyes, the certainty there disturbed him.

'Are you sure?'

'I'm certain. Trust me, Father. I know he got out. I just know.'

Tolonen sniffed then looked back at the squad leader. 'Go in another five *ch'i*. If there's nothing there we'll call it off.'

They waited, Tolonen's hopes fading by the moment. But then there was a shout from one of the men controlling the remote. He looked up from his screen and laughed. 'She's right. Damn me if she isn't right!'

They went across and looked. There, enhanced on the screen, was a set of clear prints, hidden behind a fold in the tunnel wall and thus untouched by the blast.

'Well?' said Tolonen, 'Are they the boy's?'

There was a moment's hesitation then the boy's prints were flashed up on the screen, the computer superimposing them over the others.

There was no doubt. They were a perfect match.

'Then he's alive!' said Tolonen. He stared at his daughter then shook his head, not understanding. 'Okay,' he said, turning to the Captain, 'this is what we'll do. I want you to contact Major Gregor Karr at Bremen Head-quarters and get him here at once. And then—'

He stopped, staring open-mouthed at the doorway. 'Hans... what are you doing here?'

Hans Ebert bowed then came forward. His face was pale, his whole manner unnaturally subdued.

'I've news,' he said, swallowing. 'Bad news, I'm afraid, Uncle Knut. It's the T'ang. I'm afraid he's dead.'

Hans Ebert paused on the terrace, looking out across the gardens at the centre of the mansion where the Marshal's daughter stood, her back to him.

Jelka was dressed in the southern Han fashion, a tight silk *sam fu* of a delicate eggshell blue wrapped about her strong yet slender body. Her hair had been plaited and coiled at the back of her head, but there was no mis-taking her for Han. She was too tall, too blonde to be anything but *Hung Mao*. And not simply *Hung Mao* but Nordic. New European.

He smiled then made his way down the steps quietly, careful not to disturb her reverie. She was standing just beyond the bridge, looking down into the tiny stream, one hand raised to her neck, the other holding her folded fan against her side.

His wife. Or soon to be.

He was still some way from her when she turned, suddenly alert, her whole body tensed, as if prepared against attack.

'It's all right,' he said, raising his empty hands in reassurance. 'It's only me.'

He saw how she relaxed – or tried to, for there was still a part of her that held out against him – and smiled inwardly. There was real spirit in the girl; an almost masculine hardness that he admired. His father had been right for once: she would make him the perfect match.

'What is it?' she asked, looking back at him as if forcing herself to meet his eyes. Again he smiled.

'I'm sorry, Jelka, but I have to go. Things are in flux and the new T'ang has asked for me. But please... our home is yours. Make yourself comfortable. My *mui tsai*, Sweet Flute, will be here in a while to look after you.'

She stared back at him a moment, her lips slightly parted, then gave a small bow of her head. 'And my father?'

'He feels it best that you stay here for the moment. As I said, things are in flux and there are rumours of rioting in the lower levels. If it spreads...'

She nodded then turned away, looking across at the ancient pomegranate trees, flicking her fan open as she did so. It was a strange, almost nervous gesture and for a moment he wondered what it meant. Then, bowing low, he turned to go. But he had gone only a few paces when she called to him.

'Hans?'

He turned, pleased that she had used his name. 'Yes?'

'Will you be General now?'

He took a long breath then shrugged. 'If the new T'ang wishes it. Why?'

She made a small motion of her head then looked down. 'I... I just wondered, that's all.'

'Ah...' He stood there a moment longer, watching her, then turned and made his way back along the path towards the house. And if he was? Well, maybe it would be a reason for bringing his marriage forward. After all, a general ought to have a wife, a family, oughtn't he? He grinned then spurred himself on, mounting the steps two at a time. Yes. He would speak to Tolonen about it later.

★

She stood there after he was gone, her eyes following the slow swirl of a mulberry leaf as it drifted on the artificial current.

So the boy, Kim, was alive. But how had she known?

She turned, hearing footsteps on the pathway. It was a young woman – a girl little older than herself. The mui tsai.

The girl came closer then stopped, bowing low, her hands folded before her. 'Excuse me, Hsiao Chi, but my master asked me to see to your every wish.'

Jelka turned, smiling at the girl's use of Hsiao Chi – Lady – to one clearly no older than herself. But it was obvious that the girl was only trying to be respectful.

'Thank you, Sweet Flute, but I wish only to wait here until my father comes.'

The mui tsai glanced up at her then averted her eyes again. 'With respect, Hsiao Chi, I understand that might be some while. Would you not welcome some refreshments while you wait? Or perhaps I could summon the musicians. There is a pavilion...'

Jelka smiled again, warmed by the girl's manner. Even so, she wanted to be left alone. The matter with the boy disturbed her. The preliminary search of the levels below the Project had found no trace of him.

She sighed then gave a tiny laugh. 'All right, Sweet Flute. Bring me a drink. A cordial. But no musicians. The birds sing sweetly enough for me. And I do wish to be left alone. Until my father comes.'

The mui tsai bowed. 'As you wish, Hsiao Chi.'

Jelka looked about her, letting herself relax for the first time since she had heard of the attack on the Project, drinking in the harmony of the garden. Then she stiffened again.

From the far side of the gardens came a strange, high-pitched keening, like the sound of an animal in pain. For almost a minute it continued and then it stopped, as abruptly as it had begun.

What in the gods' names...?

She hurried across the bridge and down the path, then climbed the wooden steps up on to the terrace. It had come from here, she was sure of it.

She paused, hearing the low murmur of male voices from the doorway just ahead of her. Slowly, step by step, she crept along the terrace until she stood there, looking in.

There were four of them, dressed in the pale green uniforms of the Ebert household. In the midst of them, a gag tied tightly about her mouth, was a woman. A Han woman in her late twenties.

Jelka watched, astonished, as the woman kicked out wildly and threw herself about, trying to escape her captives, her face dark, contorted. But there was no escaping. As Jelka watched, the men subdued her, forcing her into a padded jacket, the over-long arms of which they fastened at the back.

Shuddering with indignation, she stepped inside. 'Stop it! Stop it at once!'

The men turned, disconcerted by her sudden appearance, the woman in their midst suddenly forgotten. She fell and lay there on the floor, her legs kicking impotently.

Jelka took another step, her whole body trembling with the anger she felt. 'What in the gods' names do you think you're doing?'

They backed away as she came on, bowing abjectly.

'Forgive us, Mistress Tolonen,' one of them said, recognizing her. 'But we are only acting on our master's orders.'

She looked at the man witheringly then shook her head. 'Unbind her. Unbind her at once.'

'But, Mistress, you don't understand –'

'Quiet, man!' she barked, the strength in her voice surprising him. He fell to his knees, head bowed, and stayed there, silent. She shivered then looked at the others. 'Well? Must I ask you again?'

There was a quick exchange of glances then the men did as she said, unbinding the woman and stepping back, as if afraid of the consequences. But the woman merely rolled over and sat up, easing the jacket from her, calm now, the fit – if that was what it had been – gone from her.

'Good,' Jelka said, not looking at them, her attention fixed upon the strange woman. 'Now go. I wish to be alone with her.'

'But, Mistress –'

'Go!'

There was no hesitation this time. Bowing furiously, the four men departed. She could hear the dull murmur of their voices outside, then nothing. She was alone with the woman.

Jelka went across and knelt over her, letting her hand rest on her arm. 'What is it?'

The woman looked up at her. She was pretty. Very pretty. In some ways more like a child than Jelka herself. 'What's your name?' Jelka asked, touched by the expression of innocence in the woman's eyes.

'My baby...' the woman said, looking past Jelka distractedly. 'Where's my baby?'

Jelka turned, looking about the room, then saw it. A cot, there, on the far side of the room. And as she saw she heard it – a strange, persistent snuffling.

'There,' she said gently. 'Your baby's there.'

She stood to one side as the woman got up and, casting the straitjacket aside, went across to the cot, bending down over it to lift and cradle the child. 'There, there...' she heard her say, a mother's softness in her voice. 'There, they'll not harm you. I'll see to that, my little darling. Mumma's here now. Mumma's here.'

Jelka felt a ripple of relief pass through her. But she was still angry. Angry with Hans, if it really was he who had given the order to subdue the woman. He had no right to torment her like that. She went across, touching the woman's back.

'Let me see...'

The woman turned, smiling, offering the child. A small, helpless little bundle that snuffled and snuffled...

Jelka felt herself go cold then stepped back, shaking her head, her mouth suddenly dry, appalled by what she saw. 'No...'

It stared up at her, red-eyed, its pink face too thin to be human, the hair that sprouted indiscriminately from its flesh too coarse, despite the silks in which it was wrapped. As she stared at it, one tiny three-toed hand pushed out at her, as if to grasp her hand. She jerked away, feeling the bile rise in her throat.

'Golden Heart!' The voice came from the doorway behind her. 'Put that dreadful thing away, right now! What in the gods' names do you think you're doing?'

It was the *mui tsai*, Sweet Flute. She came into the room, setting the drink down on the table, then went across to the woman, taking the bundle from her and setting it back in the cot.

'It's all right,' she said, turning back to face Jelka. 'I can explain...'

But Jelka was no longer there. She was outside, leaning over the balcony, gulping in air, the image of the tiny goat-creature like a mocking demon, burning indelibly in the redness behind her closed lids.

Tuan Ti Fo looked up from where he was making *ch'a* to where the boy lay sleeping on the bedroll in the far corner of the room. He had been asleep for some time, physically exhausted after his ordeal, but now he tossed and turned, held fast in the grip of some awful nightmare.

The old man put down the *ch'a* bowl and the cloth, then went across to the boy, balancing on his haunches beside him.

The boy seemed in pain, his lips drawn back from his teeth in what was almost a snarl, his whole body hunched into itself, as if something ate at him from within. He threshed this way and that, as if fighting himself, then, with a shudder that frightened the old man, went still.

'*Gweder...*' the boy said quietly. '*Gweder...*'

It was said softly, almost gently, yet the word itself was hard, the two sounds of which it was made stranger than anything Tuan Ti Fo had ever heard.

For a moment there was silence, then the boy spoke again, the whole of him gathered up into the movement of his lips.

'*Pandr'a bos ef, Lagasek?*'

This time the voice was harsh, almost guttural. Tuan Ti Fo felt a small ripple of fear pass through him, yet calmed himself inwardly, a still, small voice chanting the *chen yen* to dispense with fear.

'*Travyth, Gweder. Travyth...*'

He narrowed his eyes, understanding. Two voices. The first much softer, gentler than the second. Gweder and Lagasek... But what did it mean? And what was this language? He had never heard its like before.

He watched, seeing how the face changed, ugly one moment, peaceful, almost innocent, the next. Now it was ugly, the mouth distorted. Gweder was speaking again, his voice harsh, spitting out the words in challenge.

'*Praga obery why crenna? Bos why yeyn, Lagasek?*'

The boy shivered violently and the face changed, all spite, all anger draining from it. Softly now it answered, the brittle edges of the words rounded off. Yet there was pain behind the words. Pain and a dreadful sense of loss.

'*Yma gweras yn ow ganow, Gweder... gweras... ha an pyth bos tewl.*'

The abruptness of the change made him shudder. And the laughter...

The laughter was demonic. The face now shone with dark and greedy malice. With evil.

'Nyns-us pyth, Lagasek.'

There was such an awful mockery in that face that it made Tuan Ti Fo want to strike it with his fist.

Slowly, very slowly, the malice sank down into the tissue of the face. Again the boy's features settled into a kinder, more human form.

'A-dhywar-lur...' it breathed. 'A-dhywar-lur.' Then, in a cry of anguish, 'My bos yn annown... Yn annown!'

A ragged breath escaped Tuan Ti Fo. He stood abruptly then crossed the room to the tiny bookshelf. He brought the book back then squatted there again, closing his eyes and opening the pages at random, reading the first thing his eyes opened upon.

He smiled. It was a passage from midway through Book One. One of his favourites. He read, letting his voice be an instrument to soothe the boy.

'Thirty spokes share one hub. Adapt the nothing therein to the purpose in hand, and you will have the use of the cart. Knead clay in order to make a vessel. Adapt the nothing therein to the purpose in hand, and you will have the use of the vessel. Cut out doors and windows in order to make a room. Adapt the nothing therein to the purpose in hand, and you will have the use of the room. Thus what we gain is Something, yet it is by virtue of Nothing that this can be put to use.'

He looked down, seeing how still the boy had become, as if listening to his words, yet he was still asleep.

'Who are you, boy?' he asked softly, setting the book down. He reached across and pulled up the blanket until it covered the boy's chest. *Yes, he thought, and what brought you here to me? For the fates as surely directed you to me as they directed my feet this morning to a path I never took before.*

He leaned back then took up the book and began to read again, letting Lao Tzu's words – words more than two and a half thousand years old – wash over the sleeping boy and bring him ease.

'Well?'

Karr stared back morosely at his friend then set his ch'a bowl down.

'Nothing. The trail's gone cold. I tracked the boy as far as the factory, but there it ended. It's as if he vanished. There's no way he could have got past that guard post.'

Chen sat down, facing Karr across the table. 'Then he's still there. In the factory.'

Karr shook his head. 'We've taken it apart. Literally. I had a hundred men in there, dismantling the place back to the bare walls. But nothing.'

'We've missed something, that's all. I'll come back with you. We can go through it again.'

Karr looked down. 'Maybe. But I've been through it a dozen, twenty times already. It's as if he was spirited away.'

Chen studied his friend a moment. He had never seen Karr looking so down in the mouth.

'Cheer up,' he said. 'It can't be that bad.'

'No?' Karr sat back, drawing himself up to his full height. 'It seems Ebert's to be appointed General. The old T'ang accepted Nocenzi's resignation before he died. Tolonen was to step back into the job, but it seems the new T'ang wants a new man in the post.'

Chen grimaced then sat back. 'Then our lives aren't worth a beggar's shit.'

Karr stared at him a moment then laughed. 'You think?'

'And you don't?'

Karr stood up. 'Let a thousand devils take Hans Ebert. We'll concentrate on finding the boy. After all, that's our job, isn't it – finding people?'

Li Yuan was the first to arrive. Walking from the hangar, he felt detached, as if outside himself, watching. The meaning of this death had come to him slowly; not as grief but as nakedness, for this death exposed him. There was no one now but him; a single link from a broken chain.

Outside his father's rooms he stopped, in the grip of strong reluctance, but the eyes of others were upon him. Steeling himself, he ordered the doors unlocked then went inside.

The doors closed, leaving him alone with his dead father.

Li Shai Tung lay in his bed, as if he slept, yet his face was pale, like carved ivory, his chest still.

Li Yuan stood there, looking down at him. The old man's eyes were closed, the thin lids veined, mauve leaf patterns on the milky white. He knelt, studying the patterns in the white, but like the rest it meant nothing. It was merely a pattern, a repetition.

He shook his head, not understanding, knowing only that he had never seen his father sleeping. Never seen those fierce, proud eyes closed before this moment.

He put his hand out, touching his father's cheek. The flesh was cold. Shockingly cold. He drew his hand back sharply then shuddered. Where did it go? Where did all that warmth escape to?

Into the air.

He stood then drew the covers back. Beneath the silken sheets his father lay there naked, the frailty of his body revealed. Li Yuan looked, feeling an instinctive pity for his father. Not love, but pity. Pity for what time had done to him.

Death had betrayed him. Had found him weak and vulnerable.

His eyes moved down the body, knowing that others had looked before him. Surgeons with their dispassionate eyes; looking, as he looked now.

He shuddered. The body was thin, painfully emaciated, but unmarked. His father had been ill. Badly ill. That surprised him, and he paused a moment before putting back the sheet. It was unlike his father not to comment on his health. Something was amiss. Some element beyond simple senility had been the cause of this.

He had no proof and yet his sense of wrongness was strong. It made him turn and look about him, noting the presence of each object in the room, questioning their function. All seemed well, and yet the sense of wrongness persisted.

He went outside, into the hallway. Surgeon Hua was waiting there with his assistants.

'How has my father been, Hua? Was he eating well?'

The old man shook his head. 'Not for some time, *Chieh Hsia*. Not since Han's death. But...' he pursed his lips, considering, '...well, enough for an old man. And your father *was* old, Li Yuan.'

Li Yuan nodded, but he was still troubled. 'Was he... clear? In his mind, I mean?'

'Yes, *Chieh Hsia*. Even last night.' Hua paused, frowning, as if he too was troubled by something. 'There was nothing evidently wrong with him. We've... examined him and...'

'Evidently?'

Hua nodded, but his eyes were watchful.

'But you think that appearances might be deceptive, is that it, Hua?'

The old surgeon hesitated. 'It isn't something I can put my finger on, *Chieh Hsia*. Just a ... a *feeling* I have. Confucius says –'

'Just tell me, Hua,' Li Yuan said, interrupting him; reaching out to hold his arm, his fondness for the old man showing in his face. 'No proverbs, please. Just tell me what made you feel something was wrong.'

'This will sound unprofessional, *Chieh Hsia*, but as you've asked.' Hua paused, clearing his throat. 'Well, he was not himself. He was sharp, alert and in a sense no different from his old self, but he was not – somehow – Li Shai Tung. He seemed like an actor, mimicking your father. Playing him exceptionally well, but not...'

He faltered, shaking his head, grief overwhelming him.

'Not like the real thing,' Li Yuan finished for him.

Hua nodded. 'He was... uncertain. And your father was *never* uncertain.'

Li Yuan considered a moment then gave his instructions. 'I want you to perform an autopsy, Hua. I want you to find out why he died. I want to know what killed him.'

Tsu Ma was dressed in white, his hair tied back in a single elegant bow. The effect was striking in its simplicity, its sobriety, while his face had a gentleness Li Yuan had never seen in it before. He came forward and embraced Li Yuan, holding him to his breast, one hand smoothing the back of his neck. It was this, more than the death, more than the coldness of his father's cheek, that broke the ice that had formed about his feelings. At last he let go, feeling the sorrow rise and spill from him.

'Good, good,' Tsu Ma whispered softly, stroking his neck. 'A man should cry for his father.' And when he moved back, there were tears in his eyes, real grief in his expression.

'And Wei Feng?' Li Yuan asked, wiping his eyes with the back of his hand.

'He's waiting below.' Tsu Ma smiled; a friend's strong smile. 'We'll go when you're ready.'

'I'm ready,' Li Yuan answered, straightening, unashamed now of his tears; feeling much better for them. 'Let us see our cousin.'

Wei Feng was waiting in the viewing room, wearing a simple robe of white, gathered at the waist. As Li Yuan came down the stairs Wei Feng came across and embraced him, whispering his condolences. But he seemed older than Li Yuan remembered him. Much older.

'Are you all right, Wei Feng?' he asked, concerned for the old man's health.

Wei Feng laughed. A short, melodic sound. 'As well as could be expected, Yuan.' His expression changed subtly. 'But your father...' He sighed. Wei Feng was the oldest now. By almost twenty years the oldest. 'So much has changed, Yuan. So much. And now this. This seems...' He shrugged, as if it were beyond words to say.

'I know.' Li Yuan frowned, releasing him. 'They killed him, Wei Feng.'

Wei Feng simply looked puzzled, but Tsu Ma came close, taking his arm. 'How do you know? Is there proof?'

'Proof? No. But I *know*. I'm sure of it, Tsu Ma. I've asked Surgeon Hua to... to look for something. Maybe that will show something but, even so, I know.'

'So what now?' Wei Feng had crossed his arms. His face was suddenly hard, his tiny figure filled with power.

'So now we play their game. Remove the gloves.'

Beside him Tsu Ma nodded.

'We know our enemies,' Li Yuan said, with an air of finality. 'We have only to find them.'

'DeVore, you mean?' Tsu Ma looked across at Wei Feng. The old man's face was troubled, but his jaw was set. Determination weighed the heavier in his conflicting emotions. Tsu Ma narrowed his eyes, considering. 'And then?'

Li Yuan turned. His eyes seemed intensely black, like space itself; cold, vacant, all trace of life and warmth gone from them. His face was closed, expressionless, like a mask. 'Arrange a meeting of the Council, Tsu Ma. Let Chi Hsing host it. We must talk.'

Li Yuan was barely eighteen, yet the tone, the small movement of the left hand that accompanied the final words, were uncannily familiar. As if the father spoke and acted through the son.

PART FIFTEEN   **FIGURES OF SMOKE**

Autumn 2207

Chapter 62

CHEN YEN

The ch'a bowl lay to one side, broken, its contents spilled across the floor. Beside it Tuan Ti Fo crouched, his back to the door, facing the boy.

'Yn-mes a forth, cothwas!' the boy snarled, the sound coming from the back of his throat. 'Yn-mes a forth!'

Tuan Ti Fo felt the hairs rise on the back of his neck. The boy was down on all fours, his face hideously ugly, the features distorted with rage, the chin thrust forward aggressively, his round, dark eyes filled with animal menace. He made small movements with his body, feinting this way and that, gauging Tuan Ti Fo's response to each, a low growling coming from his throat.

It was the third time the boy had tried to get past him, and, as before, he seemed surprised by the old man's quickness; shocked that, whichever way he moved, Tuan Ti Fo was there, blocking his way.

The old man swayed gently on his haunches then, as the boy threw himself to the left, moved effortlessly across, fending off the child with his palms, using the least force possible to achieve his end. The boy withdrew, yelping with frustration, then turned and threw himself again, like a dog, going for Tuan's throat.

This time he had to fight the boy. Had to strike him hard and step back, aiming a kick to the stomach to disable him. Yet even as the boy fell back, gasping for breath, that strange transformation overcame him again. As

Tuan Ti Fo watched, the harshness faded from the boy's features, becoming something softer, more human.

'Welcome back, Lagasek,' he said, taking a long, shuddering breath. But for how long? He looked about him, noting the broken bowl, the spilled *ch'a*, and shook his head. He would have to bind the boy while he slept, for in time he would have to sleep. He could not guard against this 'Gweder' thing for ever.

He moved closer, crouching over the boy. He was peaceful now, his face almost angelic in its innocence. But beneath? Tuan Ti Fo narrowed his eyes, considering, then began to speak, softly, slowly, as if to himself.

'Look at you, child. So sweet you look just now. So innocent. But are you good or evil? Is it Gweder or Lagasek who rules you? And which of them brought you here to my rooms?' He smiled then got up, moving across to fetch a small towel to mop up the *ch'a*, a brush to gather up the tiny pieces of broken porcelain. And as he did so he continued to speak, letting his voice rise and fall like a flowing stream, lulling the sleeping child.

'Kao Tzu believed that each man, at birth, was like a willow tree, and that righteousness was like a bowl. To become righteous, a man had therefore to be cut and shaped, like the willow, into the bowl. The most base instincts – the desire for food or sex – were, he argued, all that one could ever find in the unshaped man, and human nature was as indifferent to good or evil as free-flowing water is to the shape it eventually fills.'

He turned, looking at the child, seeing how the boy's chest now rose and fell gently, as if soothed by his voice, then turned back, smiling, beginning to mop up the spill.

'Meng Tzu, of course, disagreed. He felt that if what Kao Tzu said were true, then the act of becoming righteous would be a violation of human nature – would, in fact, be a calamity. But I have my own reason for disagreeing with Kao Tzu. If it *were* so – if human nature were as Kao Tzu claimed – then why should any goodness come from evil circumstances? And why should evil come from good?' He gave a soft laugh. 'Some men *are* water drops and willow-sprouts, it's true, but not all. For there are those who determine their own shape, their own direction, and the mere existence of them demonstrates Kao Tzu's claim to be a misrepresentation.'

He finished mopping then carried the towel to the basin in the corner and dropped it in. Returning, he set the two large pieces of the broken bowl to one side, then began to sweep the tiny slivers of porcelain into a pile.

'Of course, there is another explanation. It is said that shortly after the Earth was separated from Heaven, Nu Kua created human beings. It appears that she created the first men by patting yellow earth together. She laboured at this a long time, taking great care in the shaping and moulding of the tiny, human forms, but then she grew tired. The work was leaving her little time for herself and so she decided to simplify the task. Taking a long piece of string, she dragged it to and fro through the mud, heaping it up and turning that into men. But these were crude, ill-formed creatures compared to those she had first made. Henceforth, it is said, the rich and the noble are those descended from the creatures who were formed before Nu Kua tired of her task – the men of yellow earth – whereas the poor and the lowly are descendants of the cord-made men – the men of mud.'

He laughed quietly then looked up again, noting how restful the boy now was.

'But, then, as the T'ien Wen says, "Nu Kua had a body. Who formed and fashioned it?"'

He turned, taking the thin paper box in which the ch'a brick had come and setting it down, sweeping the fragments up into it, then dropped in the two largest pieces.

'Ah, yes, but we live in a world gone mad. The bowl of righteousness was shattered long ago, when Tsao Ch'un built his City. It is left to indi-vidual men to find the way – to create small islands of sanity in an ocean of storms.' He looked about him. 'This here is such an island.'

Or had been. Before the child had come. Before the bowl had been broken, his peace disturbed.

For a moment Tuan Ti Fo closed his eyes, seeking that inner stillness deep within himself, his lips forming the chen yen – the 'true words' – of the mantra. With a tiny shudder he passed the hard knot of tension from him then looked up again, a faint smile at the corners of his mouth.

'Food,' he said softly. 'That's what you need. Something special.'

He stood, then went across to the tiny oven set into the wall on the far side of the room and lit it. Taking a cooking bowl from the side, he part-filled it from the water jar and set it down on the ring.

Tuan Ti Fo turned, looking about him at the simple order of his room.

'Chaos. The world is headed into chaos, child, and there is little you or I can do to stop it.' He smiled sadly then went across and took up the basin, carrying it across to the door. He would empty it later, after the child had been fed.

The boy had turned on to his side, the fingers of one hand lightly touching his neck. Tuan Ti Fo smiled and, taking a blanket, took it across and laid it over the child.

He crouched there a moment, watching him. 'You know, the Chou believed that Heaven and Earth were once inextricably mixed together in a state of undifferentiated chaos, like a chicken's egg. *Hun tun* they called that state. *Hun tun...*'

He nodded then went back to the oven, taking a jar from the shelf on the wall and emptying out half of its contents on to the board beside the oven. The tiny, sac-like dumplings looked like pale, wet, unformed creatures in their uncooked state. Descendants of the mud men. He smiled and shook his head. *Hun tun*, they were called. He had made them himself with the things the girl, Marie, had brought last time she'd come. It was soy, of course, not meat, that formed the filling inside the thin shells of dough, but that was as he wished it. He did not believe in eating flesh. It was not The Way.

As the water began to boil he tipped the dumplings into the bowl and stirred them gently before leaving them to cook. There were other things he added – herbs sent to him from friends on the Plantations and other, special things. He leaned forward, sniffing the concoction delicately, then nodded. It was just what the child needed. It would settle him and give him back his strength.

That precious strength that 'Gweder' spent so thoughtlessly.

He turned, expecting to see the child sitting up, his face transformed again into a snarl, but the boy slept on.

He turned back, for a while busying himself preparing the food. When it was cooked, he poured half of the broth into a small ceramic bowl and took it across.

It was a shame to wake the boy, but it was twelve hours now since he had eaten. And afterwards he would sleep. The herbs in the soup would ensure that he slept.

He set the bowl down then lifted the boy gently, cradling him in a half-sitting position. As he did so the boy stirred and struggled briefly then relaxed. Lifting the spoon from the bowl, Tuan Ti Fo placed it to the boy's lips, tilting it gently.

'Here, child. I serve you Heaven itself.'

The boy took a little of the warm broth, then turned his head slightly. Tuan Ti Fo persevered, following his mouth with the spoon, coaxing a little of the liquid into him each time until the child's mouth was opening wide for each new spoonful.

At last the bowl was empty. Tuan Ti Fo smiled, holding the boy to him a while, conscious yet again of how insubstantial he seemed. As if he were made of something finer than flesh and bone, finer than yellow earth. And again he wondered about his presence in the dream. What did that mean? For it had to mean something.

He drew a pillow close then set the boy's head down, covering him with the blanket.

'Maybe you'll tell me, eh? When you wake. That's if that strange tongue is not the only one you speak.'

He went back to the oven and poured the remains of the *Hun tun* into the bowl, spooning it down quickly, then took the bowls and basin outside, locking the door behind him, going to the washrooms at the far end of the corridor. It didn't take long, but he hurried about his tasks, concerned not to leave the child too long. And when he returned he took care in opening the door, lest 'Gweder' should slip out past him. But the boy still slept.

Tuan Ti Fo squatted, his legs folded under him, watching the boy. Then, knowing it would be hours before he woke, he got up and fetched his *wei chi* set, smoothing the cloth 'board' out on the floor before him then setting the bowls to either side, the white stones to his left, the black to his right. For a time he lost himself in the game, his whole self gathered up into the shapes the stones made on the board, until it seemed the board was the great Tao and he the stones.

Once he had been The First Hand Supreme in all Chung Kuo, Master of Masters and eight times winner of the great annual championship held in Suchow. But that had been thirty, almost forty years ago. Back in the days when he had yet concerned himself with the world.

He looked up from the board, realizing his concentration had been broken. He laughed, a quotation of Ch'eng Yi's coming to mind.

'Within the universe all things have their opposite: when there is the Yin, there is the Yang; where there is goodness, there is evil.'

And in the boy? He took a deep breath, looking across at him. Gweder and Lagasek. Yin and Yang. As in all men. But in this one the Tao was at war with itself. Yin and Yang were not complementary but antagonistic. In that sense the child was like the world of Chung Kuo. There too the balance had been lost. Like the boy, Chung Kuo was an entity at war with itself.

But the thought brought with it an insight. Just as this world of theirs had been tampered with, so too had the child. Something had happened to split him and make him fight himself. He had lost his oneness.

Or had had it taken from him.

Tuan Ti Fo cleared the board slowly, concerned for the boy. Yet maybe that was his role in this – to make the boy whole again: to reconcile the animal and the human in him. For what was a man without balance?

'Nothing,' he answered himself softly. 'Or worse than nothing.'

He began again, the shapes of black and white slowly filling the board until he knew there were no more stones to play, nothing left to win or lose.

Tuan Ti Fo looked up. The boy was sitting up, watching him, his dark, over-large eyes puzzling over the shapes that lay there on the cloth.

He looked down, saying nothing, then cleared the board and set up another game. He began to play, conscious now of the boy watching, of him edging slowly closer as the stones were laid, the board filled up again.

Again he laid the final stone, knowing there was no more to be won or lost. He looked up. The boy was sitting there, not an arm's length from him now, studying the patterns of black and white with a fierce intensity, as if to grasp some meaning from them.

He cleared the board and was about to play again when the boy's hand reached out and took a white stone from the bowl to his left. Tuan Ti Fo made to correct him – to make him take from the bowl of black stones – but the boy was insistent. He slapped a stone down, in the corner nearest him on the right. In *tsu*, the north.

They played, slowly at first, then faster, Tuan Ti Fo giving nothing to the boy, punishing him for every mistake he made. Yet when he made to take a line of stones he had surrounded from the board, the boy placed his hand over Tuan's, stopping him, lifting his hand so that he might study the position, his face creased into a frown, as if trying to take in what he had done wrong. Only then did he move his hand back, indicating that Tuan Ti Fo should take the stones away.

The next game was more difficult. The boy repeated none of the simple errors he had made first time round. This time Tuan Ti Fo had to work hard to defeat him. He sat back, his eyes narrowed, staring at the boy, surprised by how well he'd played.

'So,' he said. 'You can play.'

The boy looked up at him, wide-eyed, then shook his head. No, Tuan thought; it's not possible. You *must* have played before.

He cleared the board then sat back, waiting, feeling himself go very still, as if something strange – something wholly out of the ordinary – was about to happen.

This time the boy set the stone down in the south, in *shang*, only a hand's length from Tuan Ti Fo's knee. It was a standard opening – the kind of play that made no real difference to the final outcome – yet somehow the boy made it seem a challenge. An hour later Tuan Ti Fo knew he had been defeated. For the first time in over forty years someone had humbled him on the board he considered his own.

He sat back, breathing deeply, taking in the elegance of the shapes the boy had made, recollecting the startling originality of the boy's strategies – as if he had just re-invented the game. Then he bowed low, touching his forehead almost to the board.

The boy stared back at him for a moment, then returned his bow.

So you are human after all, Tuan Ti Fo thought, shaking his head, amused by the gesture. *And now I'm certain that the gods sent you.* He laughed. *Who knows? Perhaps you're even one of them.*

The boy sat there, his legs crossed under him, perfectly still, watching Tuan Ti Fo, his eyes narrowed, as if trying to understand why the old man was smiling.

Tuan Ti Fo leaned forward, beginning to clear the board, when a knock sounded at the door. A casual rapping that he knew at once was Marie.

He saw how the boy froze – how his face grew rigid with fear – and reached out to hold his arm.

'It's all right...' he whispered. 'There!' he said, indicating the blanket. 'Get under there, boy, and stay hidden. I'll send them away.'

★

Marie turned, hearing noises behind her, then broke into a smile, bowing to the two elderly gentlemen who were passing in the corridor. She turned back, frowning. Where was he? It was not like him to delay.

Marie Enge was a tall, good-looking woman in her late twenties with the kind of physical presence that most men found daunting. They preferred their women more delicately made, more deferent. Neither was the impression of physical strength deceptive. She was a powerful woman, trained in the arts of self-defence, but that was not to say that she lacked feminine charm. At a second glance one noticed signs of a softer side to her nature: in the delicate primrose pattern of the edging to her tunic; in the strings of pearl and rose-coloured beads at her wrists; in the butterfly bow on her otherwise masculine-looking pigtail.

She waited a moment longer then knocked again. Harder this time, more insistent.

'Tuan Ti Fo? Are you there? It's me. Marie. I've come for our game.'

She heard a shuffling inside and gave a small sigh of relief. For a moment she had thought he might be ill. She moved back, waiting for the door to open, but it remained firmly shut.

'Tuan Ti Fo?'

The slightest edge of concern had entered her voice now. She moved forward, about to press her ear against the door, when it slid open a little.

'What is it?' the old man said, eyeing her almost suspiciously.

'It's me, Shih Tuan. Don't you remember? It's time for our game.'

'Ah...' He pulled the door a fraction wider, at the same time moving forward, blocking her view into the room. 'Forgive me, Marie, I've just woken. I didn't sleep well and...'

'You're not ill, are you?' she said, concerned

'No...' He smiled then gave a bow. 'However, I do feel tired. So if, for once, you'll excuse me?'

She hesitated then returned his bow. 'Of course, Shih Tuan. Tomorrow, perhaps?'

He tilted his head slightly then nodded. 'Perhaps...'

She stood back, watching the door slide closed, then turned away. But she had gone only a few paces before she turned and stared back at the door, a strong sense of oddness – of wrongness – holding her in its grip. He had never before spoken of sleepless nights; neither, as far as she knew, had he ever complained of any kind of illness. Indeed, a fitter old boy she had never known. Nor had he ever put her off before. She frowned then turned away again, moving slowly, reluctantly, away.

For a moment she hesitated, not quite knowing what to do, then she nodded to herself and began to move quicker. She would go straight to the Dragon Cloud. Would ask Shang Chen if she could work an extra hour this end of her shift and leave an hour earlier. Yes. And then she would return.

Just in case the old man needed her.

The Dragon Cloud filled one end of Main, dominating the market that spread below its eaves. It was a big, traditional-looking building with a steeply sloping roof of red tile, its five storeys not walled in but open to the surroundings, each level linked by broad mock-wooden steps. Greenery was everywhere, in bowls and screens and hanging from the open balustrades, giving the teahouse the look of an overgrown garden. Waiters dressed in pale blue gowns – male and female, Han and *Hung Mao* – hurried between the levels, carrying broad trays filled with exquisite ceramics, the bowls and pots a pure white, glazed with a blue marking. At strategic points about the house the *ch'a* masters, specialists in *ch'a shu*, the art of tea, sat at their counters, preparing their special infusions.

At a stretch the Dragon Cloud could seat five thousand. More than enough, one would have thought, to cater for the surrounding levels. Even so, it was packed when they got there, not a table free. Chen looked about him then looked back at Karr.

'Let's go elsewhere, Gregor. It'll be an hour at least before we get a table.'

Karr turned, beckoning to one of the waiters. Chen saw how the man came across, wary of Karr, eyeing the big man up and down as if to assess how much trouble he might be. Behind him, at the counter, several of the other waiters, mostly Han, turned, following him with their eyes.

Chen watched; saw Karr press something into the waiter's hand; saw the man look down, then up again, wide-eyed. Karr muttered something then pressed a second tiny bundle into the man's hand. This time the waiter bowed. He turned and, summoning two of his fellows across, hurried away, whispering something to his companions.

In a little while the waiter was back, bowing, smiling, leading them up two flights of steps then through to a table at the centre of the house. As they moved between the tables, three elderly Han came towards them, bowing and smiling.

Chen leaned towards Karr, keeping his voice low. 'You bought their table?'

Karr smiled, returning the old gentlemen's bows before allowing one of the waiters to pull a chair out for him. When Chen was seated across from him, he answered.

'I've heard that the Dragon Cloud is the cultural centre of these levels. The place where everybody who is anybody comes. Here, if anywhere, we shall hear news of the boy. You understand?'

'Ah...' Chen smiled then sat back, relaxing. It was not like Karr to use his privilege so crudely and for a moment he had been concerned by his friend's behaviour.

'Besides,' Karr added, accepting the *ch'a* menu the waiter held out to him, 'I have heard that the Dragon Cloud is the paragon among teahouses. Its fame spreads far and wide, even to the heavens.'

This was said louder, clearly for the benefit of the waiters. The one who had first dealt with Karr bowed his head slightly, responding to Karr's words.

'If the *ch'un tzu* would like something... special?'

Karr leaned back. Even seated he was still almost a head taller than the Han.

'You would not have a *hsiang p'ien*, by any chance?'

The waiter bowed his head slightly lower, a smile of pleasure splitting his face. 'It is the speciality of the Dragon Cloud, *ch'un tzu*. What kind of *hsiang p'ien* would you like?'

Karr looked across at his friend. 'Have you any preference, Kao Chen?'

Chen studied the menu a moment, trying to recognize something he knew amongst the hundred exotic brews, then looked up again, shrugging. 'I don't know. I guess I'll have what you have.'

Karr considered a moment then turned his head, looking at the waiter. 'Have you a *ch'ing ch'a* with a lotus fragrance?'

'Of course, Master. A *pao yun*, perhaps?'

Karr nodded. 'A Jewelled Cloud would be excellent.'

The man bowed, then, his head still lowered, took the *ch'a* menus from them. 'I will have the girl bring the *ch'a* and some sweetmeats. It will be but a few minutes, *ch'un tzu.*' He bowed again then backed away.

Chen waited a moment, until the man had gone, then leaned across, keeping his voice low. 'What in the gods' names is a *hsiang p'ien?*'

Karr smiled, relaxing for the first time in almost twelve hours of searching. '*Hsiang p'ien* are flower *ch'a.* And a *ch'ing ch'a* is a green, unfermented *ch'a.* The one we're having is placed into a tiny gauze bag overnight with the calix of a freshly plucked lotus.' He laughed. 'Have you not read your Shen Fu, Chen?'

Chen laughed and shook his head. 'When would I have time, my friend? With three children there is barely time to shit, let alone read!'

Karr laughed then studied him a moment. He reached out and touched his arm gently. 'Maybe so, Kao Chen, but a man ought to read. I'll give you a copy of Shen Fu some time. His *Six Records of a Floating Life.* He lived four centuries ago, before the great City was built. It was another age, I tell you, Chen. Cruder, and yet in some ways better than ours. Even so, some things don't change. Human nature, for instance.'

Chen lowered his head slightly. So it was. He looked about him, enjoying the strange peacefulness of the place. Each table was cut off from the next by screens of greenery; even so, from where he sat he had a view of what was happening at other tables and on other levels. He turned, looking about him. Above the nearest serving counter a huge banner portrait of the *ch'a* god, Lu Yu, fluttered gently in the breeze of the overhead fans. It was an image that even Chen recognized, flying, as it did, over every teahouse in Chung Kuo.

'Where do we begin?' Chen asked after a moment. 'I mean, we can't simply go from table to table asking, can we?'

Karr had been staring away almost abstractedly; now he looked back at Chen. 'No. You're quite right, Chen. It must be done subtly. Quietly. If necessary, we will sit here all day, and all tomorrow too. Until we hear something.'

'And if we don't?' Chen shook his head. 'Besides, I hate all this sitting and waiting. Why don't we just empty this whole deck and search it room by room?'

Karr smiled. 'You think that would be a good idea, Chen? And what reason would we give?'

'What reason would we need to give? We are on the T'ang's business, surely?'

Karr leaned towards him, lowering his voice to a whisper. 'And if rumour were to go about the levels that the T'ang has lost something important and would clear a deck to find it? Surely such a rumour would have a price? Would find ears we'd rather it didn't reach?'

Chen opened his mouth then closed it again. 'Even so, there must be something else we can do?'

Karr shook his head. 'The trail has gone cold. It would not do to rush about blindly elsewhere. The boy is here somewhere. I know it. The only course now is to wait. To bide our time and listen to the faint whispers from the tables.'

Chen leaned forward, about to say something, then sat back again. One of the waiters was approaching their table – a woman this time, a tall, blonde-haired *Hung Mao*. He glanced at her as she set the tray down on the table between them then frowned, seeing how Karr was staring at her.

'Your *hsiang p'ien*,' she said, moving back slightly from the table, her head bowed. 'Shall I pour for you, *ch'un tzu*?'

Karr smiled. 'That would be most pleasant.'

The teapot was square in shape with a wicker handle; a white-glazed, ceramic pot with a blue circular pattern on each side – the stylized pictogram for 'long life'. Beside it was a *chung*, a lidded serving bowl, and two ordinary *ch'a* bowls. Moving forward, the woman poured some of the freshly brewed *ch'a* into their bowls, then the rest into the *chung*, setting the lid back on.

She was a big woman, yet her movements had been precise, almost delicate. She touched the bowls as if each were alive, while the *ch'a* itself fell daintily, almost musically into the bowls, not a drop splashed or spilled.

Chen, watching Karr, saw a small movement in the big man's face; saw him look up at the woman appreciatively.

'Thank you,' Karr said, smiling up at her. 'It is good to be served by someone who cares so much for the art.'

She looked at him for the first time then lowered her eyes again. 'We try our best to please, *ch'un tzu*.'

'And these bowls...' Karr continued, as if reluctant to let her go. 'I have rarely seen such elegance, such grace of line, such sobriety of colour.'

For the first time she smiled. 'They are nice, aren't they? I've often commented how pleasant it is to serve *ch'a* from such bowls. They have... *yu ya*, no?'

Karr laughed softly, clearly delighted. 'Deep elegance. Yes...' He sat back, appraising her more closely. 'You know a great deal, *Fu Jen*... ?'

Again she lowered her eyes, a faint colour coming to her neck and cheeks. 'I had a good teacher. And it is *Hsiao Chieh* Enge, not *Fu Jen*. I am not married, you understand?'

Karr's smile faded momentarily. 'Ah... forgive me.' He sat forward slightly. 'Anyway, I thank you again, *Hsiao Chieh* Enge. As I said, it is very pleasing to be served by one who knows so much about the great art of *ch'a shu*.'

She bowed one final time, and turned to go. Then, as if changing her mind, she turned back, leaning closer to Karr. 'And if it is not too forward, *ch'un tzu*, you might call me Marie. It is how I am known here in these levels. Ask for Marie. Anyone will know me.'

Chen watched her go then turned, looking back at Karr. The big man was still watching her, staring across at where she was preparing her next order.

'You like her, Gregor?'

Karr looked back at him almost blankly then gave a brief laugh. 'I think we have our contact, Chen. What did she say? Anyone will know me. And likewise, she will know anyone, neh?' He raised one eyebrow.

Chen was smiling. 'You didn't answer me, Gregor. You like her, don't you?'

Karr stared back at him a moment longer, then shrugged and looked away. As he did so, a commotion started up behind them, at the *ch'a* counter.

Chen turned to look. There were three men – Han, dressed in dark silks with blood-red headbands about their foreheads. He glanced at Karr knowingly then looked back.

'Triad men,' he said quietly. 'But what are they doing up this high?'

Karr shook his head. 'Things are changing, Chen. They've been spreading their net higher and higher these last few years. The unrest has been their making.'

'Even so...' He shook his head, angered by what he saw.

Karr reached out and held his arm, preventing him from getting up.

'Remember why we're here. We can't afford to get involved.'

One of them was shouting at the men behind the counter now, a stream of threats and curses in *Kuo Yu* – Mandarin – while the two behind him looked about them threateningly. It was a classic piece of Triad mischief – an attempt to unsettle the owners of the Dragon Cloud before they moved into it in force.

'I'd like to kick their arses out of here,' Chen said beneath his breath.

Karr smiled. 'It would be fun, neh? But not now. After the boy's found, maybe. We'll find out who's behind it and pay them a visit, neh? In force.'

Chen looked at him and smiled. 'That would be good.'

'In the meantime...' Karr stopped then leaned forward, his eyes suddenly narrowed.

Chen turned and looked across. The leader of the three was still shouting, but now his curses were directed at the woman who was confronting him. Chen stood up, a cry coming to his lips as he saw the bright flash of a knife being drawn.

This time Karr made no attempt to stop him. Rather, Karr was ahead of him, moving quickly between the tables.

Chen saw the knife describe an arc through the air and felt himself flinch. But then the Triad thug was falling backwards, the knife spinning away harmlessly through the air. A moment later he saw the second of the men go down with a sharp groan, clutching his balls. The third turned and made to run, but the woman was on him like a tigress, pulling him backwards by his hair, her hand chopping down viciously at his chest.

Chen pulled up sharply, almost thudding into Karr who stood there, his hands clenched at his sides, his great chest rising and falling heavily as he stared down at the three prone gangsters.

The woman turned, meeting Karr's eyes briefly, her own eyes wide, her whole body tensed as if to meet some other threat, then she turned away, a faint shudder passing through her, letting her co-workers carry the three men off.

Karr hesitated a moment then went after her. He caught up with her on the far side of the teahouse, in an area that was roped off for the staff's use only.

She turned, seeing he was following her, and frowned, looking down. 'What do you want?'

Karr shook his head. 'That was... astonishing. I...' He shrugged and opened his hands. 'I meant to help you, but you didn't need any help, did you?' He laughed strangely. 'Where did you learn to fight like that?'

Again she looked at him, almost resentful now; a reaction to the fight beginning to set in. He could see that her hands were trembling faintly and remembered how that felt. He nodded, feeling mounting respect for her.

'I've never seen a woman fight like that,' he began again.

'Look,' she said, angry suddenly. 'What do you want?'

'I'm looking for someone,' he said, trusting her; knowing that she had acted from more than self-interest. 'My nephew. He had an accident, you see, and he ran away. He can't remember who he is, but I know he's here somewhere. I tracked him down here, but now he's disappeared.'

'What's that to do with me?'

He swallowed, conscious that others were listening. 'Just that you might be able to help me. You know these levels. Know the people. If anything odd happened, you'd know about it, neh?'

She gave a grudging nod. 'I guess so.'

'Well, then. You'll help me, neh? He's my dead brother's son and he means a great deal to me. I...'

He looked down, as if unable to go on, then felt her move closer.

'All right,' she said quietly, touching his arm. 'I'll help. I'll listen out for you.'

He looked up, meeting her eyes. 'Thanks. My name's Karr. Gregor Karr.'

She looked back at him a moment longer then smiled. 'Well... you'd best get back to your ch'a, Gregor Karr. *Hsiang p'ien* tastes awful when it's cold.'

As before, the old man was slow coming to the door, but this time she was ready for him. This time when he slid the door back, she moved towards him, as if expecting him to let her pass, beginning to tell him about the incident at the Dragon Cloud, the wicker basket of leftovers from the teahouse held out before her.

It almost worked, almost got her into the room, but then, unexpectedly, she found herself blocked.

'I am sorry, Marie, but you cannot stay. It would benefit neither of us to have our session now.'

She turned her head, staring at him, noting how he looked down rather than meet her eyes, and knew at once that he was lying to her. It came as a shock, but it was also confirmation of the feeling she had had back at the restaurant when the man, Karr, had spoken to her.

The boy was here. She knew he was. But what was Tuan Ti Fo up to?

'Forgive me,' he was saying, the gentle pressure of his hand forcing her slowly back, 'but I am in the worst of humours, Marie. And when a man is in an ill humour he is fit company only for himself, neh?'

The faint, apologetic smile was more like the old Tuan Ti Fo.

She tried to look past him, but it was almost impossible to see what or who was in the room beyond. Stalling for time, she pushed the basket at him.

'You will at least take these, Master Tuan. You must eat, after all, bad humour or no.'

He looked down at the basket, then up at her, smiling. 'I am extremely grateful, Marie, and, yes, I would be a foolish old man indeed if I did not welcome your gift.'

The small bow he made was all she needed. For that brief moment she could see the room beyond him and there, jutting out from what seemed at first glance to be a pillow beneath the blanket, was the naked foot of a youth.

She shivered, then, backing away a step, returned Tuan Ti Fo's bow.

'Tomorrow,' he said. 'When the mood has passed.'

'Tomorrow,' she said, watching the door slide shut again. Then, turning away, she began to make her way back to her apartment, confused, a dark uncertainty at the core of her.

Tuan Ti Fo stood there for some time, staring at the door, the wicker basket resting lightly in his hand. Then, hearing a movement behind him, he turned.

The boy had crawled out from beneath the blanket and knelt there, looking across at Tuan Ti Fo, his eyes wide with fear.

'It was a friend,' the old man said reassuringly. 'But it seems best not to take any chances, neh?'

He set the basket down on the low table by the oven then turned back, looking at the boy.

'But we must leave here now. I cannot stall her for ever, and soon she will grow suspicious, if she hasn't already. She is not a bad woman – quite the contrary – but curiosity can be a destructive thing.'

He eyed the boy a moment, not certain how much of what he was saying was understood, then gave a small shrug.

'I have lived in this world a long time, child. I have been many things in my time. I have worked in their factories and on their Plantations. I have served in their officialdom and lived among the criminal element down beneath the Net. I know their world. Know it for the madhouse it is. Even so, sometimes the way ahead is uncertain. So it is now. We must leave here. That much is clear. But where should we go?'

'The Clay,' the boy answered him, staring back at him with a strange intensity. 'Take me down to the Clay. That's where I belong. Where I came from.'

'The Clay...' he whispered, then nodded, understanding. As in the dream he had had. 'Spiders,' he said, and saw the boy nod his head slowly. Yes, spiders. Tiny, beautiful spiders, infused with an inner light, spinning their vast webs across the endless darkness. He had seen them, their strong yet delicate webs anchored to the Clay. And there – how clearly he remembered it suddenly – *there*, watching them climb into the dark, was the boy, smiling beatifically, his big, dark eyes filled with wonder.

Tuan Ti Fo shivered, awed by the power of the vision.

'What's your name, boy? What did they call you in the Clay?'

The boy looked away, as if the memory disturbed him, then looked back, his eyes searching Tuan Ti Fo's.

'Lagasek,' he said finally. 'Lagasek, they called me. *Starer*.'

Tuan Ti Fo caught his breath. 'And Gweder?'

The boy frowned and looked down, as if he was having trouble recollecting the word. 'Gweder? Gweder means mirror. Why? What have I been saying? I...' He shuddered and looked about him. 'Something happened, didn't it? Something...' He shook his head. 'I feel funny. My voice – it's... different.' He stared down at his hands. 'And my body, it's...'

He looked back at Tuan Ti Fo, puzzled. 'It feels like I've been asleep for a long time. Trapped in a huge, deep well of sleep. I was working in the Casting Shop. I remember now. Chan Shui was away. And then...' His face creased into a fierce frown of concentration then he let it go, shaking his head. 'I don't understand. T'ai Cho was going to –'

'T'ai Cho? Who's T'ai Cho?'

The boy looked up again. 'Why, T'ai Cho's my friend. My tutor at the Project. He...'

The frown came back. Again the boy looked down at his hands, staring at his arms and legs as if they didn't belong to him.

'What's the matter, Lagasek? What's wrong?'

'Laga...' The boy stared at him, then shook his head again. 'No. It's Kim. My name is Kim. Lagasek was down there.'

'In the Clay?'

'Yes, and...' He shook his head. 'I feel... strange. My body... It doesn't feel like it's mine. It's as if...'

He stopped, staring up at the old man, his face filled with an intent curiosity.

'What did I say? Those words. You must have heard me say them. So what else did I say?'

Tuan Ti Fo met his eyes, remembering the savagery of the face within his face – the face of Gweder, the mirror – then shook his head.

'You said nothing, Kim. Nothing at all. But come. We must pack now and be away from here. Before they find us here.'

Kim stood there a moment longer, staring up at the old man. Then, letting his eyes fall, he nodded.

'Shih Karr! Please... stop a moment!'

Karr turned, prepared for trouble, then relaxed, seeing who it was. 'Ah, it's you, Marie Enge. How did you find me?'

She drew one hand back through her hair then smiled uncertainly. 'As I said, I know everyone in these levels. And you...' She looked him up and down admiringly. 'Well, who could overlook a man like you, Shih Karr?'

He laughed. 'That's true. But what can I do for you?'

'The thing you were talking of...'

'The boy,' he said quietly, leaning towards her. 'You know where he is?'

She hesitated, but he pre-empted her.

'Look. I've a private room. We can talk more easily there, if you wish.'

She nodded and let herself be led through to his room on the second level of the travellers' hostel. As such places went it was a clean, respectably furnished room, but it was a 'transient' all the same and, looking at him, she could not help but think he looked out of place there. She had seen at once, back in the Dragon Cloud, how his brutish exterior concealed a cultured manner.

He offered her the only chair then set himself down on the edge of the bed, facing her. 'Well? What do you know?'

She looked away momentarily, thinking of Tuan Ti Fo. Was she doing the right thing in coming to see Karr? Or was this all a mistake? She looked back. 'I've heard something. Nothing definite, but...'

She saw how Karr narrowed his eyes. Saw him look down then look back at her, some small change having taken place in his face.

'Can I trust you, Marie Enge?'

The strange openness of his deeply blue eyes took her by surprise. Some quality that had previously been hidden now shone through them. She stared back at him, matching his openness with her own.

'I'm honest, if that's what you mean, *Shih* Karr. And I can keep a secret if I'm asked. That is, if it's someone I trust.'

He lifted his chin slightly. 'Ah... I understand. You're thinking, Can I trust *Shih* Karr? Well, let's see what we can do about that. First I'll take a chance on you. And then, if you still want to help me, maybe you'll trust me, neh?'

She studied him a moment then nodded.

'Good. Then first things first. My name is Karr, but I'm not *Shih* Karr.' He fished into his tunic pocket and took out his ID, handing it across to her. 'As you can see, I'm a major in the T'ang's Security forces and my friend, Chen, whom you met earlier, is a captain. The boy we're looking for is not my nephew but we still need to find him. Alive and unharmed.'

She looked up from the ID card then handed it across. 'Why do you need to find him? I don't understand. If he's just a boy...'

Karr slipped the card back and took out something else – a flat, matt black case – and handed that to her.

'That's a hologram of the boy. You can keep that. I've others. But that'll help you check he's the one we're looking for.'

She rested the case on her knee then pressed her palm on it briefly, the warmth of her flesh activating it. She studied the image a while then killed it, looking back at Karr.

'He's a strange-looking boy. Why are you interested in him?'

'Because he's the only survivor of a terrorist raid on one of the T'ang's installations. A very important scientific installation. The whole place was destroyed and all Kim's fellow workers killed.'

'Kim?'

'That's his name. But as I was saying—'

She reached out and touched his arm, stopping him. 'I don't follow you. You said "his fellow workers". But he's just a boy. What would he be doing on a scientific installation?'

Karr looked down at her hand then sat back slightly. 'Don't under-estimate him, Marie Enge. He may be just a boy, but he's also something of a genius. Or was, before the attack. And he might be the only surviving link we have to the Project. That's if he's still alive. And if we can get to him before the terrorists find out that he escaped.'

She was looking at him strangely. 'This is very important, then?'

Karr narrowed his eyes. 'You want payment for your help?'

'Did I say that?'

He winced slightly at the sharpness in her voice then bowed his head. 'I'm sorry. It's just...'

'It's all right, Major Karr. I understand. You must deal with some un-savoury types in the work you do.'

He smiled. 'Yes... But to answer you – I have the T'ang's own personal authority to find the boy. If I wanted to, I could tear this place apart to find him. But that's not my way. Besides, I want the boy unharmed. Who knows what he might do if he felt threatened.'

'I see...' She looked down, suddenly very still.

'Look,' he said, 'why don't we simplify this? Why don't you act as inter-mediary? It might be best if you and not one of us were to deal with the boy. He might find it easier to trust you.'

She looked back at him, grateful.

Karr smiled. 'Then you know where he is.'

She caught her breath, a strange little movement in her face betraying the fact that she thought she had been tricked by him. Then she nodded, looking up at him.

'Yes. At least, I think so.'

She watched him a moment longer, a lingering uncertainty in her face, then gave a small laugh. 'You mean it, then? You'll let me handle it?'

He nodded. 'I gave my word to you, didn't I? But take this.' He handed her a necklace. 'When you're ready, just press the stud on the neck. We'll trace it and come.'

Again the uncertainty returned to her face.

He smiled reassuringly. 'Trust me, Marie Enge. Please. We will do nothing until you call for us. I shall not even have you followed when you leave this room. But I'm relying on you, so don't let me down. Much depends on this.'

'All right.' She stood, slipping the necklace over her head. 'But what if he's afraid? What if he doesn't want to go back?'

Karr nodded then reached into his tunic pocket yet again. 'Give this to him. He'll understand.'

It was a pendant. A beautiful silver pendant. And inside, in the tiny, circular locket, was the picture of a woman. A beautiful, dark-haired woman. She snapped it closed then held it up, watching it turn, flashing, in the light.

She slipped the pendant into her apron pocket and turned to leave, but he called her back. 'By the way,' he said, 'how good are you at *wei chi*?'

She turned in the doorway and looked back at him, smiling. 'How good? Well, maybe I'll play you some time and let you find out for yourself, neh, Major Karr?'

Karr grinned. 'I'd like that, Marie Enge. I'd like that very much.'

She was standing there when the door opened. It was just after two in the morning and the corridors were empty. Tuan Ti Fo took one step towards her then stopped, seeing her there in the shadows.

'Marie...'

'I know,' she said quickly, seeing how he was dressed; how he was carrying his bedroll on his back. Behind him the boy looked out, wide-eyed, wondering what was going on.

He took a breath. 'Then you will understand why we must go. The boy is in great danger here.'

She nodded. 'I know that, too. There are men trying to kill him. They killed his friends.'

He narrowed his eyes, his voice a whisper. 'How do you know all this, Marie?'

'Inside,' she said, moving closer. 'Please, Tuan Ti Fo. I must talk with you.' When he hesitated, she reached out and touched his arm. 'Please, Master Tuan. For the boy's sake.'

They went inside. The boy had backed away. He was crouched against the back wall, his eyes going from Tuan Ti Fo to the newcomer, his body tensed.

'It's all right, Kim,' Tuan Ti Fo said, going across and kneeling next to him. 'She's a friend.' He half turned, looking back at Marie. 'This is Kim. Kim, this is Marie.'

She came across and stood there, shaking her head. 'You're the boy, all right, but it doesn't make sense.' She looked from him to Tuan Ti Fo. 'I was told he was a scientist, a genius, but...' She turned back. 'Well, he's just a boy. A frightened boy.'

Tuan Ti Fo's eyes had widened at her words. Now he laughed. 'A boy he may be, but *just* a boy he's certainly not. Do you know something, Marie? He beat me. In only his third game.'

'I don't understand you, Master Tuan. Beat you at what?'

'At the game. At *wei chi*. He's a natural.'

She stared at Tuan Ti Fo then looked back at the boy, new respect entering her expression. 'He *beat* you?' Her voice dropped to a whisper. 'Gods...'

'Yes...' Tuan Ti Fo chuckled. 'And by five stones, no less. Not just beaten, but humiliated.' He looked back at Kim and gave him a small bow. 'Which makes our friend here unofficial First Hand Supreme of all Chung Kuo, neh?'

She laughed; a small laugh of astonishment. 'No wonder they want him back.'

Tuan Ti Fo stiffened, his face hardening. 'They?'

Marie nodded, suddenly more sober. 'Li Yuan. The new T'ang. Kim was working for him.'

She explained.

Tuan Ti Fo sighed. 'I see... And you're certain of this?'

'I...' She hesitated, remembering her meeting with Karr, then nodded. 'Yes. But there's something I have to give the boy. They said it would mean something to him.'

She took the pendant from her pocket and crouched down, holding it out to the boy.

For a moment he seemed almost not to see the bright silver circle that lay in her palm. Then, growing wonder filling his eyes, he reached out and touched the hanging chain.

She placed it in his hand then moved back slightly, watching him.

Slowly the wonder faded, shading into puzzlement. Then, like cracks appearing in the wall of a dam, his face dissolved, a great flood of pain and hurt overwhelming him.

He cried out – a raw, gut-wrenching sound in that tiny room – then pressed the pendant to his cheek, his fingers trembling, his whole face ghastly now with loss.

'T'ai Cho,' he moaned, his voice broken, wavering. 'T'ai Cho... they killed T'ai Cho!'

CHUNG KUO

Chapter 63

NEW BLOOD

The statue stood at the centre of the Hall of Celestial Destinies in Nantes spaceport, the huge, bronze figures raised high above the executive-class travellers who bustled like ants about its base. Thrice life-size and magnificently detailed, the vast human figures seemed like giants from some golden age, captured in the holo-camera's trebled eye and cast in bronze.

'Kan Ying bows to Pan Chao after the Battle of Kazatin', read the description, the huge letters cut deep into the two-*ch'i*-thick base, the Mandarin translation given smaller underneath, as though to emphasize the point that the message was aimed at those who had been conquered in that great battle – the *Hung Mao*.

Michael Lever stopped and stared up at it. Kazatin was where the dream of Rome, of the great *Ta Ts'in* emperors, had failed. The defeat of Kan Ying – Domitian as he had been known by his own people – had let the Han into Europe. The rest was history.

'What do you make of it?' Kustow said into his ear. 'It looks like more of their crowing to me.'

Like Lever, Bryn Kustow was in his late twenties, a tall man with close-cropped blond hair. He wore the same sombre clothes as Lever, a wine-red *pau* that made them seem more like clerks than the heirs to great Companies. Facially the two men were very different, Kustow's face blunt and Lever's hawkish, but the similarity of dress and the starkness of their haircuts made them seem like brothers, or members of some strange cult. So, too, the third of them, Stevens, who stood to one side, looking back at the wall-length window and its view of the great circle of the spaceport's landing apron.

They were strangers here. Americans. Young men over here on their fathers' business. Or so their papers claimed. But there were other reasons for coming to City Europe. This was where things were happening just now. The pulsing heart of things. And they had come to feel that pulse. To find out if there was something they could learn from looking around.

Lever turned, smiling back at his best friend. 'They say Kan Ying was a good man, Bryn. A strong man and yet fair. Under him the lands of Ta Ts'in were fairly governed. Had his sons ruled, they say there would have been a golden age.'

Kustow nodded. 'A good man, yes, until the great Pan Chao arrived.'

The two men laughed quietly then looked back at the statue.

Kan Ying knelt before Pan Chao, his back bent, his forehead pressed into the bare earth. He was unarmed, while Pan Chao stood above him, legs apart, his great sword raised in triumph, two daggers in his belt. Behind Kan Ying stood his four generals, their arms and insignia stripped from them, their faces gashed, their beards ragged from battle. There was honour in the way they held themselves, but also defeat. Their armies had been slaughtered on the battlefield by the superior Han forces. They looked tired, and the great, empty coffin they carried between them looked too much for their wasted strength to bear.

Neither would it grow any lighter. For, so the story went, Pan Chao had decapitated Kan Ying there and then and sent his body back to Rome where it had lain out in the open in the great square, slowly rotting, waiting for the young Emperor Ho Ti's triumphal entry into the city three years later.

Two thousand years ago. And still the Han crowed about it. Still they raised great statues to celebrate the moment when they had laid the Hung Mao low.

Lever turned. 'Carl! Bryn! Come on! We're meeting Ebert in an hour.'

Stevens turned, smiling, then hurried across. 'I was just watching one of the big interplanetary craft go up. They're amazing. You could feel the floor trembling beneath you as it turned on the power and climbed.'

Kustow laughed. 'So that's what it was... And there was I thinking it was the chow mein we had on the flight.'

Stevens smiled back at them then put his arms about their shoulders. He was the eldest of the three, an engineering graduate whose father owned a near-space research and development company. His fascination with anything to do with space and spaceflight bordered on obsession and he had been horrified when *The New Hope* had been blown out of the sky by the Seven. Something had died in him that day; and, at the same time, something had been born. Determination to get back what had been taken from them. To change the Edict and get out there, into space again, whatever it took.

'We'll be building them one day, I tell you,' he said softly. 'But bigger than that, and faster.'

Kustow frowned. 'Faster than that?' He shook his head. 'Well, if you say so, Carl. But I'm told some of those craft can make the Mars trip in forty days.'

Stevens nodded. 'The *Tientsin* can do it in thirty. Twenty-six at perihelion. But, yes, Bryn. Give me ten years and I'll make something that can do it in twenty.'

'And kill all the passengers! I can see it now. It's bad enough crossing the Atlantic on one of those things, but imagine the g-forces that would build up if you –'

'*Please...*' Lever interrupted, seeing how things were developing. 'Hans will be waiting for us. So let's get on.'

They went through to the main City Transfer barrier, ignoring the long queue of passengers formed up at the gates, going directly to the duty officer, a short, broad-shouldered man with neat black hair.

'Forgive me, Captain,' Lever began, 'but could you help us?' He took his documentation from his pocket and pushed it into the officer's hand. 'We've an appointment with Major Ebert at eleven and –'

The officer didn't even look at the card. 'Of course, *Shih* Lever. Would you mind following me? You and your two companions. There's a transporter waiting up above. Your baggage will be sent on.'

Lever gave a small nod of satisfaction. So Ebert had briefed his men properly. 'And the other two in our party?'

The officer smiled tightly. His information was not one hundred per cent perfect, then. 'They'll join you as quickly as possible.'

'Good.' Lever smiled. No, even Ebert hadn't known he was bringing two experts with him. Neither had he wanted him to know. In business – even in this kind of business – it was always best to keep your opponent wrong-footed, even when your opponent was your friend. To make him feel uncertain, uninformed. That way you kept the advantage.

'Then lead on,' he said. 'Let's not keep our host waiting.'

Stevens was the first to note it. He leaned across and touched Lever's arm. 'Michael... something's wrong.'

'What do you mean?'

Stevens leaned closer. 'Look outside, through the window. There are mountains down below. And the sun... it's to the left. We're heading south. At a guess I'd say we're over the Swiss Wilds.'

Lever sat up, staring outward, then turned, looking down the aisle of the transporter.

'Captain? Can you come here a moment?'

The Security officer broke off his conversation with his adjutant and came across, bowing respectfully.

'What is it, Shih Lever?'

Lever pointed out at the mountains. 'Where are we?'

The Captain smiled. 'You've noticed. I'm sorry, ch'un tzu, but I couldn't tell you before. My orders, you understand. However, Shih Stevens is right. We're heading south. And those below are the Swiss Wilds.' He reached into his tunic and withdrew a folded, handwritten note, handing it to Lever. 'Here, this will explain everything.'

Lever unfolded the note and read it quickly. It was from Ebert.

Lever smiled, his fingers tracing the wax seal at the foot of the note, then looked up again. 'And you, Captain? What's your role in this?'

The officer smiled then began to unbutton his tunic. He peeled it off and threw it to one side then sat facing the three Americans.

'Forgive the deception, my friends, but let me introduce myself. My name is Howard DeVore and I'm to be your host for the next eight hours.'

Lehmann sat at the back of the room, some distance from the others. A huge viewing screen filled the wall at the far end, while to one side, on a long, wide table made of real mahogany, a detailed map of City Europe was spread out, the Swiss Wilds and the Carpathians marked in red, like blood-stains on the white.

DeVore, Lever and the others sat in big leather chairs, drinks in hand, talking. Above them, on the screen, the funeral procession moved slowly through the walled northern garden at Tongjiang: the Li family; the seven T'ang; their generals; and their chief retainers. Thirty shaven-headed servants followed, the open casket held high above their heads.

DeVore raised his half-filled glass to indicate the slender, dark-haired figure in white who led the mourners.

'He carries his grief well. But, then, he must. It's a quality he'll need to cultivate in the days ahead.'

DeVore's smile was darkly ironic. Beside him, Lever laughed then leaned forward, cradling his empty glass between his hands. 'And look at our friend Hans. A study in solemnity, neh?'

Lehmann watched them laugh, his eyes drawn to the man who sat to the extreme right of the group. He was much older than Lever and his friends, his dark hair tied back in two long pigtails. There was a cold elegance about him that contrasted with the brashness of the others. He was a proud, even arrogant man; the way he sat, the way he held his head, expressed that eloquently. Even so, he was their servant, not they his, and that fact bridled his tongue and kept him from being too familiar with them.

His name was Andrew Curval and he was an experimental geneticist; perhaps the greatest of the age. As a young man he had worked for GenSyn as a commodity slave, his time and talents bought by them on a fifteen-year contract. Twelve years back that contract had expired and he had set up his own Company, but that venture had failed after only three years. Now he was back on contract; this time to Old Man Lever.

Lehmann looked back at the others. Kustow was talking, his deep voice providing a commentary on the proceedings. He was pointing up at Li Yuan, there at the centre of the screen.

'Look at him! He's such an innocent. He hasn't the faintest idea of how things really stand.'

'No,' Lever agreed. 'But that's true of all of them. They're cut off from the reality of what's happening in the Cities. There's real dissent down there, real bitterness, and the Seven simply don't know about it. They're like the emperors of old: they don't like bad news, so their servants make sure the truth never gets through to them. That's bad enough, but, as we all know, the system's corrupt to the core. From the pettiest official to the biggest Minister, there's not one of them you can't put a price to.'

The camera closed in. Li Yuan's face, many times its natural size, filled the screen. His fine, dark hair was drawn back tightly from his forehead, secured at the nape in a tiny porcelain bowl of purest white. His skin was unmarked, unlined; the flesh of youth, untouched by time or the ravages of experience.

Even so, he knows, Lehmann thought, looking up into the young T'ang's eyes. *He knows we murdered his father. Or, at least, suspects.*

Irritated by their arrogance, he stood then went across, filling Lever's glass from the wine kettle. 'I think you underestimate our man,' he said quietly. 'Look at those eyes. How like his father's eyes they are. Don't misjudge him. He's no fool, this one.' He turned, looking directly at DeVore. 'You've said so yourself often enough, Howard.'

'I agree,' said DeVore, eyeing Lehmann sharply. 'But there are things he lacks. Things the Seven miss now that Li Shai Tung is dead. Experience, wisdom, an intuitive sense of when and how to act. Those things are gone from them now. And without them...' He laughed softly. 'Without them the Seven are vulnerable.'

On the screen the image changed, the camera panning back, the figures diminishing as the larger context was revealed. A grey stone wall, taller than a man, surrounded everything. Beyond it the mountains of the Ta Pa Shan formed faint shapes in the distance. The tomb was to the left, embedded in the earth, the great white tablet stretching out towards its open mouth. To the right was the long pool, still, intensely black, its surface like a mirror. Between stood the seven T'ang and their retainers, all of them dressed in white, the colour of mourning.

'One bomb,' said Kustow, nodding to himself. 'Just one bomb and it would all be over, neh?' He turned in his seat, looking directly at DeVore. 'How do you come by these pictures? I thought these ceremonies were private?'

'They are,' DeVore said, taking a sip from his glass. He leaned forward, smiling, playing the perfect host, knowing how important it was for him to win these young men over. 'The camera is a standard Security surveillance device. They're all over Tongjiang. I've merely tapped into the system.'

All three of the Americans were watching DeVore closely now, ignoring what was happening on the screen.

'I thought those systems were discrete,' Lever said.

'They are.' DeVore set his drink down on the table at his side, then took a small device from his pocket and handed it across. 'This was something my friend Soren Berdichev developed at SimFic before they shut him down. It looks and functions like the back-up battery packs they have on those Security cameras, but there's more to it than that. What it does is to send a tight beam of information up to a satellite. There the signal is scrambled into code and re-routed here, where it's decoded.'

Lever studied the device then handed it to Kustow. He turned, look-ing back at DeVore. 'Astonishing. But how did you get it into place? I'm told those palaces are tighter than a young whore's arse when it comes to security.'

DeVore laughed. 'That's true. But whatever system you have, it always relies on men. Individual men. And men can be bought, or won, or simply threatened. It was relatively easy to get these installed.'

Lehmann, watching, saw how that impressed the young men, but it was only half-true. The device worked exactly as DeVore had said, but the truth was that he had access only to Tongjiang, and that only because Hans Ebert had been daring enough to take the thing in, risking the possibility that an over-zealous officer might search him, Tolonen's favourite or no. Elsewhere his attempts to plant the devices had failed.

They looked back at the screen. Li Yuan stood at the edge of the family tablet, the freshly inscribed name of his father cut into the whiteness there. Behind the young T'ang stood the rest of the Seven, and at their back the generals. Bringing up the rear of this small but powerful gathering stood members of the Li Family – cousins and uncles, wives, concubines and close relations – a hundred in all. The ranks were thin, the weakness of the Family exposed to view, and yet Li Yuan stood proudly, his eyes looking straight ahead into the darkness of the tomb.

'All the trappings of power,' said Kustow, shaking his head as if in dis-approval. 'Like the Pharaohs, they are. Obsessed with death.'

Lehmann studied Kustow a moment, noting the strange mixture of awe and antagonism in his blunt, almost rectangular face. *You admire this,* he thought. *Or envy it, rather. Because you too would like to create a dynasty and be buried in a cloth of gold.*

For himself, he hated it all. He would have done with kings and dynasties.

They watched as the casket was carried to the mouth of the tomb. Saw the six strongest carry it down the steps into the candlelit interior. And then the camera focused once more on Li Yuan.

'He's strong for one so young.'

They were the first words Curval had spoken since he had come into the room. Again Lehmann looked, admiring the manner of the man, his single-ness of being. In his face there was a hard, uncompromising certainty about things; in some strange way it reminded Lehmann of Berdichev. Or of how Berdichev had become, after his wife's death.

On the screen Li Yuan bowed to the tablet then turned, making his slow way to the tomb.

'He looks strong,' DeVore said after a moment, 'but there are things you don't know about him. That outward presence of his is a mask. Inside he's a writhing mass of unstable elements. Do you know that he killed all his wife's horses?'

All eyes were on DeVore, shocked by the news. To kill horses – it was unthinkable!

'Yes,' DeVore continued. 'In a fit of jealousy, so I understand. So, you see, beneath that calm exterior lies a highly unstable child. Not unlike his headstrong brother. And a coward, too.'

Lever narrowed his eyes. 'How so?'

'Fei Yen, his brother's wife, is heavily pregnant. Rumour has it that it is not his child. The woman has been sent home to her father in disgrace. And they say he knows whose bastard it is. Knows and does nothing.'

'I see,' Lever said. 'But that doesn't necessarily make the man a coward.'

DeVore gave a short laugh. 'If you were married you would understand it better, Michael. A man's wife, his child, these things are more than the world to him. He would kill for them. Even a relatively passive man. But Li Yuan holds back, does nothing. That, surely, is cowardice?'

'Or a kind of wisdom?' Lever looked back up at the screen, watching the young T'ang step down into the darkness. 'Forgive me, *Shih* DeVore, but I feel your friend here is right. It would not do to underestimate Li Yuan.'

'No?' DeVore shrugged.

'Even so,' Lever said, smiling, 'I take your point. The Seven have never been weaker than they are right now. And their average age has never been younger. Why, we're old men by comparison to most of them!'

There was laughter at that.

DeVore studied the three Americans, pleased by Lever's unconscious echo of his thoughts. It was time.

He raised his hand. At the prearranged signal the screen went dark and a beam of light shone out from above, spotlighting the table and the map on the far side of the room.

'Ch'un tzu...' DeVore said, rising to his feet, one arm extended, indicating the table. 'You've seen how things stand with the Seven. How things are now. Well, let us talk of how things might be.'

Lever stood, studying DeVore a moment, as if to weigh him, then smiled and nodded. 'All right, Shih DeVore. Lead the way. We're all ears.'

Back inside, Li Yuan drew Wang Sau-leyan aside.

'Cousin Wang,' he said softly. 'May I speak to you in private? News has come.'

Wang Sau-leyan stared back at him, faintly hostile. 'News, cousin?'

Li Yuan turned slightly to one side, indicating the door to a nearby room. Wang hesitated, then nodded and went through. Inside, Li Yuan pulled the doors closed then turned, facing his fellow T'ang.

'Your grain ships...' he began, watching Wang Sau-leyan's face closely.

'Yes?' Wang's expression was mildly curious.

'I'm afraid your ships are at the bottom of the ocean, cousin. An hour back. It seems someone blew them up.'

Wang's expression of angry surprise was almost comical. He shook his head as if speechless then, unexpectedly, he reached out and held Li Yuan's arm. 'Are you certain, Li Yuan?'

Li Yuan nodded, looking down at the plump, bejewelled hand that rested on the rough cloth of his sleeve. 'It's true. Your Chancellor, Hung Mien-lo, has confirmed it.'

Wang Sau-leyan let his hand fall. He turned his head away then looked back at Li Yuan, a strange hurt in his eyes.

'I am so sorry, Li Yuan. So very sorry. The grain was my gift to your father.

My final gift to him.' He shook his head, pained. 'Oh, I can spare more grain – and, indeed, you will have it, cousin – but that's not the point, is it? Someone destroyed my gift! My gift to your father!'

Li Yuan's lips parted slightly in surprise. He had not expected Wang to be so upset, so patently indignant. Neither had he for one moment expected Wang to offer another shipment. No, he had thought this all some kind of clever ruse, some way of shirking his verbal obligation. He frowned then shook his head, confused.

'Your offer is very generous, cousin, but you are in no way to blame for what has happened. Indeed, I understand that the Ping Tiao have claimed responsibility for the act.'

'The Ping Tiao!' Again there was a flash of anger in Wang's face that took Li Yuan by surprise. 'Then the Ping Tiao will pay for their insult!'

'Cousin...' Li Yuan said softly, taking a step closer. 'The matter is being dealt with, I assure you. The insult will not be allowed to pass.'

Wang gave a terse nod. 'Thank you, cousin. I–'

There was a loud knocking on the door. Li Yuan half turned then looked back at Wang. 'You wished to say...?

A faint smile crossed Wang's features. 'Nothing, cousin. But again, thank you for telling me. I shall instruct my Chancellor to send a new ship-ment at once.'

Li Yuan lowered his head. 'I am most grateful.'

Wang smiled and returned the bow to the precise degree – tacitly acknowledging their equality of status – then moved past Li Yuan, pulling the door open.

Hans Ebert stood outside, in full dress uniform, his equerry three paces behind him. Seeing Wang Sau-leyan, he bowed low.

'Forgive me, Chieh Hsia. I didn't realize...'

Wang Sau-leyan smiled tightly. 'It is all right, Major Ebert. You may go in. Your master and I have finished now.'

Ebert turned then, taking a deep breath, stepped into the doorway, present-ing himself.

'Chieh Hsia?'

Li Yuan was standing on the far side of the room, beside the ceremonial *kang*, one foot up on the ledge of it, his right hand stroking his unbearded chin. He looked across then waved Ebert in almost casually.

Ebert marched to the centre of the room and came smartly to attention, lowering his head respectfully, waiting for his T'ang to speak.

Li Yuan sighed then launched into things without preamble. 'These are troubled times, Hans. The old bonds must be forged stronger than ever, the tree of State made firm against the storm to come, from root to branch.'

Ebert raised his head. 'And my role in this, *Chieh Hsia*?'

Li Yuan looked down. 'Let me explain. Shortly before his death, my father went to see General Nocenzi in hospital. As you may have heard, he accepted Nocenzi's resignation. There was no other choice. But who was to be general in his place?' He paused significantly. 'Well, it was my father's intention to ask Marshal Tolonen to step down from his post of seniority to be general again, and he drafted a memorandum to that effect. There were good reasons for his decision, not least of which was the stability that the old man's presence would bring to the Security forces. He also felt that to bring in a *lao wai* – an outsider – might cause some resentment. Besides which, it takes some time for a new general to adapt to his command, and time was something we did not have.'

Li Yuan turned away, silent a moment, then looked back at him. 'Don't you agree, Hans?'

Ebert bowed his head. 'It is so, *Chieh Hsia*. Moreover, there is no one in all Chung Kuo with more experience than the Marshal. Indeed, I can think of nobody your enemies would welcome less in the post.'

He saw Li Yuan smile, pleased by his words. Even so, his sense of disappointment was acute. After what Tolonen had said to him earlier he had hoped for the appointment himself.

Li Yuan nodded then spoke again. 'However, my father's death changes many things. Our enemies will think us weak just now. Will think me callow, inexperienced. We need to demonstrate how wrong they are. Tolonen's appointment as General would certainly help in that regard, but I must also show them that I am my own man, not merely my father's shadow. You understand me, Hans?'

'I understand, *Chieh Hsia*.'

Only too well.

'Yes...' Li Yuan nodded thoughtfully. 'In that we are alike, neh, Hans?

We know what it is to have to wait. To be our fathers' hands. Yet in time we must become them, and more, if we are to gain the respect of the world.'

'It is so,' Ebert said quietly.

'Besides which,' Li Yuan continued, 'things are certain to get worse before they get better. In consequence we must grow harder, more ruthless than we were in the days of ease. In that, Wang Sau-leyan is right. It is a new age. Things have changed, and we must change with them. The days of softness are past.'

Ebert watched Li Yuan's face as he spoke the words and felt genuine admiration for the young T'ang. Li Yuan was much harder, much more a pragmatist than his father – his ideas about the Wiring Project were proof of that.

But Ebert was too far along his own road now to let that colour his think-ing; too deeply committed to his own dream of inheritance.

One day he would have to kill this man, admire him or not. It was that or see his own dream die.

'Trust,' Li Yuan said. 'Trust is the cornerstone of the State. In that, as in many things, my father was right. But in an age of violent change who should the wise man trust? Who *can* he trust?' He looked back at Ebert, narrowing his eyes. 'I'm sorry, Hans. It's just that I must talk this through. You understand?'

Ebert bowed his head. 'I am honoured that you feel you can talk so freely in my presence, *Chieh Hsia*.'

Li Yuan laughed then grew serious again. 'Yes, well... I suppose it is because I consider you almost family, Hans. Your father had been chief amongst my father's counsellors since Shepherd's illness and will remain among my council of advisors. However, it is not about your father that I summoned you today, it is about you.'

Ebert raised his head. '*Chieh Hsia*?'

'Yes, Hans. Haven't you guessed, or have I been too indirect? I want you for my general – my most trusted man. I want you to serve me as Tolonen served my father. To be my sword arm and my scourge, the bane of my enemies and the defender of my children.'

Ebert's mouth had fallen open. 'But, *Chieh Hsia*, I thought–'

'Oh, Tolonen is appointed temporarily. As caretaker general. He agreed an hour past. But it is you I want to stand behind me at my coronation three days from now. You who will receive the ceremonial dagger that morning.'

Ebert stared at him, open-mouthed, then fell to his knees, bowing his head low. 'Chieh Hsia, you do me a great honour. My life is yours to command.'

He had rehearsed the words earlier, yet his surprise at Li Yuan's sudden reversal gave them force. When he glanced up, he could see the pleasure in the young T'ang's face.

'Stand up, Hans. Please.'

Ebert got to his feet slowly, keeping his head bowed.

Li Yuan came closer. 'It might surprise you, Hans, but I have been watching you for some time now. Seeing how well you dealt with your new responsibilities. It did not escape my notice how loyal your officers were to you. As for your courage...' He reached out and touched the metal plate on the back of Ebert's head then moved back again. 'Most important of all, though, you have considerable influence among the elite of First Level. An important quality in a general.'

Li Yuan smiled broadly. 'Your appointment will be posted throughout the levels tonight at twelfth bell. But before then I want you to prepare a plan of action for me.'

'A plan, Chieh Hsia?'

Li Yuan nodded. 'A plan to eradicate the Ping Tiao. To finish off what my father began. I want every last one of them dead, a month from now. Dead, and their bodies laid out before me.'

Ebert stood there, his mouth fallen open again. Then he bowed his head. For a moment he had almost laughed. Eradicate the Ping Tiao? Little did Li Yuan know. It was done already! And done by Li Yuan's chief enemy, DeVore!

Li Yuan touched his shoulder. 'Well... go now, Hans. Go and tell your father. I know he will be proud. It was what he always wanted.'

Ebert smiled then bowed his head again, surprised by the pride he felt. To be this man's servant – what was there to be proud of in that? And yet, strangely enough, he was. He turned, making to leave, but Li Yuan called him back.

'Oh, and, Hans... we found the boy.'

Ebert turned back, his stomach tightening. 'That's excellent, Chieh Hsia. How was he?'

Li Yuan smiled. 'It could not have been better, Hans. He remembered everything. Everything...'

*

DeVore took his eye from the lens of the electron-microscope and looked across at the geneticist, smiling, impressed by what he'd seen.

'It's clever, *Shih* Curval. Very clever indeed. And does it always behave like that, no matter the host?'

Curval hesitated a moment then turned back, reaching across DeVore to take the sealed slide from the microscope, handling it with extreme delicacy. As indeed he ought, for the virus it contained was deadly. He looked back at DeVore.

'If the host has had the normal course of immunization then, yes, it should follow near enough the same evolutionary pattern. There will be slight statistical variations, naturally, but such "sports" will be small in number. For all intents and purposes you could guarantee a one hundred per cent success rate.'

DeVore nodded thoughtfully. 'Interesting. So, in effect, what we have here is a bug that evolves. That's harmless when it's first passed on but which, in only a hundred generations, evolves into a deadly virus. A brain-killer.' He laughed. 'And what's a hundred generations in the life of a bug?'

For the first time, Curval laughed. 'Exactly...'

DeVore moved back, letting the scientist past, his mind reeling with an almost aesthetic delight at the beauty of the thing. 'Moreover, the very thing that triggers this evolutionary pattern is that which is normally guaranteed to defend the body against disease – the immunization programme!'

'Exactly. The very thing that every First Level child has pumped into their system as a six-month foetus.'

DeVore watched him place the sealed slide back into the padded, shock-safe case and draw another out.

'Come... here's another. Slightly different this time. Same principle, but more specific.'

DeVore leaned forward, fascinated. 'What do you mean, more specific?'

Curval slipped the slide into the slot then stood back. 'Just watch. I'll trigger it when you're ready.'

He put his eye to the lens. Again he saw the thing divide and grow and change, like the ever-evolving pattern in a kaleidoscope, but this thing was real, *alive* – as alive as only a thing whose sole purpose was to kill could be.

DeVore looked up. 'It looks the same.'

Curval looked at him closely. 'You noticed no difference, then?'

DeVore smiled. 'Well, there were one or two small things, midway through. There was a brief stage when the thing seemed a lot bigger than before. And afterwards there was a slight colour change. Then it normalized. Was the same as before.'

Curval laughed. 'Good. So you did see.'

'Yes, but what did I see?'

Curval took out the slide – it seemed not as carefully as before – and set it down on the table beside him.

'This...' he tapped it almost carelessly '...is as harmless to you or me as spring water. We could take in a huge dose of it and it wouldn't harm us one tiny little bit. But to a Han...'

DeVore's eyes widened.

Curval nodded. 'That's right. What you saw was the virus priming itself genetically, like a tiny bacteriological time-bomb, making itself racially specific.'

DeVore laughed then reached across to pick it up. The slide seemed empty, yet its contents could do untold damage. Not to him or his kind, but to the Han. He smiled broadly. 'Wonderful! That's wonderful!'

Curval laughed. 'I thought you'd like it. You know, I had you in mind constantly while I was making it. I would sit there late nights and laugh, imagining your reaction.'

DeVore looked at him a moment then nodded. The two had known each other more than twenty years, ever since their first fateful meeting at one of Old Man Ebert's parties. Curval had been restless even then – wanting to break out on his own, burdened by the remaining years of his contract. It had been DeVore who had befriended him. DeVore who had found him his first, important contacts in City America. DeVore who had shown him the top-security files detailing the deals Klaus Ebert had struck with various Companies to destroy Curval's own enterprise. DeVore who had arranged the deal whereby he worked for the Levers and yet had his own private laboratories.

And now Curval was returning the favour. With only one string attached. A minor thing. DeVore could have the virus, but first he must promise to kill Old Man Ebert.

He had agreed.

'Does Michael know about this?'

Curval smiled. 'What do you think? Michael Lever is a nice young man, for all his revolutionary fervour. He wants to change things – but fairly. He'll fight if he must, but he won't cheat. He'd kill me if he knew I'd made something like this.'

DeVore considered that a while then nodded. 'You're sure of that?'

Curval laughed sourly. 'I know that young man too well. He seems different, but underneath it all he's the same as the rest of them. They've had it too easy, all of them. What fires them isn't ambition but a sense of bitterness. Bitterness that their fathers still treat them as children. For all they were saying back there in the screen-room, they don't want change. Not real change, like you and I want. When they talk of change, what they mean is a change of leadership. They'd as soon relinquish their privileges as the Seven.'

'Maybe,' DeVore said, watching Curval pack up the microscope. 'By the way, has the virus a name?'

Curval clicked the case shut and turned, looking back at DeVore. 'Yes, as a matter of fact it does. I've named it after the viral strain I developed it from. That too was a killer, though not as lethal or efficient as mine. And it was around for centuries before people managed to find a cure for it. Syphilis they called it. What the Han call *yang mei ping*, "willow plum sickness".'

DeVore laughed, surprised. 'So it's sexually transmitted?'

Curval stared at DeVore then laughed quietly. 'Of course! I thought you understood that. It's the only way to guarantee that it will spread, and spread widely. Fucking... it's the thing the human race does most of and says least about. And when you consider it, it's the perfect way of introducing a new virus. After all, they're all supposed to be immune to sexual disease. From birth.'

DeVore touched his tongue against his top teeth then nodded. Errant husbands and their unfaithful wives, bored concubines and their casual lovers, lecherous old men and randy widows, sing-song girls and libertine young sons – he could see it now, spreading like the leaves and branches of a great tree, until the tree itself rotted and fell. He laughed then slapped Curval on the back.

'You've done well, Andrew. Very well.'

Curval looked at him. 'And you, Howard? You'll keep your promise?'

DeVore squeezed his shoulder. 'Of course. Have I ever let you down? But come, let's go through. Our young friends will be wondering why we've been gone so long. Besides, I understand our friend Kustow has brought his *wei chi* champion with him and I fancied trying myself out against him.'

Curval nodded. 'He's good. I've seen him play.'

DeVore met his eyes. 'As good as me?'

Curval turned and took the tiny, deadly slide from off the table. 'They say he might even challenge for the championship next year.'

DeVore laughed. 'Maybe so, but you still haven't answered me. You've seen me play. Would you say he's as good as me?'

Curval slotted the slide back into the case and secured the lid, then looked back at DeVore, hesitant, not certain how he'd take the truth.

'To be honest with you, Howard, yes. Every bit as good. And maybe a lot better.'

DeVore turned away, pacing the tiny room, lost in his own thoughts. Then he turned back, facing Curval again, a smile lighting his face.

'Our friend Kustow... do you know if he likes to gamble?'

DeVore looked up from the board then bowed to his opponent, conceding the game. It was the fifth the two had played and the closest yet. This time he had come within a stone of beating the Han. Even so, the result of the tournament was conclusive: Kustow's champion had triumphed five–nil, two of those games having been won by a margin of more than twenty stones.

'Another five?' Kustow said, smiling. He had done well by the contest – DeVore had wagered five thousand *yuan* on each game and a further ten thousand on the tournament.

DeVore looked back at him, acknowledging his victory. 'I wish there was time, my friend, but you must be at the Ebert Mansion by nine and it's six already. I'll tell you what, though. When I come to America, I'll play your man again. It will give me the opportunity to win my money back.'

Lever leaned forward in his chair. 'You plan to come to America, then, *Shih* DeVore? Wouldn't that be rather dangerous for you?'

DeVore smiled. 'Life *is* dangerous, Michael. And while it pays to take care, where would any of us be if we did not take risks?'

Lever looked to his two friends. 'True. But one must choose one's friends well in these uncertain times.'

DeVore bowed his head slightly, understanding what was implied. They were inclined to work with him, but had yet to commit themselves fully. He would need to give them further reasons for allying with him. 'And one's lieutenants. My man Mach, for instance. He served me well in the attack on the T'ang's Plantations.'

Lever gave a laugh of surprise. 'That was you? But I thought...'

'You thought as everyone was meant to think. That it was the *Ping Tiao*. But, no, they were my men.'

'I see. But why? Why not claim credit for yourself?'

'Because sometimes it suits one's purpose to make one's enemies believe the truth is other than it is. You see, the *Ping Tiao* is now defunct. I destroyed the last vestiges of that organization two days back. Yet as far as the Seven are concerned, it still exists – still poses a threat to them. Indeed, the new T'ang, Li Yuan, plans to launch a major campaign against them. He has given instructions to his new General to use whatever force it takes to destroy them, and at whatever cost. Such a diversion of funds and energies is to be welcomed, wouldn't you say?'

Lever laughed. 'Yes! And at the same time it draws attention away from your activities here in the Wilds. I like that.'

DeVore nodded, pleased. Here were young men with fire in them. They were not like their European counterparts. Their anger was pure. It had only to be channelled.

He stood and, with one final bow to his opponent, came round the table, facing the three young men.

'There's one more thing before you go from here. Something I want to give you.'

Lever looked at his friends then lowered his head. 'We thank you, *Shih* DeVore, but your hospitality has been reward enough.'

DeVore understood. Lever was accustomed to the use of gifts in business to create obligations. It was a trick the Han used a great deal. He shook his head. 'Please, my friends, do not mistake me – this gift carries no obligation. Indeed, I would feel greatly offended if you took it otherwise. I am no trader. I would not dream of seeking any material advantage from our meeting. Let this be a simple token of our friendship, neh?'

He looked at each of them, at Lever, Kustow and finally at Stevens, seeing how each had been won by the simplicity of his manner.

'Good. Then wait here. I have it in the other room.'

He left them, returning a moment later with a bulky, rectangular parcel wrapped in red silk.

'Here,' he said, handing it to Lever. 'You are to open it later – on the flight to Ebert's if you must, but later. And whatever you finally decide to do with it, bear in mind that great sacrifices have been made to bring this to you. Let no one see it whom you do not trust like a brother.'

Lever stared at the parcel a moment, his eyes burning with curiosity, then looked up again, smiling.

'I've no idea what this is, but I'll do as you say. And thank you, Howard. Thank you for everything. You must be our guest when you come to America.'

DeVore smiled. 'That's kind of you, Michael. Very kind indeed.'

'Well, Stefan, what do you think?'

Lehmann stood there a moment longer at the one-way mirror then turned back, looking at DeVore. He had witnessed everything.

'The contest... You lost it deliberately, didn't you?'

DeVore smiled, pleased that Lehmann had seen it.

'I could have beaten him. Not at first maybe, but from the third game on. There's a pattern to his game. So with these Americans. There's a pattern to their thinking and I feel as if I'm beginning to discern it. Which is why I have to go there myself. Europe is dead as far as we're concerned. We've milked it dry. If we want to complete the fortresses, we've got to get funds from the Americans. We've got to persuade them to invest in us – to make them see us as the means by which they can topple the Seven.'

'And Curval? You promised him you'd kill Old Man Ebert. Is that wise?'

DeVore laughed. 'If the gods will it that the old man dies in the next six months, he will die, and I will claim the credit. But I shall do nothing to aid them. I have no great love for Klaus Ebert – I think he's a pompous old windbag, to tell the truth – but he is Hans's father. Kill him and we risk all. No, we will leave such things to fate. And if Curval objects...' He laughed. 'Well, we can deal with that as and when, neh? As and when.'

CHUNG KUO

Chapter 64

MIRRORS

It was night. Li Yuan stood there on the bridge, staring down into the lake, watching the full moon dance upon the blackness. Tongjiang was quiet now, the guests departed. Guards stood off at a distance, perfectly still, like statues in the silvered darkness.

It had been a long and busy day. He had been up at four, supervising the final arrangements for his father's funeral, greeting the mourners as they arrived. The ceremony had taken up the best part of the morning, followed by an informal meeting of the Seven. Interviews with ministers and various high officials had eaten up the rest of the afternoon as he began the task of tying up the loose strands of his father's business and making preparations for his own coronation ceremony three days hence.

And other things. So many other things.

He felt exhausted, yet there was still more to do before he retired.

He turned, looking back at the palace, thinking how vast and desolate it seemed without his father's presence. There was only him now – only Li Yuan, second son of Li Shai Tung. The last of his line. The last of the house of Li.

A faint wind stirred the reeds at the lake's edge. He looked up, that same feeling of exposure – that cold, almost physical sense of isolation – washing over him again. Where were the brothers, the cousins he should have had? Dead, or never born. And now there was only him.

A thin wisp of cloud lay like a veil across the moon's bright face. In the distance a solitary goose crossed the sky, the steady beat of its wings carrying to where he stood.

He shivered. Today he had pretended to be strong, had made his face thick, like a wall against his inner feelings. And so it had to be, from this time on, for he was T'ang now, his life no longer his own. All day he had been surrounded by people – countless people, bowing low before him and doing as he bid – and yet he had never felt so lonely.

No, never in his life had he felt so desolate, so empty.

He gritted his teeth, fighting back what he felt. Be strong, he told himself. Harden yourself against what is inside you. He took a deep breath, looking out across the lake. His father had been right. Love was not enough. Without trust – without those other qualities that made of love a solid and substantial thing – love was a cancer, eating away at a man, leaving him weak.

And he could not be weak, for he was T'ang now, Seven. He must put all human weakness behind him. Must mould himself into a harder form.

He turned away, making his way quickly down the path towards the palace.

At the door to his father's rooms he stopped, loath to go inside. He looked down at the ring that rested, heavy and unfamiliar, on the middle finger of his right hand, and realized that nothing could have prepared him for this. His father's death and the ritual of burial had been momentous occasions, yet neither had been quite as real as this simpler, private moment.

How often had he come in from the garden and found his father sitting there at his desk, his secretaries and ministers in attendance? How often had the old man looked up and seen him, there where he now stood, and, with a faint, stern smile, beckoned him inside?

And now there was no one to grant him such permission. No one but himself.

Why, then, was it so difficult to take that first small step into the room? Why did he feel an almost naked fear at the thought of sitting at the desk – of looking back at where he was now standing?

Perhaps because he knew the doorway would be empty.

Angry with himself, he took a step into the room, his heart hammering in his chest as if he were a thief. He laughed uncomfortably then looked about him, seeing it all anew.

It was a long, low-ceilinged room, furnished in the traditional manner, his father's desk, its huge scrolled legs shaped like dragons, raised up on a massive plinth at the far end of the chamber, a low, gold-painted balustrade surrounding it, like a room within a room, the great symbol of the *Ywe Lung* set into the wall behind. Unlike his own, it was a distinctly masculine room, no hanging bowls, no rounded pots filled with exotic plants breaking up its rich Yang heaviness; indeed, there was not a single trace of greenery, only vases and screens and ancient wall hangings made of silk and golden thread.

He moved further in, stopping beside a huge bronze cauldron. It was empty now, but he recalled when it had once contained a thousand tiny objects carved from jade; remembered a day when he had played there on his father's floor, the brightly coloured pieces – exquisite miniatures in blue and red and green – scattered all about him. He had been four then, five at most, but he could still see them vividly; could feel the cool, smooth touch of them between his fingers.

He turned. On the wall to his right was a mirror; an ancient, metallic mirror of the T'ang dynasty, its surface filled with figures and lettering, arrayed in a series of concentric circles emanating outwards from the central button. Li Yuan moved closer, studying it. The button – a simple unadorned circle – represented the indivisibility of all created things. Surrounding it were the animals of the Four Quadrants: the Tiger, symbol of the west and of magisterial dignity, courage and martial prowess; the Phoenix, symbol of the south and of beauty, peace and prosperity; the Dragon, symbol of the east, of fertility and male vigour; and the Tortoise, symbol of the north, of longevity, strength and endurance. Beyond these four were the Eight Trigrams and surrounding those the Twelve Terrestrial Branches of the zodiac – rat, ox and tiger, hare, dragon and serpent, horse, goat and monkey, cock, dog and boar. A band of twenty-four pictograms separated that from the next circle of animals – twenty-eight in all – representing the constellations.

He looked past the figures a moment, seeing his face reflected back at him through the symbols and archetypes of the Han universe. Such a mirror was *hu-hsin ching* and was said to have magic powers, protecting its owner from evil. It was also said that one might see the secrets of futurity in such a mirror. But he had little faith in what men said. Why, he could barely see his own face, let alone the face of the future.

He turned his head away, suddenly bitter. Mirrors: they were said to symbolize conjugal happiness, but his own was broken now, the pieces scattered.

He went across to the desk. Nan Ho had been in earlier to prepare it for him. His father's things had been cleared away and his own set in their place: his ink block and brushes; his sandbox and the tiny statue of Kuan Ti, the God of War, which his brother, Han Ch'in, had given him on his eighth birthday. Beside those were a small pile of folders and one large, heavy-bound book, its thick spine made of red silk decorated with a cloud pattern of gold leaf.

Mounting the three small steps, he stood there, his hands resting on the low balustrade, his head almost brushing the ceiling, looking across at the big, tall-backed chair. The great wheel of seven dragons – the *Ywe Lung* or Moon Dragon – had been burned into the back of the chair, black against the ochre of the leather, mirroring the much larger symbol on the wall behind. This chair had been his father's and his father's father's before that, back to his great-great-great-grandfather in the time of Tsao Ch'un.

And now it was his.

Undoing the tiny catch, he pushed back the gate and entered this tiny room-within-a-room, conscious of how strange even that simple action felt. He looked about him again then lowered himself into the chair. Sitting there, looking out into the ancient room, he could feel his ancestors gathered close: there in the simple continuity of place, but there also in each small movement that he made. They lived, within him. He was their seed. He understood that now. Had known it even as they had placed the lid on his father's casket.

He reached across and drew the first of the folders from the pile. Inside was a single sheet, from Klaus Ebert at GenSyn: a document relinquishing thirteen patents granted in respect of special food production techniques. Before his father's death, Ebert had offered to release the patents to his competitors to help increase food production in City Europe. They were worth an estimated two hundred and fifty million *yuan* on the open market, but Ebert had given them freely, as a gift to his T'ang.

Li Yuan drew the file closer then reached across and took his brush, signing his name at the bottom of the document.

He set the file aside and took another from the pile. It was the summary of the post-mortem report he had commissioned on his father. He read it through then signed it and set it atop the other. Nothing. They had found nothing. According to the doctors, his father had died of old age. Old age and a broken heart.

Nonsense, he thought. Utter nonsense.

He huffed out his impatience and reached across for the third file, opening it almost distractedly. Then, seeing what it was, he sat back, his mouth gone dry, his heart beating furiously. It was the result of the genotyping test he had had done on Fei Yen and her child.

He closed his eyes in pain, his breathing suddenly erratic. So now he would know. Know for good and certain who the father was. Know to whom he owed the pain and bitterness of the last few months.

He leaned forward again. It was no good delaying. No good putting off what was inevitable. He drew the file closer, forcing himself to read it, each word seeming to cut and wound him. And then it was done.

He pushed the file away and sat back. So...

For a moment he was still, silent, considering his options, then reached across, touching the summons bell.

Almost at once the door to his right swung back. Nan Ho, his Master of the Inner Chamber, stood there, his head bowed low.

'Chieh Hsia?'

'Bring ch'a, Master Nan. I need to talk.'

Nan Ho bobbed his head. 'Should I send for your Chancellor, Chieh Hsia?'

'No, Master Nan, it is you I wish to speak with.'

'As you wish, Chieh Hsia.'

When he had gone, Li Yuan leaned across and drew the large, heavy-bound book towards him. A stylized dragon and phoenix – their figures drawn in gold – were inset into the bright red silk of the cover. Inside, on the opening page, was a handwritten quotation from the Li Chi, the ancient Book of Rites, the passage in the original Mandarin.

The point of marriage is to create a union between two persons of
different families, the object of which is to serve, first, the ancestors
in the temple, and, second, the generation to come.

He shivered. So it was. So it had always been amongst his kind. Yet he had thought it possible to marry for love. In so doing he had betrayed his kind. Had tried to be what he was not. For he was Han. Han to the very core of him. He recognized that now.

But it was not too late. He could begin again. Become what he had failed to be. A good Han, leaving all ghosts of other selves behind.

He flicked through the pages desultorily, barely seeing the faces that looked up at him from the pages. Here were a hundred of the most eligible young women, selected from the Twenty-Nine, the Minor Families. Each one was somewhat different from the rest, had some particular quality to recommend her, yet it was all much the same to him. One thing alone was important now – to marry and have sons. To make the family strong again, and fill the emptiness surrounding him.

For anything was better than to feel like this. Anything.

He closed the book and pushed it away, then sat back in the chair, closing his eyes. He had barely done so when there was a tapping on the door.

'Chieh Hsia?'

'Come!' he said, sitting forward again, the tiredness like salt in his blood, weighing him down.

Nan Ho entered first, his head bowed, the tray held out before him. Behind him came the She t'ou – the 'tongue', or taster. Li Yuan watched almost listlessly as Nan Ho set the ch'a things down on a low table then poured, offering the first bowl to the She t'ou.

The man sipped then offered the bowl back, bowing gracefully, a small smile of satisfaction crossing his lips. He waited a minute then turned to Li Yuan and bowed low, kneeling, touching his head against the floor before he backed away.

Nan Ho followed him to the door, closing it after him, then turned, facing Li Yuan.

'Shall I bring your ch'a up to you, Chieh Hsia?'

Li Yuan smiled. 'No, Nan Ho. I will join you down there.' He stood, yawning, stretching the tiredness from his bones, then leaned forward, picking up the heavy-bound volume.

'Here,' he said, handing it to Nan Ho, ignoring the offered bowl.

Nan Ho set the bowl down hastily and took the book from his T'ang. 'You have decided, then, Chieh Hsia?'

Li Yuan stared at Nan Ho a moment, wondering how much he knew

– whether he had dared look at the genotyping – then, dismissing the thought, he smiled.

'No, Master Nan. I have not decided. But you will.'

Nan Ho looked back at him, horrified. '*Chieh Hsia?*'

'You heard me, Master Nan. I want you to choose for me. Three wives I need. Good, strong, reliable women. The kind that bear sons. Lots of sons. Enough to fill the rooms of this huge, empty palace.'

Nan Ho bowed low, his face a picture of misery. 'But, *Chieh Hsia*... It is not my place to do such a thing. Such responsibility...' He made to shake his head then fell to his knees, his head pressed to the floor. 'I beg you, *Chieh Hsia*. I am unworthy for such a task.'

Li Yuan laughed. 'Nonsense, Master Nan. If anyone, you are the very best of men to undertake such a task for me. Did you not bring Pearl Heart and Sweet Rose to my bed? Was your judgment so flawed then? No! So, please, Master Nan, do this for me, I beg you.'

Nan Ho looked up, wide-eyed. '*Chieh Hsia*... you must not say such things! You are T'ang now.'

'Then do this thing for me, Master Nan,' he said tiredly. 'For I would be married the day after my coronation.'

Nan Ho stared at him a moment longer then bowed his head low again, resigned to his fate. 'As my lord wishes.'

'Good. Now let us drink our *ch'a* and talk of other things. Was I mistaken or did I hear that there was a message from Hal Shepherd?'

Nan Ho set the book down beside the table then picked up Li Yuan's bowl, turning back and offering it to him, his head bowed.

'Not Hal, *Chieh Hsia*, but his son. Chung Hu-yan dealt with the matter.'

'I see. And did the Chancellor happen to say what the message was?'

Nan Ho hesitated. 'It was... a picture, *Chieh Hsia*.'

'A picture? You mean, there were no words? No actual message?'

'No, *Chieh Hsia*.'

'And this picture – what was in it?'

'Should I bring it, *Chieh Hsia*?'

'No. But describe it, if you can.'

Nan Ho frowned. 'It was odd, *Chieh Hsia*. Very odd indeed. It was of a tree – or rather of twinned apple trees. The two were closely intertwined, their trunks twisted about each other, yet one of the trees was dead, its leaves shed, its branches broken and rotting. Chung Hu-yan set it aside for you to look at after your coronation.' He averted his eyes. 'He felt it was not something you would wish to see before then.'

Like the gift of stones his father had tried to hide from him – the white *wei chi* stones DeVore had sent to him on the day he had been promised to Fei Yen.

Li Yuan sighed. For five generations the Shepherds had acted as advisors to his family. Descended from the original architect of the City, they lived beyond its walls, outside its laws. Only they, in all Chung Kuo, stood equal to the Seven.

'Chung Hu-yan acted as he felt he ought, but in future any message – worded or otherwise – that comes from the Shepherds must be passed directly to me, at once, Master Nan. This picture – you understand what it means?'

'No, *Chieh Hsia*.'

'No. And neither, it seems, does Chancellor Chung. It means that Hal Shepherd is dying. The tree was a gift from my father to him. I must go and pay my respects at once.'

'But, *Chieh Hsia*...'

Li Yuan shook his head. 'I know, Master Nan. I have seen my schedule for tomorrow. But the meetings will have to be cancelled. This cannot wait. He was my father's friend. It would not do to ignore such a summons, however strangely couched.'

'A summons, *Chieh Hsia*?'

'Yes, Master Nan. A summons.'

He turned away, sipping at his *ch'a*. He did not look forward to seeing Hal Shepherd in such a state, yet it would be good to see his son again; to sit with him and talk.

A faint, uncertain smile came to his lips. Yes, it would be good to speak with him, for in truth he needed a mirror just now: someone to reflect him back clearly to himself. And who better than Ben Shepherd? Who better in all Chung Kuo?

The man staggered past him then leaned against the wall unsteadily, his head lowered, as if drunk. For a moment he seemed to lapse out of consciousness, his whole body hanging loosely against his outstretched arm, then he lifted his head, stretching himself strangely, as if shaking something off. It was only then that Axel realized what he was doing. He was pissing.

Axel looked away then turned back, hearing the commotion behind him. Two burly-looking guards – Han, wearing the dark green of GenSyn, not the powder blue of Security – came running across, batons drawn, making for the man.

They stood either side of the man as he turned, confronting him.

'What the fuck you think you do?' one of them said, prodding him brutally, making him stagger back against the wall.

He was a big man, or had been, but his clothes hung loosely on him now. They were good clothes, too, but, like those of most of the people gathered there, they were grime-ridden and filthy. His face, too, bore evidence of maltreatment. His skin was blotched, his left eye almost closed, a dark, yellow-green bruise covering the whole of his left cheek. He stank, but again that was not uncommon, for most were beggars here.

He looked back at the guards blearily then lifted his head in a remembered but long-redundant gesture of pride.

'I'm here to see the General,' he said uncertainly, his pride leaking from him slowly until his head hung once again. 'You know...' he muttered, glancing up apologetically, the muscle in his cheek spasming now. 'The handout... I came for that. It was on the newscast. I heard it. Come to this place, it said, so I came.'

The guard who had spoken grunted his disgust. 'You shit bucket,' he said quietly. 'You fucking shit bucket. What you think you up to, pissing on the T'ang's walls?' Then, without warning, he hit out with his baton, catching the beggar on the side of the head.

The man went down, groaning loudly. As he did, the two guards waded in, standing over him, striking him time and again on the head and body until he lay still.

'Fucking shit bucket!' the first guard said as he stepped back. He turned, glaring at the crowd that had formed around him. 'What you look at? Fuck off! Go on! Fuck off! Before you get same!' He raised his baton threateningly, but the message had got through already. They had begun to back off as soon as he had turned.

Axel stood there a moment longer, tensed, trembling with anger, then turned away. There was nothing he could do. Nothing, at least, that would not land him in trouble. Two he could have handled, but there were more than fifty of the bastards spread out throughout the hall, jostling whoever got in their way and generally making themselves as unpleasant as they could. He knew the type. They thought themselves big men – great fighters, trained to take on anything – but most of them had failed basic training for Security or had been recruited from the Plantations, where standards were much lower. In many cases their behaviour was simply a form of compensation for the failure they felt at having to wear the dark green of a private security force and not the imperial blue.

He backed away then turned, making his way through the crowd towards the end of the hall, wondering how much longer they would be forced to wait. They had started queuing three hours back, the corridors leading to the main transit packed long before Axel had arrived. For a brief while he had thought of turning back – even the smell of the mob was enough to make a man feel sick – but had stayed, determined to be among the two thousand 'fortunates' who would be let into the grounds of the Ebert Mansion for the celebrations.

He had dressed specially. Had gone out and bought the roughest, dirtiest clothes he could lay his hands on. Had put on a rough workman's hat – a hard shell of dark plastic, like an inverted rice bowl – and dirtied his face. Now he looked little different from the rest. A beggar. A shit-bucket bum from the lowest of the levels.

He looked about him, his eyes travelling from face to face, seeing the anger there and the despair, the futility and the incipient madness. There was a shiftiness to their eyes, a pastiness to their complexions, that spoke of long years of deprivation. And they were thin, every last one of them; some of them so painfully undernourished that he found it difficult to believe that they were still alive, still moving their wasted, fragile limbs. He stared at them, fascinated, his revulsion matched by a strong instinctive pity for them; for many, he knew, there had been no choice. They had fallen long before they were born, and nothing in this world could ever redeem them. In that he differed. He too had fallen, but for him there had been a second chance.

Lowering his head, he glanced at the timer at his wrist, keeping it hidden beneath the greasy cuff of his jacket. It was getting on towards midnight.

They would have to open the gates soon, surely?

Almost at once he felt a movement in the crowd, a sudden surge forward, and knew the gates had been opened. He felt himself drawn forward, caught up in the crush.

Hei were manning the barriers, the big GenSyn half-men herding the crowd through the narrow gates. Above the crowd, on a platform to one side, a small group of Han officials looked on, counting the people as they went through.

Past the gates, crush barriers forced the crowd into semi-orderly lines, at the head of which more officials – many of them masked against the stench and the possibility of disease – processed the hopeful.

As movement slowed and the crush grew more intense, he heard a great shouting from way back and knew the gates had been closed, the quota filled. But he was inside.

The pressure on him from all sides was awful, the stink of unwashed bodies almost unbearable, but he fought back his nausea, reminding himself why he was there. To bear witness. To see for himself the moment when Hans Ebert was declared General-elect.

As he passed through the second barrier, an official drew him aside and tagged his jacket with an electronic trace, then thrust a slice of cake and a bulb of drink into his hands. He shuffled on, looking about him, seeing how the others crammed their cake down feverishly before emptying the bulb in a few desperate swallows. He tried a mouthful of the cake then spat it out. It was hard, dry and completely without flavour. The drink was little better. Disgusted, he threw them down, and was immediately pushed back against the wall as those nearby fought for what he had discarded.

The big transit lift was just ahead of them now. Again Hei herded them into the space, cramming them in tightly, until Axel felt his breath being forced from him. Like the others surrounding him, he fought silently, desperately, for a little space – pushing out with his elbows, his strength an asset.

The doors closed, the huge elevator – used normally for goods, not people – began its slow climb up the levels. As it did, a voice sounded overhead, telling them that they must cheer when the masters appeared on the balcony; that they would each receive a five-yuan coin if they cheered loud enough.

'The cameras will be watching everyone,' the voice continued. 'Only those who cheer loudly will get a coin.'

The journey up-level seemed to last an eternity. Two hundred and fifty levels they climbed, up to the very top of the City.

Coming out from the transit was like stepping outside into the open. Overhead was a great, blue-black sky, filled with moonlit cloud and stars, the illusion so perfect that for a moment Axel caught his breath. To the right, across a vast, landscaped park, was the Ebert Mansion, its imposing facade lit up brilliantly, the great balcony festooned with banners. A barrier of Hei prevented them from going that way – the brute, almost porcine faces of the guards lit grotesquely from beneath. All around him people had slowed, astonished by the sight, their eyes wide, their mouths fallen open, but masked servants hurried them on, ushering them away to the left, into an area that had been fenced off with high transparent barriers of ice.

They stumbled on, only a low murmur coming from them now, most of them awed into silence by the sight of such luxury, intimidated by the sense of openness, by the big sky overhead. But for Axel, shuffling along slowly in their midst, it reminded him of something else – of that day when he and Major DeVore had called on Representative Lehmann at his First Level estate. And he knew, almost without thinking it, that there was a connection between the two. As if such luxury bred corruption.

Stewards herded them down a broad gravel path and out into a large space in front of the mansion. Here another wall barred their way, the translucent surface of it coated with a non-reflective substance that to the watching cameras would make it seem as if there was no wall – no barrier – between the Eberts and the cheering crowd.

As the space filled up, he noticed the stewards going out into the crowd, handing out flags and streamers – the symbols of GenSyn and the Seven distributed equally – before positioning themselves at various strategic points. Turning, he sought out one of the stewards and took a banner from him, aiming to conceal himself behind it when the cheering began. It was unlikely that Hans Ebert would study the film of his triumph that closely, but it was best to take no chances.

He glanced at his timer. It was almost twelve.

The stewards began the cheering, turning to encourage the others standing about them. 'Five *yuan!*' they shouted. 'Only those who shout will get a coin!'

As the Eberts stepped out on to the balcony, the cheering rose to a crescendo. The cameras panned about the crowd, then focused on the scene on the balcony again. Klaus Ebert stood there in the foreground, a broad beam of light settling on him, making his hair shine silver-white, his perfect teeth sparkle.

'Friends!' he began, his voice amplified to carry over the cheering. 'A notice has been posted throughout our great City. It reads as follows.' He turned and took a scroll from his secretary, then turned back, clearing his throat. Below the noise subsided as the stewards moved among the crowd, damping down the excitement they had artificially created.

Ebert opened out the scroll, then began.

'"I, Li Yuan, T'ang designate of *Ch'eng Ou Chou*, City Europe, declare the appointment of Hans Joachim Ebert, currently Major in my Security services, as Supreme General of my forces, this appointment to be effective from midday on the fifteenth day of September in the year two thousand two hundred and seven."'

He stepped back, beaming with paternal pride.

There was a moment's silence and then a ragged cheer went up, growing stronger as the stewards whipped the crowd into a fury of enthusiasm.

Up on the balcony, Hans Ebert stepped forward, his powder-blue uniform immaculate, his blond hair perfectly groomed. He grinned and waved a hand as if to thank them for their welcome, then stepped back, bowing, all humility.

Axel, watching from below, felt a wave of pure hatred pass through him. If they knew – if they only knew all he had done. The cheating and lying and butchery, the foulness beneath the mask of perfection. But they knew nothing. He looked about him, seeing how caught up in it they suddenly were. They had come for the chance of food and drink and for the money, but now they were here their enthusiasm was genuine. Up there they saw a king – a man so high above them that to be at such proximity was a blessing. Axel saw the stewards look among themselves and wink, laughing, sharing the joke, and felt more sick than he had ever felt among the unwashed mass. They, at least, did not pretend that they were clean. One could smell what they were. But Ebert?

Axel looked past the fluttering banner; saw how Ebert turned to talk to those behind him, so at ease in his arrogance, and swore again to bring him low. To pile the foul truth high, burying his flawless reputation.

He shuddered, frightened by the sheer intensity of what he felt; knowing that had he a gun and the opportunity, he would have tried to kill the man, right there and then. Up on the balcony, the Eberts turned away, making their way back inside. As the doors closed behind them the lights went down, leaving the space before the mansion in darkness.

The cheering died. Axel threw the banner down. All about him the crowd was dispersing, making for the barriers. He turned, following them, then stopped, looking back. Was it that? Was it excess of luxury that corrupted a man? Or were some men simply born evil and others good?

He looked ahead, looked past the barriers to where small knots of beggars had gathered. Already they were squabbling, fighting each other over the tiny pittance they had been given. As he came closer he saw one man go down and several others fall on him, punching and kicking him, robbing him of the little he had. Nearby the guards looked on, laughing among themselves.

Laughing... He wiped his mouth, sickened by all he'd seen, then pushed past the barrier, ignoring the offered coin.

Inside the mansion the celebrations were about to begin. At the top of the great stairway Klaus Ebert put his arm about his son's shoulders and looked out across the gathering that filled the great hall below.

'My good friends!' he said, then laughed. 'What can I say? I am so full of pride! My son...'

He drew Hans close and kissed his cheek, then looked about him again, beaming and laughing, as if he were drunk.

'Come, Father,' Hans said in a whisper, embarrassed by his father's sudden effusiveness. 'Let's get it over with. I'm faint with hunger.'

Klaus looked back at him, smiling broadly, then laughed, squeezing his shoulder again. 'Whatever you say, Hans.' He turned back, putting one arm out expansively. 'Friends! Let us not stand on formalities tonight. Eat, drink, be merry!'

They made their way down the stairs, father and son, joining the crowd gathered at the foot. Tolonen was amongst those there, lean and elegant in his old age, his steel-grey hair slicked back, the dress uniform of General worn proudly for the last time.

'Why, Knut,' Klaus Ebert began, taking a glass from a servant, 'I see you are wearing Hans's uniform!'

Tolonen laughed. 'It is but briefly, Klaus. I am just taking the creases out of it for him!'

There was a roar of laughter at that. Hans smiled and bowed, then looked about him. 'Is Jelka not here?'

Tolonen shook his head. 'I'm afraid not, Hans. She took an injury in her practice session this morning. Nothing serious – only a sprain – but the doctor felt she would be better off resting. She was most disappointed, I can tell you. Why, she'd spent two whole days looking for a new dress to wear tonight!'

Hans lowered his head respectfully. 'I am sorry to hear it, Father-in-law. I had hoped to dance with her tonight. But perhaps you would both come here for dinner – soon, when things have settled.'

Tolonen beamed, delighted by the suggestion. 'That would be excellent, Hans. And it would make up for her disappointment, I am sure.'

Hans bowed and moved on, circulating, chatting with all his father's friends, making his way slowly towards a small group on the far side of the hall, until, finally, he came to them.

'Michael!' he said, embracing his old friend.

'Hans!' Lever held Ebert to him a moment, then stood back. They had been classmates at Oxford in their teens, before Lever had gone on to Business College and Ebert to the Academy. But they had stayed in touch all this time.

Ebert looked past his old friend, smiling a greeting to the others.

'How was your journey?'

'As well as could be expected!' Lever laughed then leaned closer. 'When in the gods' names are they going to improve those things, Hans? If you've any influence with Li Yuan, make him pass an amendment to the Edict to enable them to build something more comfortable than those transatlantic rockets.'

Ebert laughed then leaned closer. 'And my friend? Did you enjoy his company?'

Lever glanced at his companions then laughed. 'I can speak for us all in saying that it was a most interesting experience. I would never have guessed...'

Ebert smiled. 'No. And let's keep it that way, neh?' He turned, looking about him, then took Lever's arm. 'And his gift?'

Lever's eyes widened. 'You knew about that?'

'Of course. But come. Let's go outside. It's cool in the garden. We can talk as we go. Of Chung Kuo and *Ta Ts'in* and dreams of empire.'

Lever gave a soft laugh then bowed his head. 'Lead on...'

It was just after four when the last of the guests left the Ebert Mansion. Hans, watching from the balcony, stifled a yawn, then turned and went back inside. He had not been drinking and yet he felt quite drunk – buoyed up on a vast and heady upsurge of well-being. Things had never been better. That very evening his father had given over a further sixteen companies to him, making it almost a quarter of the giant GenSyn empire that he now controlled. Life, at last, was beginning to open to him. Earlier he had taken Tolonen aside to suggest that his marriage to Jelka be brought forward, and while, at first, the old man had seemed a little put out, when Hans had spoken of the sense of stability it would bring him, Tolonen had grown quite keen – almost as if the idea had been his own.

Ebert went down the stairs and out into the empty hall, standing there a moment, smiling, recollecting Tolonen's response.

'Let me speak to her,' Tolonen had said, as he was leaving. 'After the coronation, when things have settled a little. But I promise you, Hans, I'll do my best to persuade her. After all, it's in no one's interest to delay, is it?'

No, he thought. *Especially not now.* At least, not now that they had come to an arrangement with the Americans.

He went out and said goodnight to his father and mother then came back, running across the hall and out through the back doors into the garden. The night seemed fresh and warm and for the briefest moment he imagined himself outside, beneath a real moon, under a real sky. Well, maybe that would happen soon. In a year or two perhaps. When he was King of Europe.

On the ornamental bridge he slowed, looking about him. He felt a great restlessness in his blood, an urge to do something. He thought of the *mui tsai*, but for once his restlessness was pure, uncontaminated by a sense of sexual urgency. No, it was as if he needed to go somewhere, do something. All this waiting – for his inheritance, his command, his wife – seemed suddenly a barrier to simple *being*. Tonight he wanted to *be*, to *do*. To break heads or ride a horse at breakneck speed.

He kicked out, sending gravel into the water below, watching the ripples spread. Then he moved on, jumping down the steps to the path and vaulting up on to the balcony above. He turned, looking back. A servant had stopped, watching him. Seeing Ebert turn, he moved on hurriedly, his head bowed, the huge bowl he held making slopping sounds in the silence.

Ebert laughed. There were no heads to break, no horses here to ride. So maybe he would fuck the *mui tsai* anyway. Maybe that would still his pulse and purge the restlessness from his system. He turned, making his way along to his suite of rooms. Inside he began to undress, unbuttoning his tunic. As he did so, he went over to the comset and touched in the code.

He turned away, throwing his tunic down on a chair, then went across and tapped on the inner door. At once a servant popped his head round the door.

'Bring the *mui tsai* to my room then go. I'll not need you any more tonight, Lo Wen.'

The servant bowed and left. Ebert turned back, looking at the screen. There were a great number of messages for once, mainly from friends, congratulating him on his appointment. But amongst them was one he had been expecting. DeVore's.

He read it through then laughed. So the meeting with the Americans had gone well. Good. The introduction was yet another thing DeVore owed him for. What's more, DeVore wanted him to do something else.

He smiled then sat down, pulling off his boots. Slowly, by small degrees, DeVore was placing himself in his debt. More and more he had come to rely on him – for little things at first, but now for ever larger schemes. And that was good. For he would keep account of all.

There was a faint tapping at the inner door.

He turned in the chair, looking across. 'Come in,' he said softly.

The door slid back. For a moment she stood there, naked, looking in at him, the light behind her. She was so beautiful, so wonderfully made that his penis grew hard simply looking at her. Then she came across, fussing about him, helping him with the last few items of his clothing.

Finished, she looked up at him from where she knelt on the floor in front of him. 'Was your evening good, master?'

He pulled her up on to his lap then began to stroke her neck and shoulder, looking up into her dark and liquid eyes, his blood inflamed now by the warmth of her flesh against his own. 'Never better, Sweet Flute. Never in my whole life better.'

DeVore slipped the vial back into its carrying case, sealed the lid, and handed it to Lehmann.

'Don't drop it, Stefan, whatever else you do. And make sure that Hans knows what to do with it. He knows it's coming, but he doesn't properly know what it is. He'll be curious, so it's best if you tell him something, if only to dampen down his curiosity.'

The albino slipped the cigar-shaped case into his inner pocket then fastened his tunic tight. 'So what should I say?'

DeVore laughed. 'Tell him the truth for once. Tell him it kills Han. He'll like that.'

Lehmann nodded, then bowed and turned away.

He watched Lehmann go then went across and took his furs from the cupboard in the corner. It was too late now to sleep. He would go hunting instead. Yes, it would be good to greet the dawn on the open mountainside.

DeVore smiled, studying himself in the mirror as he pulled on his furs, then, taking his crossbow from the rack on the wall, went out, making his way towards the old tunnels, taking the one that came out on the far side of the mountain beside the ruins of the ancient castle.

As he walked along he wondered, not for the first time, what Lever had made of the gift he'd given him.

The Aristotle File. A copy of Berdichev's original, in his own handwriting. The true history of Chung Kuo. Not the altered and sanitized version the Han peddled in their schools, but the truth, from the birth of Western thought in Aristotle's yes/no logic, to the splendours of space travel, mass communications and artificial intelligence systems. A history of the West systematically erased by the Han. Yes, and that was another kind of virus. One, in its own way, every bit as deadly for the Han.

DeVore laughed, his laughter echoing down the tunnel. All in all it had been a good day. And it was going to get better. Much better.

It was exactly ten minutes past five when the scouts moved into place on the mountainside, dropping the tiny gas pellets into the base's ventilation outlets. At the entrance to the hangar, four masked men sprayed ice-eating acids on to the snow-covered surface of the doors. Two minutes later Karr, wearing a mask and carrying a lightweight air canister, kicked his way inside.

He crossed the hangar at a quick march, then ran down the corridor linking it to the inner fortress, his automatic moving this way and that as he looked for any sign of resistance, but the colourless, odourless gas had done its work. Guards lay slumped in several places. They would have had no chance to issue any kind of warning.

He glanced down at his timer then turned, looking back. Already the first squad was busy, binding and gagging the unconscious defenders before the effects of the gas wore off. Behind them a second squad was coming through, their masked faces looking from side to side, double-checking as they came along.

He turned back, pushing on, hyper-alert now, knowing that it would not be long before he lost the advantage of surprise.

There were four lifts, spaced out along a single broad corridor. He stared at them a moment then shook his head. A place like this, dug deep into the mountainside, would be hard to defend unless one devised a system of independent levels, and of bottlenecks linking them – bottlenecks that could be defended like the barbican in an ancient castle – the killing ground. So here. These lifts – seemingly so innocuous – were their barbican. But unlike in a castle there would be another way into the next level of the fortress. There had to be, because if the power ever failed, they had to have some way of ensuring that they still got air down in the lower tunnels.

There would be shafts. Ventilation shafts. As above.

Karr turned and beckoned the squad leader over.

'Locate the down shafts. Then I want one man sent down each of them straight away. They're to secure the corridors beneath the shafts while the rest of the men come through. Understand?'

The young lieutenant bowed then hurried away, sending his men off to do as Karr had ordered. He was back a moment later.

'They're sealed, Major Karr.'

'Well? Break the seals!'

'But they're alarmed. Maybe even boobytrapped.'

Karr grunted, impatient now. 'Show me!'

The shaft was in a tiny corridor leading off what seemed to be some kind of storeroom. Karr studied it a moment, noting its strange construction, then, knowing he had no alternative, raised his fist and brought it down hard. The seal cracked but didn't break. He struck it again, harder this time, and it gave, splintering into the space below.

Somewhere below he could hear a siren sounding, security doors slamming into place.

'Let's get moving. They know we're here now. The sooner we hit them the better, neh?'

He went first, bracing himself against the walls of the narrow tunnel as he went down, his shoulders almost too wide for the confined space. Others followed, almost on top of him.

Some five *ch'i* above the bottom seal he stopped and brought his gun round, aiming it down between his legs. He opened fire. The seal shattered with a great upward hiss of air, tiny splinters thrown up at him.

He narrowed his eyes then understood. The separate levels were kept at different pressures, which meant there were air-locks. But why? What were they doing here?

He scrambled down then dropped. As he hit the floor he twisted about. A body lay to one side of the shaft's exit point, otherwise the corridor was empty.

It was a straight stretch of corridor, sixty *ch'i* long at most, ending in a T-junction at each end. There were no doors, no windows and, as far as he could make out, no cameras.

Left or right? If the groundplan followed that of the level above, the lifts would be somewhere off to the left, but he didn't think it would be that simple. Not if DeVore had designed this place.

Men were jumping down behind him, forming up either side, kneeling, their weapons raised to their shoulders, covering both ends of the corridor.

Last down was the squad leader. Karr quickly despatched him off to the left with six men, while he went right with the rest.

He had not gone more than a dozen paces when there was a loud clunk and a huge metal firedoor began to come down.

From the yells behind him he knew at once that the same was happening at the other end of the corridor. No cameras, eh? How could he have been so naïve!

He ran, hurling himself at the diminishing gap, half sliding, half rolling beneath the door just before it slammed into the floor. As he thudded into the end wall he felt his gun go clattering away from him, but there was no time to think of that. As he came up from the floor the first of them was on him, slashing down with a knife the length of his forearm.

Karr blocked the blow and counter-punched, feeling the man's jaw shatter. Behind him, only a few paces off, a second guard was raising his automatic. Karr ducked, using the injured guard as a shield, thrusting his head into the man's chest as he began to fall, pushing him upward and back, into the second man.

Too late, the guard opened fire, the shells ricocheting harmlessly off the end wall as he stumbled backwards.

Karr kicked him in the stomach then stood over him, chopping down savagely, finishing him off. He stepped back, looking about him. His gun was over to the right. He picked it up and ran on, hearing voices approaching up ahead.

He grinned fiercely. The last thing they would expect was a single man coming at them. Even so, it might be best to give himself some additional advantage.

He looked up. As he'd thought, they hadn't bothered to set the pipework and cabling into the rock but had simply secured it to the ceiling of the tunnel with brackets. The brackets looked firm enough – big metallic things – but were they strong enough to bear his weight?

There was only one way to find out. He tucked his gun into his tunic and reached up, pulling himself up slowly. Bringing his legs up, he reached out with his boots to get a firmer grip. So far so good. If he could hold himself there with his feet and one hand he would be above them when they came into view. The rest should be easy.

They were close now. At any moment they would appear at the end of the corridor. Slowly he drew the gun from his tunic, resting the stock of it against his knee.

There! Four of them, moving quickly but confidently, talking among themselves, assuming there was no danger. He let them come on four, five paces, then squeezed the trigger.

As he opened fire, the bracket by his feet jerked, then came away from the wall. At once a whole section of cabling slewed towards him, his weight dragging it down. Along the whole length of the ceiling the securing brackets gave, bringing down thick clouds of rock and debris.

Karr rolled to one side, freeing himself from the tangle, bringing his gun up to his chest. Through the dust he could see that two of them were down. They lay still, as if dead, pinned down by the cables. A third was getting up slowly, groaning, one hand pressed to the back of his head where the cabling had struck him. The fourth was on his feet, his gun raised, looking straight at Karr.

There was the deafening noise of automatic fire. Shells hammered into the wall beside him, cutting into his left arm and shoulder, but he was safe. His own fire had ripped into the guards an instant earlier, throwing them backwards.

Karr got up slowly, the pain in his upper arm intense, the shoulder wound less painful but more awkward. The bone felt broken – smashed probably. He crouched there a moment, feeling sick, then straightened up, gritting his teeth, knowing there was no option but to press on. It was just as it had been in the Pit all those years ago. He had a choice. He could go on and he could live, or he could give up and let himself be killed.

A choice? He laughed sourly. No, there had never really been a choice. He had always had to fight. As far back as he could remember, it had always been the same. It was the price for being who he was, for living where he'd lived, beneath the Net.

He went on, each step jolting his shoulder painfully, taking his breath. The gun was heavy in his right hand. Designed for two-handed use, its balance was wrong when used one-handed, the aim less certain.

Surprise. It was the last card left up his sleeve. Surprise and sheer audacity.

He was lucky. The guard outside the control-room had his back to him as he came out into the main corridor. There was a good twenty ch'i between them, but his luck held. He was on top of the man before he realized he was there, smashing the stock of the gun into the back of his head.

As the man sank to his knees, Karr stepped past him into the doorway and opened fire, spraying the room with shells. It was messy – not the way he'd normally have done it – but effective. When his gun fell silent again, there were six corpses on the floor of the room.

One wall had been filled with a nest of screens, like those they'd found in the Overseer's House in the Plantation. His gunfire had destroyed a number of them, but more than three-quarters were still functioning. He had the briefest glimpse of various scenes, showing that fighting was still going on throughout the fortress, and then the screens went dead, the overhead lights fading.

He turned, listening for noises in the corridor, then turned back, knowing his only hope was to find the controls that operated the doors and let his men into this level.

He scanned the panels quickly, cursing the damage he'd done, then set his gun down beside a keyboard inset into the central panel. Maybe this was it.

The keyboard was unresponsive to his touch. The screen stayed blank. Overhead a red light began to flash. Karr grabbed his gun and backed out. Not before time. A moment later a metal screen fell into place, sealing off the doorway.

What now?

Karr turned, looking to his left. It was the only way. But did it lead anywhere? Suddenly he had a vision of DeVore sitting somewhere, watching him, laughing as he made his way deeper and deeper into the labyrinth he had built; knowing that all of these tunnels led nowhere. Nowhere but into the cold, stone heart of the mountain.

He shuddered. The left side of his tunic was sodden now, the whole of his left side warm, numb yet tingling, and he was beginning to feel light-headed. He had lost a lot of blood and his body was suffering from shock, but he had to go on. It was too late now to back off.

He went on, grunting with pain at every step, knowing he was close to physical collapse. Every movement pained him, yet he forced himself to keep alert, moving his head from side to side, his whole body tensed against a sudden counter-attack.

Again his luck held. The long corridor was empty, the rooms leading off deserted. But did it go anywhere?

Karr slowed. Up ahead the wall lighting stopped abruptly, but the tunnel went on into the darkness.

He turned, looking back, thinking he'd heard something, but there was nothing. No one was following him. But how long would it be before someone came? He had to keep going on.

Had to.

He threw off his mask then pulled the heat-sensitive glasses down over his eyes and went on.

After a while the tunnel began to slope downwards. He stumbled over the first of the steps and banged his damaged shoulder against the wall. For a moment he crouched there, groaning softly, letting the pain ease, then went on, more careful now, pressing close to the right-hand wall in case he fell.

At first they were not so much steps as broad ledges cut into the rocky floor, but soon that changed as the tunnel began to slope more steeply. He went on, conscious of the sharp hiss of his breathing in the silent darkness.

Partway down he stopped, certain he had made a mistake. The wall beside him was rough, as if crudely hacked from the rock. Moreover, the dank, musty smell of the place made him think that it was an old tunnel, cut long before DeVore's time. For what reason he couldn't guess, but it would explain the lack of lighting, the very crudeness of its construction.

He went on, slower now, each step an effort, until, finally, he could go no further. He sat, shivering, his gun set down beside him in the darkness.

So this was it? He laughed painfully. It was not how he had expected to end his days – in the cold, dank darkness at the heart of a mountain, half his shoulder shot away – but if this was what the gods had fated, then who was he to argue? After all, he could have died ten years back had Tolonen not bought out his contract, and they had been good years. The very best of years.

Even so, he felt bitter regret wash over him. Why now? Now that he had found Marie. It made no sense. As if the gods were punishing him. And for what? For arrogance? For being born the way he was? No... it made no sense. Unless the gods were cruel by nature.

He pulled the heat-sensitive glasses off then leaned back a little, seeking some posture in which the pain would ease, but it was no good. However he sat, the same fierce, burning ache would seize him again after a few moments, making him feel feverish, irrational.

What, then? Go back? Or go on, ever down?

The question was answered for him. Far below he heard a heavy rustling noise then the sharp squeal of an unoiled door being pushed back. Light spilled into the tunnel. Someone was coming up, hurriedly, as if pursued.

He reached beside him for his gun then sat back, the gun laid across his lap, its barrel facing down towards the light.

It was too late now to put his glasses back on, but what the hell? Whoever it was, they had the light behind them, while he sat in total darkness. Moreover, he knew they were coming, while they had no idea he was there. The advantages were all his. Even so, his hand was trembling so badly now that he wondered if he could even pull the trigger.

Partway up the steps the figure stopped, moving closer to the right-hand wall. There was a moment's banging then it stopped, the figure turning towards him again. It sniffed the air then began to climb the steps, slower now, more cautiously, as if it sensed his presence. Up it came, closer and closer, until he could hear the steady pant of its breath, not twenty ch'i below.

Now! he thought, but his fingers were dead, the gun a heavy weight in his lap.

He closed his eyes, awaiting the end, knowing it was only a matter of time. Then he heard it. The figure had stopped; now it was moving back down the steps. He heard it try the lock again and opened his eyes.

For a moment his head swam then, even as his eyes focused, the door below creaked open, spilling light into the dimly lit passageway.

Karr caught his breath, praying the other wouldn't turn and see him there. Yet even as the figure disappeared within, he recognized the profile.

DeVore! It had been DeVore!

CHUNG KUO

Chapter 65

IN THE TEMPLE OF HEAVEN

The tower was built into the side of the mountain, a small, round, two-storey building, dominated by a smooth, grey overhang of rock. Beneath it only the outlines of ancient walls remained, huge rectangles laid out in staggered steps down the mountainside, the low brickwork overgrown with rough grasses and alpine flowers.

Lehmann stood there at the edge of the ruins, looking out across the broad valley towards the east. There was nothing human here, nothing but the sunlit mountains and, far below, the broad stretch of the untended meadows, cut by a slow-moving river. Looking at it, he could imagine it remaining so a thousand years, while the world beyond the mountains tore itself apart.

And so it would be. Once the disease of humanity had run its course.

He looked across. On the far side of the valley bare rock fell half a li to the green of the valley floor, as if a giant had cut a crude path through the mountains. Dark stands of pine crested the vast wall of rock then, as the eye travelled upwards, that too gave way – to snow and ice and, finally, to the clear, bright blue of the sky.

He shivered. It was beautiful. So beautiful it took his breath. All else – all art, however fine – was mere distraction compared to this. This was real. Was like a temple. A temple to the old gods. A temple of rock and ice, of tree and stream, thrown up into the heavens.

He turned, looking back at Reid. The man was standing by the tower, hunched into himself, his furs drawn tight about him, as if unaware of the vast mystery that surrounded him. Lehmann shook his head then went across.

It was only a hunch, but when he had seen the Security craft clustered on the slopes, his first thought had been of the old tunnel. *He'll be there*, he'd thought. Now, an hour later, he wasn't quite so sure.

'What are we doing?' Reid asked anxiously. He too had seen the extent of the Security operation, had seen the rows of corpses stretched out in the snow.

Lehmann stared back at him a moment then climbed the narrow path to the tower. The doorframe was empty. He went inside and stood there, looking about him. The tower was a shell, the whole thing open to the sky, but the floor was much newer. The big planks there looked old, but that was how they were meant to look. At most they were ten years old.

Reid came and stood there in the doorway, looking in at him. 'What is this? Are we going to camp here until they've gone?'

Lehmann shook his head then turned and came out, searching the nearby slope. With a grunt of satisfaction he crouched down, parting the spiky grasses with his gloved hands.

'Here,' he said. 'Give me a hand.'

Reid went across. It was a hatch of some kind. An old-fashioned circular metal plate less than a *ch'i* in circumference. There were two handles, set into either side of the plate. Lehmann took one, Reid the other. Together they heaved at the thing until it gave.

Beneath was a shallow shaft. Lehmann leaned inside, feeling blindly for something.

'What are you doing?' Reid asked, looking out past him, afraid that a passing Security craft would spot them.

Lehmann said nothing, simply carried on with his search. A moment later he sat back, holding something in his hand. It looked like a knife. A broad, flat knife with a circular handle. Or a spike of some kind.

Lehmann stood then went back to the tower.

He went inside and crouched down, setting the spike down at his side. Groaning with the effort, he pushed one of the planks back tight against the far wall, revealing a small depression in the stonework below, its shape matching that of the spike perfectly. Lehmann hefted the spike a moment then slotted it into the depression. Reid, watching from the open doorway, laughed. It was a key.

Lehmann stepped back into the doorway. As he did so there was a sharp click and the whole floor began to rise, pushing up into the shell of the tower, until it stopped, two ch'i above their heads.

It was a lift. Moreover, it was occupied. Reid made a small sound of surprise then bowed his head hurriedly. It was DeVore.

'About time!' DeVore said, moving out past the two men, his face livid with anger. 'Another hour and they'd have had me. I could hear them working on the seal at the far end of the tunnel.'

'What happened?' Lehmann asked, following DeVore out into the open.

DeVore turned, facing him. 'Someone's betrayed us! Sold us down the fucking river!'

Lehmann nodded. 'They were Security,' he said. 'The craft I saw were special elite. That would take orders from high up, wouldn't you say?'

There was an ugly movement in DeVore's face. His incarceration in the tunnel had done nothing for his humour. 'Ebert! What's that bastard up to? What game's that little fucker playing?'

'Are you sure it's him?'

DeVore looked away. 'No. I can't see what he'd gain from it. But who else could it be? Who else knows where we are? Who else could hit me without warning?'

'So what are you going to do?'

DeVore laughed sourly. 'Nothing. Not until I've spoken to the little weasel. But if he hasn't got a bloody good explanation he's dead. Useful or not, he's dead, hear me?'

Hal Shepherd turned his head, looking up at the young T'ang, his eyes wet with gratitude.

'Li Yuan... I'm glad you came.'

His voice was thin, almost transparently so, matching perfectly the face from which it issued: a thin-fleshed, ruined face that was barely distinguishable from a skull. It pained Li Yuan to see him like this. To see all the strength leached from the man and death staring out from behind his eyes.

'Ben sent me a note,' he said gently, almost tenderly. 'But you should have sent for me before now. I would have spared the time. You know I would.'

The ghost of a smile flickered on Shepherd's lips. 'Yes. You're like Shai Tung in that. It was a quality I much admired in him.'

It took so long for him to say the words – such effort – that Li Yuan found himself longing for him to stop. To say nothing. Simply to lie there, perhaps. But that was not what Shepherd wanted. He knew his death lay but days ahead of him and, now that Li Yuan was here, he wanted his say. Neither was it in Li Yuan's heart to deny him.

'My father missed you greatly after you returned here. He often remarked how it was as if he had had a part of him removed.' Li Yuan looked aside, giving a small laugh. 'You know, Hal, I'm not even sure it was your advice he missed, simply your voice.'

He looked back, seeing how the tears had formed again in Shepherd's eyes, and found his own eyes growing moist. He looked away, closing his eyes briefly, remembering another time, in the long room at Tongjiang, when Hal had shown him how to juggle. How, with a laugh, he had told him that it was the one essential skill a ruler needed. So he always had been – part playful and part serious, each game of his making a point, each utterance the distillation of a wealth of unspoken thought. He had been the very best of counsellors to his father. In that the Li Family had always been fortunate, for who else, among the Seven, could draw from such a deep well as they did with the Shepherds? It was what gave them their edge. Was why the other Families always looked to Li for guidance. But now that chain was broken. Unless he could convince Hal's son otherwise.

He looked back at Shepherd and saw how he was watching him, the eyes strangely familiar in that unrecognizably wasted face.

'I'm not a pretty sight, I realize, Yuan. But look at me. Please. I have something important to say to you.'

Li Yuan inclined his head. 'Of course, Hal. I was... remembering.'

'I understand. I see it all the time. In Beth. You grow accustomed to such things.'

Shepherd hesitated, a brief flicker of pain passing across his face, then went on, his voice a light rasp.

'Well... let me say it simply. Change has come, Yuan, like it or not. Now you must harness it and ride it like a horse. I counselled your father differently, I know, but things were different then. Much has changed, even in this last year. You must be ruthless now. Uncompromising. Wang Sau-leyan is your enemy. I think you realize that. But do not think he is the only one who will oppose you. What you must do will upset friend as well as foe, but do not shrink from it merely because of that. No. You must steer a hard course, Yuan. If not, there is no hope. No hope at all.'

Hal lay there afterwards, quiet, very still, until Yuan realized that he was sleeping. He sat there, watching him a while. There was nothing profound in what Hal had said, nothing he had not heard a thousand times before. No. What made it significant was that it was Hal who had said it. Hal, who had always counselled moderation, even during the long War with the Dispersionists. Even after they had seeded him with the cancer that now claimed him.

He sat there until Beth came in. She looked past him, seeing how things were, then went to the drawer and fetched another blanket, laying it over her husband. Then she turned, looking at Li Yuan.

'He's not... ?' Li Yuan began, suddenly concerned.

Beth shook her head. 'No. He does this often now. Sometimes he falls asleep in mid-sentence. He's very weak now, you understand. The excite-ment of you coming will have tired him. But, please, don't worry about that. We're all pleased that you came, Li Yuan.'

Li Yuan looked down, moved by the simplicity of her words. 'It was the least I could do. Hal has been like a father to me.' He looked up again, meet-ing her eyes. 'You don't know how greatly it pains me to see him like this.'

She looked away, only a slight tightening of her cheek muscles revealing how much she was holding back. Then she looked back at him, smiling.

'Well... let's leave him to sleep, neh? I'll make some ch'a.'

He smiled then gave the smallest bow, understanding now why his father had talked so much about his visit here. Hal's pending death or no, there was contentment here. A balance.

And how find that for himself? For the wheel of his own life was broken, the axle shattered.

He followed her out down the narrow twist of steps then stood there, staring out through the shadows of the hallway at the garden – at a brilliant square of colour framed by the dark oak of the doorway.

He shivered, astonished by the sight; by the almost hallucinatory clarity of what could be seen within that frame. It was as if, in stepping through, one might enter another world. Whether it was simply a function of the low ceiling and the absence of windows here inside and the contrasting openness of the garden beyond he could not say, but the effect took away his breath. It was like nothing he had ever seen. The light seemed embedded in the darkness, like a lens. So vivid it was. As if washed clean. He went towards it, his lips parted in wonder, then stopped, laughing, putting his hand against the warm wood of the upright.

'Ben?'

The young man was to the right, in the kitchen garden, close by the hinged door. He looked up from where he was kneeling at the edge of the path, almost as if he had expected Li Yuan to appear at that moment.

'Li Yuan...'

Li Yuan went across and stood there over him, the late morning sunlight warming his neck and shoulders. 'What are you doing?'

Ben patted the grass beside him. 'I'm playing. Won't you join me?'

Li Yuan hesitated then, sweeping his robes beneath him, knelt at Ben's side.

Ben had removed a number of the rocks from the border of the flowerbeds, exposing the dark earth beneath. Its flattened surface was criss-crossed with tiny tunnels. On the grass beside him lay a long silver box with rounded edges, like an over-long cigar case.

'What's that?' Li Yuan asked, curious.

Ben laughed. 'That's my little army. I'll show you in a while. But look. It's quite extensive, isn't it?'

The maze of tiny tunnels spread out several ch'i in each direction.

'It's part of an ants' nest,' Ben explained. 'Most of it's down below, under the surface. A complex labyrinth of tunnels and levels. If you could dig it out in one big chunk it would be huge. Like a tiny City.'

'I see,' said Li Yuan, surprised by Ben's interest. 'But what are you doing with it?'

Ben leaned forward slightly, studying the movement in one of the tracks. 'They've been pestering us for some while. Getting in the sugar jar and scuttling along the back of the sink. So Mother asked me to deal with them.'

'Deal with them?'

Ben looked up. 'Yes. They can be a real nuisance if you don't deal with them. So I'm taking steps to destroy their nest.'

Li Yuan frowned then laughed. 'I don't understand, Ben. What do you do – use acid or something?'

Ben shook his head. 'No. I use these.' He picked up the silver case and handed it across to the young T'ang.

Li Yuan opened the case and immediately dropped it, moving back from it sharply.

'It's all right,' Ben said, retrieving the case. 'They can't escape unless I let them out.'

Li Yuan shivered. The box was full of ants. Big, red, brutal-looking things. Hundreds of them, milling about menacingly.

'You use them?'

Ben nodded. 'Amos made them. He based them on *polyergus* – Amazon ants, as they're known. They're a soldier caste, you see. They go into other ants' hives and enslave them. These are similar, only they don't enslave, they simply destroy.'

Li Yuan shook his head slowly, horrified by the notion.

'They're a useful tool,' Ben continued. 'I've used them a lot out here. We get new nests every year. It's a good job Amos made a lot of these. I'm forever losing half a dozen or so. They get clogged up with earth and stop functioning or, just occasionally, the real ants fight back and take them apart. Usually, however, they encounter very little resistance. They're utterly ruthless, you see. Machines, that's all they are. Tiny, super-efficient little machines. The perfect gardening tool.'

Ben laughed, but the joke was lost on Li Yuan.

'Your father tells me I must be ruthless.'

Ben looked up from the ants and smiled. 'It was nothing you didn't know.'

Li Yuan looked back at Ben. As on the first occasion they had met – the day of his engagement to Fei Yen – he had the feeling of being with his equal, of being with a man who understood him perfectly.

'Ben? Would you be my counsellor? My Chief Advisor? Would you be to me what your father was to my father?'

Ben turned, looking out across the bay, as if to take in his surroundings, then he looked back at Li Yuan.

'I am not my father.'

'Nor I mine.'

'No.' Ben sighed and looked down, tilting the case, making the ants run this way and that. There was a strange smile on his lips. 'You know, I didn't think it would tempt me, but it does. To try it for a while. To see what it would be like.' He looked up again. 'But, no, Li Yuan. It would simply be a game. My heart wouldn't be in it. And that would be dangerous, don't you think?'

Li Yuan shook his head. 'You're wrong. Besides, I need you, Ben. You were bred to be my helper, my advisor...'

He stopped, seeing how Ben was looking at him.

'I can't be, Li Yuan. I'm sorry, but there's something else I have to do. Something more important.'

Li Yuan stared at him. Something more important? How could *anything* be more important than the business of government?

'You don't understand,' Ben said. 'I knew you wouldn't. But you will. It may take twenty years, but one day you'll understand why I said no today.'

'Then I can't persuade you?'

Ben smiled. 'To be your Chief Advisor – to be what my father was to Li Shai Tung – that I can't be. But I'll be your sounding board if you ever need me, Li Yuan. You need only come here. And we can sit in the garden and play at killing ants, neh?'

Li Yuan stared back at him, not certain whether he was being gently mocked, then let himself relax, returning Ben's smile.

'All right. I'll hold you to that promise.'

Ben nodded. 'Good. Now watch. The best bit is always at the start. When they scuttle for the holes. They're like hounds scenting blood. There's something pure – something utterly pure – about them.'

Li Yuan moved back, watching as Ben flipped back the transparent cover to the case, releasing a bright red spill. They fell like sand on to the jet-black earth, scattering at once into the tiny tracks, the speed at which they moved astonishing. And then they were gone, like blood-soaked water drained into the thirsty earth, seeking out their victims far below.

It was as Ben had said: there was something pure – something quite fascinating – about them. Yet at the same time they were quite horrifying. Tiny machines, they were. Not ants at all. He shuddered. What in the gods' names had Amos Shepherd been thinking when he'd made such things? He looked at Ben again.

'And when they've finished... what happens then?'

Ben looked up at him, meeting his eyes. 'They come back. They're pro-grammed to come back. Like the *Hei* you use beneath the Net. It's all the same, after all. All very much the same.'

Hans Ebert sat back in his chair, his face dark with anger.

'Karr did *what?*'

Scott bowed his head. 'It's all here, Hans. In the report.'

'*Report?*' Ebert stood and came round the desk, snatching the file from the Captain. He opened it, scanning it a moment, then looked back at Scott.

'But this is to Tolonen.'

Scott nodded. 'I took the liberty of making a copy. I knew you'd be interested.'

'You did, eh?' Ebert took a breath, then nodded. 'And DeVore?'

'He got away. Karr almost had him, but he slipped through the net.'

Ebert swallowed. He didn't know what was worse: DeVore in Karr's hands or DeVore loose and blaming him for the raid.

He had barely had time to consider the matter when his equerry appeared in the doorway.

'There's a call for you, sir. A *Shih* Beattie. A business matter, I understand.'

He felt his stomach tighten. Beattie was DeVore.

'Forgive me, Captain Scott. I must deal with this matter rather urgently. But thank you. I appreciate your prompt action. I'll see that you do not go unrewarded for your help.'

Scott bowed then left, leaving him alone. For a moment he sat there, steeling himself, then leaned forward.

'Put *Shih* Beattie through.'

He sat back, watching as the screen containing DeVore's face tilted up from the desk's surface, facing him. He had never seen DeVore so angry.

'What the fuck are you up to?'

Ebert shook his head. 'I only heard five minutes back. Believe me, Howard.'

'Crap! You must have known something was going on. You've got your finger on the pulse, haven't you?'

Ebert swallowed back his anger. 'It wasn't *me*, Howard. I can prove it wasn't. And I didn't know a fucking thing until just now. All right? Look...'

He held up the file, turning the opening page so that it faced the screen.

DeVore was silent a moment, reading through, then he swore.

'You see?' Ebert said, glad for once that Scott had acted off his own initiative. 'Tolonen ordered it. Karr carried it out. Tsu Ma's troops were used. I was never, at any stage, involved.'

DeVore nodded. 'All right. But why? Have you asked yourself that yet, Hans? Why were you excluded from this?'

Ebert frowned. He hadn't considered it. He had just assumed that they had done it because he was so busy, preparing to take over the generalship. But now that he thought about it, it was odd. Very odd indeed. Tolonen, at the very least, ought to have let him know that *something* was going on.

'Do you think they suspect some kind of link?'

DeVore shook his head. 'Tolonen would not have recommended you, and Li Yuan certainly wouldn't have appointed you. No, this has to do with Karr. I'm told his men were poking about the villages recently. I was going to deal with that, but they've pre-empted me.'

'So what do we do?'

DeVore laughed. 'That's very simple. You'll be General in a day or so. Karr, instead of being your equal, will be your subordinate.'

Ebert shook his head. 'That's not strictly true. Karr is Tolonen's man. He always was. He took a direct oath to the old man when he joined Security eleven years ago. He's only technically in my command.'

'Then what about that friend of his. Kao Chen? Can't you start court martial proceedings against him?'

Ebert shook his head, confused. 'Why? What will that achieve?'

'They're close. Very close, so I've heard. If you can't get at Karr, attack his friends. Isolate him. I'm sure you can rig up enough evidence to convict the Han. You've friends who would lie for you, haven't you, Hans?'

Hans laughed. More than enough. Even so, he wasn't sure he wanted to take on Karr. Not just yet.

'Isn't there an alternative?'

'Yes. You might have Karr killed. And Tolonen, too, while you're at it.'

'Kill Tolonen?' Ebert sat forward, startled by the suggestion. 'But he's virtually my father-in-law!'

'So? He's dangerous. Can't you see that, Hans? He almost had me killed last night. And where would we have been then, neh? Besides, what if he discovers the link between us? No, Hans, this is no time to play *Shih* Conscience. If you don't have him killed, I will.'

Ebert sat back, a look of sour resignation on his face. 'All right. I take your point. Leave it with me.'

'Good. And, Hans... congratulations. You'll make a good general. A very good general.'

Ebert sat there afterwards, thinking back on what had been said. To kill Karr: he could think of nothing more satisfying, or – when he considered it – more difficult. In contrast, having Tolonen killed would be all too easy, for the old man trusted him implicitly.

He understood DeVore's anger – understood and even agreed with the reasons he had given – yet the thought of killing the old man disturbed him. Oh, he had cursed the old man often enough for a fool, but he had never been treated badly by him. No, Tolonen had been like a father to him these past years. More of a father than his own. At some level he rather liked the old dog. Besides, how could he marry Jelka, knowing he had murdered her father?

And yet, if he didn't, DeVore would. And that would place him at a disadvantage in his dealings with the Major. Would place him in his debt. He laughed bitterly. In reality there was no choice at all. He had to have Tolonen killed. To keep the upper hand. And to demonstrate to DeVore that, when it came to such matters, he had the steel in him to carry through such schemes.

He paused, contemplating the map. As from tomorrow all this was his domain. Across this huge continent he was the arbiter, the final word, speaking with the T'ang's tongue. Like a prince, trying out the role before it became his own.

There was a tapping on the door behind him. He turned. 'Come!'

It was the Chancellor, Chung Hu-yan.

'What is it, Chung? You look worried.'

Chung held out a sheaf of papers to him, the great seal of the T'ang of Europe appended to the last of them.

'What are these?'

Chung shook his head, clearly flustered. 'They are my orders for the coronation ceremony tomorrow, Major Ebert. They outline the protocol I am to follow.'

Ebert frowned. 'So what's the problem? You follow protocol. What's unusual in that?'

'Look!' Chung tapped the first sheet. 'Look at what he wants them all to do.'

Ebert read the passage Chung was indicating then looked up at him, wide-eyed. 'He wants them to do *that*?'

Chung nodded vigorously. 'I tried to see him this morning, but he is not at the palace. And the rehearsal is to be in an hour. What shall I do, Major Ebert? Everyone who is to be there tomorrow is attending – the very cream of the Above. They are bound to feel affronted by these demands. Why, they might even refuse.'

Ebert nodded. It was a distinct possibility. Such a ritual had not been heard of since the tyrant Tsao Ch'un's time, and he had modelled it on the worst excesses of the Ch'ing dynasty – the Manchu.

'I feel for you, Chung Hu-yan, but we are our masters' hands, neh? And the T'ang's seal is on that document. My advice to you is to follow it to the letter.'

Chung Hu-yan stared at the sheaf of papers a moment longer, quickly furled them and, with a bow to Ebert, turned, hurrying away. Ebert watched him go, amused by how ruffled the normally implacable Chancellor was. Even so, he had to admit to a small element of unease on his own account. What Li Yuan was asking for was a radical departure from the traditional ceremony and there was bound to be resentment, even open opposition. It would be interesting to see how he dealt with that. Very interesting indeed.

The big man mounted the steps, pressing his face close to the Chancellor's, ignoring the guards who hurried to intercede.

'Never!' he said, his voice loud enough to carry to the back of the packed hall. 'I'd as soon cut off my own bollocks as agree to that!'

There was laughter at that, but also a fierce murmur of agreement. They had been astonished when Chung Hu-yan had first read Li Yuan's instructions to them. Now their astonishment had turned to outrage.

Chung Hu-yan waved the guards back then began again. 'Your T'ang instructs you–' But his words were drowned out by a roar of disapproval.

'*Instructs* us?' the big man said, turning now, looking back into the hall. 'By what right does he instruct us?'

'You must do as you are told,' Chung Hu-yan began again, his voice quavering. 'These are the T'ang's orders.'

The man shook his head. 'It is unjust. We are not *hsiao jen* – little men. We are the masters of this great City. It is not right to try to humiliate us in this manner.'

Once more a great roar of support came from the packed hall. Chung Hu-yan shook his head. This was not his doing. Not his doing at all. Even so, he would persist.

'You must step down, *Shih* Tarrant. These are the T'ang's own instructions. Would you disobey them?'

Tarrant puffed out his huge chest. 'You've heard what I have to say, Chancellor Chung. I'll not place my neck beneath any man's foot, T'ang or no. Neither will anyone in this room, I warrant. It is asking too much of us. Too much by far!'

This time the noise was deafening. But as it faded the great doors behind Chung Hu-yan swung back and the T'ang himself entered, a troop of his elite guards behind him.

A hush fell upon the crowd.

Li Yuan came forward until he stood beside his Chancellor, looking back sternly at the big man, unintimidated by his size.

'Take him away,' he said, speaking over his shoulder to the captain of the guard. 'What he has said is in defiance of my written order. Is *treason*. Take him outside at once and execute him.'

There was a hiss of disbelief. Tarrant stepped back, his face a picture of astonishment, but four of the guards were on him at once, pinning his arms behind his back. Shouting loudly, he was frogmarched past the T'ang and out through the doors.

Li Yuan turned his head slowly, looking out across the sea of faces in the hall, seeing their anger and astonishment, their fear and surprise.

'Who else will defy me?'

He paused, looking about him, seeing how quiet, how docile they had become. 'No. I thought not.'

'This is a new age,' he said, lifting his chin commandingly. 'And a new age demands new rules, new ways of behaving. So do not mistake me for my father, *ch'un tzu*. I am Li Yuan, T'ang of City Europe. Now bow your heads.'

★

He was like the sun, stepping down from the *Tien Tan*, the Temple of Heaven. His arms were two bright flashes of gold as he raised the imperial crown and placed it on his brow. Sunlight beat from his chest in waves as he moved from side to side, looking out across the vast mass of his subjects who were stretched out prone before him in the temple grounds.

No one looked. Only the cameras took this in. All other eyes were cast into the dust, unworthy of the sight.

'This is a new age,' Li Yuan said softly to himself. 'A new time. But old are the ways of power. As old as Man himself.'

One by one his servants came to him, stretched out on the steps beneath him, their heads turned to one side, their necks exposed. And on each proffered neck he trod, placing his weight there for the briefest moment before releasing them. His vassals. This time they'd learn their lesson. This time they would know whose beasts they were.

Officers and Administrators, Representatives and Company Executives, Ministers and Family Heads – all bowed before him and exposed their necks, each one acknowledging him their lord and master.

Last was Tolonen. Only here did Li Yuan's reluctance take a shape, his naked sole touching the old man's neck as if he kissed it, no pressure behind the touch.

Then it was done. The brute thing made manifest to all. He was an emperor, like the emperors of old, powerful and deadly. And afterwards he saw how changed they were by this, how absolute he'd made them think his power. He almost smiled, wondering what his father would have made of this. So powerful was this ritual, so naked its meaning.

You are mine, it said, *to crush beneath my heel or raise to prominence.*

The ceremony over, he dismissed all but those closest to him, holding audience in the great throne-room. First to greet him there were his fellow T'ang. They climbed the marble steps to bow their heads and kiss his ring, welcoming him to their number. Last of these was Wei Feng, wearing the white of mourning. Wei's eyes were filled with tears, and when he had kissed the ring, he leaned forward to hold Li Yuan to him a moment, whispering in his ear.

Li Yuan nodded and held the old man's hands a moment, then relinquished them. 'I shall,' he said softly, moved deeply by the words his father's friend had uttered.

Others came, pledging loyalty in a more traditional way. And last of all his officers, led by General Tolonen.

The General knelt, unsheathing his ceremonial dagger and offering it up to his T'ang, hilt first, his eyes averted. Li Yuan took it from him and laid it across his lap.

'You served my father well, Knut. I hope you'll serve me just as well in future. But new lords need new servants. I must have a general to match my youth.'

The words were a formality, for it was Tolonen who had pushed to have Ebert appointed. The old man nodded and lifted his head. 'I wish him well, *Chieh Hsia*. He is as a son to me. I have felt honoured to have served, but now my time is done. Let another serve you as I tried to serve your father.'

Li Yuan smiled then summoned the young man forward.

Hans Ebert came towards the throne, his head bowed, his shoulders stooped, and knelt beside Tolonen. 'I am yours,' he said ritually, lowering his forehead to touch the step beneath the throne, once, twice and then a third time. The sheath at his belt was empty. No mark of rank lay on his powder-blue uniform. He waited, abased and 'naked' before his lord.

'Let it begin here,' said Li Yuan, speaking loudly over the heads of the kneeling officers to the gathered eminences. 'My trust goes out from me and into the hands of others. So it is. So it must be. This is the chain we forge; the chain that links us all.'

He looked down at the young man, speaking more softly, personally now. 'Raise your head, Hans Ebert. Look up at your lord, who is as the sun to you and from whom you have your life. Look up and take from me my trust.'

Ebert raised his head. 'I am ready, *Chieh Hsia*,' he said, his voice steady, his eyes meeting those of Li Yuan unflinchingly.

'Good.' Li Yuan nodded, smiling. 'Then take the badge of your office.'

He lifted the dagger from his lap and held it out. Ebert took it carefully then sheathed it, lowering his head once more. Then both he and Tolonen backed down the steps, their eyes averted, their heads bowed low.

That same evening they met in a room in the Purple Forbidden City: the Seven who ruled Chung Kuo. One thing remained before they went from there, one final task to set things right.

Tsu Ma stood before Li Yuan, grasping his hands firmly, meeting him eye to eye. 'You're sure you want this?'

'The genotyping is conclusive. It must be done now, before the child is born. Afterwards is too late.'

Tsu Ma held him a moment longer, then released his hands. 'So be it, then. Let us all sign the special Edict.'

Each signed his name and sealed it with his ring, in the old manner. Later it would be confirmed with retinal prints and ECG patterning, but for now this was sufficient.

Wei Feng was last to sign and seal the document. He turned, looking back at the new T'ang. 'Good sits with ill this day, Li Yuan. I would not have thought it of her.'

'Nor I,' said Li Yuan, staring down at the completed Edict. And so it was done. Fei Yen was no longer his wife. The child would not inherit.

'When is the marriage to be?' Tsu Ma stood close. His voice was gentle, sympathetic.

'Tomorrow,' Yuan answered, grateful for Tsu Ma's presence. 'How strange that is. Tonight I lose a wife. And tomorrow...'

'Tomorrow you gain three.' Tsu Ma shook his head. 'Do you know who it was, Yuan? Whose son Fei Yen is carrying?'

Li Yuan looked at him then looked away. 'That does not concern me,' he said stiffly. Then, relenting, he laid his hand on Tsu Ma's arm. 'It was a mistake ever to have begun with her. My father was right. I know that now. Only my blindness kept it from me.'

'Then you are content?'

Li Yuan shook his head. 'Content? No. But it is done.'

Tolonen turned from the screen and the image of the boy and faced the Architect.

'From what I've seen, the experience seems not to have done Ward too much harm, but what's your opinion? Is he ready for this yet, or should we delay?'

The Architect hesitated, remembering the last time, years before, when he had been questioned about the boy's condition. Then it had been Berdichev, but the questions were much the same. How is the boy? Is he ready to be used? He smiled tightly then answered Tolonen.

'It's too early to know what the long-term effects are going to be, but in the short term you're right. He's emerged from this whole episode extremely well. His reaction to the attack – the trauma and loss of memory – seems to have been the best thing that could have happened to him. I was concerned in case it had done lasting damage, particularly to his memory, but if anything the experience seems to have...' he shrugged '...toughened him up, I guess you'd say. He's a resilient little creature. Much tougher than we thought. The psychological blocks we created during his restructuring four years ago seem to have melted away – as if they'd never been. But instead of regressing to that state of savagery in which we first encountered him, he appears to have attained a new balance. I've never seen anything like it, to be honest. Most minds are too inflexible – too set in their ways – to survive what Kim has been through without cracking. He, on the other hand, seems to have emerged stronger, saner than ever.'

Tolonen frowned. 'Maybe. But you say that the psychological blocks have gone. That's a bad thing, surely? I thought they were there to prevent the boy from reverting into savagery.'

'They were.'

'Then there's a chance he might still be dangerous?'

'There's a chance. But that's true of anyone. And I mean anyone. We've all of us a darker side. Push us just so far and we'll snap. I suspect now that that was what happened the first time, that Kim was simply responding to extreme provocation from the other boy. My guess is that unless Kim were pushed to the same extreme again he'd be perfectly safe. After all, he's not a bomb waiting to go off, he's only a human being, like you or I.'

'So he's not dangerous. He won't be biting people's ears off or clawing out their eyes?'

'I doubt it. The fact that his friend survived has helped greatly. Their reunion was a major factor in his recuperation. If T'ai Cho had been killed our problems might have been of a different order but, as it is, I'd say Kim's fine. As fine as you or I.'

'Then you think he's up to it?'

The Architect laughed. 'I do. In fact, I think it would be positively good for him. He has a mind that's ever-hungry for new things and an instinct for seeking them out. From what I've heard of it, the North American scene should prove a good hunting ground in that regard.'

Tolonen frowned, not certain he liked the sound of that, but it was not in his brief to query what was happening in Wu Shih's City; his job was to find out whether Kim was fit to travel to North America, and from all indications he was.

He sniffed deeply then nodded, his mind made up. 'Good. Then prepare the boy at once. There's a flight from Nantes spaceport at tenth bell. I want Ward and his tutor on it.'

'And the wire? Shall we remove that now that our tests are finished?'

Tolonen looked away. 'No. Leave it in. It won't harm, after all.' He looked back at the Architect, his face a mask. 'Besides, if something does go badly wrong – if he goes missing again – we'd be able to trace him, wouldn't we?'

The Architect looked down, beginning to understand what was really happening. 'Of course.'

'Would you like anything, sir?'

The boy looked up, startled, his dark eyes wide, then settled back in his seat again, shaking his head.

'Nothing... I... I'm all right.'

The Steward backed off a pace, noting how tense the bodyguards had grown, and bowed his head. 'Forgive me, sir, but if you change your mind you have only to press the summons button.'

The boy returned a tense smile. 'Of course.'

He moved on, settling the passengers, checking they were securely strapped into the seats, asking if there was anything he could do for them before the launch, but all the while his mind was on the boy.

Who was he? he wondered. After all, it wasn't every day they received an order direct from Bremen, neither was it customary for Security to reserve a whole section of the cabin for a single passenger. Knowing all this, he had expected some high-ranking Han – a Minor Family prince at the very least, or a Minister – so the boy's appearance had surprised him. At first he had thought he might be a prisoner of some kind, but the more he thought about it the more that seemed ridiculous. Besides, he wasn't bound in any way, and the men with him were clearly bodyguards, not warders. He had only to ask for something and one of them would go running.

No. Whoever he was, he was important enough to warrant the kind of treatment reserved only for the very highest of the Above – the *Supernal*, as they were known these days – and yet he seemed merely a boy, and a rather odd, almost ugly little boy at that. There was a curious angularity to his limbs, a strange darkness in his over-large eyes.

The Steward came to the end of the walkway and turned, looking back down the cabin. It was five minutes to take-off. The young Americans were settled now. Like so many of their kind they were almost totally lacking in manners. Only the quiet one – Lever – had even seemed to notice he was there. The rest had snapped their fingers and demanded this and that, as if he were not Steward but some half-human creature manufactured in the GenSyn vats. It was things like that that he hated about this new generation. They were not like their fathers. Not at all. Their fathers understood that other men had their own pride, and that it was such pride that held the vast fabric of society together. These youngsters had no idea. They were blind to such things. And one day they would pay – and pay dearly – for their blindness.

He turned and went through the curtain. The Security Captain was sitting there, the file open on his knee. He looked up as the Steward came in, giving him a brief smile.

'Are they all settled?'

The Steward nodded. 'Even the two women. I had to give them both a sedative, but they seem all right now.' He shook his head. 'They shouldn't let women travel. I've nothing but trouble with them.'

The Captain laughed, closing the file. 'And the boy?'

'He's fine. I wondered...'

The Captain shook his head. 'Don't ask me. All I was told was that there was to be a special guest on board. A guest of the T'ang himself. But who he is or what...' He shrugged then laughed again. 'I know. I'm as curious as you. He's a strange one, neh?'

The Steward nodded then moved away, satisfied that the Captain knew no more than him. Even so, he thought he had glimpsed a picture of the boy, earlier, when he had first come back behind the curtain – in the file the Captain was reading. He could have been mistaken, but...

'Are you on business?' he asked, pulling the webbing harness out from the wall behind the Captain.

'Liaison,' the Captain answered, moving forward in his seat, letting himself be fastened into the harness. 'My job is to increase cooperation between the two Cities.'

The Steward smiled politely. 'It sounds very interesting. But I'd have thought there was little need.'

'You'd be surprised. The days of isolation are ended for the Cities. The Triads have spread their nets wide these days. And not only the Triads. There's a lot of illicit trade goes on. Some of it via these rockets, I've no doubt!'

The Steward stared at him a moment then turned away. 'Anyway, I'll leave you now. I have one last check to make before I secure myself.'

The Captain nodded then called him back. 'Here. I almost forgot. I was told to deliver this to the boy before we took off.' He handed the Steward a sealed envelope. 'It was in my file. Along with a picture of the boy. All very mysterious, neh?'

The Steward stared at the envelope a moment then nodded. He turned away, disappearing through the curtain once again.

DeVore watched the man go, breathing a sigh of relief. Then he laughed. It was easy – all so bloody easy. Why, he could have taken the boy out earlier, in the lobby, if he'd wished. He'd had a clear shot. But that wasn't what he wanted. No, he wanted the boy. Besides, Li Yuan was up to something. It would be interesting to find out what.

He smiled then opened the file again, picking up from where he'd left off. After a moment he looked up, nodding thoughtfully. Ebert had done him proud. There was everything here. Everything. The report Tolonen had made on the attack on the Project, the medical and psychological reports on Ward and a full transcript of the debriefing. The only thing missing – and it was missing only because it didn't exist – was something to indicate just why Li Yuan had decided to ship the boy off to North America.

Well, maybe he could clarify things a little over the next few days. Maybe he could find out – through the Levers – what it was Li Yuan wanted. And at the same time he might do a little business on his own account: would take up young Lever's invitation to meet his father and have dinner.

Yes, and afterwards he would put his proposal to the son. Would see just how deep his enthusiasm for change was. And then...?

He smiled and closed the file. And then he would begin again, building new shapes on a new part of the board; constructing his patterns until the game was won. For it would be won. If it took him a dozen lifetimes he would win it.

Chapter 66

GHOSTS

I t was a cold, grey morning, the sky overcast, the wind whipping off the surface of the West Lake, bending back the reeds on the shoreline of Jade Spring Island. In front of the great pavilion – a huge, circular, two-tiered building with tapered roofs of vermilion tile – the thousand bright red and gold dragon banners of the T'ang flapped noisily, the ranks of armoured bearers standing like iron statues in the wind, their red capes fluttering behind them.

To the south of the pavilion a huge platform had been built, reaching almost to the lake's edge. In its centre, on a dais high above the rest, stood the throne, a great canopy of red silk shielding it from the rain that gusted intermittently across the lake.

Li Yuan sat there on the throne, his red silks decorated with tiny golden dragon and phoenix emblems. Behind him, below the nine steps of the great dais, his retainers and Ministers were assembled, dressed in red.

Facing Li Yuan, no more than a hundred ch'i distant, a wide bridge linked the island to the eastern shore. It was an ancient bridge, built in the time of the Song dynasty, more than a thousand years before, its white stone spans decorated with lions and dragons and other mythical beasts.

Li Yuan stared at it a moment then turned his head, looking out blank-eyed across the lake, barely conscious of the great procession that waited on the far side of the bridge. News had come that morning. Fei Yen had had her child. A boy it was. A boy.

The music of the ceremony began, harsh, dissonant – bells, and drums and cymbals. At once the New Confucian officials came forward, making their obeisance to him before they backed away. On the eastern shore the procession started forward, a great tide of red, making its slow way across the bridge.

He sighed and looked down at his hands. It was only two days since he had removed her wedding ring. Two days… He shivered. So simple it had been. He had watched himself remove it from his finger and place it on the gold silk cushion Nan Ho had held out to him. Had watched as Nan Ho had turned and taken it from the room, ending the life he had shared with her, destroying the dream for good and all.

He took a shuddering breath then looked up again. This was no time for tears. No. Today was a day for celebrations, for today was his wedding day.

He watched them come. The heads of the three clans walked side by side at the front of the procession: proud old men, each bearing his honour in his face like a badge. Behind them came the ranks of brothers and cousins, sisters and wives, many hundreds in all, and beyond them the lung t'ing – the 'dragon pavilions' – each one carried by four bare-headed eunuch servants. The tiny sedan chairs were piled high with dowry gifts for the T'ang – bolts of silk and satin, boxes of silver, golden plates and cups, embroidered robes, delicate porcelain, saddles and fans and gilded cages filled with songbirds. So much, indeed, that this single part of the procession was by far the longest, with more than a hundred lung t'ing to each family.

An honour guard was next. Behind that came the three feng yu, the phoenix chairs, four silver birds perched atop each canopy, each scarlet and gold sedan carried aloft by a dozen bearers.

His brides…

He had told Nan Ho to get the Heads of the three clans to agree to waive the preliminary ceremonies – had insisted that the thing be done quickly if at all – yet it had not been possible to dispense with this final ritual. It was, after all, a matter of face. Of pride. To marry a T'ang – that was not done without due celebration, without due pomp and ceremony. And would the T'ang deny them that?

He could not. For to be T'ang had its obligations as well as its advantages. And so here he was, on a cold, wet, windy morning, marrying three young women he had never seen before this day.

Necessary, he told himself. *For the Family must be strong again.* Even so, his heart ached and his soul cried out at the wrongness of it.

He watched them come, a feeling of dread rising in him. These were the women he was to share his life with. They would bear his sons, would lie beneath him in his bed. And what if he came to hate them? What if they hated him? For what was done here could not easily be undone.

No. A man was forgiven one failure. But any more and the world would condemn him, wherever lay the fault.

Wives. These strangers were to be his wives. And how had this come about? He sat there, momentarily bemused by the fact. Then, as the music changed and the chant began below, he stood and went to the top of the steps, ready for the great ceremony to begin.

An hour later it was done. Li Yuan stepped back, watching as his wives knelt, bowing low, touching their foreheads to the floor three times before him.

Nan Ho had chosen well, had shown great sensitivity, for not one of the three reminded him in the least of Fei Yen and yet each was, in her own way, quite distinct. Mien Shan, the eldest and officially his First Wife, was a tiny thing with a strong build and a pleasantly rounded face. Fu Ti Chang, the youngest, just seventeen, was also the tallest, a shy, elegant willow of a girl. By way of contrast, Lai Shi seemed quite spirited; she was a long-faced girl, hardly a beauty, but there was a sparkle in her eye that made her by far the most attractive of the three. Li Yuan had smiled when she'd pulled back her veil, surprised to find an interest in her stirring in himself.

Tonight duty required him to visit the bed of Mien Shan. But tomorrow?

He dismissed his wives then turned, summoning Nan Ho to him.

'*Chieh Hsia?*'

He lowered his voice. 'I am most pleased with this morning's events, Master Nan. You have done well to prepare things so quickly.'

Nan Ho bowed low. 'It was but my duty, *Chieh Hsia.*'

'Maybe so, but you have excelled yourself, Nan Ho. From henceforth you are no longer Master of the Inner Chamber but Chancellor.'

Nan Ho's look of amazement was almost comical. '*Chieh Hsia!* But what of Chung Hu-yan?'

Li Yuan smiled. 'I am warmed by your concern, Nan Ho, but do not worry. I informed Chung yesterday evening. Indeed, he confirmed my choice.'

Nan Ho's puzzlement deepened. '*Chieh Hsia?*'

'I should explain, perhaps, Master Nan. It was all agreed long before my father's death. It was felt that I would need new blood when I became T'ang, new men surrounding me. Men I could trust. Men who would grow as I grew and would be as pillars, supporting me in my old age. You understand?'

Nan Ho bowed his head. 'I understand, *Chieh Hsia*, and am honoured. Honoured beyond words.'

'Well… Go now. Chung Hu-yan has agreed to stay on as your advisor until you feel comfortable with your new duties. Then he is to become my counsellor.'

Nan Ho gave the briefest nod, understanding. Counsellor. It would make Chung virtually an uncle to Li Yuan, a member of Li Yuan's inner council, discussing and formulating policy. No wonder he had not minded relinquishing his post as Chancellor.

'And when am I to begin, *Chieh Hsia*?'

Li Yuan laughed. 'You began two days ago, Master Nan, when you came to my room and took the book of brides from me. I appointed you then, in here.' He tapped his forehead. 'You have been my Chancellor ever since.'

Jelka was standing at her father's side, among the guests in the great pavilion, when Hans Ebert came across and joined them.

'Marshal Tolonen…' Ebert bowed to the old man then turned, smiling, to Jelka. In his bright red dress uniform he looked a young god, his golden hair swept back neatly, his strong, handsome features formed quite pleasantly. Even his eyes, normally so cold, seemed kind as he looked at her. But still, Jelka hardened herself against the illusion, reminding herself of what she knew about him.

He lowered his head, keeping his eyes on her face. 'It's good to see you here, Jelka. I hope you're feeling better.'

His enquiry was soft-spoken, his words exactly what a future husband ought to have said, yet somehow she could not accept them at face value. He was a good actor – a consummately good actor, for it seemed almost as if he really liked her – but she knew what he was beneath the act. A shit. A cold, self-centred shit.

'I'm much better, thank you,' she said, lowering her eyes, a faint blush coming to her cheeks. 'It was only a sprain.'

The blush was for the lie she had told. She had not sprained her ankle at all. It was simply that the idea of seeing Hans Ebert made general in her father's place had been more than she could bear. To have spent the evening toasting the man she most abhorred! She could think of nothing worse.

She kept her eyes averted, realizing the shape her thoughts had taken. Was it really that bad? Was Hans Ebert really so abhorrent? She looked up again, meeting his eyes, noting the concern there. Even so, the feeling persisted. To think of marrying this man was a mistake. A horrible mistake.

His smile widened. 'You will come and dine with us, I hope, a week from now. My father is looking forward to it greatly. And I. It would be nice to speak with you, Jelka. To find out who we are.'

'Yes...' She glanced up at him then lowered her eyes again, a shiver of revulsion passing through her at the thought. Yet what choice had she? This man was to be her husband – her life partner.

Ebert lifted her hand, kissing her knuckles gently before releasing it. He smiled then bowed, showing her the deepest respect. 'Until then...' He turned slightly, bowing to her father, then turned away.

'A marvellous young man,' Tolonen said, watching Ebert make his way back through the crowd towards the T'ang. 'Do you know, Jelka, if I'd had a son, I'd have wished for one like Hans.'

She shivered. The very thought of it made her stomach tighten, reminded her of the mad girl in the Ebert Mansion and of that awful pink-eyed goat-baby. A son like Hans... She shook her head. No! It could never be!

In the sedan travelling back to Nanking, Jelka sat there, facing her father, listening to him, conscious, for the first time in her life, of how pompous, how vacuous his words were. His notion that they were at the beginning of a new 'Golden Age', for instance. It was a nonsense. She had read the special reports on the situation in the lower levels and knew how bad things were. Every day brought growing disaffection from the Seven and their rule – brought strikes and riots and the killing of officials – yet he seemed quite blind to all that. He spoke of growth and stability and the glorious years to come. Years that would recapture the glory of his youth.

She sat there a long while, simply listening, her head lowered. Then, suddenly, she looked up at him.

'I can't.'

He looked across at her, breaking off. 'Can't what?'

She stared back into his steel-grey eyes, hardening herself against him. 'I can't marry Hans Ebert.'

He laughed, shocked. 'Don't be silly, Jelka. It's all arranged. Besides, Hans is General now.'

'I don't care!' she said, the violence of her words surprising him. 'I simply *can't* marry him!'

He shook his head then leaned forward. 'You mustn't say that, Jelka. You mustn't!'

She glared back at him defiantly. 'Why not? It's what I feel. To marry Hans would kill me. I'd shrivel up and die.'

'Nonsense!' he barked, angry now. 'You're being ridiculous! Can't you see the way that boy looks at you? He's besotted!'

She looked down. 'You really don't understand, do you?' She shuddered then looked up at him again. 'I don't *like* him, Daddy. I...' She gave a small, pained laugh. 'How can I possibly marry someone I don't like?'

He had gone very still, his eyes narrowed. 'Listen, my girl, you *will*, and sooner than you think. I've agreed a new date for the wedding. A month from now.'

She sat back, open-mouthed, staring at him.

He leaned closer, softening his voice. 'It's not how I meant to tell you but, there, it's done. And no more of this nonsense. Hans is a fine young man. The very best of young men. And you're a lucky girl, if only you'd get these silly notions out of your head. You'll come to realize it. And then you'll thank me for it.'

'*Thank* you?' The note of incredulity in her voice made him sit back, bristling.

'Yes. *Thank* me. Now, no more. I insist.'

She shook her head. 'You don't know him, Father. He keeps a girl in his house – a mad girl whose baby he had killed – and I've heard –'

'Enough!'

Tolonen got to his feet, sending the sedan swaying. As it slowed, he sat again, the colour draining slowly from his face.

'I won't hear another word from you, my girl. Not another word. Hans is a fine young man. And these lies...'

'They're not lies. I've seen her. I've seen what he did to her.'

'*Lies...*' he insisted, shaking his head. 'Really... I would not have believed it of you, Jelka. Such behaviour. If your mother were alive...'

She put her head down sharply, trembling with anger. Gods! To talk of her mother at such a time. She slowed her breathing, calming herself, then said it one more time.

'I *can't.*'

She looked up and saw how he was watching her: coldly, so far from her in feeling that it was as if he were a stranger to her.

'You will,' he said. 'You will because I say you will.'

The doctor was still fussing over Karr's shoulder when they brought the man in. Karr turned, wincing, waving the doctor away, then leaned across the desk, studying the newcomer.

'You're sure this is him?' he asked, looking past the man at Chen.

Chen nodded. 'We've made all the checks. He seems to be who he claims he is.'

Karr smiled then sat back, a flicker of pain passing across his face. 'All right. So you're Reid, eh? Thomas Reid. Well, tell me, *Shih* Reid, why are you here?'

The man looked down, betraying a moment's fear, then he girded up his courage again and spoke.

'I was there, you see. After you raided the fortress. I was there with the Man's lieutenant...'

'The Man?'

'DeVore. That's what we call him. The Man.'

Karr glanced at Chen. 'And?'

'Just that I was there, afterwards. Lehmann and I...'

'Lehmann?'

'Stefan Lehmann. The albino. Under-Secretary Lehmann's son.'

Karr laughed, surprised. 'And he's DeVore's lieutenant?'

'Yes. I was with him, you see. We'd been off to deliver something for the Man. But when we got back, shortly after eight, we saw your transporters from some distance away and knew there had been trouble. We flew south then doubled back, crossing the valley on foot, then climbed up to the ruins.'

'The ruins?'

'Yes, there's a castle... or, at least, the remains of one. It's on the other side of the mountain from the base. There's an old system of tunnels beneath it. The Man used them when he built the base. Linked up to them.'

'Ah...' The light of understanding dawned in Karr's eyes. 'But why did you go there?'

'Because Lehmann had a hunch. He thought DeVore might be there, in the old tunnel.'

'And was he?'

'Yes.'

Karr looked at Chen. It was as he'd said. But now they knew for sure. DeVore had got out: was loose in the world to do his mischief.

'Do you know where he is?'

Reid shook his head.

'So why are you here? What do you want?'

Reid looked aside. 'I was... afraid. Things were getting desperate out there. Out of hand. DeVore, Lehmann... they're not people you can cross.'

'And yet you're here. Why?'

'Because I'd had enough. And because I felt that you, if anyone, could protect me.'

'And why should I do that?'

'Because I know things. Know where the other bases are.'

Karr sat back, astonished. *Other bases...* 'But I thought...' He checked himself and looked at Chen, seeing his own surprise mirrored back at him. They had stumbled on to the Landek base by complete chance in the course of their sweep of the Wilds, alerted by its heat emission patterns. They had blessed their luck, but never for an instant had they thought there would be others. They assumed all along that DeVore was working on a smaller scale: that he'd kept his organization much tighter.

This changed things.

Reid was watching Karr. 'I know how things are organized out there. I was in charge of several things in my time. I've pieced things together in my head. I know where their weak spots are.'

'And you'll tell us all of this in return for your safety?'

Reid nodded. 'That and ten million *yuan*.'

Karr sat back. 'I could have you tortured. Could wring the truth from you.'

'You could. But then Ebert might come to know about it, mightn't he? And that would spoil things for you. I understand he's already instigated a special investigation into your activities.'

Karr jerked forward, grimacing, the pain from his shoulder suddenly intense. 'How do you know that?'

Reid smiled, amused by the effect his words had had. 'I overheard it. The Man was speaking to Ebert. It seems the new General plans a purge of his ranks. And you and your friend, Kao Chen, are top of the list.'

'But ten million. Where would I get hold of ten million *yuan*?'

Reid shrugged. 'That's your problem. But until you agree to my terms I'm telling you nothing. And the longer you wait, the more likely it is that Ebert will close you down.'

Chen broke his silence. 'And what good would that do you, *Shih* Reid?'

Reid turned, facing Chen. 'The way I figure it, Kao Chen, is that I'm either dead or I'm safe and very, very rich. It's the kind of choice I understand. The kind of risk I'm willing to take. But how about you? You've children, Kao Chen. Can you look at things so clearly?'

Chen blanched, surprised that Reid knew so much. It implied that DeVore had files on them all: files that Ebert, doubtlessly, had provided. It was a daunting thought. The possibility of Wang Ti and the children being threatened by DeVore made him go cold. He looked past Reid at Karr.

'Gregor...'

Karr nodded then looked back at Reid, his expression hard. 'I'll find the money, *Shih* Reid. I give you my word. You'll have it by this evening. But you must tell me what you know. Now. While I can still act on it. Otherwise my word won't be worth a dead whore's coonie.'

Reid hesitated then nodded. 'All right. Get me a detailed map of the Wilds. I'll mark where the bases are. And then we'll talk. I'll tell you a story. About a young General and an ex-Major, and about a meeting the two had at an old skiing lodge a year ago.'

Li Yuan sat in his chair in the old study at Tongjiang, the package on the desk before him. He looked about him, remembering. Here he had learned what it was to shoulder responsibility; to busy himself with matters of State. Here he had toiled – his father's hands – until late into the night, untangling the knotted thread of event to find solutions to his father's problems.

And now those problems were his. He looked down at the package and sighed.

He turned, looking across at the big communications screen. 'Connect me with Wu Shih,' he said, not even glancing at the overhead camera. 'Tell him I have something urgent to discuss.'

There was a short delay and then the screen lit up, the T'ang of North America's face filling the screen, ten times life-size.

'Cousin Yuan. I hope you are well. And congratulations. How are your wives?'

'They are wives, Wu Shih. But listen. I have been considering that matter we talked about and I believe I have a solution.'

Wu Shih raised his eyebrows. Some weeks before, his Security sources had discovered the existence of a new popular movement, 'The Sons of Benjamin Franklin'. Thus far there was nothing to link them to anything even resembling a plot against the Seven, neither could any acts of violence or incitement be laid at their door. In that respect they kept scrupulously within the letter of the law. However, the mere existence of such a secret society – harking, as its name implied, back to a forbidden past – was cause for grave concern. In other circumstances he might simply have rounded up the most prominent figures and demoted them. But these were no ordinary hotheads. The 'Sons' were, without exception, the heirs to some of the biggest Companies in North America. Wu Shih's problem was how to curtail their activities without alienating their powerful and influential fathers. It was a tricky problem, made worse by the fact that because no 'crime' had been committed, there was also no pretext upon which he might act.

'A solution, Li Yuan? What kind of solution?'

'I have sent someone into your City, Wu Shih. As my envoy, you might say, though he himself does not know it.'

Wu Shih frowned and sat forward slightly, his image breaking up momentarily then re-forming clearly. 'An envoy?'

Li Yuan explained.

Afterwards Wu Shih sat back, considering. 'I see. But why do you think this will work?'

'There is no guarantee that it will, but if it fails we have lost nothing, neh?'

Wu Shih smiled. 'That sounds reasonable enough.'

'And you will look after the boy for me?'

'Like my own son, Li Yuan.'

'Good. Then I must leave you, Wu Shih. There is much to do before this evening.'

Wu Shih laughed. 'And much to do tonight, neh?'

There was a momentary hesitation in Li Yuan's face then he returned Wu Shih's smile tightly, bowing his head slightly to his fellow T'ang before he cut contact.

Tonight. He shivered. Tonight he wished only to be alone. But that was not his fate. He was married now. He had duties to his wives. And to his ancestors. For it was up to him now to provide a son. To continue the line. So that the chain should remain unbroken, the ancestral offerings made, the graves tended.

Even so, his heart felt dead in him. Ever since this morning he had kept thinking of the new child, seeing it in his mind, resting in Fei Yen's arms as she lay there propped up in bed on her father's estate.

He shook his head then stood. It hurt. It hurt greatly, but it was behind him now. It had to be. His life lay ahead of him, and he could not carry his hurt about like an open wound. Neither could he wait for time to heal the scars. He must press on. For he was T'ang now. T'ang.

He stood with his hands resting against the edge of the desk, staring down at the package, still undecided whether he should send it, then leaned forward, pressing the summons bell. 'Send in Nan Ho.'

The boy's debriefing had proved more successful than any of them had dared hope and had put the lie to what Director Spatz had said about Ward's 'nil contribution' to the Project. Ward had remembered everything. In fact, the extent of his knowledge about the Wiring Project had surprised them all. With what he had given them, they would be able to reconstruct the facility within months. A facility that, in theory anyway, would be far more advanced than the one Spatz had so spectacularly mismanaged.

This time he would do it right. Would ensure that the right men were appointed, that it was adequately funded and properly protected. No, there would be no mistakes this time.

Mistakes. He shook his head. He had misjudged things badly. He ought to have trusted to his instinct about the boy, but he had been off balance. That whole business with Fei Yen had thrown him. He had been unable to see things clearly. But now he could put things right. Could reward the boy. Indeed, what better way was there of making Ward loyal to him than through the ties of gratitude? And he needed the boy to be loyal. He saw that now. Saw what he had almost lost through his inadvertence.

Such talent as Kim possessed appeared but rarely in the world. It was a priceless gift. And whoever had the use of it could only benefit. Change was coming to Chung Kuo, like it or not, and they must find a way to harness it. Ward's skills – his genius, if you like – might prove effective, not in preventing Change, for who could turn back the incoming tide, but in giving it a shape better suited to the wishes of the Seven.

For now, however, Li Yuan would use him in a different role. As an eye, peering into the darkness of his enemies' hearts. As an ear, listening to the rhythms of their thought. And then, when he was done with that, he would fly him on a long leash, like a young hawk, giving him the illusion of freedom, letting him stretch his wings, even as he restrained and directed him.

There was a faint knock. 'Come,' he said.

'You sent for me, *Chieh Hsia*?'

He picked up the package and offered it to his Chancellor. 'Have this sent to *Shih* Ward at once. I want it to be in his room when he returns tonight.'

'Of course, *Chieh Hsia*.' Nan Ho hesitated. 'Is that all?'

As ever, he had read Li Yuan's mood. Had understood without the need for words.

'One thing, Nan Ho. You will carry a note for me. Personally. To Fei Yen. To wish her well.'

Nan Ho bowed his head. 'Forgive me, *Chieh Hsia*, but is that wise? There are those who might construe such a note to mean...'

Li Yuan cut him off. 'Nan Ho! Just do it. Wise or not, I *feel* it must be done. So, please, take my message to her and wish her well. I would not be bitter about the past, understand me? I would be strong. And how can I be strong unless I face the past clear-eyed, understanding my mistakes?'

Nan Ho bowed, impressed by his master's words. 'I will go at once, *Chieh Hsia*.'

'Good. And when you return you will find me a new Master of the Inner Chambers. A man who will serve me as well as you have served me.'

Nan Ho smiled. 'Of course, *Chieh Hsia*. I have the very man in mind.'

★

It was after midnight and Archimedes Kitchen was packed. The club was dimly lit, like the bottom of the ocean, the air heavy with exotic scents. As one stepped inside, under the great arch, the deep growl of a primitive bass rhythm obliterated all other sound, like a slow, all-pervasive heartbeat, resonating in everything it touched.

The architecture of the club was eccentric but deliberate. All things Han were absent here. Its fashions looked backwards, to the last years of the American Empire, before the Great Collapse.

From its position at the top edge of the City, the Kitchen overlooked the dark green, island-strewn waters of Buzzard Bay. Through the vast, clear windows of the upper tiers you could, on a clear day, see the south-western tip of Martha's Vineyard, distant and green, unspoiled by any structure. Few were so inclined. For most of the time the magnificent view windows were opaqued; arabesques of vivid colour swirling across their blinded surfaces.

Inside, the place was cavernous. Tier after tier spiralled up about the central circle of the dance floor, a single, broad ramp ascending smoothly into the darkened heights. Along the slowly winding length of this elegantly carpeted 'avenue', tables were set. Ornate, impressive tables, in 'Empire' style, the old insignia of the sixty-nine States carved into the wooden surfaces, bronzed eagles stretching their wings across the back of each chair. Gold-and-black-suited waiters hovered – literally hovered – by the rail to take orders. Their small backpack jets, a memory of the achievements of their technological past, flaunted the Edict. Like bees, they tended the needs of the crowded tiers, fetching and carrying, issuing from the darkness high above their patrons' heads.

In the centre of all was a huge light sculpture, a twisting double band of gold stretching from floor to ceiling. It was a complex double helix, detailed and flowing, pulsing with the underlying bass rhythm, by turns frail and intense, ghostly thin and then broad, sharply delineated, like a solid thing. This, too, bordered on the illicit; was a challenge of sorts to those who ruled.

Membership of the Kitchen was exclusive. Five, almost six thousand members crowded the place on a good night – which this was – but five times that number were members and twenty times that were on the club's waiting list. More significantly, membership was confined to just one section of the populace. No Han were allowed here, or their employees. In this, as in so many other ways, the club was in violation of statutes passed in the House some years before, though the fact that every one of the North American Representatives was also a member of the Kitchen had escaped no one's notice.

It was a place of excess. Here, much more was permitted than elsewhere. Eccentricity seemed the norm, and nakedness, or partial nakedness that concealed little of importance, was much in evidence. Men wore their genitalia dressed in silver, small fins sprouting from the sides of their drug-aroused shafts. The women were no less overt in their symbolism; many wore elaborate rings of polished metal about their sex – space gates, similar in form to the docking apertures on spacecraft. It was all a game, but there was a meaning behind its playfulness.

Of those who were dressed – the majority, it must be said – few demonstrated a willingness to depart from what was the prevalent style: a style which might best be described as Techno-Barbarian, a mixture of space suits and ancient chain-mail. Much could be made of the curious opposition of the fine, in some cases beautiful, aristocratic faces and the brutish, primitive dress. It seemed a telling contrast, illustrative of some elusive quality in the society itself. Of the unstated yet ever-present conflict in their souls. Almost a confession.

It was nearly two in the morning when Kim arrived at the 'Gateway' and presented his invitation. The sobriety of his dress marked him out as a visitor, just as much as his diminutive status. People stared at him shamelessly as he was ushered through the crowded tunnel and out into the central space.

He boarded a small vehicle to be taken to his table – a replica of the four-wheeled, battery-powered jeep that had first been used on the moon two hundred and thirty-eight years before. At a point halfway up the spiral it stopped. There was an empty table with spaces set for five. Nearby two waiters floated, beyond the brass and crystal rail.

Kim sat beside the rail, looking down at the dance floor more than a hundred ch'i below. The noise was not so deafening up here. Down there, however, people were thickly pressed, moving slowly, sensually, to the stimulus of a Mood Enhancer. Small firefly clouds of hallucinogens moved erratically amongst the dancers, sparking soundlessly as they made contact with the moist warmth of naked flesh.

Kim looked up. His hosts had arrived. They stood there on the far side of the table: two big men, built like athletes, dressed casually in short business *pau*, as if to make him more at ease.

The older of the two came round the table to greet him.

'I'm glad you could come,' he said, smiling broadly. 'My name is Charles Lever.'

'I know,' Kim said simply, returning his smile.

Old Man Lever; he was Head of the biggest pharmaceuticals company in North America, possibly in the whole of Chung Kuo. The other man, his personal assistant, was his son, Michael. Kim shook Lever's hand then looked past him at his son, noting how alike they were.

They sat, the old man leaning towards him across the table. 'Do you mind if I order for you, Kim? I know the specialties of this place.'

Kim nodded and looked around, noting the occupants of the next table down. His eyes widened in surprise. Turning, he saw it was the same at the next table up.

A group of aristocrats now sat at each table. They had not been there before, so they must have slipped into their places after the Levers had arrived. There was nothing especially different about the way they dressed, yet they were immediately noticeable. They were bald. That absence of hair first drew the eye, but then another detail held the attention: a cross-hatching of scars, fine patterns like a wiring grid in an ancient circuit. These stood out, blue against the whiteness of each scalp – like some alien code.

Kim studied them a moment, fascinated, not certain what they were, then looked back to find Old Man Lever watching him, a faint smile of amusement on his lips.

'I see you've noticed my friends.'

Lever rose and went from table to table, making a show of introducing them. Kim watched, abstracted from the reality of what was happening, conscious only of how uniform they seemed despite a wide variation of features; of how this one thing erased all individuality in their faces, making *things* of them.

'What you see gathered here, Kim, is the first stage of a grand experiment. One I'd like you to help me in.' The old man stood there, his arms folded against his broad chest, relaxed in his own power and knowledge, confident of Kim's attention. 'These here are the first to benefit from a breakthrough in ImmVac's research programme. Trailblazers, you might call them. Pioneers of a new way of living.'

Kim nodded, but he was thinking how odd it was that Lever should do this all so publicly; should choose this way of presenting things.

'These...' Lever paused and smiled broadly, as if the joke was all too much for him. 'These are the first immortals, Kim. The very first.'

Kim pursed his lips, considering, trying to anticipate the older man. He was surprised. He hadn't thought anyone was close enough yet. But if it was so, what did it mean? Why did Lever want to involve him? What was the flaw that needed ironing out?

'Immortals,' the old man repeated, his eyes afire with the word. 'What Mankind has always dreamed of. The defeat of death itself.'

There was a whisper from the nearby tables, like the rustle of paper-thin metal streamers in a wind. At Kim's back the coiled and spiralling threads of light pulsed and shimmered, while waiters floated between the levels. The air was rich with distracting scents. It all seemed dreamlike, almost absurd.

'Congratulations,' he said. 'I assume...'

He paused, holding the old man's eyes. What *did* he assume? That it worked? That Lever *knew* he was flouting the Edict? That it *was* 'what Mankind had always dreamed of'? All of these, perhaps, but he finished otherwise. 'I assume you'll pay me well for my help, *Shih* Lever.'

The son turned his head sharply and looked at Kim, surprised. His father considered a moment then laughed heartily and took his seat again.

'Why, of course you'll be paid well, *Shih* Ward. Very well indeed. If you can help us.'

The waiters arrived, bringing food and wine. For a moment all speech was suspended as the meal was laid out. When it was done Kim reached across and poured himself a glass of water from the jug, ignoring the wine. He sipped the ice-cool liquid then looked across at Old Man Lever again.

'But why all this? Why raise the matter here, in such a *public* place?'

Lever smiled again and began to tuck into his starter. He chewed for a while then set his fork down. 'You aren't used to our ways yet, are you? All this...' he gestured with his knife '...it's a marketplace. And these...' He indicated his friends. 'These are my product.' He grinned and pointed at Kim with his knife. 'You, so I'm told on good authority, come with a reputation second to none. Forget connections.' There was a brief flicker in the corner of one eye. 'By meeting you here, like this, I signal my intention to work with you. The best with the best.' He took a second forkful and chewed and swallowed. Beside him his son watched, not eating.

'So it's all publicity?'

'Of a kind.' The son spoke for the father. 'It does our shares no harm. Good rumour feeds a healthy company.'

Old Man Lever nodded. 'Indeed. So it is, Kim. And it won't harm your own career one jot to be seen in harness with ImmVac.'

Yes, thought Kim, *unless the Seven start objecting to what you're doing and close you down*. Aloud he said, 'You know I've other plans.'

The old man nodded. 'I know everything about you, Kim.'

It sounded ominous and Kim looked up from his plate, momentarily alarmed, but it was only a form of words. *Not everything*.

'It would be... theoretical work,' continued Lever. 'The sort of thing I understand you're rather good at. *Synthesizing*.'

Kim tilted his head, feeling uneasy, but not knowing quite why he had the feeling. Perhaps the words had simply thrown him. He didn't like to be *known* so readily.

'We have a drug that works. A stabilizer. Something that in itself prevents the *error catastrophe* that creates ageing in human beings. But we don't want to stop there. Longevity shouldn't just be for the young, neh, Kim?' There was a slight nervousness in his laughter that escaped no one at the table. The son looked disconcerted by it, embarrassed. To Kim, however, it was the most significant thing Lever had said. He knew now what it was that drove him.

You want it for yourself. And the drug you have won't give it to you. It doesn't reverse the process, it only holds it in check. You want to be young again. You want to live for ever. And right now you can't have either.

'And your terms?'

Again Lever laughed, as if Kim was suddenly talking his own language. 'Terms we'll discuss when we meet. For now just enjoy this marvellous food. Tuck in, Kim. Tuck in. You've never tasted anything like this fish, I guarantee.'

Kim took a bite and nodded. 'It's good. What is it?'

There was laughter at the surrounding tables. Lever raised a hand to silence it then leaned across the table towards the boy. 'They only serve one kind of fish here. Shark.'

Kim looked across at the watchful faces of the new immortals then back at the Levers, father and son, seeing how much they enjoyed this little joke.

'Like Time,' he said.

'How's that?' asked the old man, sitting back in his chair, one arm curled about the eagle's wing.

'Time,' said Kim, slowly cutting a second mouthful from the fish steak in front of him. 'It's like a shark in a bloodied sea.'

He saw their amusement fade, the biter bit, a flicker in the corner of the old man's eye. And something else. Respect. He saw how Lever looked at him, measuring him anew. 'Yes,' he said, after a moment. 'So it is, boy. So it is.'

Tolonen climbed the twist of stairs easily, two at a time, like a man half his age, yet as he turned to say something to the leader of the honour guard, he realized he was alone. The stairs behind were empty, the door at their foot closed. Up ahead the corridor was silent, dimly lit, doors set off either side. At the far end a doorway led through to the central control room.

'What in hell...?' he began, then fell silent. Something had not been right. His instincts prickled, as if to alert him. Something about their uniforms...

He reacted quickly, turning to shoot the first of them as they came through the far door, but they were moving fast and the second had aimed his knife before Tolonen could bring him down.

He fell to his knees, crumpled against the right-hand wall, blood oozing from his left arm, his gun arm, his weapon fallen to the floor. He could hear shooting from below, from back the way he'd come, but there was no time to work out what it meant. As he pulled the knife from his arm and straightened up, another of the assassins appeared at the far end of the corridor.

Grabbing up the gun, he opened fire right-handed, hitting the man almost as he was on him. The assassin jerked backwards then lay there, twitching, his face shot away, the long knife still trembling in his hand.

He understood. They had instructions to take him alive. If not, he would have been dead already. But who was it wanted him?

He barely had time to consider the question when he heard the door slide open down below and footsteps on the stairs. He swung round, a hot stab of pain shooting up his arm as he aimed his gun down into the stairwell.

It was Haavikko. Tolonen felt a surge of anger wash through him. 'You bastard!' he hissed, pointing his gun at him.

'No!' Haavikko said urgently, putting his hands out at his sides, the big automatic he carried pointing away from the Marshal. 'You don't understand! The honour guard. Their chest patches... Think, Marshal! Think!'

Tolonen lowered his gun. That was right. The recognition band on their chest patches had been the wrong colour. Had been the green of an African banner, not the orange of a European one.

Haavikko started up the steps again. 'Quick! We've got to get inside.'

Tolonen nodded then turned, covering the corridor as Haavikko came alongside.

'I'll check the first room out,' Axel said into his ear. 'We can hole up there until help comes. It'll be easier to defend than this.'

The old man nodded, gritting his teeth against the pain in his arm. 'Right. Go. I'll cover you.'

He moved out to the right, covering the doorway and the corridor beyond as Haavikko tugged the door open and stepped inside. Then Haavikko turned back, signalling for him to come.

Inside, the room was a mess. This whole section was supposed to be a 'safe area' – a heavily guarded resting place for visiting Security staff – but someone had taken the place apart. The mattresses were ripped, the standing lockers kicked over. Papers littered the floor.

Haavikko pointed across the room. 'Get behind there – between the locker and the bed. I'll take up a position by the door.'

Tolonen didn't argue. His arm was throbbing painfully now and he was beginning to feel faint. He crossed the room as quickly as he could then slumped against the wall, a wave of nausea sweeping over him.

It was not a moment too soon. Tolonen heard the door slam further down the corridor and the sound of running men. Then Haavikko's big gun opened up, deafening in that confined space.

Haavikko turned, looking back at him. 'There are more of them coming. Down below. Wait there. I'll deal with them.'

Through darkening vision Tolonen saw him draw the grenade from his belt and move out into the corridor. It was a big thing: the kind they used to blast their way through a blocked Seal. He closed his eyes, hearing the grenade clatter on the steps.

And then nothing.

Axel crossed the room swiftly, throwing himself on top of the locker, shielding the Marshal with his body. It was not a moment too soon. An instant later the blast shook the air, ripping at his back, rocking the whole room.

He pulled himself upright. There was a stinging pain in his right shoulder and a sudden warmth at his ear and neck. He looked down. Tolonen was unconscious now and the wound in his arm was still seeping blood, but the blast seemed not to have harmed him any further.

Axel turned. The room was slowly filling with smoke and dust. Coughing, he half lifted the old man then dragged him across the room and out into the corridor. He stopped a moment, listening, then hauled the old man up on to his shoulder, grunting with the effort, his own pain forgotten. Half-crouching, the gun strangely heavy in his left hand, he made his way along the corridor, stepping between the fallen bodies. At the far end he kicked the door open, praying there were no more of them.

The room was empty, the door on the far side open. Taking a breath, he moved on, hauling the old man through the doorway. He could hear running feet and shouts from all sides now, but distant, muted, as if on another level.

Ping Tiao? If so, he had to get the Marshal as far away as possible.

The Marshal was breathing awkwardly now, erratically. The wound in his arm was bad, his uniform soaked with blood.

He carried the old man to the far side of the room then set him down gently, loosening his collar. He cut a strip of cloth from his own tunic and twisted it into a cord, then bound it tightly about the Marshal's arm, just above the wound. The old man hadn't been thinking. Pulling the knife out had been the worst thing he could have done. He should have left it in. Now it would be touch and go.

He squatted there on his haunches, breathing slowly, calming himself, the gun balanced across his knee, one hand combing back his thick blond hair. Waiting...

Seconds passed. A minute… He had almost relaxed when he saw it.

The thing scuttled along the ceiling at the far end of the corridor. Something new. Something he had never seen before. A probe of some kind. Slender, camouflaged, it showed itself only in movement, in the tiny shadows it cast.

It came a few steps closer then stopped, focusing on them. Its tiny camera eye rotated; the smallest of movements of the lens.

He understood at once. This was the assassin's 'eyes'. The man himself would be watching, out of sight, ready to strike as soon as he knew how things stood.

Axel threw himself forward, rolling, coming up just as the assassin came round the corner.

The tactic worked. It gave him the fraction of a second that he needed. He was not where the man thought he'd be, and in that split second of uncertainty the assassin was undone.

Axel stood over the dead man, looking down at him. His limbs shook badly now, adrenalin changed to a kind of naked fear as he realized how close it had been.

He turned away, returning to Tolonen. The bleeding had stopped, but the old man was still unconscious, his breathing slow, laborious. His face had an unhealthy pallor.

Axel knelt astride the Marshal, tilting his head backwards, lifting his neck. Then, pinching the Marshal's nostrils closed, he breathed into his mouth.

Where was the back-up? Where was the regular squad? Or had the Ping Tiao taken out the entire deck?

He shuddered and bent down again, pushing his breath into the old man, knowing he was fighting for his life.

And then there was help. People were milling about behind him in the room – special elite Security and medics. Someone touched his arm, taking over from him. Another drew him aside, pulling him away.

'The Marshal will be all right now. We've regularized his breathing.'

Haavikko laughed. Then it had failed! The assassination attempt had failed! He made to turn, to go over to Tolonen and tell him, but as he moved a huge wave of blackness hit him.

Hands grabbed for him as he keeled over, cushioning his fall, then settled him gently against the wall.

'Kuan Yin!' said one of them, seeing the extent of his burns. 'We'd better get him to a special unit fast. It's a wonder he got this far.'

Ten thousand li away, on the far side of the Atlantic, DeVore was sitting down to breakfast at the Lever Mansion. The Levers – father and son – had come straight from Archimedes Kitchen. DeVore had got up early to greet them, impressed by the old man's energy. He seemed as fresh after a night spent wining and dining as he had when he'd first greeted DeVore more than thirty hours before.

While servants hurried to prepare things, they went through to the Empire Room. It was a big, inelegant room, its furnishings rather too heavy, too overbearing for DeVore's taste. Even so, there was something impressive about it, from the massive pillars that reached up into the darkness overhead to the gallery that overlooked it on all four sides. The table about which they sat was huge – large enough to sit several dozen in comfort – and yet it had been set for the three of them alone. DeVore sat in the tall-backed chair, his hands resting on the polished oak of the arms, looking down the full length of the table at Lever.

The old man smiled, raising a hand to summon one of his servants from the shadows. 'Well, Howard? How did you get on?'

DeVore smiled. Lever was referring to the return-match against Kustow's *wei chi* champion.

'I was very fortunate. I lost the first two. But then...'

Lever raised an eyebrow. 'You *beat* him?'

DeVore lowered his head, feigning modesty, but it had been easy. He could have won all five. 'As I say, I was fortunate.'

Michael Lever stared at him, surprised.

'Your friends were most hospitable,' DeVore said. 'They're good fellows, Michael. I wish we had their like in City Europe.'

'And you, Howard? Did you win your money back?'

DeVore laughed. 'Not at all. I knew how weak Kustow's man was. It would not have been fair to have wagered money on the outcome.'

Michael Lever nodded. 'I see...' But it was clear he was more impressed than he was willing to say. So it had been with the others last night: their eyes had said what their mouths could not. He had seen the new respect with which they looked at him. Ten stones he had won by, that last game. Kustow's champion would never live it down.

The old man had been watching them from the far end of the table. Now he interrupted.

'It's a shame you're not staying longer, Howard. I would have liked to have taken you to see our installations.'

DeVore smiled. He had heard rumours of how advanced they were, how openly they flouted the Edict's guidelines. But, then, the War with the Dispersionists, which had so completely and devastatingly crushed the Above in City Europe, had barely touched them here. Many of the Dispersionists' natural allies here had kept out of that war. As a result, things were much more buoyant, the Company Heads filled with a raw self-confidence that was infectious. Everywhere he'd been there was a sense of optimism; a sense that here, if nowhere else, change could be forced through, Seven or no.

He looked back at Old Man Lever, bowing his head. 'I would have liked that, Charles. But next time, perhaps? I've been told your factories are most impressive: a good few years ahead of their European counterparts.'

Lever laughed then leaned forward. 'And so they should be! I've spent a great deal of money rebuilding them these past few years. But it hasn't been easy. No. We've had to go backwards to go forwards, if you see what I mean.'

DeVore nodded, understanding. Indeed, if he needed any further clue to what Lever meant, he had only to look about him. Mementoes of the American Empire were everywhere in the room, from the great spread eagles on the backs of the chairs to the insignia on the silverware. Most prominent of all was the huge map on the wall behind Old Man Lever: a map of the American Empire at its height in 2043, five years after the establishment of the sixty-nine States. The year of President Griffin's assassination and the Great Collapse.

On the map, the red, white and blue of the Empire stretched far into the southern continent. Only the triple alliance of Brazil, Argentina and Uruguay had survived the massive American encroachments, forming the last outposts of a one-time wholly Latin continent, while to the north the whole of Canada had been swallowed up, its vastness divided into three huge administrative areas.

He looked down. To him such maps were vivid testimonies to the ephemerality of empires, to the certain dissolution of all things human in the face of Time. But to Lever and his kind they were something different. To them the map represented an ideal, a golden age to which they must return.

America. He had seen how the word lit them from within; how their eyes came alive at its sound. Like their European cousins, they had been seduced by the great dream of return. A dream that his gift of the Aristotle File was sure to feed, like coals on the fire of their disaffection, until this whole vast City erupted in flames.

He sighed. Yes, the day would come. And he would be there when it did. To see the Cities in flames, the Seven cast down.

He turned in his chair, taking a coffee from the servant, then looked across again, meeting Lever's eyes. 'And the boy? How was your dinner? I understand you took him to the Kitchen.'

Lever smiled thoughtfully. 'It went well. He's sharp, that one. Very sharp. And I'm grateful for your introduction, Howard. It could prove a most valuable contact.'

'That's what I thought–'

'However,' Lever interrupted, 'I've been wondering.'

DeVore took a sip of his coffee then set the cup down, pushing it away from him. 'Wondering?'

'Yes. Think a moment. If the boy is so valuable, why has Li Yuan sent him here? Why hasn't he kept him close at hand, in Europe, where he can use him?'

DeVore smiled. 'To be honest with you, Charles, I'm not sure. I do know that the old T'ang intended to have the boy terminated. Indeed, if it wasn't for the attack on the Project, the boy wouldn't be here now. It seems Li Yuan must have reconsidered.'

'Yes. But what's he up to now?'

DeVore laughed. 'That's what we'd all like to know, neh? But to be serious, I figure it like this. The boy suffered a great shock. Certain psychological blocks that were induced in him during his personality reconstruction aren't there any longer. In a very real sense he's not the same person he was before the attack. Li Yuan has been told that. He's also been told that, as a result, the boy is not one hundred per cent reliable. That he needs a rest and maybe a change of setting. So what does he do? He ships the boy off here, with complete medical back-up, hoping that the trip will do him good and that he'll return refreshed, ready to get to work again.'

Lever nodded thoughtfully. 'So you think Li Yuan will use him after all?'

'Maybe. But maybe not. I have heard rumours.'

'Rumours?'

DeVore shrugged apologetically. 'More I can't say just yet. But when I hear more I'll let you know, I promise you.'

Lever huffed impatiently then turned in his chair, snapping his fingers. 'Come! Quickly now! I'm starving.'

Across from him his son laughed. 'But, Father, you only ate three hours back. How can you be starving?'

Lever stared back at his son a moment then joined his laughter. 'I know. But I am, all the same.' He looked back at DeVore. 'And you, Howard, what will you eat?'

DeVore smiled. *The world*, he thought. *I'll eat the world.* But aloud he said, 'Coffee will do me fine, Charles. I've no appetite just now. Maybe later, neh?'

He turned, looking at the son. 'Are you eating, Michael, or can I interest you in a breath of air?'

The young man sat back, drawing one hand through his short blond hair. 'I was going to get a few hours' sleep, but half an hour won't make much difference.' He turned, looking across. 'You'll excuse us, Father?'

Lever nodded. 'That's fine, Michael. But remember there's a lot still to be done before Friday night.'

Young Lever smiled. 'It's all in hand.'

'Good!' Lever lifted his fork, pointing at DeVore. 'Why don't you change your mind and stay over, Howard? We're holding a Thanksgiving Ball. You could see how we Americans celebrate things. Besides, there'll be a lot of interesting and important people there. People you ought to meet.'

DeVore bowed his head. 'Thanks, but I really must get back tonight. Another time, perhaps?'

Lever shrugged then waved them away, lowering his head as he dug into his breakfast.

Outside it was cooler. Subtle lighting gave the impression that it really was morning, that they really were walking beneath a fresh, early autumn sky, a faint breeze whispering through the branches of the nearby trees.

DeVore, watching the younger Lever, saw how he changed once out of his father's presence; how the tense pose of formality slipped from him.

'Was I right?' he asked, as soon as they were out of earshot of the mansion.

Lever turned. 'You're a clever man, Howard, but don't underestimate my father.'

'Maybe. But was I right?'

Lever nodded. 'It was all he talked about. But, then, that's not surprising. It's an obsession with him. Immortality...'

DeVore put his hand on the young man's arm. 'I understand how you must feel, Michael. I've not said anything before now – after all, it would hardly be good manners to talk of it in front of your father – but to you I can speak freely. You see, I find the idea of living for ever quite absurd. To think that we could outwit death – that we could beat the old Master at his own game!' He laughed and shook his head ruefully, seeing how he had struck a chord in the other man.

'Well, I'm sure you agree. The very idea is ludicrous. Besides, why perpetuate the weakness of the old creature – the *mei yu jen wen*? Why not strive to make some better, finer being?'

'What do you mean?'

DeVore lowered his voice. 'You've seen what I've achieved so far. Well, much more has yet to be done. The fortresses are but a small part of my scheme. It's my belief that we must look beyond the destruction of the Seven and anticipate what happens afterwards. And not merely anticipate. The wise man seeks to shape the future, surely?'

Lever nodded thoughtfully. 'It's what I've always said.'

'Good. Then hear me out, for I've a plan that might benefit us both.'

'A plan?'

'Yes. Something that will keep everyone happy.'

Lever laughed. 'That's a tall order.'

'But not impossible. Listen. What if we were to set up an Immortality Research Centre in the Wilds?'

Lever started. 'But I thought you said...?'

'I did. And I meant what I said. But look at it this way: you want one thing; your father another. However, he has the power – the money, to be precise – and you have nothing. Or as good as.'

He could see from the sourness in the young man's face that he had touched a raw nerve.

'Well, why not channel a little of that money into something for yourself, Michael?'

Lever's eyes widened, understanding. 'I see. When you talk of a research centre, you don't mean that, do you? You're talking of a front. A way of channelling funds.'

'Of course.'

'You're asking me to fool my father. To draw on his obsession, hoping he'll be blind to what I'm doing.'

DeVore shook his head. 'I'm asking nothing of you, Michael. You'll act as you choose to act. And if that accords with what I want, all well and good. If not...' He shrugged and smiled pleasantly, as if it didn't matter.

'And what *do* you want?'

DeVore hesitated. He had been asked that question so many times now that he had even begun to ask it of himself. For a brief moment he was tempted to spell it out – the whole grand scheme he carried in his head – then changed his mind.

'I think you know what I want. But let me just ask you this, Michael. If your father got his dearest wish – if he finally found a way of becoming immortal – what then? Wouldn't that simply prove a curse to all involved? After all, if he *were* to live for ever, when would you inherit?'

Lever met DeVore's eyes briefly then looked away. But DeVore, watching, had seen how his words had touched him to the quick. It was what he feared – what his whole generation feared. To be a son for ever, bound by a living ghost.

Lever shivered then shook his head. 'And this centre... how would you go about selling the idea to my father?'

DeVore smiled and took the young man's arm again, leading him on, beginning to outline his plan. The most difficult part now lay behind him. The rest would be easy.

Immortality. It was a nonsense, but a useful nonsense. And he would milk it to the last drop. But before then he would carry out a few last schemes of his own. To tidy things up, and settle a few last scores.

★

It was after six when Kim got back to the high-security complex where he was staying. The guards checked his ID then passed him through.

The apartment was in darkness, only the faint glow of the console display showing from the room at the far end of the hallway. He stood there a moment, feeling uneasy. His bedroom was just up a little on the right. He went through, closing the door behind him, then turned on the bedside lamp.

He stiffened then turned slowly, looking about him. The red silk package on the bedside table had not been there when he had left. Someone had been into the room.

He stared at it a moment, wondering what to do. If it was a bomb it might already be too late – merely coming into the room could have triggered the timer. Then he saw the note, poking out from beneath, and smiled, recognizing the hand.

He sat, placing the package beside him on the bed while he read the note. It was in Mandarin, the black ink characters formed with confident, fluent strokes. At the foot of the small, silken sheet was the young T'ang's seal, the *Ywe Lung* impressed into the bright gold wax. He read it quickly.

Shih Ward,
At our first meeting I said that if you did as I wished I would tear up my father's warrant. You have more than fulfilled your part of our agreement, therefore I return my father's document, duly enacted.
   I would be honoured if you would also accept these few small gifts with my sincere gratitude for your help in restoring the Project.
I look forward to seeing you on your return from my cousin's City.
With deepest respect,
Li Yuan

Kim looked up. The note was most unusual. *With deepest respect*. These were not words a T'ang normally used to a subject. No, he knew enough of the social mechanics of Chung Kuo to know that this was exceptional behaviour on the young T'ang's part. But why? What did he want from him?

Or was that fair? Did Li Yuan *have* to want something?

He set the note down and picked up the package. Beneath the silk wrapping was a tiny box: a black, lacquered box, the letters of Kim's name impressed into the lid in bright gold lettering. He felt a tiny tremor of antic-ipation ripple through him then opened it. Inside the box, wrapped in the torn pieces of Li Shai Tung's warrant, were four small cards. He spilled them on to the bed. They were little different from the computer cards that were in use everywhere throughout Chung Kuo: multipurpose cards that served to store information in every shape and form. There was no guessing what these were until he fed them into a comset. They might be credit chips, for instance, or holograms, or special programmes of some kind. The only clue he had was the number Li Yuan had handwritten on each.

He scooped them up and went through to the end room, putting on the desk lamp beside the console before slipping the first of the cards – numbered *yi* – one – into the slot in front of him.

He sat back, waiting.

There was the sound of a tiny bell being rung, the note high and pure, then a word appeared on the screen.

PASS-CODE?

He placed his hand palm down on the touch-pad and leaned forward over the dark, reflective surface, opening his eyes wide, letting the machine verify his retinal print. He spoke four words of code then sat back.

There was a fraction of a second's delay before the response came up on the screen.

AUDIO OR VISUAL?

'Visual,' he said softly.

The screen rippled in acknowledgment, like the calm surface of a pool disturbed by a single small stone falling cleanly into its centre. A moment later the screen lifted smoothly from the desktop, tilting up to face him.

He gave the code again. At once the screen filled with information. He scanned through quickly then sat back. It was an amended copy of his con-tract with SimFic, buying out their interest in him. And the new owner? It was written there at the foot of the contract. Kim Ward. For the first time in his life he owned himself.

He shivered then took the file from the slot and replaced it with the one marked *er* – two.

As the screen lit up again, he nodded to himself. Of course. It would have meant nothing to be his own master without this – his citizenship papers. But Li Yuan had gone further: he had authorized an all-levels pass.

That gave Kim clearance to travel anywhere within the seven Cities, and few – even among the Above – were allowed that.

Two more... He stared at the tiny cards a moment, wondering, then placed the third – marked *san* – into the slot.

At first he didn't understand. Maybe one of Li Yuan's servants had made a mistake and placed the wrong card in the package. Then, as the document scrolled on, he caught his breath, seeing his name, there in the column marked 'Registered Head'.

A company! Li Yuan had given him his own company – complete with offices, patents and enough money to hire staff and undertake preliminary research. He shook his head, bewildered. All this... He didn't understand.

He closed his eyes. It was like a dream, a dream he would shortly wake up from, yet when he opened his eyes again, the information was still there on the screen, Li Yuan's personal verification codes rippling down the side of the file.

But why? Why had Li Yuan given him all this? What did he want in return?

He laughed strangely then shook his head again. It always came back to that. He had grown so used to being owned – to being *used* – that he could not think of such a gesture in any other way. But what if Li Yuan wanted nothing? What if he meant what he had said in his note? What had he to lose in making such a gesture?

And what to gain?

He frowned, trying to see through the confusion of his feelings to the objective truth, but for once it proved too difficult. He could think of no reason for Li Yuan's generosity. None but the one his words appeared to give.

He removed the file and placed the last of the cards – *si* – into the slot.

What now? What else could Li Yuan possibly give him?

It was a different kind of file – he saw that at once. For a start, Li Yuan's personal code was missing. But it was more than that. He could tell by the length and complexity of the file that it had been prepared by experts.

He gave the access code. At once the screen filled with brilliant colours, like a starburst, quickly resolving itself into a complex diagram. He sat back, his mouth wide open. It was a genotyping.

No. Not just a genotyping. He knew at once what it was without needing to be told. It was *his* genotyping.

He watched, wide-eyed, as the programme advanced, one detail after another of the DNA map boldly emphasized on the screen. Then, lifting the details from the flat screen one by one, it began to piece the building blocks together until a holo-image of a double helix floated in the air above the desk, turning slowly in the darkness.

He studied the slow turning spiral, memorizing it, his heart pounding in his chest, then gave the verbal cue to progress the file.

The next page gave a full probability set. It numbered just short of six billion possible candidates: the total number of adult male *Hung Mao* back in 2190. He shivered, beginning to understand, then cued the file again. The next display itemized close-match candidates. Ten names in all. He scanned the list, his mouth falling open again. His father... One of these was his father.

One by one he was given details of the ten: genotypes; full face portraits; potted biographies; each file quite frightening in its detail.

When the last had faded from the screen he called hold then sat back, his eyes closed, his breathing shallow. He felt strange, as if he were standing on the edge of a deep well, ill balanced, about to fall. He shivered, knowing he had never felt like this before. Knowledge had always been an opening – a breaching of the dark – but this...

For once he was afraid to know.

He let the giddiness pass then opened his eyes again, steeling himself. 'All right. Move on...'

There was a full second's hesitation and then the screen lit up. This time it gave details of the known movements of the ten candidates over a three-month period in the winter of 2190; details compiled from Security files.

It narrowed things down to a single candidate. Only one of the ten had visited the Clay during that period. Only one, therefore, could possibly have been his father.

He swallowed drily then cued the file again.

The image appeared immediately, as sharp as if it had been made earlier that day. A youngish man in his late twenties or early thirties; a tall, slightly built man, fine-boned and elegant, with distinctly aristocratic features. His light brown hair was cut neatly but not too severely and his dark green eyes seemed kind, warm. He was dressed simply but stylishly in a dark red *pau*, while about both of his wrists were a number of slender *tiao tuo* – bracelets of gold and jade.

Kim narrowed his eyes, noticing an oddity about the man. It was as if his head and body were parts of two different, separate beings: the head too large somehow, the chin and facial features too strong for the slender, almost frail body that supported them. Kim frowned then mouthed his father's name.

'Wyatt... Edmund Wyatt.'

It was an old image. Looking at it, he felt something like regret that he would never meet this man or come to know him, for, as the file indicated, Edmund Wyatt had been dead eight years – executed for the murder of the T'ang's minister, Lwo Kang. A crime for which he had later, privately, been pardoned.

Kim shuddered. Was that the reason for Li Yuan's generosity? To square things up? Or was a T'ang above such moral scruples?

He leaned forward, about to close the file, when the image of Wyatt vanished. For a moment the screen was blank then it lit up again.

GENOTYPE PREDICT: FEMALE SOURCE.

He called hold, his voice almost failing him, his heart hammering.

For a long time he sat there, hunched forward in his chair, staring at the heading, then, in a voice that was almost a whisper, he gave the cue.

First came the genotype: the puzzle pieces of DNA that would interlock with Edmund Wyatt's to produce his own. He watched as they formed a double helix in the air. Then, dramatically, they vanished, replaced not by further figures but by a computer graphics simulation – a full-length 3-D portrait of a naked woman.

He gasped then shook his head, not quite believing what he saw. It was his mother. Though he had not seen her in almost a dozen years, he knew at once that it was her. But not as she had been. No, this was not at all like the scrawny, lank-haired, dugless creature he had known.

He almost laughed at the absurdity of the image, but a far stronger feeling – that of bitterness – choked back the laughter.

He moaned and looked away, the feeling of loss so great that, for a moment, it threatened to unhinge him.

'Mother...' he whispered, his eyes blurring over. 'Mother...'

The computer had made assumptions. It was programmed to assume a normal Above diet, normal Above life-expectations. These it had fed into its simulation, producing something that, had such conditions prevailed down there in the Clay, would have been quite accurate. But as it was...

Kim looked at the image again, staring open-mouthed at a portrait of his mother as she might have been: at a dark-haired beauty, strong-limbed and voluptuous, full-breasted and a good two ch'i taller than she had been in life. A strong, handsome woman.

He shuddered, angered – it was awful, like some dreadful mockery – then shook his head. No. The reality – the truth – that was grotesque. And this?

He hesitated, afraid to use the word; but there was no other way of describing the image that floated there in the darkness.

It was beautiful.

The image was a lie. And yet it was his mother. There was no doubt of that. He had thought her gone from mind, all trace of her erased. After all, he had been little more than four when the tribe had taken him. But now the memories came back, like ghosts, taunting, torturing him.

He had only to close his eyes and he could see her crouched there beneath the low stone wall, just after they had escaped from the Myghtern's brothel, her eyes bright with excitement. Could see her lying beside him in the darkness, reaching out to hold him close, her thin arms curled about him. Could see her, later, scrambling across the rocks in the shadow of the Wall, hunting, her emaciated form flexing and unflexing as she tracked some pallid, rat-like creature. Could see her turn, staring back at him, a smile on her lips and in her dark, well-rounded eyes.

Could see her...

He covered his eyes, pressing his palms tight into the sockets as if to block out these visions, a single, wavering note of hurt – a low, raw, animal sound, unbearable in its intensity – welling up from deep inside him.

For a time there was nothing but his pain. Nothing but the vast, unendurable blackness of loss. Then, as it ebbed, he looked up once more and, with a shuddering breath, reached out to touch her.

His fingers brushed the air; passed through the beautiful, insubstantial image.

He sighed. Oh, he could see her now. Yes. And not only as she had been but as she should have been. Glorious. Wonderful...

He sat back, wiping the wetness from his cheeks, then shook his head, knowing that it was wrong to live like this – the City above, the Clay below.

Knowing, with a certainty he had never felt before, that something had gone wrong. Badly wrong.

He leaned forward, closing the file, then sat back again, letting out a long, shuddering breath. Yes, he knew it now. Saw it with a clarity that allowed no trace of doubt. Chung Kuo was like himself – motherless, ghost-haunted, divided against itself. It might seem teeming with life, yet in reality it was a great, resounding shell, its emptiness echoing down the levels.

Kim picked up the four tiny cards and held them a moment in his palm. Li Yuan had given him back his life. More than that, he had given him a future. But who would give Chung Kuo such a chance? Who would give the great world back its past and seek to heal it?

He shook his head. No, not even Li Yuan could do that. Not even if he wished it.

CHUNG KUO

IN TIMES TO COME...

Chung Kuo: The Broken Wheel is the seventh volume of a vast dynastic saga that covers more than half a century of this vividly realized future world. In the fourteen volumes that follow, the Great Wheel of fate turns through a full historical cycle, transforming the social climate of Chung Kuo utterly. *Chung Kuo* is the portrait of these turbulent – and often apocalyptic – times and the people who lived through them.

In *Chung Kuo: The White Mountain*, Kim Ward has been rewarded by Li Yuan with his freedom and the funds to set up his own Company, in North America. Only the 'Old Men' want to buy his services. They want an Immortality treatment. When Kim refuses, they destroy his Company. But Kim will not bow to them. He would rather become a 'commodity slave' and sell his services for seven years to the great SimFic Corporation than do so.

Among the Minor Families, chief supporters of the Seven, a sudden epidemic of 'willow plum sickness' now strikes: a virulent and fast-acting form of syphilis – a brain-killer that destroys its victims in days. Li Yuan, knowing he must act quickly, is utterly ruthless, killing all those who have the sickness and stamping it out. He is successful, but his actions alienate some of the Minor Family Heads and they seek out Wang Sau-leyan to become his allies. The one-time solidity of the Seven has been reduced to 'Four against Three'.

When Ben Shepherd visits Li Yuan, we discover that Li Yuan was the father of Fei Yen's son, Han; that he divorced her so that his son would never become T'ang and thus a 'target' in the way his own brother Han had been. It was why he never confronted Tsu Ma. Because he never knew.

But it is Kao Chen's experiences as a guard at Kwibesi, a detention camp in Africa (in view of Kilimanjaro, the White Mountain), that colour this volume. His experience of Li Yuan's camp for captured terrorists changes Chen's belief in what he's doing. The sheer inhumanity of it makes him challenge his sense of duty. He realizes that there are no real solutions, 'only degrees of wrongness'.

CHARACTER LISTING

MAJOR CHARACTERS

Ascher, Emily
: Trained as an economist, she joined the *Ping Tiao* revolutionary party at the turn of the century, becoming one of its policy-formulating 'Council of Five'. A passionate fighter for social justice, she was also once the lover of the *Ping Tiao*'s unofficial leader, Bent Gesell.

DeVore, Howard
: A one-time major in the T'ang's Security forces, he has become the leading figure in the struggle against the Seven. A highly intelligent and coldly logical man, he is the puppetmaster behind the scenes as the great 'War of the Two Directions' takes a new turn.

Ebert, Hans
: Son of Klaus Ebert and heir to the vast GenSyn Corporation, he is a captain in the Security forces, admired and trusted by his superiors. Ebert is a complex young man: a brave and intelligent officer, he also has a selfish, dissolute and rather cruel streak.

Fei Yen
: Daughter of Yin Tsu, one of the heads of the 'Twenty Nine', the minor aristocratic families of Chung Kuo. The classically beautiful 'Flying Swallow', her marriage to the murdered Prince Li Han Ch'in nullified, then married Han's brother, the young Prince Li Yuan. Fragile in appearance, she is surprisingly strong-willed and fiery.

Haavikko, Axel
: Smeared by the false accusations of his fellow officers, Lieutenant Haavikko spent the best part of a decade in debauchery and self-negation.

At core, however, he is a good, honest man, and circumstances have raised him from the pit into which he had fallen.

Kao Chen
Once an assassin from the Net, the lowest levels of the great City, Chen has raised himself from his humble beginnings to become an officer in the T'ang's Security forces. As friend and helper to Karr, he is one of the foot-soldiers in the War against DeVore.

Karr, Gregor
A major in the Security forces, he was recruited by Marshal Tolonen from the Net. In his youth he was an athlete and, later, a 'blood' – a to-the-death combat fighter. A giant of a man, he is to become the 'hawk' Li Shai Tung flies against his adversary, DeVore.

Lehmann, Stefan
Albino son of the former Dispersionist leader, Pietr Lehmann, he has become a lieutenant to DeVore. A cold, unnaturally dispassionate man, he seems to be the very archetype of nihilism, his only aim to bring down the Seven and their great City.

Li Shai Tung
T'ang of City Europe and one of the Seven, the ruling Council of Chung Kuo, Li Shai Tung is now in his seventies. For many years he was the fulcrum of the Council and unofficial spokesman for the Seven, but the murder of his heir, Han Ch'in, has weakened him, undermining his once strong determination to prevent Change at all costs.

Li Yuan
Second son of Li Shai Tung, he becomes heir to City Europe after the murder of his elder brother. Thought old before his time, his cold, thoughtful manner conceals a passionate nature, expressed in his wooing of his dead brother's wife, Fei Yen.

Shepherd, Ben
Son of Hal Shepherd, the T'ang's chief advisor, and great-great-grandson of City Earth's Architect. Shepherd was born and brought up in the Domain, an idyllic valley in the south-west of England where, deciding not to follow in his father's footsteps and become advisor to Li Yuan, he pursues instead his calling as an artist, developing a whole new art form, the Shell, which will eventually have a cataclysmic effect on Chung Kuo's society.

Tolonen, Jelka
Daughter of Marshal Tolonen, Jelka has been brought up in a very masculine environment, lacking a mother's influence. However, her genuine interest

	in martial arts and in weaponry and strategy mask a very different side to her nature; a side brought out by violent circumstances.
Tolonen, Knut	Marshal of the Council of Generals and one-time General to Li Shai Tung, Tolonen is a big, granite-jawed man and the staunchest supporter of the values and ideals of the Seven. Possessed of a fiery, fearless nature, he will stop at nothing to protect his masters, yet after long years of war even his belief in the necessity of stasis has been shaken.
Tsu Ma	T'ang of West Asia and one of the Seven, the ruling Council of Chung Kuo, Tsu Ma has thrown off his former dissolute ways as a result of his father's death and become one of Li Shai Tung's greatest supporters in Council. A strong, handsome man, he has still, however, a weakness in his nature: one that is almost his undoing.
Wang Sau-leyan	Fourth and youngest son of Wang Hsien, T'ang of Africa, the murder of his two eldest brothers has placed him closer to the centre of political events. Thought of as a wastrel, he is, in fact, a shrewd and highly capable political being who is set – through circumstances of his own devising – to become the harbinger of Change inside the Council of the Seven.
Ward, Kim	Born in the Clay, that dark wasteland beneath the great City's foundations, Kim has a quick and unusual bent of mind. His vision of a giant web, formulated in the darkness, has driven him up into the light of the Above. However, after a traumatic fight and a long period of personality reconstruction, he has returned to things not quite the person he was. Or so it seems, for Kim has lost none of the sharpness that has made him the most promising young scientist in the whole of Chung Kuo.

THE SEVEN AND THE FAMILIES

An Sheng	head of the An family (one of the 'Twenty-Nine' Minor Families)
Chi Hsing	T'ang of the Australias
Chi Hu Wei	T'ang of the Australias
Fu Ti Chang	Minor Family princess
Hou Tung-po	T'ang of South America

Hsiang K'ai Fan	Minor Family prince
Hsiang Shao-erh	head of the Hsiang family (one of the 'Twenty-Nine' Minor Families) and father of Hsiang K'ai Fan and Hsiang Wang
Hsiang Wang	Minor Family prince
Lai Shi	Minor Family princess
Li Ch'i Chan	brother and advisor to Li Shai Tung
Li Feng Chiang	brother and advisor to Li Shai Tung
Li Shai Tung	T'ang of Europe
Li Yuan	second son of Li Shai Tung and heir to City Europe
Li Yun Ti	brother and advisor to Li Shai Tung
Mien Shan	Minor Family princess
Pei Chao Yang	son and heir of Pei Ro-hen
Pei Ro-hen	head of the Pei family (one of the 'Twenty-Nine' Minor Families)
Tsu Ma	T'ang of West Asia
Tsu Tao Chu	third son of Tsuchang, deceased first son of Tsu Tiao
Wang Sau-leyan	fourth son of Wang Hsien and T'ang of Africa
Wei Chan Yin	eldest son of Wei Feng and heir to City East Asia
Wei Feng	T'ang of East Asia
Wu Shih	T'ang of North America
Yi Shan-ch'i	Minor Family prince
Yin Chang	Minor Family prince; son of Yin Tsu and elder brother to Fei Yen
Yin Fei Yen	'Flying Swallow', Minor Family princess; daughter of Yin Tsu; widow of Li Han Ch'in
Yin Sung	Minor Family prince; elder brother of Fei Yen and son and heir of Yin Tsu
Yin Tsu	head of Yin family (one of the 'Twenty-Nine' Minor Families)
Yin Wei	younger brother of Fei Yen
Yin Wu Tsai	Minor Family princess and cousin of Fei Yen

FRIENDS AND RETAINERS OF THE SEVEN

Auden, William	captain in Security
Chang Li	Chief Surgeon to Li Shai Tung
Chang Shih-sen	personal secretary to Li Yuan
Ch'in Tao Fan	Chancellor of East Asia
Chuang Ming	Minister to Li Shai Tung
Chung Hu-Yan	Chancellor to Li Shai Tung

Ebert, Berta	wife of Klaus Ebert
Ebert, Hans	major in Security and heir to GenSyn
Ebert, Klaus Stefan	head of GenSyn (Genetic Synthetics) and advisor to Li Shai Tung
Fan Liang-wei	painter to the court of Li Shai Tung
Fu	servant to Wang Hsien
Haavikko, Axel	lieutenant in Security
Haavikko, Vesa	sister of Axel Haavikko
Heng Yu	son of Heng Fan and nephew of Heng Chi-Po
Hua	personal surgeon to Li Shai Tung
Hung Feng-chan	Chief Groom at Tongjiang
Hung Mien-lo	advisor to Wang Ta-hung; Chancellor of City Africa
Kao Chen	captain in Security
Karr, Gregor	'blood', and later major in Security
Lo Wen	Hans Ebert's servant
Lung Mei Ho	secretary to Tsu Ma
Nan Ho	Li Yuan's Master of the Inner Chambers
Nocenzi, Vittorio	General of Security, City Europe
Pearl Heart	maid to Li Yuan
Scott	captain of Security
Shepherd, Ben	son of Hal Shepherd
Shepherd, Beth	wife of Hal Shepherd
Shepherd, Hal	advisor to Li Shai Tung and head of the Shepherd family
Shepherd, Meg	daughter of Hal Shepherd
Sweet Rain	maid to Wang Hsien
Sweet Rose	maid to Li Yuan
Tolonen, Helga	aunt of Jelka Tolonen
Tolonen, Jelka	daughter of Knut Tolonen
Tolonen, Jon	brother of Knut Tolonen
Tolonen, Knut	Marshal of the Council of Generals and father of Jelka Tolonen
Wang Ta Chuan	Li Shai Tung's Master of the Inner Palace at Tongjiang
Wu Ming	servant to Wang Ta-hung
Yen Shih-fa	groom at Tongjiang

DISPERSIONISTS

DeVore, Howard	former major in Li Shai Tung's Security forces
Ecker, Michael	company head

Kubinyi	lieutenant to DeVore
Lehmann, Stefan	albino son of former Dispersionist leader, Pietr Lehmann and lieutenant to DeVore
Reid, Thomas	lieutenant to DeVore
Ross, Alexander	company head
Schwarz	lieutenant to DeVore
Scott	alias of DeVore
Turner	alias of DeVore
Wiegand, Max	lieutenant to DeVore
Weiss, Anton	banker

PING TIAO

Ascher, Emily	economist and member of the 'Council of Five'
Gesell, Bent	unofficial leader of the Ping Tiao and member of the 'Council of Five'
Mach, Jan	maintenance official for the Ministry of Waste Recycling and member of the 'Council of Five'
Mao Liang	Minor Family princess and member of the 'Council of Five'
Quinn	New member of the 'Council of Five'
Shen Lu Chua	computer expert and member of the 'Council of Five'
Yun Ch'o	lieutenant to Shen Lu Chua

OTHER CHARACTERS

Beattie, Douglas	alias of DeVore
Curval, Andrew	company director; experimental geneticist
DeValerian, Rachel	alias of Emily Ascher
Ebert, Lutz	half-brother of Klaus Ebert
Ellis, Michael	assistant to Director Spatz
Endfors, Pietr	best friend of Knut Tolonen
Enge, Marie	serving woman at the Dragon Cloud teahouse
Ganz, Joseph	alias of DeVore
Golden Heart	young prostitute bought by Hans Ebert for his household
Hammond, Joel	Senior Technician on the Wiring Project
Heng Chian-ye	son of Heng Chi-po and nephew of Heng Yu
Jennings, Mary	alias of Emily Ascher
Kao Ch'iang Hsin	infant daughter of Kao Chen
Kao Wu	infant son of Kao Chen

Kustow, Bryn	company director
Lever, Charles	company head; father of Michael Lever
Lever, Michael	company director; son of and assistant to Charles Lever
Loehr	alias of DeVore
Lo Wen	personal servant to Hans Ebert
Lu Cao	amah (maidservant) to Jelka Tolonen
Lu Ming Shao	'Whiskers Lu', Triad boss
Mu Chua	'Madam' of the House of the Ninth Ecstasy, a sing-song house, or brothel
Reynolds	alias of DeVore
Siang Che	martial arts instructor to Jelka Tolonen
Spatz, Gustav	Director of the Wiring Project
Stevens, Carl	company director
Sweet Flute	*mui tsai* to Hans Ebert
Sweet Honey	sing-song girl in Mu Chua's
T'ai Cho	tutor and 'guardian' to Kim Ward
Tarrant	company head
Tissan, Catherine	student at Oxford
Tolonen, Hannah	aunt to Knut Tolonen
Tsang Yi	friend of Heng Chian-ye
Tuan Ti Fo	Master of *wei chi*
Tung Liang	boy in the Casting Shop
Tung T'an	Senior Consultant at the Melfi Clinic
Turner	alias of DeVore
Wang Ti	wife of Kao Chen
Ward, Kim	Lagasek, or 'Starer'; 'Clayborn', orphan and scientist
White Orchid	sing-song girl in Mu Chua's
Yung Pi-chi	Head of the Yung family

THE DEAD

Aaltonen	Marshal and Head of Security for City Europe
Alex	close friend of Jake Reed and fiancée of Jenny. Security captain in Special Forces
Anders	a mercenary
Anderson	Director of 'The Project'
Ascher, Mary	mother of Emily Ascher
Ascher, Mikhail	junior credit agent in the *Hu Pu* (the Finance Ministry) and father of Emily Ascher
Ascher, Walter	Account Overseer for Hinton Industries

Bakke	Marshal in Security
Barrow, Chao	member of the House of Representatives Dispersionist
Bates, Alan	English actor
Beatrice	daughter of Cathy Hubbard, granddaughter of Mary Reed
Berdichev, Soren	owner of the SimFic Corporation and leading Dispersionist
Big Wen	a landowner
Boss Yang	an exploiter of the people
Branagh, William	King of Wessex
Brogan, Margaret	Old Ma Brogan resident of Church Knowle
Buck, John	Head of Development at the Ministry of Contracts
Buckland, Eddie	framer from Corfe
Captain Sensible	English pop musician
Chang Hsuan	Han painter from the 8th century
Chang Lai-hsun	nephew of Chang Yi Wei
Chang Li Chen	Junior Dragon in charge of drafting the Edict of Technological Control
Chang Lui	woman who adopted Pavel
Chang Te	Han soldier member of Jiang Lei's bodyguard
Chang Yan	guard on the Plantations
Chang Yi Wei	senior brother of the Chang clan owners of MircoData
Chang Yu	Tsao Ch'un's new appointment as First Dragon, during the War of Liberation
Chao Ni Tsu	Grand Master of *wei chi* and a computer genius. Servant of Tsao Ch'un
Ch'eng I	Minor Family prince and son of Ch'eng So Yuan
Ch'eng So Yuan	Minor Family head
Chen So I	Head of the Ministry of Contracts
Chen Yu	steward to Tsao Ch'un in Pei Ch'ing
Cheng Ro	Song Dynasty painter
Cheng Yu	one of the original Seven, advisor to Tsao Ch'un, subsequently T'ang
Chi Fei Yu	an usurer
Chi Lin Lin	legal assistant to Yang Hong Yu
Ching Su	friend of Jiang Lei
Chiu Fa	Media commentator on the Mids news channel
Cho	Han soldier servant to Wang Yu-lai
Cho Yi Yi	Master of the Bedchamber at Tongjiang

Chris	close friend of Jake Reed, gay partner of Hugo and multi-millionaire industrialist
Christie, Julie	English actress
Chung Hsun	"loyalty" a bond servant to Li Shai Tung
Coldplay	an English pop group
Cooke, Dick	famer from Cerne Abbas
Cooper, Charlie	son of Jed and Judy Cooper
Cooper, Jed	husband of Judy Cooper and father of Charlie and John
Cooper, John	son of Jed and Judy Cooper
Cooper, Judy	wife of Jed Cooper and mother of Charlie and John
Cooper, Will	farmer from Corfe
Croft, Leopold	father of Becky
Croft, Rebecca	'Becky', daughter of Leopold, with the Lazy eye
Curtis, Tim	Head of Human Resources, GenSyn
Daas	DAAS4 – the Data Automated Analysis System – an enhanced intelligence unit belonging to Hinton Industries
Dag	a mercenary
Denny, Sandy	English folk singer
Depp, Johnny	American actor
Dick, Philip K	American science fiction writer
Douglas, John	businessman and Dispersionist
Drake, Nick	English folk singer
Duchck, Albert	Administrator of Lodz and Dispersionist
Ebert, Gustav	genetics genius and co-founder of GenSyn (Genetic Synthetics)
Ebert, Ludovic	son of Gustav Ebert and GenSyn director
Ebert, Wolfgang	financial genius and co-founder of GenSyn (Genetic Synthetics)
Einor	a mercenary
Endfors, Jenny	wife of Knut Tolonen and mother of Jelka Tolonen
Fan Chang	a member of the original Seven, and advisor to Tsao Ch'un
Fan Cho	son of Fan Chang
Fan Lin	son of Fan Chang
Fan Peng	eldest wife of Fan Chang
Fan Si-pin	Master of *wei chi* from the eighteenth century
Fan Ti Yu	son of Fan Chang
Feng I	Colonel in charge of Tsao Ch'un's elite force
Fu Jen Maitland	Stefan Lehmann's mother

Gaughan, Dick	Scottish folk singer
Gifford, Dick	farmer from Corfe and son of Ted
Gifford, Ted	farmer from Corfe and father of Dick
Goodman, Frank	farmer from Langton Maltravers
Gosse	elite guard at the Domain
Grant, Thomas	captain in Security
Griffin, James B	Sixtieth president of the United States of America (the 69 States)
Grove, Dick	resident of Corfe
Gurney, Tom	watchman from Corfe
Haavikko, Knut	major in Security
Haines, Billy	landlord of The Wessex Arms in Wool
Hamilton, Jack	Landlord of The Quay Inn in Wareham
Hammond, Matthew	butcher from Church Knowle
Hart	doctor from Church Knowle
Hendrix, Jimi	American rock guitarist
Heng Chi-po	Li Shai Tung's Minister of Transportation
Henrik	a mercenary
Hewitt	lieutenant to Branagh, leader of a horse patrol
Hinton, Charles	CEO of Hinton Industries
Hinton, George	Senior Executive at Hinton Industries
Hinton, Henry	'Harry' Head of Strategic Planning, Hinton Industries
Ho	Steward Ho body servant of Jiang Lei when in the field
Horsfield, Geoff	historian and resident of Corfe
Hou Hsin-Fa	one of the original Seven, advisor to Tsao Chun and subsequently T'ang
Hsieh Ho	art critic and author of *The Six Principles*
Hsu Jung	friend of Jiang Lei
Huang Tzu Kung	Seventh Dragon servant of the 'Ministry', "The Thousand Eyes"
Hubbard, Beth	second daughter of Tom and Mary Hubbard
Hubbard, Cathy	eldest daughter of Tom and Mary Hubbard
Hubbard, Mary	wife of Tom Hubbard and mother of Cathy, Meg and Beth. Second wife of Jake Reed
Hubbard, Meg	youngest daughter of Tom and Mary Hubbard and girlfriend of Peter Reed
Hubbard, Tom	farmer, resident of Church Knowle, husband of Mary and father of Beth, Meg and Cathy. Best friend of Jake Reed

Hugo	close friend of Jake Reed and gay partner of Chris, acclaimed classical composer
Hui	receptionist for GenSyn
Hui Chang Ye	Senior Legal Advocate for the Chang clan
Hung	Tsao Ch'un's spy in Jiang Lei's camp
Hwa	a master 'blood', or to-the-death fighter from below the Net
Jenny	a close friend of Jake Reed and fiancé of Alex
Jiang Ch'iao-chieh	eldest daughter of Jiang Lei
Jiang Chun Hua	wife of Jiang Lei
Jiang Lei	general of Tsao Chun's Eighteenth Banner Army, also known as Nai Liu
Jiang San-chieh	youngest daughter of Jiang Lei
Joel	Senior engineer in the datascape for Hinton Industries
Jones, Micky	lead guitarist of Man, a welsh rock band
Jung	steward to Tobias Lahm
Karl	a mercenary
Ku	Marshal of the Fourth Banner Army
Kurt	Chief Technician at GenSyn
Lahm, Tobias	Eight Dragon at the 'Ministry', "The Thousand Eyes"
Lampton, Sir Henry	Head of Security, Hinton Industries
Lao Jen	Junior Minister to Li Shai Tung
Leggat, Brian	farmer from Abbotsbury
Lehmann, Pietr	Under Secretary of the House of Representatives, father of Stefan Lehmann and leader of the Dispersionists
Li	Han soldier, servant to Wang Yui-lai
Li Chang So	sixth son of Li Chao Ch'in
Li Chao Ch'in	one of the original Seven, advisor to Tsao Ch'un and subsequently T'ang
Li Fa	Han soldier and technician, working for Jiang Lei
Li Fu Jen	third son of Li Chao Ch'in
Li Han Ch'in	first son of Li Shai Tung and heir to City Europe
Li Kuang	fifth son of Li Cao Ch'in
Li Peng	eldest son of Li Chao Ch'in
Li Po	T'ang Dynasty poet
Li Shen	second son of Li Chao Ch'in
Li Weng	fourth son of Li Chao Ch'in
Lin Yua	first wife of Li Shai Tung
Ling	steward at the Black Tower

Little Bee	maid to Wang Hsien
Liu Ke	Han soldier; member of Jiang Lei's bodyguard; an adept at the *pi-p'a* or Chinese lute
Lo Wen	granddaughter of Jiang Lei
Lovegrove, John	farmer from Purbeck
Lu Tung	merchant; third cousin to Lu Wang-pei
Lu Wang-pei	third cousin of Lu Tung
Ludd, Drew	biggest grossing actor in Hollywood and star of Ubik
Lung Ti	secretary to Edmund Wyatt
Lwo Kang	son of Lwo Chun-yi and Li Shai Tung's Minister of the Edict of Technological Control
McKenzie, Liam	owner of The Stables in Dorchester
Ma Feng	Han soldier; member of Jiang Leis bodyguard
Mao Shao Tu	senior servant to Li Chao Ch'in
Man	Welsh rock band
Mao Tse T'ung	first *Ko Ming* emperor of China (ruled 1948–1976 AD)
Mason, Harry	landlord of The Thomas Hardy inn in Dorchester
Melfi, Charles	father of Alexandra Shepherd
Mi Feng	"Little Bee"; maidservant to Wang Hsien
Ming Hsin-Fa	senior advocate for GenSyn
Ming Huang	T'ang Dynasty emperor; the Purple Emperor
Nai Liu	'Enduring Willow', pen name of Jiang Lei and the most popular Han poet of his age
Nicolson, Jack	American actor
Nietzsche, Friedrich	German nineteenth-century philosopher
Oatley, Jennifer	young Englishwoman 'processed' by Jiang Lei
Padgett	retired doctor from Wool
Palmer, Joshua	'Old Josh', father of Will and an avid record collector
Palmer, Will	landlord of the Banks Arms Hotel, Corfe and son of Josh
Pan Chao	the great 'hero' of Chung Kuo, who conquered Asia in the First Century AD
Pan Tsung-yen	friend of Jiang Lei
Pavel	young worker on the Plantations, with a crooked back
Pei Ko	one of the original Seven, advisor to Tsao Ch'un and subsequently T'ang
Pei Lin-Yi	eldest son of Pei Ko
P'eng Chuan	Sixth Dragon at the Ministry, "The Thousand Eyes"
P'eng K'ai-chi	nephew of P'eng Chuan
Presley, Elvis	American rock and roll singer

Ragnar	a mercenary
Raikkonen	Marshal in Security
Randall, Jack	farmer from Church Knowle and husband of Jenny
Randall, Jenny	wife of Jack
Reed, Annie	first wife of Jake Reed; mother of Peter Reed and sister of Mary Hubbard (Jake's second wife)
Reed, Jake	'Login' or 'webdancer' for Hinton Industries; father of Peter Reed
Reed, Mary	second wife of Peter Reed
Reed, May	sister of Jake Reed
Reed, Peter	son of Jake and Annie Reed. GenSyn executive
Reed, Tom	son of Jake and Mary Reed
Rheinhardt	Media Liaison for GenSyn
Rory	Music store holder in Dorchester; owner of 'Rory's Record Shack', father of Roxanne
Sam	'Hopper' pilot, working for Hinton Industries
Sanders	captain in Security
Schwarz	aide to Marshal Tolonen
Shan	Han soldier; captain and one of Jiang Lei's men
Shao Shu	First Steward at Chun Hua's mansion
Shao Yen	major in Security; friend of Ming Hsin-fa
Shen	Han soldier; bodyguard to Jiang Lei
Shen Chen	son of Shen Fu
Shen Fu	First Dragon, Head of the Ministry, "The Thousand Eyes"
Shen Lu Chua	computer expert and member of the *Ping Tiao* 'Council of Five'
Shepherd, Alexandra	wife of Amos Shepherd and daughter of Charles Melfi
Shepherd, Amos	great-great grandfather of Hal Shepherd. Chief advisor to Tsao Ch'un and architect of City Earth
Shepherd, Augustus Raedwald	great grandfather of Hal Shepherd
Shepherd, Beth	daughter of Amos Shepherd
Shu Liang	Senior Legal Advocate
Shuh San	Junior Minister to Lwo Kang
Si Wu Ya	'Silk Raven' wife of Supervisor Sung
Spirit	Californian rock band
Su Ting-an	Eighteenth-century Master of *wei chi*
Ssu Lu Shan	official of the Ministry, "The Thousand Eyes"
Stamp, Terence	English actor
Su Ting-an	master of *wei chi* from the eighteenth century

Su Tung-p'o	Han official and poet of the eleventh century
Sung	supervisor on the Plantations
Svensson	Marshal in Security
Sweet Rain	maid to Wang Hsien
Tai Yu	'Moonflower'; maid to Augustus Ebert, a GenSyn clone
Tender Willow	maid to Wang Hsien
Teng	"Master Teng", a '*shou*' (literally "a hand"); a servant of The First Dragon, the first lord of the Ministry or "Thousand Eyes"
Teng Fu	guard on the plantations
Teng Liang	Minor Family princess betrothed to Pring Ch'eng I
Trish	artificial intelligence 'filter avatar' for Jake Reed's penthouse apartment
Ts'ao P'I	"Number Three" steward at Tsao Ch'un's court in Pei Ch'ing
Tsao Ch'i Yuan	youngest son of Tsao Ch'un
Tsao Ch'un	ex-member of the standing committee of the Communist Party politburo and architect of 'The Collapse'. Mass murderer and tyrant. 'Creator' of the world state of Chung Kuo
Tsao Heng	second son of Tsao Ch'un
Tsao Hsiao	Tsau Ch'un's elder brother
Tsao Wang-po	eldest son of Tsao Ch'un
Tsu Chen	one of the original Seven, advisor to Tsao Ch'un and subsequently T'ang
Tsu Lin	eldest son of Tsu Chen
Tsu Shi	steward to Gustav Ebert. A GenSyn clone
Tsu Tiao	T'ang of West Asia
Tu Mu	assistant to Alison Winter at GenSyn
Tung Ch'i-ch'ang	Ming dynasty *shanshui* artist
Tung Men-tiao	artist of the original *Chou* (or 'State') cards
The Verve	English pop group
Waite, Charlie	landlord of The New Inn, Church Knowle
Wang An-Shih	Han official and poet from the eleventh century
Wang Chang Ye	eldest son of Wang Hsien, heir to City Africa
Wang Hsien	T'ang of Africa
Wang Hui So	one of the original Seven, advisor to Tsao Ch'un and subsequently T'ang
Wang Lieh Tsu	second son of Wang Hsien
Wang Lung	eldest son of Wang Hui So
Wang Ta-hung	third son of Wang Hsien

Wang Yu-lai	'cadre'; servant of the Ministry, "The Thousand Eyes", instructed to report back on Jiang Lei
Webber, Sam	youth from Corfe
Wei	a judge
Wei Shao	Chancellor to Tsao Ch'un
Weis, Anton	banker and Dispersionist
Wen	captain in Security on Mars
Wen P'ing	close acquaintance and body servant of Tsa Ch'un; a man of great power
Williams, Charles	husband of Margaret and father of Kate. Retired head of a stockbroking company
Williams, Kate	fiancé of Jake Reed and daughter of Charles and Margaret
Williams, Margaret	wife of Charles and mother of Kate
Wilson, Dougie	farmer from Kimmeridge
Winter, Alison	ex-fiancé of Jake Reed; head of Evaluation at GenSyn and mother of Jake Winter
Winter, Jake	only son of Alison
Wolf	elite guard on The Domain
Wu Chi	AI (Artificial Intelligence) for Tobias Lahm
Wu Hsien	one of the original Seven, advisor to Tsao Ch'un and, subsequently, T'ang
Wyatt, Edmund	Company head, Dispersionist and (unknown to him) father of Kim Ward
Yang Hong Yu	Legal Advocate
Yang Kuei Fei	the famous concubine of T'ang emperor Ming Huang
Yates, Andrew Isiah	Prime Minister of the UK in 2043
Ying Chai	assistant to Sun Li Hua, brother to Ying Fu
Ying Fu	assistant to Sun Li Hua, brother to Ying Chai
Yo Jou Hsi	a judge
Young, Neil	Canadian singer-songwriter
Yu Ch'o	family retainer to Wang Hui So

GLOSSARY OF MANDARIN TERMS

t is not intended to belabour the reader with a whole mass of arcane Han expressions here. Some – usually the more specific – are explained in context. However, as a number of Mandarin terms are used naturally in the text, I've thought it best to provide a brief explanation of those terms.

aiya!	a common expression of surprise or dismay
amah	a domestic maidservant
Amo Li Jia	the Chinese gave this name to North America when they first arrived in the 1840s. Its literal meaning is 'The Land Without Ghosts'
an	a saddle. This has the same sound as the word for peace, and thus is associated in the Chinese mind with peace
catty	the colloquial term for a unit of measure formally called a *jin*. One catty – as used here – equals roughly 1.1 pounds (avoirdupois), or (exactly) 500 gm. Before 1949 and the standardization of Chinese measures to a metric standard, this measure varied district by district, but was generally regarded as equalling about 1.33 pounds (avoirdupois)
ch'a	tea; it might be noted that *ch'a shu*, the Chinese art of tea, is an ancient forebear of the Japanese tea ceremony *chanoyu*. *Hsiang p'ien* are flower teas, *Ch'ing ch'a* are green, unfermented teas
ch'a hao t'ai	literally, a 'directory'
ch'a shu	the art of tea, adopted later by the Japanese in their tea ceremony. The *ch'a* god is Lu Yu and his

	image can be seen on banners outside teahouses throughout Chung Kuo
chan shih	a 'fighter', here denoting a *tong* soldier
chang	ten *ch'i*, thus about 12 feet (Western)
Chang-e	the goddess of the Moon, and younger sister of the Spirit of the Waters. The moon represents the very essence of the female principal, *Yin*, in opposition to the Sun, which is *Yang*. Legend has it that Chang-e stole the elixir of immortality from her husband, the great archer Shen I, then fled to the Moon for safety, where she was transformed into a toad, which, so it is said, can still be seen against the whiteness of the moon's surface
chang shan	literally 'long dress', which fastens to the right. Worn by both sexes. The woman's version is a fitted, calf-length dress similar to the *chi pao*. A south China fashion, it is also known as a *cheung sam*
chao tai hui	an 'entertainment', usually, within *Chung Kuo*, of an expensive and sophisticated kind
chen yen	true words; the Chinese equivalent of a mantra
ch'eng	The word means both 'City' and 'Wall'
Ch'eng Ou Chou	City Europe
Ch'eng Hsiang	'Chancellor', a post first established in the Ch'in court more than two thousand years ago
ch'i	a Chinese 'foot'; approximately 14.4 inches
ch'i	'inner strength'; one of the two fundamental 'entities' from which everything is composed. Li is the 'form' or 'law', or (to cite Joseph Needham) the 'principal of organization' behind things, whereas *ch'i* is the 'matter-energy' or 'spirit' within material things, equating loosely to the *Pneuma* of the Greeks and the *prana* of the ancient Hindus. As the sage Chu Hsi (AD 1130–1200) said, 'The li is the *Tao* that pertains to "what is above shapes" and is the source from which all things are produced. The *ch'i* is the material [literally instrument] that pertains to "what is within shapes", and is the means whereby things are produced... Throughout the universe there is no *ch'i* without li. Or li without *ch'i*.'
chi ch'i	common workers, but used here mainly to denote the ant-like employees of the Ministry of Distribution
Chia Ch'eng	Honorary Assistant to the Royal Household

chi'an	a general term for money
chiao tzu	a traditional North Chinese meal of meat-filled dumplings eaten with a hot spicy sauce
Chieh Hsia	term meaning 'Your Majesty', derived from the expression 'Below the Steps'. It was the formal way of addressing the Emperor, through his Ministers, who stood 'below the steps'
chi pao	literally 'banner gown', a one-piece gown of Manchu origin, usually sleeveless, worn by women
chih chu	a spider
ch'in	a long (120 cm), narrow, lacquered zither with a smooth top surface and sound holes beneath, seven silk strings and thirteen studs marking the harmonic positions on the strings. Early examples have been unearthed from fifth century BC tombs, but it probably evolved in the fourteenth or thirteenth century BC. It is the most honoured of Chinese instruments and has a lovely mellow tone
Chin P'ing Mei	*The Golden Lotus*, an erotic novel, written by an unknown scholar – possibly anonymously by the writer Wang Shih-chen – at the beginning of the seventeenth century as a continuation of the *Shui Hui Chuan*, or 'Warriors of the Marsh', expanding chapters 23 to 25 of the *Shan Hui*, which relate the story of how Wu Sung became a bandit. Extending the story beyond this point, *The Golden Lotus* has been accused of being China's great licentious (even, perhaps, pornographic) novel. But as C.P. Fitzgerald says, 'If this book is indecent in parts, it is only because, telling a story of domestic life, it leaves out nothing.' It is available in a three-volume English-language translation
ch'ing	pure
ching	literally 'mirror', here used also to denote a perfect GenSyn copy of a man. Under the Edict of Technological Control, these are limited to copies of the ruling T'ang and their closest relatives. However, mirrors were also popularly believed to have certain strange properties, one of which was to make spirits visible. Buddhist priests used special 'magic mirrors' to show believers the form into which they would be reborn. Moreover, if a man looks into one of these mirrors and fails to recognize his own face, it is a

	sign that his own death is not far off. [See also *hu hsin chung*.]
ch'ing ch'a	green, unfermented teas
Ch'ing Ming	the Festival of Brightness and Purity, when the graves are swept and offerings made to the deceased. Also known as the Festival of Tombs, it occurs at the end of the second moon and is used for the purpose of celebrating the spring, a time for rekindling the cooking fires after a three-day period in which the fires were extinguished and only cold food eaten
Chou	literally, 'State', but here used as the name of a card game based on the politics of Chung Kuo
chow mein	this, like chop suey, is neither a Chinese nor a Western dish, but a special meal created by the Chinese in North America for the Western palate. A transliteration of *chao mian* (fried noodles), it is a distant relation of the *liang mian huang* served in Suchow
ch'u	the west
chun hua	literally, 'Spring Pictures'. These are, in fact, pornographic 'pillow books', meant for the instruction of newly-weds
ch'un tzu	an ancient Chinese term from the Warring States period, describing a certain class of noblemen, controlled by a code of chivalry and morality known as the *li*, or rites. Here the term is roughly, and sometimes ironically, translated as 'gentlemen'. The *ch'un tzu* is as much an ideal state of behaviour – as specified by Confucius in the *Analects* – as an actual class in Chung Kuo, though a degree of financial independence and a high standard of education are assumed a prerequisite
chung	a lidded ceramic serving bowl for *ch'a*
chung hsin	loyalty
E hsing hsun huan	a saying: 'Bad nature follows a cycle'
er	two
erh tzu	son
erhu	a traditional Chinese instrument
fa	punishment
fen	a unit of currency; see *yuan*. It has another meaning, that of a 'minute' of clock time, but that usage is avoided here to prevent any confusion

feng yu   a 'phoenix chair', canopied and decorated with
                   silver birds. Coloured scarlet and gold, this is the
                   traditional carriage for a bride as she is carried to her
                   wedding ceremony

fu jen   'Madam', used here as opposed to *t'ai t'ai*, 'Mrs'

fu sang   the hollow mulberry tree; according to ancient
                   Chinese cosmology this tree stands where the
                   sun rises and is the dwelling place of rulers. *Sang*
                   (mulberry), however, has the same sound as *sang*
                   (sorrow) in Chinese

Han   term used by the Chinese to describe their own race,
                   the 'black-haired people', dating back to the Han
                   dynasty (210 BC–AD 220). It is estimated that some
                   ninety-four per cent of modern China's population
                   are Han racially

Hei   literally 'black'. The Chinese pictogram for this
                   represents a man wearing war paint and tattoos.
                   Here it refers specifically to the genetically
                   manufactured half-men, made by GenSyn and used
                   as riot police to quell uprisings in the lower levels
                   of the City

ho yeh   *Nelumbo Nucifera*, or lotus, the seeds of which are
                   used in Chinese medicine to cure insomnia

Hoi Po   the corrupt officials who dealt with the European
                   traders in the nineteenth century, more commonly
                   known as 'hoppos'

Hsia   a crab

hsiang p'en   flower *ch'a*

hsiao   filial piety. The character for *hsiao* is comprised of
                   two parts, the upper part meaning 'old', the lower
                   meaning 'son' or 'child'. This dutiful submission of
                   the young to the old is at the heart of Confucianism
                   and Chinese culture generally

Hsiao chieh   'Miss', or an unmarried woman. An alternative to
                   nu shi

hsiao jen   'little man/men'. In the *Analects*, Book XIV, Confucius
                   writes, 'The gentleman gets through to what is
                   up above; the small man gets through to what is
                   down below.' This distinction between 'gentlemen'
                   (*ch'un tzu*) and 'little men' (*hsiao jen*), false even
                   in Confucius's time, is no less a matter of social
                   perspective in Chung Kuo

hsien	historically an administrative district of variable size. Here the term is used to denote a very specific administrative area, one of ten stacks – each stack composed of thirty decks. Each deck is a hexagonal living unit of ten levels, two li, or approximately one kilometre, in diameter. A stack can be imagined as one honeycomb in the great hive that is the City. Each hsien of the city elects one Representative to sit in the House at Weimar
Hsien Ling	Chief Magistrate, in charge of a Hsien. In Chung Kuo these officials are the T'ang's representatives and law enforcers for the individual hsien. In times of peace each hsien would also elect one Representative to sit in the House at Weimar
hsueh pai	'snow white', a derogatory term here for Hung Mao women
Hu pu	the T'ang's Finance Ministry
hu hsin chung	see ching, re Buddhist magic mirrors, for which this was the name. The power of such mirrors was said to protect the owner from evil. It was also said that one might see the secrets of futurity in such a mirror. See the chapter 'Mirrors' in The White Mountain for further information
hu t'ieh	a butterfly. Anyone wishing to follow up on this tale of Chuang Tzu's might look to the sage's writings and specifically the chapter 'Discussion on Making All Things Equal'
hua pen	literally 'story roots', these were précis guidebooks used by the street-corner storytellers in China for the past two thousand years. The main events of the story were written down in the hua pen for the benefit of those storytellers who had not yet mastered their art. During the Yuan or Mongol dynasty (AD 1280–1368) these hua pen developed into plays, and, later on – during the Ming dynasty (AD 1368–1644) – into the form of popular novels, of which the Shui Hu Chuan, or 'Outlaws of the Marsh', remains one of the most popular. Any reader interested in following this up might purchase Pearl Buck's translation, rendered as All Men Are Brothers and first published in 1933
Huang Ti	originally Huang Ti was the last of the 'Three Sovereigns' and the first of the 'Five Emperors' of ancient Chinese tradition. Huang Ti, the Yellow

Emperor, was the earliest ruler recognized by the historian Ssu-ma Ch'ien (136–85 BC) in his great historical work, the *Shih Chi*. Traditionally, all subsequent rulers (and would-be rulers) of China have claimed descent from the Yellow Emperor, the 'Son of Heaven' himself, who first brought civilization to the black-haired people. His name is now synonymous with the term 'emperor'

hun — the higher soul or 'spirit soul', which, the Chinese believe, ascends to Heaven at death, joins Shang Ti, the Supreme Ancestor, and lives in his court for ever more. The *hun* is believed to come into existence at the moment of conception (see also *p'o*)

hun tun — 'the Chou believed that Heaven and Earth were once inextricably mixed together in a state of undifferentiated chaos, like a chicken's egg. Hun Tun they called that state' (*The Broken Wheel*, Chapter 37). It is also the name of a meal of tiny sack-like dumplings

Hung Lou Meng — *The Dream of Red Mansions*, also known as *The Story of the Stone*, a lengthy novel written in the middle of the eighteenth century. Like the *Chin Ping Mei*, it deals with the affairs of a single Chinese family. According to experts the first eighty chapters are the work of Ts'ao Hsueh-ch'in, and the last forty belong to Kao Ou. It is, without doubt, the masterpiece of Chinese literature, and is available from Penguin in the UK in a five-volume edition

Hung Mao — literally 'redheads', the name the Chinese gave to the Dutch (and later English) seafarers who attempted to trade with China in the seventeenth century. Because of the piratical nature of their endeavours (which often meant plundering Chinese shipping and ports) the name continues to retain connotations of piracy

Hung Mun — the Secret Societies or, more specifically, the Triads

huo jen — literally, 'fire men'

I Lung — the 'First Dragon', Senior Minister and Great Lord of the 'Ministry', also known as 'The Thousand Eyes'

jou tung wu — literally 'meat animal': 'It was a huge mountain of flesh, a hundred *ch'i* to a side and almost twenty *ch'i* in height. Along one side of it, like the teats of a giant pig, three dozen heads jutted from the flesh,

	long, eyeless snouts with shovel jaws that snuffled and gobbled in the conveyor-belt trough...'
kai t'ou	a thin cloth of red and gold that veils a new bride's face. Worn by the Ch'ing empresses for almost three centuries
kan pei!	'good health!' or 'cheers!' – a drinking toast
kang	the Chinese hearth, serving also as oven and, in the cold of winter, as a sleeping platform
k'ang hsi	a Ch'ing (or Manchu) emperor whose long reign (AD 1662–1722) is considered a golden age for the art of porcelain-making. The lavender-glazed bowl in 'The Sound Of Jade' is, however, not kang-hsi but Chun chou ware from the Sung period (960–1127) and considered amongst the most beautiful (and rare) wares in Chinese pottery
kao liang	a strong Chinese liquor
Ko Ming	'revolutionary'. The Tien Ming is the Mandate of Heaven, supposedly handed down from Shang Ti, the Supreme Ancestor, to his earthly counterpart, the Emperor (Huang Ti). This Mandate could be enjoyed only so long as the Emperor was worthy of it, and rebellion against a tyrant – who broke the Mandate through his lack of justice, benevolence and sincerity – was deemed not criminal but a rightful expression of Heaven's anger
k'ou t'ou	the fifth stage of respect, according to the 'Book of Ceremonies', involves kneeling and striking the head against the floor. This ritual has become more commonly known in the West as kowtow
ku li	'bitter strength'. These two words, used to describe the condition of farm labourers who, after severe droughts or catastrophic floods, moved off their land and into the towns to look for work of any kind – however hard and onerous – spawned the word 'coolie' by which the West more commonly knows the Chinese labourer. Such men were described as 'men of bitter strength', or simply 'ku li'
Kuan Hua	Mandarin, the language spoken in mainland China. Also known as kuo yu and pai hua
Kuan Yin	the Goddess of Mercy. Originally the Buddhist male bodhisattva, Avalokitsevara (translated into Han as 'He who listens to the sounds of the world', or 'Kuan Yin'), the Han mistook the well-developed breasts of

	the saint for a woman's and, since the ninth century, have worshipped Kuan Yin as such. Effigies of Kuan Yin will show her usually as the Eastern Madonna, cradling a child in her arms. She is also sometimes seen as the wife of *Kuan Kung*, the Chinese God of War
Kuei Chuan	'Running Dog', here the name of a Triad
kuo yu	Mandarin, the language spoken in most of Mainland China. Also rendered here as *kuan hua* and *pai hua*
kwai	an abbreviation of *kwai tao*, a 'sharp knife' or 'fast knife'. It can also mean to be sharp or fast (as a knife). An associated meaning is that of a 'clod' or 'lump of earth'. Here it is used to denote a class of fighters from below the Net, whose ability and self-discipline separate them from the usual run of hired knives
Lan Tian	'Blue Sky'
Lang	a covered walkway
lao chu	sing-song girls, slightly more respectable than the common *men hu*
lao jen	'old man' (also *weng*); used normally as a term of respect
lao kuan	a 'Great Official', often used ironically
lao shih	term that denotes a genuine and straightforward man – bluff and honest
lao wai	an outsider
li	a Chinese 'mile', approximating to half a kilometre or one third of a mile. Until 1949, when metric measures were adopted in China, the li could vary from place to place
Li	'propriety'. See the *Li Ching* or 'Book Of Rites' for the fullest definition
Li Ching	'The Book Of Rites', one of the five ancient classics
liang	a Chinese ounce of roughly 32gm. Sixteen *liang* form a *catty*
liu k'ou	the seventh stage of respect, according to the 'Book of Ceremonies'. Two stages above the more familiarly known 'k'ou t'ou' (kowtow) it involves kneeling and striking the forehead three times against the floor, rising to one's feet again, then kneeling and repeating the prostration with three touches of the forehead to the ground. Only the *san*

	kuei chiu k'ou – involving three prostrations – was more elaborate and was reserved for Heaven and its son, the Emperor (see also *san k'ou*)
liumang	punks
lu nan jen	literally 'oven man', title of the official who is responsible for cremating all of the dead bodies
lueh	'that invaluable quality of producing a piece of art casually, almost uncaringly'
lung t'ing	'dragon pavilions', small sedan chairs carried by servants and containing a pile of dowry gifts
Luoshu	the Chinese legend relates that in ancient times a turtle crawled from a river in Luoshu province, the patterns on its shell forming a three by three grid of numeric pictograms, the numbers of which – both down and across – equalled the same total of fifteen. Since the time of the Shang (three thousand-plus years ago) tortoise shells were used in divination, and the Luoshu diagram is considered magic and is often used as a charm for easing childbirth
ma kua	a waist-length ceremonial jacket
mah jong	whilst, in its modern form, the 'game of the four winds' was introduced towards the end of the nineteenth century to Westerners trading in the thriving city of Shanghai, it was developed from a card game that existed as long ago as AD 960. Using 144 tiles, it is generally played by four players. The tiles have numbers and also suits – winds, dragons, bamboos and circles
mao	a unit of currency. See *yuan*
mao tai	a strong, sorghum-based liquor
mei fa tzu	common saying, 'It is fate!'
mei hua	'plum blossom'
mei mei	sister
mei yu jen wen	'subhumans'. Used in *Chung Kuo* by those in the City's uppermost levels to denote anyone living in the lower hundred
men hu	literally, 'the one standing in the door'. The most common (and cheapest) of prostitutes
min	literally 'the people'; used (as here) by the Minor Families in a pejorative sense, as an equivalent to 'plebeian'

Ming	the dynasty that ruled China from 1368 to 1644. Literally, the name means 'Bright' or 'Clear' or 'Brilliant'. It carries connotations of cleansing
mou	a Chinese 'acre' of approximately 7,260 square feet. There are roughly six mou to a Western acre, and a 10,000-mou field would approximate to 1,666 acres, or just over two and a half square miles
Mu Ch'in	'Mother', a general term commonly addressed to any older woman
mui tsai	rendered in Cantonese as 'mooi-jai'. Colloquially, it means either 'little sister' or 'slave girl', though generally, as here, the latter. Other Mandarin terms used for the same status are pei-nu and yatou. Technically, guardianship of the girl involved is legally signed over in return for money
nan jen	common term for 'Man'
Ni Hao?	'How are you?'
niao	literally 'bird', but here, as often, it is used euphemistically as a term for the penis, often as an expletive
nu er	daughter
nu shi	an unmarried woman, a term equating to 'Miss'
Pa shi yi	literally 'Eighty-One', here referring specifically to the Central Council of the New Confucian officialdom
pai nan jen	literally 'white man'
pai pi	'hundred pens', term used for the artificial reality experiments renamed 'Shells' by Ben Shepherd
pan chang	supervisor
pao yun	a 'jewelled cloud' ch'a
pau	a simple long garment worn by men
pau shuai ch'i	the technical scientific term for 'half-life'
pi-p'a	a four-stringed lute used in traditional Chinese music
Pien Hua!	Change!
p'ing	an apple, symbol of peace
ping	the east
Ping Fa	Sun Tzu's The Art Of War, written over two thousand years ago. The best English translation is probably Samuel B. Griffith's 1963 edition. It was a book Chairman Mao frequently referred to

Ping Tiao	levelling. To bring down or make flat. Here, in Chung Kuo, it is also a terrorist organization.
p'o	The 'animal soul' which, at death, remains in the tomb with the corpse and takes its nourishment from the grave offerings. The *p'o* decays with the corpse, sinking down into the underworld (beneath the Yellow Springs) where – as a shadow – it continues an existence of a kind. The *p'o* is believed to come into existence at the moment of birth (see also *hun*)
sam fu	an upper garment (part shirt, part jacket) worn originally by both males and females, in imitation of Manchu styles; later on a wide-sleeved, calf-length version was worn by women alone
san	three
San chang	the three palaces
san kuei chiu k'ou	the eighth and final stage of respect, according to the 'Book Of Ceremonies', it involves kneeling three times, each time striking the forehead three times against the ground before rising from one's knees (in *k'ou t'ou* one strikes the forehead but once). This most elaborate form of ritual was reserved for Heaven and its son, the Emperor. See also *liu k'ou*
san k'ou	abbreviated form of *san kuei chiu k'ou*
San Kuo Yan Yi	*The Romance of the Three Kingdoms*, also known as the *San Kuo Chih Yen I*. China's great historical novel, running to 120 chapters, it covers the period from AD 168 to 265. Written by Lo Kuan-chung in the early Ming dynasty, its heroes, Liu Pei, Kuan Chung and Chang Fei, together with its villain, Ts'ao Ts'ao, are all historical personages. It is still one of the most popular stories in modern China
sao mu	the 'Feast of the Dead'
shang	the south
shan shui	the literal meaning is 'mountains and water', but the term is normally associated with a style of landscape painting that depicts rugged mountain scenery with river valleys in the foreground. It is a highly popular form, first established in the T'ang dynasty, back in the seventh to ninth centuries AD
shao lin	specially trained assassins, named after the monks of the *shao lin* monastery

shao nai nai	literally, 'little grandmother'. A young girl who has been given the responsibility of looking after her siblings
she t'ou	a 'tongue' or taster, whose task is to safeguard his master from poisoning
shen chung	'caution'
shen mu	'she who stands in the door': a common prostitute
shen nu	'god girls': superior prostitutes
shen t'se	special elite force, named after the 'palace armies' of the late T'ang dynasty
Shih	'Master'. Here used as a term of respect somewhat equivalent to our use of 'Mister'. The term was originally used for the lowest level of civil servants, to distinguish them socially from the run-of-the-mill 'Misters' (*hsian sheng*) below them and the gentlemen (*ch'un tzu*) above
shou hsing	a peach brandy
Shui Hu Chuan	*Outlaws of the Marsh*, a long historical novel attributed to Lo Kuan-chung but re-cast in the early sixteenth century by 'Shih Nai-an', a scholar. Set in the eleventh century, it is a saga of bandits, warlords and heroes. Written in pure *pai hua* – colloquial Chinese – it is the tale of how its heroes became bandits. Its revolutionary nature made it deeply unpopular with both the Ming and Manchu dynasties, but it remains one of the most popular adventures among the Chinese populace
siang chi	Chinese chess, a very different game from its Western counterpart
Ta	'Beat', here a heavily amplified form of Chinese folk music, popular amongst the young
ta lien	an elaborate girdle pouch
Ta Ssu Nung	the Superintendency of Agriculture
tai	literally 'pockets' but here denoting Representatives in the House at Weimar. 'Owned' financially by the Seven, historically such *tai* have served a double function in the House, counterbalancing the strong mercantile tendencies of the House and serving as a conduit for the views of the Seven. Traditionally they had been elderly, well-respected men, but more recently their replacements were young, brash and

	very corrupt, more like the hoppoes of the Opium Wars period
t'ai chi	the Original, or One, from which the duality of all things (*yin* and *yang*) developed, according to Chinese cosmology. We generally associate the *t'ai chi* with the Taoist symbol, that swirling circle of dark and light supposedly representing an egg (perhaps the *Hun Tun*), the yolk and the white differentiated
tai hsiao	a white wool flower, worn in the hair
Tai Huo	'Great Fire'
T'ai Shan	Mount T'ai, the highest and most sacred of China's mountains, located in Shantung province. A stone pathway of 6,293 steps leads to the summit and for thousands of years the ruling emperor has made ritual sacrifices at its foot, accompanied by his full retinue, presenting evidence of his virtue. T'ai Shan is one of the five Taoist holy mountains, and symbolizes the very centre of China. It is the mountain of the sun, symbolizing the bright male force (*yang*). 'As safe as T'ai Shan' is a popular saying, denoting the ultimate in solidity and certainty
Tai Shih Lung	Court Astrologer, a title that goes back to the Han dynasty
T'ang	literally, 'beautiful and imposing'. It is the title chosen by the Seven, who were originally the chief advisors to Tsao Ch'un, the tyrant. Since overthrowing Tsao Ch'un, it has effectively had the meaning of 'emperor'
Ta Ts'in	the Chinese name for the Roman Empire. They also knew Rome as Li Chien and as 'the land West of the Sea'. The Romans themselves they termed the 'Big Ts'in' – the Ts'in being the name the Chinese gave themselves during the Ts'in dynasty (AD 265–316)
te	'spiritual power', 'true virtue' or 'virtuality', defined by Alan Watts as 'the realization or expression of the Tao in actual living'
t'e an tsan	'innocent westerners'. For 'innocent' perhaps read naive
ti tsu	a bamboo flute, used both as a solo instrument and as part of an ensemble, playing traditional Chinese music

ti yu	the 'earth prison' or underworld of Chinese legend. There are ten main Chinese Hells, the first being the courtroom in which the sinner is sentenced and the last being that place where they are reborn as human beings. In between are a vast number of sub-Hells, each with its own Judge and staff of cruel warders. In Hell, it is always dark, with no differentiation between night and day
Tian	'Heaven', also, 'the dome of the sky'
tian-fang	literally 'to fill the place of the dead wife'; used to signify the upgrading of a concubine to the more respectable position of wife
tiao tuo	bracelets of gold and jade
T'ieh Lo-han	'Iron Goddess of Mercy', a ch'a
T'ieh Pi Pu Kai	literally, 'the iron pen changes not', this is the final phrase used at the end of all Chinese government proclamations for the last three thousand years
ting	an open-sided pavilion in a Chinese garden. Designed as a focal point in a garden, it is said to symbolize man's essential place in the natural order of things
T'ing Wei	the Superintendency of Trials, an institution that dates back to the T'ang dynasty. See Book Eight, The White Mountain, for an instance of how this department of government – responsible for black propaganda – functions
T'o	'camel-backed', a Chinese term for 'hunch-backed'
tong	a gang. In China and Europe these are usually smaller and thus subsidiary to the Triads, but in North America the term has generally taken the place of Triad
tou chi	Glycine Max, or the black soybean, used in Chinese herbal medicine to cure insomnia
Tsai Chien!	'Until we meet again!'
Tsou Tsai Hei	'the Walker in the Darkness'
tsu	the north
tsu kuo	the motherland
ts'un	a Chinese 'inch' of approximately 1.4 Western inches. Ten ts'un form one ch'i
Tu	Earth
tzu	'Elder Sister'

wan wu	literally 'the ten thousand things'; used generally to include everything in creation, or, as the Chinese say, 'all things in Heaven and Earth'
Wei	Commandant of Security
wei chi	'the surrounding game', known more commonly in the West by its Japanese name of Go. It is said that the game was invented by the legendary Chinese Emperor Yao in the year 2350 BC to train the mind of his son, Tan Chu, and teach him to think like an emperor
wen ming	a term used to denote civilization, or written culture
wen ren	the scholar-artist; very much an ideal state, striven for by all creative Chinese
weng	'Old man'. Usually a term of respect
Wu	a diviner; traditionally, these were 'mediums' who claimed to have special psychic powers. Wu could be either male or female
Wu	'non-being'. As Lao Tzu says: 'Once the block is carved, there are names.' But the Tao is unnameable (wu-ming) and before Being (yu) is Non-Being (wu). Not to have existence, or form, or a name, that is wu
Wu ching	the 'Five Classics' studied by all Confucian scholars, comprising the Shu Ching (Book Of History), the Shih Ching (Book of Songs), the I Ching (Book of Changes), the Li Ching (Book of Rites, actually three books in all), and the Ch'un Chui (The Spring and Autumn Annals of the State of Lu)
wu fu	the five gods of good luck
wu tu	the 'five noxious creatures' – which are toad, scorpion, snake, centipede and gecko (wall lizard)
Wushu	the Chinese word for Martial Arts. It refers to any of several hundred schools. Kung fu is a school within this, meaning 'skill that transcends mere surface beauty'
wuwei	non-action, an old Taoist concept. It means keeping harmony with the flow of things – doing nothing to break the flow
ya	homosexual. Sometimes the term 'a yellow eel' is used
yamen	the official building in a Chinese community
yang	the 'male principle' of Chinese cosmology, which, with its complementary opposite, the female yin,

forms the *t'ai ch'i*, derived from the Primeval One. From the union of *yin* and *yang* arise the 'five elements' (water, fire, earth, metal, wood) from which the 'ten thousand things' (the *wan wu*) are generated. Yang signifies Heaven and the South, the Sun and Warmth, Light, Vigor, Maleness, Penetration, odd numbers and the Dragon. Mountains are *yang*

yang kuei tzu	Chinese name for foreigners, 'Ocean Devils'. It is also synonymous with 'Barbarians'
yang mei ping	'willow plum sickness', the Chinese term for syphilis, provides an apt description of the male sexual organ in the extreme of this sickness
yi	the number one
yin	the 'female principle' of Chinese cosmology (see *yang*). Yin signifies Earth and the North, the Moon and Cold, Darkness, Quiescence, Femaleness, Absorption, even numbers and the Tiger. The *yin* lies in the shadow of the mountain
yin mao	pubic hair
Ying kuo	English, the language
ying tao	'baby peach', a term of endearment here
ying tzu	'shadows' – trained specialists of various kinds, contracted out to gangland bosses
yu	literally 'fish', but, because of its phonetic equivalence to the word for 'abundance', the fish symbolizes wealth. Yet there is also a saying that when the fish swim upriver it is a portent of social unrest and rebellion
yu ko	a 'Jade Barge', here a type of luxury sedan
Yu Kung	'Foolish Old Man!'
yu ya	deep elegance
yuan	the basic currency of Chung Kuo (and modern-day China). Colloquially (though not here) it can also be termed *kuai* – 'piece' or 'lump'. Ten *mao* (or, formally, *jiao*) make up one *yuan*, while 100 *fen* (or 'cents') comprise one *yuan*
yueh ch'in	a Chinese dulcimer, one of the principal instruments of the Chinese orchestra
Ywe Lung	literally 'The Moon Dragon', the wheel of seven dragons that is the symbol of the ruling Seven throughout Chung Kuo: 'At its centre the snouts

of the regal beasts met, forming a rose-like hub,
huge rubies burning fiercely in each eye. Their lithe,
powerful bodies curved outward like the spokes
of a giant wheel while at the edge their tails were
intertwined to form the rim.' (Chapter 4 of *The Middle
Kingdom*)

AUTHOR'S NOTE

The transcription of standard Mandarin into European alphabetical form was first achieved in the seventeenth century by the Italian Matteo Ricci, who founded and ran the first Jesuit Mission in China from 1583 until his death in 1610. Since then several dozen attempts have been made to reduce the original Chinese sounds, represented by some tens of thousands of separate pictograms, into readily understandable phonetics for Western use. For a long time, however, three systems dominated – those used by the three major Western powers vying for influence in the corrupt and crumbling Chinese Empire of the nineteenth century: Great Britain, France, and Germany. These systems were the Wade-Giles (Great Britain and America – sometimes known as the Wade System), the Ecole Francaise de l'Extreme Orient (France) and the Lessing (Germany).

Since 1958, however, the Chinese themselves have sought to create one single phonetic form, based on the German system, which they termed the *hanyu pinyin fang' an* (Scheme for a Chinese Phonetic Alphabet), known more commonly as *pinyin*, and in all foreign-language books published in China since 1 January 1979 *pinyin* has been used, as well as being taught now in schools alongside the standard Chinese characters. For this work, however, I have chosen to use the older and to my mind far more elegant transcription system, the Wade-Giles (in modified form). For those now used to the harder forms of *pinyin*, the following may serve as a basic conversion guide, the Wade-Giles first, the *pinyin* after:

p for b	ch' for q
ts' for c	j for r
ch' for ch	t' for t
t for d	hs for x
k for g	ts for z
ch for j	ch for zh

The effect is, I hope, to render the softer, more poetic side of the original Mandarin, ill-served, I feel, by modern *pinyin*.

David Wingrove
April 1990

CHUNG KUO

ACKNOWLEDGMENTS

The translations of Li Ho's 'On and On Forever' and 'On The Frontier' are by A. C. Graham from his excellent *Poems of the Late T'ang*, published by Penguin Books, London, 1965, and are used with their kind permission. The translation of Li Shangyin's 'Fallen Flowers' is by Tao Jie and is taken from *300 T'ang Poems, A New Translation*, Commercial Press, Hong Kong. The passage from *On Protracted War* is from Mao Tse-tung's *Selected Works*, Volume II, Peking Press.

The passages quoted from Book One (XI) and (XXXVII) of Lao Tzu's *Tao Te Ching* are from the D. C. Lau translation, published by Penguin Books, London, 1963, and used with their kind permission. The quotation from Confucius, *The Analects*, Book XII, is once again from a D. C. Lau translation, published by Penguin Books, 1979, and used with their permission.

The passage from Sun Tzu's classic *The Art of War* is from the Samuel B. Griffith translation, published by Oxford University Press, 1963.

Thanks must go to the following for their help. To my editors – Nick Sayers, Brian DiFiore, John Pearce and Alyssa Diamond – for their sheer niceness and (of course) for their continuing enthusiasm, and to Carolyn Caughey, fan-turned-editor, for seeing where to cut the cake.

To Mike Cobley, thanks not merely for encouragement but for Advanced Cheerfulness in the face of Adversity. May both your patience and your talent be rewarded. And to Andy Sawyer, for a thoughtful reading of the text. I hope I can reciprocate one of these days.

To my first-line critic and safety net, the stalwart Brian Griffin, may I say yet again how much all of this is appreciated. The notes you've done will make a wonderful book some day!

To family and friends, particularly my girls (Susan, Jessica, Amy and Georgia) go the usual thanks in the face of my at-times monomaniacal neglect. And especial thanks this time to everyone I met on my travels to the Universities of Leeds, Manchester, Oxford, Cambridge, Southampton, Brighton, Canterbury and Dublin. And, of course, to the Glasgow group. *Slainte Mhath!*